Praise for

THE FAT ARTIST

"Benjamin Hale writes from an altitude that is entirely his own. The view from up there—a hilariously zoological panorama of Americans at their most frail, feral, and blundering—is also entirely his own. *The Fat Artist* is a brilliant, ceaselessly engaging book."

—Joseph O'Neill, award-winning author of *Netherland* and *The Dog*

"Generous, unfolding at a decidedly unhurried pace, the stories in *The Fat Artist* seem at first to be so precise in the portraits they draw and so specific in their emotional concerns that it takes a while to recognize the fine strands connecting them to American history, culture, and everyday life, strands that will ensnare the lucky readers of this collection as well. Benjamin Hale's writing has range, depth, soul, and music."

—Christopher Sorrentino, author of *The Fugitives* and *Trance*

"[An] excellent new story collection from Hale . . . Hale's heroes and antiheroes don't glide through the world around them; they stumble, fall, and get kicked while they're on the ground . . . It's a beautiful reflection on what people are willing to do for art, or what they're willing to let art do to them. . . . Hale treats all of [his characters] with care, and like the flare of a satellite that will one day decay and crash back down to Earth, it's oddly beautiful and impossible to look away from."

—Michael Schaub, *Los Angeles Times*

"You may have read Benjamin Hale's 'Don't Worry Baby' in our Spring issue. It's my favorite from his new collection, *The Fat Artist*, because it's the most hallucinatory and unhinged display of his prose . . . The other story that stands out as something truly special is 'If I Had Possession over Judgment Day' . . . While Hale's characters are quick to attribute the chaos that ensues to forces cosmic, the orbiting satellites are the only vestiges of order that remain after the bloodbath; in all three points of view, this passage appears at least once: 'The tiny prick of light traveled in a smooth, shallow arc, gradually gathering in brightness until it became a bright white flash. . . .' He's saying something here about our impulse to blame our most entropic mistakes on the actually quite regimented universe."

—*The Paris Review*

"A steadily growing professional talent . . . There is a true seriousness to the [title] story: Hale means to say something about art and death, just as elsewhere he means to take us into modes of being that are sometimes torqued a little beyond ordinary reality . . . [His] stories are wry . . . the questions he raises are interesting all the same."

—*Kirkus Reviews*

"Wonderfully weird short stories . . . at his best: turning to the dark and absurd to lay bare the unexpected consequences of one's actions and the accidents of circumstance. Sharply drawn and strange, Hale's narratives deal in secrets and egos and voracious appetites—as much a part of human tradition as sitting down together for a meal."

—*Out Magazine*

"The short story form allows Hale's own penchant for invention to further shine . . . *The Fat Artist*, which includes stories about dominatrices and performance artists, is sure to please."

—*The Millions*

"Hale's well-hewn, often violent tales are saturated with sadness and full of strange, marginal folk, but the thoughts, desires, and failures of these oddball characters are acutely recognizable . . . The reader comes away grateful for the sincerity of their melancholy quests to find meaning, love, and the purposes of their ill-fated lives. They mostly fail, some tragically, but not before leaving behind tidbits of wisdom about what it means to be human. This book is at once absurd, morbid, melancholy, ridiculous, and disturbing. It is also erudite and very nearly pretentious, all of which, for like-minded skeptics, pretty much sums up American life around the turn of the twenty-first century."

—*Publishers Weekly*

"Hale received the Bard Fiction Prize and a Michener-Copernicus Award for his debut novel, *The Evolution of Bruno Littlemore*, with a nomination for the New York Public Library's Young Lions Fiction Award to boot. This collection is just as edgy: a man's illicit tryst is interrupted by his estranged son's arrival, for instance, and a performance artist who piles on the pounds becomes an art world sensation."

—*Library Journal*

"The audacious imagination evident in Hale's acclaimed debut, *The Evolution of Bruno Littlemore* (2011), shines again in these seven stories . . . In polished prose, Hale creates memorable vignettes, as he muses on topics ranging from sailing to Kafka to sex fetishes. A provocative collection that takes a unique view of the human condition."

—*Booklist*

ALSO BY BENJAMIN HALE

The Evolution of Bruno Littlemore

THE FAT ARTIST

and other stories

BENJAMIN HALE

SIMON & SCHUSTER PAPERBACKS

New York London Toronto Sydney New Delhi

Simon & Schuster Paperbacks
An Imprint of Simon & Schuster, Inc.
1230 Avenue of the Americas
New York, NY 10020

This book is a work of fiction. Any references to historical events, real people, or real places are used fictitiously. Other names, characters, places, and events are products of the author's imagination, and any resemblance to actual events or places or persons, living or dead, is entirely coincidental.

First Simon & Schuster paperback edition May 2017

Interior design by Ruth Lee-Mui

Manufactured in the United States of America

1 3 5 7 9 10 8 6 4 2

Library of Congress Cataloging-in-Publication Data is available.

ISBN 978-1-4767-7620-0
ISBN 978-1-4767-7621-7 (pbk)
ISBN 978-1-4767-7622-4 (ebook)

For my brothers, James and John

And in memory of Ryan Gosa

THE FAT ARTIST

and other stories

DON'T WORRY BABY

When they became outlaws they gave themselves new names. He chose Miles Braintree: the first part after Miles Davis, the second after Braintree, the T's southernmost stop on the Red Line. She chose Odelia Zion: Zion for the Promised Land, and the baby name book said Odelia means "praise God," but mostly she just liked the sound of it. Hamlet's Ophelia but not quite. *Lives of the Saints* tells of the murdered virgin Odilia, patron saint of the blind. Can be shortened to Delia, Ode, O. A martyr, a lyric, a letter.

Miles had had his disagreements with SDS, split the organization before it crumbled, and formed the Obscure Reference Collective with a handful of other radicals disgruntled with the direction the movement was taking. The bloodhounds were sniffing from day one, ORC's plot to firebomb the New York Stock Exchange was botched by inside treachery, and the remaining true believers went into hiding. Odelia followed Miles to Paris, where they stayed for a few months, and then to Tangier. Money wasn't a problem. Miles had money.

In Tangier they spent two years sitting on woven mats in cafés, eating roasted dates and drinking coffee as thick as motor oil, smoking kief from hookah hoses, sometimes holing up in their second-story two-room flat for two, three, four days at a stretch without putting on clothes, drinking wine, smoking, tripping, making love, friends sometimes dropping by to join in, the daily rising and setting of the sun as inconsequential and amusing and unreal as a TV show.

They burned incense and lit candles at night, and the days were bright blue, blinding bright, their flat acrid with the smoke of goat meat crackling below their unglassed windows. Bare-footed brown legs pattered in dirt streets and in blue alleyways resonant with voices squabbling in Arabic and French. The streets were a jumble of North African and Western clothes: It wasn't uncommon to see a man wearing a keffiyeh and a double-breasted pinstripe suit. The call to prayer echoed across the city at dawn. That's why they'd come here, in part; to do the William Burroughs thing, do the Paul Bowles thing. The sunlight was sharp and harsh and made every shadow look as if it were painted on with ink. They took hashish and heroin and acid and opium and other, more exotic drugs, the names of which Miles told Odelia and Odelia forgot. Miles learned to fish for octopus: You dive down in the shallows, stick your arm under a rock, and let the octopus wrap itself around your fist, then you swim to the surface and beat it against a rock till it lets go, which also tenderizes the meat; then hang the octopus to dry on a clothesline. Dead tentacles dangling from strings. For a while they had a pet monkey, but it got sick and died. Miles and Odelia were married in a ceremony conducted in a language neither of them understood, officiated by a poet from Rhode Island in a turban with half his face painted red. Odelia gave birth to a boy they named Abraxas, after a Gnostic deity mentioned in a Hermann Hesse novel, who simultaneously embodies all eternal cosmic dualisms: life and death, male and female, good and evil. But soon they began to itch with paranoia. Strangers were following Odelia in the streets. A tall man in a gray suit and a gray hat showed up everywhere she went. Letters from friends in the States arrived with pages missing, the seals of the envelopes broken and taped back together. Miles thought he could hear the ghostly-faint feedback signal of a wiretap whenever he picked up the phone, so one night he ripped it out of the wall and threw it in the fire. It melted and stank, and then they had no phone.

Miles contacted a guy he knew in Lisbon who hooked them up with some artfully forged Canadian passports, and that August, Miles, Odelia, and their girlfriend, Tessa Doyle, sold or abandoned everything they owned except for what fit in suitcases, and they traveled, the three of them and the baby, under blandly fake names they had trained themselves to answer to, by boat from Tangier to Algeciras and by train from Algeciras to Madrid to Paris, where they would board Pan American World Airways Flight 503, with a brief layover in Miami, to Mexico City, where a contingent of former ORC were hiding and could offer asylum.

It worried the hell out of Odelia to set foot on American soil, even for a forty-five minute layover.

Miles said: "Relax, O, we're gonna be in International. We won't even leave the tarmac. Trust me. It'll just be flip flip flip, stamp stamp stamp, enjoy your flight."

• • •

They conscientiously dressed down for travel. No hippie freak shit, no saris, no serapes, no leather knee-high boots with frilled tops. Just normal drab white people in vacation clothes, nothing to see here, folks.

Miles wore cowboy boots and a yellow-and-blue Hawaiian shirt with parrots on it tucked into his tight stonewashed jeans. He'd shaved the Zappa mustache he used to have, the one he wore in the old mug shot that was on all the wanted posters, and sported a pair of yellow-tinted shooting glasses that turned his eyes as pink as a white rabbit's. Sheer vanity kept him from shaving his furry sideburns or cutting the blond hair that hung down to his jaw. Odelia pinned her hair up and wore no makeup, minimal jewelry, and a frumpy blue dress with white polka dots that buttoned down the middle so she could breastfeed Abraxas. Tessa had her long brown hair down and wore jeans and a blouse, but had a decorative bindi stuck like a little red-and-gold teardrop on her Ajna chakra, right over her third eye. Tessa Doyle was nineteen years old. Her parents probably assumed she was still in Cuba cutting sugarcane with the comrades, and had no idea she'd been sharing a bed with Miles and Odelia in North Africa for eight months.

Odelia said: "Please take off the bindi. It makes you look like Linda Kasabian. People will think we're a cult."

"Don't freak out about it," said Miles. "She's cool. She won't get us in trouble."

Tessa kept it on. Miles rubbed Odelia's knee and thigh with his hand. The hand felt firm and heavy on her leg. His hands were wide and strong. He gave each a kiss, first one and then the other. He took away his hand.

The plane began to accelerate up the tarmac and Odelia's stomach tightened. Odelia sat in the window seat with four-month-old Abraxas asleep in her lap, Tessa sat in the aisle, and Miles sat between them. An eight-hour flight from Paris to Miami, and then the layover, and then another five to Mexico City, to Tenochtitlán, where the Aztecs cut out hearts and burned them still-beating on the altar, and rolled the bodies down the steps of the pyramid, and the smoke of burnt blood swirled in the blazing New World sun. Peyote, mystery rituals. Blood running down pyramid steps. An eagle perched on a cactus with a rattlesnake thrashing in its mouth. Worship of birds, worship of snakes, worship of the sun, worship of water, worship of human blood, and worship of death. Mexico City.

The plane tipped its beak skyward, Odelia felt the wheels push off the screaming runway, and now there was nothing beneath them. Fluid sloshed around in her gut as gravity's familiar tug was suddenly waving up and down, and they were climbing, traveling along axes both vertical and horizontal, midmorning Paris rapidly expanding in scale below them, the twelve grand avenues spidering outward from the Arc de Triomphe, the tiled rooftops, the sidewalk cafés where Odelia imagined people were smoking cigarettes and eating dainty little desserts and discussing philosophy, second by second growing smaller and smaller and less real.

As the plane climbed steeper and higher Abraxas woke up and started crying. The pressure throbbing in his head. Odelia held him to her chest and rocked him as he struggled. His pink monkey face was contorted in a grimace. She kissed the top of his head.

"Shh——. Shhh——."

How confused, how exhausted he must be. They had already been traveling by boat and bus and train for days and were ragged and dirty and tired before they even got on the plane. *Sleep*, *sleep*, *sleep*, *sleep*, she thought-projected to the baby.

"Nnn nik ik eeaaah," said Abraxas.

"Hey, kiddo," said Miles. "Be cool."

Abraxas quit crying and flopped his head into the nook of Odelia's body where her neck met her shoulder. His tiny hand fingered the edge of her dress.

"It hurts him," Odelia said to Miles, whispering. "The pressure."

"Poor baby," said Tessa, talking across Miles's lap. "He doesn't know how to pop his ears."

"God, I hope he's not gonna cry the whole flight," said Odelia.

"No shit," said Miles. "Eight hours, Jesus. He'll be all right. Won't you?"

Miles reached over and tugged on a plump pink foot, which almost set Abraxas crying again. He uttered a couple of starting-up noises—"uk! uk!"—that could have been the prelude to a shrieking fit. Odelia saved it by kissing the top of his head and blowing on him with her lips brushing his skin. A trick she'd discovered by accident. She didn't know why it worked, but it usually did. She would kiss the top of his head and blow on his skin and say, intoning it again and again like an incantation:

"I will keep you from harm. I will keep you from harm. I will keep you from harm."

His head was downy and soft and he smelled good, sweet—he smelled new. The incantation worked. He slumped back into a zonked-out daze.

Miles produced three chocolate candy bars from the luggage under his seat, wrapped in a plastic bag and wrapped again in foil. He offered one to Odelia.

"No thanks. Not right now."

"Suit yourself. It's here when you want it."

He gently put the candy bar in her lap. Miles smiled. Miles smiled his billion-kilowatt smile, a jester's grin that could have hovered disembodied in midair, a sly smile full of fun and sex and mischief. God, how Odelia loved it. She liked to imagine what Miles must have been like as a child. She hoped he'd been a neighborhood menace, running through gardens, shooting bottle rockets at beehives. Life was a cartoon to him—Wile E. Coyote and Road Runner, explosions and music and silly sound effects and a surreal plasticity to time and space. She loved it. She loved him.

Miles and Tessa ate their candy bars. They were giggling. The chocolate muddied their teeth. The soporific purr of the jet engines put Odelia to sleep. She and the baby fell asleep together almost as a single entity melting into the corner, Paris vanishing beneath them, behind them.

The baby's squirming woke her up.

He cried a little—"uk! uk! eh!"—meaning *I'm hungry*. She unbuttoned the top three buttons of her dress and Abraxas groped frantically for her breast.

A middle-aged woman walking up the aisle slowed her gait as she passed their seats. She was wearing purple and had pearl earrings, and her brown hair was piled on top of her head like a loaf of bread. She cast a look of revulsion at Odelia.

Miles turned to her and said: "Whatcha lookin at, honey? It's nature."

The woman didn't answer and clipped away up the aisle.

"How long was I asleep?" said Odelia.

"I dunno. A while."

She blinked and smeared the ivory mucus from the corners of her eyes. The air in the cabin had become denser and mustier with cigarette smoke.

Odelia squished Abraxas to her chest. The nipple inflated into his mouth and he pulled at it with his gums, his tiny wrinkled hands hugging her breast. He latched onto her nipple. She felt the milk surge through her glands and into his mouth. One eye peeled open languidly and peeked up at her. His eyes were the same green-gold as Miles's eyes. To feed a creature who came from your body with your own bodily fluid: Odelia pondered this, its philosophical profundity, while she took the candy bar in her lap and picked back the foil with her fingernails. She was onto a deep truth. She was searching her mind for the next step in the thought, in the way you search over and over for a lost object in the place where it should be but isn't. She thought about the things she'd been reading lately: *The Golden Bough*, *The Hero with a Thousand Faces*, and the *Seven Sermons to the Dead*. She had a feeling that things were coming together in her head; that this jigsaw puzzle of interconnected ideas was almost in place. She was thinking about magic and religion and love and birth and sex and death and eternal returns and the circles of myth. She looked out the window and ate the candy bar and fed her son.

Five miles below them lay the Atlantic Ocean: blue-black and vast, its crashing waves diminished to ripples. She could see the shadow of the plane on the surface of the water, and a beaming circle of light. She thought about all the animals swimming in the ocean below them. Eels and stingrays and giant squid and fish with bioluminescent lamps dangling from their heads so they may see in the dark, who live near the bottom where we cannot go because the pressure would crush us. And whales—blue whales, these animals a hundred feet long each that glide under the surface of the water like massive phantoms and speak to one another in low haunting songs across fathoms and fathoms.

The word *fathom* would always make her think of Miles. He had been an actor in college, where they met, before they dropped out to join the revolution. He had always played spirits, sprites, tricksters, the lords of misrule. He had played Puck in *A Midsummer Night's Dream*, Mercutio in *Romeo and Juliet*, Ariel in *The Tempest*. She looked out the window at the sea below, thinking of mystery and whalesong and deep beautiful darkness, and thought, *Full fathom five thy father lies* . . . but could not remember the rest. Without looking away from the sea, the plane's shadow, its iridescent halo, her forehead resting on the windowpane that was warm from the sun, she said softly, knowing if she gave him the first line Miles would finish it:

"Full fathom five thy father lies—"

Miles immediately answered: "Of his bones are coral made, those are pearls that were his eyes: nothing of him that doth fade, but doth suffer a sea-change into something rich and strange."

She looked at Miles and smiled. Here we are in the sky, moving westbound fast enough to chase the sun over the curvature of the earth, and the sea is full of mysterious creatures and I am feeding my child with the milk of my own body. She was in love with the beauty and mystery of life on Earth.

"Miles," she said. "I love you."

She reached out her face to kiss him. Miles kissed her back. His lips felt sticky and strange. She pulled back and looked at him. His grin was crazily stretched across his face like a rubber mask. He put his wide, strong hand on her shoulder and tried to massage it a little, but the angle was awkward and his skin felt wet and bloodless, and his touch, although it was meant to be comforting, felt all wrong, like when you see a little kid petting a cat backward. His pupils were dilated.

"Oh," said Odelia. "Did you take something?"

Miles nodded and his eyebrows did a Groucho Marx up-and-down, up-and-down, and the grin stretched a little wider, the rubber mask of his face threatening to snap.

"So did Tessa," he said. "Eight-fucking-hour flight, figured might as well. You know you just did too, right?"

Tessa was doodling with a red crayon in the Moleskine notebook she'd picked up at the duty-free shop in the Aéroport de Paris-Orly, drawing roses with yonic envelopes of petals and clumsy childish houses with curlicues of smoke coiling from the chimneys that twisted into labyrinthine designs, became fans of peacock feathers with human eyes and the segmented vasculatures of dragonfly wings.

Odelia was still nursing Abraxas. She switched breasts after he sucked the heartside one dry. No noticeable effect yet.

"I guess I assumed you knew," said Miles.

"Assumed. How would I? I thought it was just a fucking candy bar."

"Relax," said Miles. "Nothing is just what it is. Everything is always something else. There is no just, only everything being something else."

He repeated this a few times, more to himself now it seemed than to her, codifying it into a mantra, trying the revelation on for size, seeing if it made any sense. When he was done he turned to her again and said: "I'm sorry. What's done is done, O. The only thing to do now is just relax and let it flow. Like Heraclitus: Everything flows. Don't fight it, baby. Don't fight it."

Odelia knew he was right about that. It only goes bad when you try to fight it. She tried to relax: breathing deeply, in through the nose and out through the mouth. Miles and Tessa had a significant head start on her. She'd been asleep, though she didn't know for how long. And they didn't know either.

Miles got out of his seat and starting walking up and down the aisle.

A stewardess rolled up with a cart. Her hair was bound in a drum-tight bun, her hips snug in a militaristic uniform with brass buttons flashing all over it.

"Steak or fish?" said the stewardess.

She startled Tessa, who was hunched over her drawings in the Moleskine.

"What?" said Tessa.

"Steak or fish?"

"What?"

The stewardess bent closer to her and articulated, her mouth opening and closing histrionically around the shape of each word:

"Steak—or—fish?"

Tessa turned away from her and shot Odelia a look of wild-eyed animal panic.

"She's asking what you want to eat," said Odelia.

"I don't want anything," said Tessa to the stewardess.

"Are you sure?"

"Yes yes I'm sure I don't want anything I don't want anything."

The stewardess turned to Odelia.

"Steak or fish?"

"Fish, please. And also white wine."

Tessa smacked her notebook shut, crossed her legs, and tried to look natural. From the seat-pocket she slid a pamphlet with colorful cartoons detailing emergency evacuation procedures and pretended to read it. Odelia unlocked the plastic table in the seat back and unfolded it out in front of her. The stewardess reached across the seats to hand her a tray with a rectangular tin, napkin, fork, and knife on it, then unscrewed a small wine bottle, filled a wineglass half full, and handed these to Odelia. Tessa's eyes followed the transferences of these objects with suspicion and a weak glimmer of hatred.

Abraxas was fine. He'd quit feeding. He wasn't asleep, but in a blissful daze: placid, smiley, making his gurgly prelinguistic baby noises.

She drank half the wine. It wasn't good. It had an unpleasantly piquant tang. She peeled back the rim of the rectangular tin container and removed the damp paper lid. Inside was a hot slimy fish dinner nestled in steamed carrots and broccoli. She picked at it with the fork, ate about half of it before she stopped because ingesting the food was making her mildly nauseated. She drank the rest of the wine and felt better. She gave the half-eaten meal on the tray back to the stewardess when she squeaked past them again with the cart.

The edges of things were beginning to get hazy. Everything was growing a thin coating of blue-gray fungus, like time-lapse footage of a mold culture growing in a Petri dish. There was a jellyfish throbbing in her stomach. Her pulse quickened and she began to feel acutely conscious of her internal organs.

She daydreamed that she was sculpting her body, molding flesh onto her skeleton like in the vision of Ezekiel, and when she was done building her body in this way she would kiss herself and breathe life into her lungs, get the heart thumping. She catalogued the systems of the body: skeletal, muscular, nervous, respiratory, circulatory, digestive, reproductive. She imagined the inside of her body, pictured herself swimming through the conduits of blood in a microscopic submarine, like in *Fantastic Voyage*. The cilia of her lungs wave around aimlessly and the spongy walls heave in and out. Billions of little wiggling fingers line the inner walls of her intestines; pulpy bits of that fish entrée come tunneling through, and the wiggling fingers grab them and pick them apart, absorb them into the walls, transferring nourishment to the blood, and the blood revitalizing the brain, and the brain converting matter into electricity and redistributing it to the rest of the body. My body is like a utopian civilization, Odelia begins to think. We all work together for the good of all. She expands on the analogy: The cardiovascular system is to the body as resource distribution is to the state, and

digestive : body :: agricultural : state
skeletal/muscular : body :: industrial : state
reproductive : body :: cultural : state
nervous : body :: political : state

Everything fits so beautifully together. All elements work integrally toward the health and benefit of the whole. She reasons that if this is possible in the naturally occurring system of a single human body then it should also be possible in human society. Look at me: I am a utopia.

Miles comes back and sits down. He's done pacing up and down the aisle. Odelia burns to tell him about this idea.

"I am a utopia," she says.

"What?"

"I am a utopia."

"What?"

"I *am* a utopia."

It doesn't occur to her that she should have to add anything else to communicate the thought.

"Hot damn," says Miles.

Miles's tongue slithers in and out of his mouth twice to wet his lips. He's waving his fingers. All of his fingers appear to undulate at slightly different wavelengths, like the tubular fingers of those medusoid creatures that lie along the ocean floor and ensnare passing fish who stray too close and absorb them into themselves. Or is she thinking of her intestines?

"Nervous body, political state," she explains.

"Me no understand," says Miles in a silly Mexican accent.

"Look. If everything in the human body communicates and works together, then there's no reason why many human bodies at the same time can't communicate and work together for the benefit of all. We all just have to think of ourselves as a single body with no individual conflicting motives. We have to all think of ourselves as parts of a single biological entity. Everybody will work just as much as everybody else and there's no need for money, no sexual jealousy . . ."

Odelia spools out her dying sentence with her fingers circling in the air.

"Oh," says Miles. "Then I see Queen Mab hath been with you."

"What?"

"Then I see Queen Mab hath been with you."

"What?"

"She is the fairies' midwife, and she comes in shape no bigger than an agate-stone on the forefinger of an alderman, drawn with a team of little atomies athwart men's noses as they lie asleep—"

"Okay, stop," says Odelia. "Not now."

Miles is quiet. He turns away from her.

A little later he gets up and leaves. So does Tessa. They both leave their seats and disappear up the aisle. Miles's yellow-and-blue Hawaiian shirt smears a wake of color in the air as he goes.

Odelia begins to see patterns on surfaces. Kaleidoscopes projected onto everything. Like a net of lace woven out of semitranslucent metallic fiber, a spiderweb mapped onto everything. Aztec stuff: the snake god, the rain god, the war god, the sun god with a mane of flames and spirals for eyes and a lolling tongue. Coyolxauhqui, whose severed head is the moon; Quetzalcoatl, the psychopomp; Tepeyollotl, the god of earthquakes, echoes, and jaguars.

The godheads slide down the concave walls of the airplane cabin and continue across the floor. Outside the window the clouds have begun to organize and form shapes, dendriform fractal sets with tendrils sprouting tendrils, curling out into infinity.

The pattern of the fabric on the backs of the seats, ugly blue-gray with orange and brown horizontal stripes and orange flecks sprinkled all over it—this pattern is only painted on. Freshly applied to the backs of the economy-class seats with wet paint, and it's dripping. The flecks of orange dribble into the blue and the colors ooze and slide down the back of the seat.

Odelia remembers to breathe, sucks in a gulp of air, shakes her head and blinks twice. The image resets itself back to normal. Then it starts dripping again.

She has to keep her fingers occupied. Her tongue thrashes in her mouth like a wounded snake. Fingers moving and muscles tensing and relaxing.

Then Abraxas begins to scream.

This is actually what reminds Odelia that he is there.

She has been holding him. Has she been holding him correctly? One hand scooped under the butt and the other supporting the back, cradling him at two points to comfortably distribute his weight, to ease the circulation of cosmic energy through his little meridians, keep his bloodflow harmonious with gravity. She holds Abraxas to her chest and sways him back and forth.

"Tsh-tsh-tsh-tsh-tsh shhhhhhh——."

He squirms in her arms like a giant earthworm. He struggles with her, smooth white fat arms and legs pumping crazily.

He's screaming.

Now she's trying to fight it. Now she's trying not to try to fight it and that makes it worse. She feels her heartbeat quicken and hears blood battering in her brain and she's sweating.

"Please," she says, whispering, unclear whether she's saying this to Abraxas or to herself. "Please stop it. Please please please please please stop it."

He doesn't stop it, nor does the (6a*R*,9*R*)-*N*,*N*-diethyl-7-methyl-4,6,6a,7,8,9-hexahydroindolo-[4,3-*fg*]quinoline-9-carboxamide that is in her brain. She sees interlocking hexagons in a chemistry textbook, valence bonds, Lewis dots. Honeycombs of hexagons latching onto the synapses, redirecting the rush of electricity like train-yard switches.

The other passengers turn their heads and filch brief looks in her direction. Maybe the men give her looks of irritation and maybe some of the women even give her looks of sympathy, but Odelia interprets every look as an indignant look, a look of condemnation. People who had been sleeping have woken up. They roll their eyes and dephlegm their throats with wet, guttural coughs. Some people stare. Other people try not to look at her.

The baby continues to thrash, he continues to cry, and not just dry wailing but full-on crying, tears running and everything, and he continues to scream.

He chokes on himself for a moment, sputters, stops, spits up. The grainy white splatter of her breast milk turned to puke slides down his chin and onto Odelia's dress. She holds him close and fumps a hand on his back. When he recovers he sucks in a deep breath and starts screaming again.

Miles and Tessa come back and sit down. Their breathing is heavy, their cheeks inflamed. Miles's yellow-and-blue Hawaiian shirt is untucked.

Miles drags his hands through his long hair and shakes it out like a wet dog drying off. He looks bewilderedly at Odelia. Abraxas screams. The baby's face is red and afraid.

"Hey, kiddo," he says, pinching a foot. "Cootchie cootchie motherfuckin' coo, little man."

Odelia looks at him.

"Whatsa matter?" says Miles.

"Miles. I don't know what to do. He won't stop screaming. He won't stop screaming."

"It's cool, it's cool, it's cool," says Miles. "He's fine. Relax. Relax. Relax."

His big hand lands on her knee and slides up her leg and squeezes the inside of her thigh. As Abraxas screams and *thump thump thumps* against her chest Miles leans over and kisses the side of her forehead. She feels the spit from his lips cooling on her temple.

Odelia looks into Abraxas's face. Abraxas opens his eyes. He opens his beautiful green-gold Miles's-eyes eyes. His pupils are dilated.

Odelia thinks of the milk, surging out of her body and into his mouth. From body to body, life to life. She thinks of threads, she thinks of wire-thin nerves spooling from the tips of her nipples into the tiny mouth, latched, gumming, draining her, swallowing her electric currents. She eats, she drinks, he drinks her. Everything that goes into her goes in some way into him. When he was in her womb, a cable of flesh connected them. They're still almost one body, their hearts still pump together in perfect syncopation, one continuum of flesh.

"O god," she says.

"What."

"O god o god o god."

"*What?*"

"O god o god o god o god o god."

Miles grabs her face with the palm of his hand and twists her head until her eyes meet his and squeezes her cheeks hard until her lips pucker. He locks eyes with her and leans in until his face is an inch away from hers and every time he pronounces the letter F she feels a hot blast of his breath on her face as he hisses:

"Please fucking get the fuck a hold of yourself and tell me what the fuck is fucking wrong with you."

Odelia points at the baby.

"He got it from the milk."

A look of some concern manifests on Miles's face. He releases the hand on her face.

"Lemme see his eyes."

"No. Don't. Don't. Don't. You'll scare him."

She clutches Abraxas and blinks several times rapidly, trying to will down the throbbing in her stomach and her chest and her brain. Tears well under her cheekbones. She tries to dam them back. Her vision blurs.

"Come on. Let me see."

Miles pries open one of Abraxas's eyes with a thumb and forefinger and the baby recoils and howls louder.

"Look, let's relax. It'll be okay. All we can do right now is fucking, you know, is just ride it out. Odelia, listen to me. Relax. It'll be all right. It'll be all right. Okay? Don't worry, baby. Everything will turn out all right."

"Okay," she whispers, so softly she almost can't hear herself. "Okay okay okay okay okay okay okay okay okay . . ."

Holding the screaming baby, rocking back and forth in her seat, she has accidentally hypnotized herself with the sound of her own speech.

The people around them whisper to one another. The world is a whisper chamber, hissing with all their secrets. The thrumming of the turbines, the peep of the wheels under the stewardess's cart, the conversations of the other passengers: Every noise becomes amplified, sharpened but not demystified, demonized to a conspiratorial whisper.

She looks out the window and sees bubble clusters sprouting, and realizes the plane is plunging underwater, fathom by fathom, into the ocean, swallowed in the maelstrom like a turd in a toilet, the massive shadows of whales gliding past, pressure pounding in her lungs, nitrogen gas frothing in her blood.

No, we're still in the air. We're in an airplane in the air, dipping and weaving through the jet stream, miracles of Newtonian mechanics keeping us strung to our vector like a bead along a wire by the thrust of stirred flame and the shape of the wings.

Look at what the human race can do!—lift us up and deliver us from one continent to another in a matter of hours, the hands of engineers animating inanimate matter, by the magic of math liberating stupid shivering primitives like us from the constrictions of time and space.

Odelia squeezes her eyes shut tight and then loosens them. The light bleeding through her eyelids makes geometric patterns, chessboards and diamonds that flicker and flash in the darkness. She sees a woman three stories tall, a huge hill of flesh. She has long black hair made of iron cables and three faces. Each of her three mouths is chewing on a pig, and the blood runs down her three faces and down her body. Her body is covered with breasts that wrap around her torso in seven rows, and a jet of blood hisses from the tip of each nipple. The blood runs down her body into a lake of boiling blood on fire that she is standing in. The lake is full of impurities and abominations, expectorate and effluvia. All the blood and piss and sweat and come and shit and puke and tears that have ever come out of anyone's body are in the lake.

She opens her eyes and looks at the thing in her lap. It won't stop screaming. For the moment she's not exactly sure what this thing is but she knows she must hold it. It will be bad if she lets go. Her hands are cold and slick.

The man in the seat in front of her turns around to look.

A mouth, a nose, and an eyeball appear in the sliver of space between the seats. The eyeball is a tender glistening globe, a prick of black rimmed in a band of blue. It is looking at her.

"Hey," the mouth says. "You going to change that kid's die purr or what?"

What? What the fuck is a die purr?

The mouth, the nose, and the eye disappear.

Oh.

The moment the face parts go away she smells the perfect smell of shit. She wonders how long it has smelled like that without her noticing. This screaming thing is my child. It is my son. This screaming thing is my son and I have to make it stop smelling like shit.

Odelia turns to Miles. He and Tessa are conversing closely. She's whispering. Her hand is on his knee.

"I have—" she says.

Miles turns to look at her. Tiny bugs are crawling around all over his face.

"I have—"

Tiny bugs are crawling around all over Miles's face. She closes her eyes.

"I have to change the diaper," Odelia says. Yes: That was a complete, coherent sentence. Good. She opens her eyes.

Miles looks at her. His face is as blank as a blank sheet of paper rolled in a typewriter in front of someone with a blank mind.

"Diaper. I have to change the diaper."

The world is receding into focus. Keep it there. Control it. Don't relax. Control it.

Miles scrunches himself sideways and Tessa folds her legs against her chest in her seat with her wrists wrapped around her ankles. Odelia squeezes past them with the screaming infant in her arms. Standing in the aisle, she asks Miles to hand her the bag underneath her seat.

"The what?" says Miles, looking at her as if she's speaking in another language.

"My bag," she says. "The bag under the seat."

Abraxas writhes. He's screaming in an almost non-baby way, screaming as if his insides are on fire. Screaming in the way she imagines the human sacrifice screamed when the Aztec priest cut a slash below the rib cage, reached under the ribs up to his elbow, groping the organs, feeling for the one that beat.

She thinks that Abraxas is thinking this: Make it stop, make it stop, make it stop, make it stop. He needs to be comforted and she cannot comfort him. He doesn't know what is happening. The bond between mother and child has been cut, and he is alone inside his own brain.

"Oh—" says Miles, finally decoding the message.

He reaches under the seat and hands her the bag with diapers and talcum powder in it.

• • •

Odelia walks down the aisle of the airplane, picking her steps like she's walking on a sheet of oiled glass. She hears decontextualized segments of people's conversations in passing, their voices hushed and accusatory, murmuring with judgment.

Orange spots appear and disappear on the carpet and the ceiling. They appear in her peripheral vision but disappear if she looks directly at them.

Inside the cramped lavatory, even with the door thumped shut and locked, she can still hear the nasty sibilance of damning whispers. The toilet and sink are made of stainless steel. So is the floor. The lighting is the color of an egg yolk. The room pitches and wobbles. She has to grasp the corner of the sink to keep her balance. She lays Abraxas on the steel floor, her hand protecting his head. He's hard to hold, he's squirming all over. He won't keep still. Streaks of orange rust are draining down the walls. She peels his diaper off. It's damp and heavy with urine and squashed pea-green shit. His skin is wrinkled from the moisture. His tiny tube of a penis. She wipes him off quickly. It's a cloth diaper, but she dumps it in the toilet anyway and flushes. The hatch roars open and sucks it down to wherever it goes. She dashes him with a puff of talcum powder and wraps him up with a fresh diaper, careful not to prick him with the safety pin. He's still screaming. Her hands are trembling. She feels so weak she might faint. She has to bend over the toilet bowl. Her stomach makes a fist and releases it. Her hands are clammy and white, gripped around the rim of the steel toilet. She leans her head over the bowl. Nothing comes out. Her hands shake. Somebody knocks on the door. She doesn't answer. There's another, angrier knock.

The baby is still screaming. She picks him up and holds him and opens the door.

• • •

Once, Odelia and Miles went hiking in the mountains outlying Tangier. Well, more than once, many times. But this once, this once, it was a blazing afternoon, the sky so bright it was almost white, the air salty, the pale green line of the sea visible from the mountains. Miles had been reading an Alan Watts book titled *The Joyous Cosmology*. They were walking and talking about the sublime harmony of the natural world. Miles told her that this was the joyous cosmology.

There was Miles, sun-browned and bare-chested in the sand-colored mountains of Morocco, stretching his lean arms out heroically, as if welcoming the embrace of the universe. The sky, the sea, the land. What a beautiful place. What a beautiful day.

"Look around you! Look! It's the joyous cosmology!"

They made love right there in the sand under the open sky in the middle of the day. His sweat smelled like truffles. She licked it off his neck.

She asked him to recite the Queen Mab speech for her. She lay smiling on the sand with their clothes bunched under her head for a pillow and felt the sun's heat on her bare stomach and watched Miles's lean, dirty, darkly tanned naked body twisting in the desert as he began, "Oh, then I see Queen Mab hath been with you . . ."—and he rocked and tumbled through the speech, shouting it at the mountains. When he came to its end, he ran to a different place and assumed a different voice, and said Romeo's line:

"Peace, peace, Mercutio, peace! Thou talk'st of nothing."

Then he ran back to Mercutio's place and answered Romeo's interruption:

"True, I talk of dreams, which are the children of an idle brain, begot of nothing but vain fantasy."

They put their clothes back on and continued hiking. They met a shepherd who was switching his flock along the trail: the dust cloud, the flies, the racket of wooden bells knocking at their necks and desultory bleating. They offered to smoke their hashish with him and he greedily accepted. They sat with him under a creaking desert palm tree and smoked the hashish. There weren't six words of language common between them, but they seemed to understand each other well enough. His brown skin was withered, weather-beaten to the texture of a crumpled brown paper sack. He had so few teeth she could count them, and his tongue was black. He got up to go.

They kept walking. A little while later they saw a stray sheep. The sheep was bashing its head against a rock. Over and over. There was a skinny boy who looked about ten years old sitting nearby on a log, watching. He was doodling in the dirt with a stick. They could tell by his face that he was the shepherd's son. The sheep kept bashing its head into the rock, over and over. Blood ran down the side of the rock and curdled in the sand. A shard of the sheep's skull had cracked open, like a little door, and a string of brains dangled out of the sheep's head.

The boy saw Miles and Odelia, and he pointed at the sheep, shrugged his shoulders.

That was before they met Tessa, and before she came to live with them, before the man in the gray suit and the gray hat started following Odelia everywhere she went, before Miles ripped the phone out of the wall and threw it in the fire, and before Abraxas was born.

The woman in purple was standing outside the lavatory door, with her pearl earrings and her brown hair piled on top of her head like a loaf of bread. She put her hand on Odelia's arm. Odelia flinched at her touch. The woman said:

"Oh dear. Did you have the fish?"

• • •

Abraxas screamed for the remaining duration of the flight. The airplane dove into Miami-Dade, and as it roared down the runway, Odelia turned to Miles and told him she had to take Abraxas to a hospital.

"He'll be fine, he'll be fine," said Miles. "You can take him to a doctor in Mexico if you want. But he'll be fine. We can't lose you. You're never gonna be able to get back to us."

"I'm not taking him to a Mexican hospital," said Odelia. "I want to be in America. I want to be in a place where people understand what I'm saying."

"You won't be safer. You'll get caught. They'll figure you out."

"I'm scared to death. Miles, I'm scared to death."

Abraxas wasn't screaming anymore. He was too tired to scream. He'd settled into a persistent tearful whimper. She held him, she tried to make him understand that she was there and that she loved him, but she knew that inside himself he was completely alone.

She kissed the top of his head, blew her warm breath on his skin, and said, incanting it, again and again: "I will keep you from harm. I will keep you from harm. I will keep you from harm."

Even though she knew he couldn't understand her, she felt like she was telling a lie.

It was light out when they descended the airstair onto the tarmac, roughly the same time here in Miami as when they'd boarded the plane in Paris. The air was oozing with humidity. Odelia left Miles and Tessa at the connecting plane. They didn't kiss good-bye. They didn't even hug. They just sort of stood there and looked at each other. Odelia was crying. Miles gave her some money. A hundred dollars. She had nothing else with her except for Abraxas. Miles and Tessa got on the plane to Mexico.

The sky was pink, the air jungly with moisture. The heat was sickening. A row of thick-trunked palm trees skirted the runway and the leaves of their brittle fronds clicked together in a slight breeze that did nothing more refreshing than blow the heat around. The tarmac was chaotic with crisscrossing streams of traffic, pedestrian and vehicular. Men in blue jumpsuits and caps walked around with bright orange batons and drove baggage trains that scuttled like grumbling, beeping caterpillars across the concrete, and all the passengers who had just deplaned from the international flights funneled into the doors of the airport in a blizzard of languages, snapping at their children and grunting miserably under the weight of their luggage. Odelia joined the crush and was carried by the crowd through the doors. With her fingers Odelia smeared tears out of her eyes, which she was sure were bloodshot and swollen-lidded from crying. Inside the airport the crowd tapered into a line that was corralled into a maze of switchbacks cordoned off with red ropes looping through rows of metal stands that looked like silver chess pawns. The floor of the large room was covered with thin gray carpet. Outside the maze of ropes men in green-and-brown military fatigues stood by with German shepherds on leashes. Several of the men in fatigues were sitting in a circle of folding chairs, drinking bottles of Coke and smoking cigarettes and watching a TV that was bolted to the wall in the corner of the ceiling. A lazily revolving metal ceiling fan whipped the rising smoke into a rapidly vanishing eddy. They were watching the commentators bicker back and forth about McGovern dumping Thomas Eagleton from the Democratic ticket. Eagleton had frail nerves. He'd undergone electroshock therapy and had troubles with drinking.

Men and women in crisp airport uniforms trawled along the line, distributing stubby pencils and customs declaration forms.

Odelia had no plan and nowhere to go. There was the question of how she was going to make it through customs, which was coming closer and closer as she shuffled toward the front of the line. There was the question of money, or rather the question of having almost no money. She thought about how she might be able to get back to her parents in Troy, New York. Maybe she could take a train or a bus. It was August 1972. She was twenty-four years old and she hadn't seen or spoken to her parents in four years. She wanted to see her parents. They did not know they had a grandson. She was going to change her son's name. A smiling young woman in a blue airport uniform handed her a customs declaration form and a stubby pencil.

"Welcome to the United States," she chirped, and moved up the line.

The baby whimpered and looked up at her, exhausted, his eyelashes caked with dried tears. Emily looked at the rectangle of starchy white paper the woman had given her. It was a hieroglyphic scramble of small print and dotted lines and boxes. Was she carrying any meats, animals, or animal products? Disease agents, cell cultures, or snails? Awkwardly balancing the baby against her shoulder with her arm and holding the form, she began to try to fill it in with the stubby pencil.

She had no legitimate identification with her. Passport, driver's license—all of that was gone, and she could not remember if they had been lost or deliberately destroyed. She only had her forged Canadian passport. Her baby did not have a social security number, and she could not even remember hers past the first three digits. She was afraid she was going to cry again. She looked around her for someone to ask for help. The people in front of her were speaking in French and the people behind her were speaking in a language she could not even guess at. Instead of filling in the customs form, she turned the card over and with the stubby pencil wrote on the back:

MY NAME IS EMILY BARROW.
I AM AN AMERICAN.
I AM A WANTED CRIMINAL.
MY CHILD IS SICK.
I AM TURNING MYSELF IN.
I WILL TELL YOU ANYTHING I KNOW
ABOUT ANYONE.
PLEASE HELP ME.

She underlined the last sentence. When she made it to the front of the line she was made to stand and wait until one of the customs officers' desks opened up. When there was a place for her the uniformed man at the head of the line unhooked a red rope from a stand and allowed her to pass through.

A thin, bored-looking bald man with glasses and a white mustache sitting at one of the high desks beckoned to her. He wore a black suit with a red-and-blue-striped tie and silver cuff links on his wrists. Emily stood in front of the desk and waited for him to speak. He was scratching at something on his desk with a fountain pen. Without looking up from the desk, the man held out a hand for her customs form and passport, and said:

"Do you have anything to declare?"

"Yes," she said, and handed him the card.

IF I HAD POSSESSION OVER JUDGMENT DAY

In November 1998 the Iridium Communications company launched sixty-six satellites into orbit. The company had ultimately intended to launch seventy-seven of these satellites to complete the network; the name Iridium was derived from the element with the atomic weight of seventy-seven. The company filed for Chapter 11 bankruptcy in 1999, the result of internal mismanagement coupled with an insufficient demand for its satellite phones. Although the Iridium global satellite communications network provided constant worldwide coverage, the phones were unwieldy and expensive, and were quickly pushed out of the market by the advent of roaming contracts between terrestrially based cellular providers who offered smaller phones with cheaper coverage plans. The Iridium network was dormant, and plans to de-orbit the satellites were drawn in 2000. However, the satellites were rescued by the company's most powerful customer, the Pentagon, which saw potential for defense applications. The sixty-six satellites remain in orbit, and today are used extensively by military intelligence. These sixty-six satellites were designed with massive panel-shaped antennae, and the mirrorlike reflectivity of their material causes intense satellite flares. If the geometry between the satellite, the sun, and the terrestrial observer aligns just right, a brilliant flare of light appears, lasting several seconds. This flare appears as a dim dot of light moving slowly across the sky, becoming brighter as the satellite moves into alignment with the observer and peaking in a flash of about –9.5 in apparent magnitude* before quickly fading away. The phenomena of Iridium satellite flares occur often, due to the large number of satellites, and, due to the regularity of the satellites' patterns of orbit, at rigidly predictable times. These satellite flares will continue until the satellites are decommissioned, or until orbital decay eventually drags them back down to Earth.

There was something Caleb Quinn used to do every afternoon, when they were the only two kids who got off the school bus at their stop. Maggie was seven and Caleb Quinn was nine, and two years' difference was nearly a third of a lifetime then. When the school bus had gone, engine grumbling, gaskets hissing, a cloud of diesel vapors left behind and a hundred hands fluttering from the half-open windows, just Caleb and Maggie standing alone on the grass at three thirty in the afternoon, Caleb would tackle her, effortlessly, pin her wrists to the ground, sit on her chest, and spit on her face.

He would dredge up a glob of snot from the back of his throat with these exaggerated sucking noises, mix it with his spit, let it dribble out, coil it onto her face in a long string. He liked to get it in her eyes and her hair. He spat on her until there was a thick sparkling sheen all over her

* Apparent magnitude is the measure of the brightness of celestial objects. The maximum brightness of Mars is –2.4, a full moon is –12.

face. Sometimes he'd drink a can of Hawaiian Punch on the way home so his spit would be pink, sticky, viscous. Maggie lashed her head from side to side, shrieked, struggled under him. He would only get bored and stop when Maggie quit struggling and resigned herself to being spat on. Eventually, he realized that just the *anticipation* of the first drop of spit was the worst part of it for her—that's when she squirmed the most. After that, the daily torture changed: First, he would tackle her, pin her wrists to the ground, and sit on her chest; then he'd summon up a frothy mouthful of spit in his cheeks and just let it ooze out between his lips, slowly extending it farther and farther down without letting go of it, and then, when the head of the strand dangled a half inch above her cheek and Maggie was wincing, burying her head into the ground trying to wiggle away from it, he would slurp it back up like a yo-yo, chew on it some more, swish it around in his cheeks, and repeat; back and forth, closer and closer, until he could no longer abstain from the pleasure of seeing it slopped on her face. Maggie began to carry a hand towel in her backpack to clean herself up with before he let her walk home, so her mother wouldn't see her like this when she got home from school.

Much later, in high school, Maggie fell in love with Caleb. They moved in together, much happened, and a year later she left him. A year after that, Maggie married Kelly Callahan, and soon after she gave birth to their son, Gabriel. One night, when Kelly was at work, Caleb Quinn came over.

Johanna was eighty-four years old and still lived in the tall, narrow house her late husband had built when they married and moved to Colorado sixty years earlier. He was a good builder but an amateur designer, and his do-it-yourself approach resulted in some strange architectural quirks.

The double doors at the end of the second-story hallway opened onto a twenty-foot drop where he'd intended to build an upper deck. The second floor was accessible not by a staircase, but by a pneumatic, pedal-operated, wrought-iron elevator, which is why Johanna kept a rope ladder upstairs, in case it ever broke and she got stuck up there. The ghosts of her late husband's hands were all over everything. Most of the people Johanna had known well in her life were dead.

Johanna was having problems with language. Words were leaving her. Simple verbs and nouns mysteriously vanishing from her vocabulary. They were moving out of her brain and leaving their empty shapes behind, like the pale outlines of pieces of furniture that have been sold or given away. She occasionally found herself wondering how to communicate actions like "listen," "eat," "give," or grasping to recall the words for objects like tables, spoons, or garbage cans, as if these things were so unremarkable that people had never bothered to waste time thinking of names for them. She was losing information. It was as if her brain was a wall from which every day someone was carefully removing a few bricks, slowly weakening the integrity of the structure.

She was alone in her house, situated at the intersection of two unpaved county roads, by a lake, a power plant, a line of railroad tracks, and an empty field of brown grass. An aluminum Christmas tree stood in the living room year round. A few years before he died, her husband had bought a telescope, which he had set up on a tripod inside the glass doors to nowhere at the end of the second-story hallway. Her phone rang routinely once a week on Sunday afternoons when her son called from Houston. The call usually came at about three o'clock, sometimes up to fifteen minutes past or fifteen minutes before the hour. She would wait until the middle of the third or fourth ring to answer it and say: "Hello?" And she would be answered by the disembodied voice of her son in the receiver, tunneling through wires or quivering along a system of strings or tubes or however it got from there to here, and she'd have a conversation with it.

Her son, who lived in Houston, would usually visit twice a year. She still drove herself to the grocery store in town and cooked her own meals.

There was also an oak grandfather clock with a brass pendulum, and it still kept time. Johanna's hearing was still good enough to predict when the clock would strike, from anywhere in the house, by the subtle ratcheting noise it made when it reared itself to bong out the count of the hour. There was a lot of silence in the house.

She read the Bible. One day, reading the Book of Ezekiel, she began to think about the following passage:

> I looked, and I saw a windstorm coming out of the north—an immense cloud with flashing lightning and surrounded by brilliant light. The center of the fire looked like glowing metal, and in the fire was what looked like four living creatures. . . . In the midst of the living creatures there was something that looked like burning coals of fire, like torches moving to and fro among the living creatures; and the fire was bright, and out of the fire went forth lightning. And the living creatures darted back and forth like flashes of lightning. Now as I looked at the living creatures, I saw a wheel upon the earth beside each living creature with its four faces. This was the appearance and structure of the wheels: They sparkled like chrysolite, and all four looked alike. Each had the appearance of a wheel inside a wheel. As they moved, they would go in any one of the four directions the creatures faced; the wheels did not turn about as the creatures went. Their rims were high and awesome, and their rims were full of eyes all around.

She began to wonder if Ezekiel had been visited by aliens. She told this to her son one day over the phone. She read the passage aloud to him, and then told him about her theory that Ezekiel had been witness to some fantastic display of extraterrestrial technology and had (only somewhat) misinterpreted it as a vision of God. Her son tried to change the subject.

Also at around this time she saw a new light in the sky at night. She had been looking in the right place at just the right time. She was standing on her front porch, looking at a spectacular vault of sky above, haunted with ribbons of starsmoke. At first it was only a speck of light. It traveled slowly across the sky in a smooth, shallow arc, gathering gradually in brightness until it became a blazing white flash, and then the bright light, though still moving in the same direction and at the same speed, began to fade away until it disappeared.

Johanna drove to the library and checked out books about astronomy.

Now Johanna spent each night awake until very late, looking through the telescope at the end of the second-story hallway, aimed at the sky through the glass doors to nowhere. She began to see more of these lights in the sky. She recorded their patterns, penciling her documentations in legal pads, with brief descriptions of what she saw, the date, the exact time of its occurrence, and its position in the firmament—its azimuth, its distance from both zenith and nadir.

She became increasingly convinced that these lights in the night sky were of extraterrestrial origin. Johanna spotted at least four of these unexplained lights per week, sometimes more. But the weekly four occurred with religious regularity. Johanna detected a pattern, or perhaps it was a small part of a larger pattern. She hoped it was part of a larger pattern, as there was much that remained a mystery, but she felt she was beginning to piece it together. In her mind the disparate threads were beginning to form a network.

The lights usually happened in the early evening, just after sunset. Every Tuesday the light would arrive at eight o'clock, almost on the dot, appearing directly south, about 30° above the nadir and 150° below the zenith: She would look at the southern sky through her telescope, listen for the subtle ratcheting noise of the grandfather clock rearing itself to strike eight times, and as soon as she heard the first strike of the clock, the light would appear in the sky. The next one came three days later, on Friday at 7:51 P.M., at the exact same altitude but about 10° west of the previous light. The next came the next day, in precisely the same heavenly position, at 7:45 P.M. The final light in the pattern appeared at the same altitude, but 15° east of Saturday's, on Sunday evening at 7:53. The pattern repeated this way, week after week, without fail or fluctuation.

Every time she saw the light in the sky, she felt something moving inside herself, in her blood, her lungs, her organs, a feeling that was not quite terror and not awe and not humility, and not a feeling that she was catching sight of something of sublime beauty, but a feeling that combined elements of all these, a feeling that must have been something akin to what early human beings felt millions of years ago when they looked up at the spectacular vault of sky above them, haunted with ribbons of starsmoke, and had no idea who they were or where they were or how big was the universe.

Johanna felt she was listening in on something.

First, foremost, Kelly's truck: what a dilapidated hunk of shit it was, how it shuddered and moaned and coughed and wheezed and didn't start half the time.

Kelly Callahan was a friend of mine, and so was Maggie. Caleb Quinn I knew, but I'd never have called him a friend. Jackson Reno I knew only peripherally. We all grew up together; we had all gone to school together. And just by a weird coincidence I knew Fred Hoffman, too. I'd briefly worked for him once, painting houses. Fred sort of fired me or I sort of quit, depending on who you ask, though even now he still calls me up once in a while and asks if I want to subcontract a job for him. His niece, Lana, I never met, but Fred showed me a picture of her once, which I thought was odd at the time, but it makes more sense to me now. That's how I stand with regard to everyone involved in this story, which is why, although I'm not in it, I'm not in the worst position to tell it.

But the truck.

It was a 1987 Ford F-150 that his father had given him, with a spiderweb crack in the windshield and rust-eaten paint, though it had been white. And as for the vehicle's problems, its many ailments, its many electrical and mechanical idiosyncrasies: The windshield wipers didn't work, the headlights went dim if the radio was on, none of the gauges on the dash were reliable, the engine was prone to overheating, and it was furthermore in dire need of new brakes, tires, transmission, air filter, fan belt, spark plugs, and an oil change, and the tank was forever low on gas. This last problem would have been ameliorable enough if not for Kelly's bigger problem, the real problem, the umbrella problem, the arch-problem from which all other problems germinate: money. Kelly's lack of it, specifically.

The truck is important because Kelly needed it for work. Kelly was working two jobs at the time. The first, his day job, was doing construction, and he worked with his friend Jackson Reno. Except for the foreman they were the only two white guys on the crew, and this was in Colorado, where nobody's unionized, and even then Kelly only got the job in the first place because the foreman was a friend of his dad's. Kelly hooked Jackson up with a job on the crew; Jackson had just gotten out of jail for dealing cocaine and nobody wanted to give him a job. Jackson was still on probation and was trying to save enough money to get out of his grandmother's basement. Jackson had sky-blue eyes and his face somehow always seemed to have four days' stubble on it. He dressed every day in ripped-up low-riding cargo shorts that came down to his ankles, a wifebeater, and a Raiders cap he always wore cocked half-sideways on his head, and had arms covered in bad tattoos. On his right bicep he had a tattoo of Cerberus, the three-headed dog that guards the gates of Hell. All the fingers on his right hand were the same length and had no fingernails, from once when he was building one of those kit cabins in the mountains and a log slammed down on his hand and set with the tips of his fingers under it, and once those things set, you can't move them; the foreman had to shoot him up with morphine and rip his hand out. He once told me it was "cauliflowering" before they even got him in the car.

Kelly's second job was driving around in the middle of the night delivering newspapers. That was what he really needed the truck for. Kelly got up around eleven at night to go to work. He'd do his paper route and get home at six in the morning, then go out again to his other job. He had to get that second job because his wife had just had the baby and Maggie couldn't work, and they were desperate for money. He was constantly trying to keep the bank account in the black. It hovered always at just about zero, and if it went under then he'd get zinged with all these Kafkaesque fees for not having any money. Kelly Callahan spent about a third of his income on bank fees. Kelly had red hair, red-red Irishman's hair, and he'd recently grown a beard. He usually wore cowboy boots and a grubby Colorado Avalanche cap. He was in pretty good shape, but he was thin and small, five foot six or so. Maggie had gotten fat. She had an eyebrow piercing and wore too much makeup, all that dark shit around her eyes making her look like a raccoon. Sometimes I would see Caleb's car parked outside their trailer when I drove by. I never told Kelly about it. Caleb Quinn and Maggie had dated in high school, if that's the word for it—they were the sort of high school couple that ditched class to go get high and screw in the bushes behind the tennis courts. They both dropped out of school and moved into an apartment together by the lake behind where the KMart used to be. They were doing a lot of drugs, and I've heard (admittedly, like, thirdhand, but I believe it) that Caleb was beating her. She left him, moved back in with her mom, and later got together with Kelly. She got pregnant and they decided to get married. Maggie and Kelly had been married for a little under a year. Gabriel, their kid, was about five months old when all this happened. They were living in that trailer park out by where 50 and 227 come together. Kelly was twenty-one years old and Maggie was twenty. I think Caleb and Jackson were twenty-two and twenty-three, maybe? I can't remember exactly.

Anyway, on the night of August 19, the night before the night in question, Kelly got up at about 11:00 P.M. Maggie was still up watching TV. He kissed her good-bye and left. The truck started and he drove to work.

Kelly figured if he turned off the engine the probability it would start again was about sixty percent. Every time he turned the key in the ignition he prayed he would hear the sound of the engine catching and vomiting to life and not *grurr-rurr-rurr-nglk!*—(silence). When he was at work, rubber banding and stacking the newspapers, he'd leave the truck's engine on while it sat in the parking lot. It leeched gas mileage leaving the truck running, but he couldn't afford to have it die on him at work, or worse, have it die in the middle of his route while he was getting gas, and he couldn't afford to have it fixed and he couldn't afford the time to fix it and sure as fuck couldn't afford a new car. After taxes, rent, food, gas for the truck, bills, cigarettes for himself and Maggie, diapers for the kid, and other necessary shit, there was pretty much nothing left. It was a good month if he could save more than twenty bucks. It was a bad month if the bank started charging him fees as this paradoxical punishment for not having any goddamn money, and all of a sudden, having done everything right, bills paid, no letters from collection agencies, no letters threatening to turn off the water, no outstanding debts, no drugs, no bounced checks, not much money in-pocket but not quite zero, and *hey!*—next day we're a hundred bucks in debt with a week till the next paycheck. Kelly wondered if having a bank account at all was costing them more than if he'd just cash all his paychecks at the liquor store and put all the money in a fucking coffee can but Maggie was against this financial plan, as she found it low-class.

And Kelly was tired. So what do you do every day, Kelly? You wake up at eleven at night and see your wife and kid for fifteen minutes, get in the truck, turn the ignition and pray it starts, if it doesn't, call work, grovel, tell them you'll be late, if it does, drive to work, a half hour up 227, pull into the lot of this converted airplane hangar with a concrete floor and corrugated aluminum walls, remember to leave the engine running, clock in, drink coffee, get one of those orange hand trucks, wait for the rig to deliver the papers from the printer, dump a stack of newspapers on the hand truck, wheel it over to the workstation, pull out a newspaper, fold it once horizontally and twice vertically, snap a rubber band on it, slip it in an orange plastic sleeve and repeat, repeat, repeat: Repeat 358 times, load them all back on the hand truck, wheel them out to the truck, put as many as will fit in the cab in the cab and the rest in the bed, all the newspapers in plastic sleeves slipping and sliding around in the truck bed like a bunch of just-caught fish in a net, refill your coffee mug with burnt-ass office coffee one more time, light the first cigarette, and drive around the suburbs of Longmont, Colorado, all night throwing newspapers out the window into people's driveways, and if you do it fast you can get home at like five thirty, six at the latest, park the truck on the gravel outside the trailer, say a little prayer for the engine and kill it, eat something, peanut butter sandwich, get into bed with your wife and child, don't wake her up, just lie there next to her and wish you'd slept, worry about money, try not to worry about money, don't take your shoes off so you don't fall asleep and miss work, then at six thirty microwave some more coffee, pack a meal in a brown paper bag, shake yourself awake and light another cigarette, watch the rising sun and wait outside on the gravel for Jackson to swing by in his Chrysler LeBaron and pick you up to take you to your other job, where you and Jackson and six Mexican guys build dream homes for people who buy organic produce and do yoga and sit at computers in air-conditioned offices and go to lunch at Chili's, Applebee's, at TGI Fridays, and who refer to theirs as "real" jobs, then go home at four thirty, so fucking tired you feel dead on your feet, see your wife and child for as long as you can manage to stay up, watch some TV, have a beer or seven, go to bed, sleep for five hours, and get ready to do it again.

Everything went as usual that night. As usual, Born Again Steve at the workstation next to his tried to give him religious pamphlets. As usual, quotes from the Book of Revelation. As usual, the oceans turned to blood and the sun was blotted out of the sky, and as usual, the riders wore breastplates the color of gleaming fire and the heads of the horses were like lions' heads and fire and smoke and sulfur issued from their mouths and a third of mankind was killed by the fire and smoke and sulfur issuing from their mouths. As usual, Kelly told Born Again Steve to fuck off. As usual, Born Again Steve clucked his tongue at him like, whatever, it's your own damnation. As usual, Kelly finished half his route and parked his truck without turning it off at his special spot. His special spot was in the gravel parking lot of Centennial Park, over on top of the hill by the lake and the power plant right off Lookout Road. There's an old cannon there with a plaque on it commemorating the site of a battle that happened in the 1870s when the National Guard slaughtered a bunch of Indians. Kelly sat on the hood of the truck and lit a cigarette and looked at the stars.

As he was looking at the sky, he saw a tiny object, a glint, like a little moving star, scrolling across the sky. The tiny prick of light traveled in a smooth, shallow arc, gradually gathering in brightness until it became a bright white flash, and then the bright light, though still moving in the same direction and at the same speed, began to fade, until it disappeared from the sky.

What had he seen? A strange light in the night sky, appearing, flashing, disappearing. He wasn't alarmed. It could be a plane or something, something explainable, something man-made, but Kelly hoped it was a UFO. In the strictest sense, that's exactly what it was, right?—an Unidentified Flying Object. He imagined a time in human history, a time that wasn't that long ago, before a third of the stars had been erased from the night, before the sky was crisscrossed with the trajectories of blinking jets, when the night was clear, dark, primeval, and mysterious new lights in it were harbingers of wars and plagues or of the supernatural nativities of prophets, portents of disaster or salvation. It made him think about that ocean of blackness, going on and on and out forever. He thought about the word *forever*. He thought about the fact that he was going to die. He remembered a thought he had once when he was a child, when he was lying in bed with strep throat, and he was feverish, swollen, sticky with sweat, so sick that for a moment he wished he would die, and in his head he sent a prayer up to God, to make him die. Then he immediately had second thoughts and wanted to take it back and so he sent up another prayer telling Him to ignore the first and hoped He would understand. Because the thought of death had made him think this: If we believe in God and be good and so on when we're alive, then we get to have eternal life after we die. Now imagine what eternal life would be like. It made him shudder. He determined that the idea of eternal life was much more terrifying than death. He realized that a material, biological death was not necessarily something to be afraid of, but rather, when checked against the terror of infinity, a comfort.

Kelly got back in his truck and finished his paper route. The sunrise as he was driving home was a good one that morning. The sky looked like it had been sprayed with fire and the faces of the mountains were glowing as if lit from within. The road shrieked under his tires as he pulled onto the deserted interstate and far ahead a flurry of birds burst over the highway and farther still the highway tapered out into a thin band of silver on the horizon. He picked up a hitchhiker on his way back. He found him sitting on his backpack on the shoulder of the interstate with his thumb out. A skinny man with a walrus mustache who slurped coffee from a Styrofoam cup. Trinkets of coffee clung to the wires of his mustache every time he took a sip. He said he was traveling because he was wanted for larceny in Wyoming and he was headed to Mexico. Kelly wished him luck, dropped him off on the exit ramp, and went home. He hadn't put any gas in the tank because the only money he had was some loose change clicking around on the dash and buying $1.36 worth of gas was hardly worth it, and because there'd been a couple of state troopers at the gas station who might have said something about Kelly filling up the tank without cutting the engine. The needle of the fuel gauge jittered right above zero. He parked the truck on the gravel outside the trailer, said a quick prayer for the engine, and turned it off. There was a guy living next door who raised dogs for fighting and kept three pit bulls all chained to the same post outside, and as always, when he pulled up they went crazy barking, scrambling all over each other and looking like one giant crazy dog with three heads. It was almost six in the morning. If the rig from the printer hadn't been late he would have been home half an hour ago. The door was unlocked. Inside the lights were off and the blinds shut to the sunrise, narrow orange bands of light striped across the room, and Maggie was sitting upright on the couch, in sweatpants and a T-shirt, feet bare, Gabriel asleep in her lap. The TV was on. The sound was muted and the picture was on snow.

"You're up early," he said.

She looked at him dully. She was mad. About what?

Kelly had been drinking coffee all night and needed to piss. He dumped his jean jacket in a chair and went to the bathroom. His urine hit the middle of the water with a violent sound, then he remembered Gabriel was asleep right in the other room and he redirected the stream to the side of the bowl to silence it. His piss smelled thickly ammoniac and was cloudy, so dark it was almost orange. Urine infection. Dehydration, too much coffee. Zip up, splash water on hands and face. Soap, scrub some of the newspaper ink from blackened palms, water. The ink from the newspapers spiraled down the drain in marbly black threads. His eyes were murky, ringed with wrinkles of gray skin, the whites dark with blood.

When he came out of the bathroom Maggie was still sitting there on the edge of the couch. She had something stuck up her nose, a twist of toilet paper crammed into one nostril to dam a nosebleed.

Kelly said: "What's wrong."

"Caleb Quinn come over when you was at work," she said.

"Caleb Quinn? What did—"

He could feel the anger coming inside him, starting in his stomach and racing up his throat.

"What did he want?"

She didn't look at him. She was watching the agitated crackle of static on the TV. It wasn't quite snow. There was some kind of image buried in it. Silent, fuzzy figures moved like shadows behind a curtain of noise.

Her voice was a decibel above a whisper, and she looked like she was conscious of being watched as she said:

"He raped me."

After he'd calmed down enough and the baby had quit crying and had gone back to sleep, Kelly sat down with her on the couch.

They sat there together, watching the figures moving behind the static on the TV, not saying anything, Gabriel asleep on Maggie's lap.

Kelly tried to hold her hand, but she didn't want him to. He tried to put his arm around her, but she flinched, she didn't want to be touched at all.

At a quarter to seven they heard the dogs barking outside.

Jackson Reno had pulled his car up on the gravel outside, and they heard him sink his palm into the horn of his green Chrysler LeBaron three times, probably guessing that Kelly had fallen asleep. Kelly had to go to work.

Fred wet the seam of the joint he'd just rolled, double-sealed it with an index finger, and presented it to Lana.

"This," he said, holding it the way one would hold up an interesting archaeological artifact for schoolchildren to see, "is a joint rolled with the inveterate craftsmanship of a dude who lived through the sixties."

Lana smiled and accepted it, almost over-casually, Fred thought, like not making too big a deal about this new illicit wickedness between them, as if to say there was nothing wrong with sharing an illegal marijuana cigarette such as this with her uncle, though it was obvious the wrongness of it thrilled her.

"Do not, I repeat, do not, tell your mother about what we're gonna do here," he said. "She wouldn't get it. This is not porn—this is art. I don't think she would get it. I don't think she would understand the difference."

"What is the difference between pornography and art, Fred?"

"That's a time-old question of aesthetics and the answer has to do with your, uh, philosophical outlook, but what I say to that question is very little actually when it comes down to it. But still. Bottom line, don't tell your mother."

"Yeah, no duh," said Lana. "She wouldn't get it."

They were sitting at Fred's kitchen table under a jittery fluorescent tube full of dead bugs, looking at books of nude photography. Fred had just dropped the needle on an album of Alan Lomax field recordings; the antique recording warbled and crackled with static, and Lead Belly sang:

Brady, Brady, Brady, you know you done wrong
busting in the room when the game was going on

Lana extended her neck out with the joint between her lips and Fred lit it for her with the feeble blue sputter of a Zippo that was running out of fuel, clacked it shut with his thumb, and set it on the table. This is what was on the table: the lighter; some empty beer bottles; two orange Fiestaware plates, on which were forks, knives, and crumbs of toasted hot dog buns and spaghetti; a brown glass ashtray Fred had stolen from a Best Western in Utah, containing the ashes and butts of the cigarettes they'd smoked; several books of art photography they'd been looking at together; some matte prints and proof sheets of Fred's own photographs. The table itself Fred had made out of tree stumps and a slab of concrete he had painted pink and decorated with Mexican Talavera tiles. Every spring he hauled the bastard thing out to the sidewalk art fairs in Denver, Boulder, Aspen, Durango, Santa Fe, Taos—along with his paintings, framed prints of his art photographs, and the other unwieldy pieces of furniture he'd made and painted with kaleidoscopic patterns, turquoise, green, neon pink, diamonds, suns, crescent moons, lizards, cacti, jaguars, dog-headed snakes, Aztec gods—and he would sit under his designated tent in a lawn chair with a cigarette and a beer and an ice-cream cone and hope for customers, and if none bit he just watched the passersby, which was entertainment enough if the weather had warmed up and all the skirts and flip-flops and bikini tops had finally come out of hibernation. Occasionally he actually sold something. Fred also photographed weddings and did high school yearbook shots, if the parents didn't take a look at Fred and decide not to drop their kids off with him (which happened), and in the summers he painted houses to supplement his income. Still, Fred Hoffman was perennially broke. He leased (not to own) this aluminum-sided fifties ranch, and had illegally converted the fallout shelter into a darkroom, where he spent a lot of time under red lights, breathing in the noxious miasmata of fixer, developer, and stop bath. Working with paint and photochemicals compounded perhaps with too much acid in the sixties (mostly the seventies, to be honest) had given Fred some nerve damage, and though he felt his wits were still intact, sometimes his words couldn't quite slide through the electrical conduits from brain to mouth syntactically unscathed—they got bogged down somewhere along the way, always arriving late and in the wrong order. He also found himself talking in a slow, nasal, pained-sounding voice; his lungs straining to push air through a smoke-hoarsened throat. And at some point in the last ten years he'd gotten really fat.

Fred wanted to shoot nudes—atmospheric close-ups of milky hips and legs and torsos and breasts, black-and-white shots with very narrow depths of field, pale dunes of skin sloping into the distance like mystical desert landscapes, or maybe something like David Hamilton, delicate-boned girls splashing around in streams, wringing hair, sighing, perched lithely on logs like forest nymphs out of some titillating Greek myth. He was thinking about starting a Web site, though Fred wasn't exactly sure what this meant, he only knew that he apparently hadn't been paying attention at the precise cultural moment when everything suddenly turned into w-w-w-dot-whatever-the-fuck-dot-com. Any technology more cutting edge than the eight-track was as good as voodoo to him. But cell phones, computers . . . technology was the thing now. Somehow technology was supposed to save us all. The future was promising and bright. It was the summer of 2001.

Fred had met Lana in Troy, New York, at his mother's funeral, when his scattered and estranged family got back together for the first time since they were kids. At the reception Mom was lying supine in a glittery electric-blue casket with a plush white interior, looking like she had passed out in the backseat of a '57 Caddy. Fred said they should have buried her facedown so when the Rapture comes and Jesus floats down from heaven to raise the dead she'll wake up and start digging in the wrong direction and we won't have to *ever* see her again, unless she eventually resurfaces somewhere in China with fingers clawed to the knucklebones, hacking up lungfuls of dirt . . . Fred's sisters didn't think it was funny when he said that. Lana had been fourteen years old at the time and had recently gone all mall punk, with a silver bauble flashing on the curl of her nostril and her pretty little head totally befouled with this psychotic haircut, her hair shaved to the skull except for a Kool-Aid–green shock in front that dangled to the corner of her mouth, and she had a disgusting habit of chewing on it. Her mother—one of Fred's older sisters—said she was "in a difficult phase." Lana was doing drugs, smoking cigarettes, listening to the Buzzcocks, dressing like a hooker, and mutilating herself with safety pins. Her mother simply didn't understand. Fred understood.

During that week, Lana and Fred would sit across from each other at dinner and exchange looks of exaggerated boredom while everybody else blithered about property values, retirement plans, PTO meetings, interest rates. Greasy, fat, bearded, long-haired Fred generally went ignored, and Lana was usually discussed by the adults (while she was present) in the third person. Lana would rearrange the food on her plate in pecks and scrapes with her silverware, makeup-blackened eyes full of murder, responding to anything asked of her as if the question were absurd. Sometimes in the course of the conversation Fred would open his mouth and attempt to contribute in some way, and when he finished talking, everybody else just sort of stared at him for a moment, and then, after a few ticks, somebody changed the subject, and people started talking again. Lana warmed to Fred.

Fred told Lana about painting backdrops in Hollywood, about his stint as a playwright in New York, about the punk scene in the East Village, about how he'd tended bar at CBGB for a while, about how he once went to live on a commune in New Mexico in the seventies but they kicked him out after three days because his stupid dog was chasing all the fucking sheep.

Lana told Fred her parents were pricks. Fred had to agree. After everybody had gone home, Lana and Fred exchanged a couple of letters, and Fred sent her some mix tapes—stuff like Television, Richard Hell and the Voidoids, (early) Sonic Youth, the Replacements, Gang of Four, Orange Juice, Josef K, The Teardrop Explodes. Meanwhile, Lana grew her hair back, washed out the dye, and quit mutilating herself with safety pins, although (as far as her mother was concerned) she still dressed like a hooker, and now that Fred was sending her the mix tapes she was listening to nastier music than ever. She was sixteen. She was still "in a difficult phase"—or maybe she was in another one.

Lana's family lived in some godawful cardboard-cutout suburb in Southern California. She saved up for a plane ticket, and now, two years after Fred's mother's funeral, Lana and Fred were sitting in Fred's kitchen together, smoking pot and talking about photography and listening to Lead Belly.

Lana gave Fred the joint, scooted back her stool, and crossed the room. Fred watched her walk: Her jeans were rolled up to her calves and her feet were bare, a flaking spot of red nail polish on each toenail. The bone-yellow linoleum of the kitchen floor made sticky noises under her feet and the rotten floorboards yowled as she walked. She yanked open the refrigerator, an old mint-green Frigidaire that looked like a sci-fi robot. The refrigerator hum kicked on and beer bottles jingled in the side door.

"Want another beer?"

"Fuck it, hon," Fred said, wheezed, emitting a burst of smoke with each word. "Uno mas cerveza, señorita. Pero uno, solamente uno."

"Your Spanish sucks, Fred." Lana gripped the necks of the beers with three fingers. "Are you a lightweight?"

"I'm driving, hon. They'll be more beer when we get back. You'd better keep a rein on yourself there. I don't want you getting all sloppy drunk on me here, man, I mean, this isn't operating like, heavy machinery here, but it does require a little, uh, cognizance."

"I don't think that's the right word. Cognizance means like, knowledge. Competence?"

They'd been talking about photography. Lana said she used to want to be a poet, but now she wanted to be a photographer. They were going to shoot photographs. Fred was going to take the photos; Lana was going to model.

She set the beers on Fred's table, took the joint from him, took the smoke deep into her lungs, let it churn there a moment, exhaled from her nostrils. Lana wedged open one of the beers with a plastic lighter, handed it to Fred, and did the same with hers. She swigged the beer, squinting. She had a tendency to squint. In the last year and a half she'd grown into her body more. Her shirt hung limp on her thin shoulders, no bra, the shadows of her nipples showing through the fabric.

They flipped through the photography books, pausing for a long time on each glossy page to soak up the image, talking about the photographs. They talked some more, a bottle of whiskey came out, they did a shot together and talked about the Delta blues. They were going to cover her body in silver paint, drive out to the woods, and do light paintings. Fred's plan was to set up the camera on the tripod in a dark place and take shots with very long exposure times, and Lana in her silver body paint was going to flit around in front of the camera like a forest nymph and Fred would shine the flashlight on her and turn it off, burning her ghostlike image into the celluloid.

The Alan Lomax recordings ended, and they moved into the living room, where the turntable was, and started rifling through the record collection that covered all four walls of the room from floor to ceiling. As Lana flipped through records, Fred mentioned Tommy Johnson, Lonnie Johnson, Robert Johnson, Skip James, Son House. Fred mentioned Blind Blake, Blind Willie Johnson, Blind Willie McTell, Blind Boy Fuller, Blind Gary Davis, Blind Lemon Jefferson. Fred mentioned Lightnin' Hopkins, Pink Anderson, Leroy Carr. On the turntable, Robert Johnson sang:

If I had possession over judgment day
Lord, the little woman I'm lovin' wouldn't have no right to pray

"Is this song about the end of the world?" said Lana, the bottle of Wild Turkey in her hand. She was sixteen. Fred was forty-nine.

Fred spoke to Lana about what Federico García Lorca called *duende*: an untranslatable word for the ineffable graveyard mysticism of only the truly great flamenco music: irrationality, earthiness, a dash of the diabolical, and a heightened awareness of death. That duende, he said, is present in these blues songs in a visceral and immediate way. All truly great music has it, he said—that skull and crossbones, that eros-thanatos, that love of darkness that infuses the sound and sentiment behind the downbeat, the minor key, the doomsday lyrics, making them so lush and so dangerously alive: a heightened awareness of death.

So next day we're at work and Kelly's telling me this bullshit about how he wants to "kill" Caleb Quinn. Kelly's pissed, I mean pissed the fuck *off*, and on top of all that he aint got no sleep cause he works his other bullshit job at night throwing newspapers in people's driveways and I'm sittin here thinkin he's gone all psycho on me here and I'm all like, hold on, slow down, motherfucker. What? No. I already told you. The thing is, Kelly don't understand women. A bitch is the only thing in the world that loves you more the worse you treat her. That's like the first fucking thing about understanding female psychology, and I don't know why but Kelly never got it. Kelly, that motherfucker is whipped. Kelly thinks he saved Maggie from a bad life, like Caleb is the bad-guy cowboy and he's the good-guy cowboy and Maggie's the bitch tied to the tracks in her panties and dun-dun-dah!, here comes Kelly on a white horse. He don't understand the bitch'd rather have a bad-guy cowboy in a black hat to come around and fuck the shit out of her than a good-guy cowboy to save her. That's the first fucking thing about like, human psychology, period. Nobody really wants to get saved, right? But whatever, she don't respect his ass and Kelly hates that she sits around all day getting fat and toking up with the kid in there. And I'm all like, what the fuck did you expect, dog? You *marry* a bitch and of course she's gonna get fat. But he don't even *know* about half the shit she does. Like, case in point. That skank calls me up on my cell some night when Kelly's gone throwing his stupid-ass newspapers and she asks me if I got any coke I wanna sell her. I say, no, fuck *you*, not only do I not have coke, I aint ever going to now cause I *just* got out of motherfucking jail, if they catch me doing *anything* while I'm still on probation they'll fuck me in the ass ten times worse, and furthermore, you stupid cunt, I know for a *fact* Kelly don't like you snorting yay or tweaking or whatever the fuck else you're doing and you got some fucking *brass* calling me up like this knowing how tight me and Kelly is, and I aint gonna tell him about it this time, but you stop this shit or I'm gonna talk some sense into Kelly and let him know the full extent of the female *parasite* he's got hanging off his ass while he's out there busting it working two goddamn jobs to make rent, you under*stand*? And Maggie, she's all crying and shit, like, *sorry, sorry, sorry,* and she starts saying something else and I just hang up on the bitch, *click*. And that's the difference between me and Kelly. But that aint Kelly's main problem. Sure as hell it aint his main problem right now.

Huh? Yeah. Yeah. No, like I fucking *told* you, I've known Kelly Callahan since we were *this* fucking tall, dude. Jesus. Whatever, dog. Okay, yeah. So we're at work, right, and Kelly's all telling me this bullshit about how he wants to kill Caleb Quinn, and he don't know what the fuck he's talking about, right? Cause Caleb Quinn, it's not like I'd call him a bud but I know him, right, and Caleb, he's a *big* motherfucker, like six three or some shit and three hunnerd pounds. And Kelly's just this little dude, and now he thinks all a sudden he can take Caleb, like he's the Incredible Hulk or some shit and just getting pissed off is gonna turn him into this big scary green-ass monster? But Kelly's good, man. He's good people, you know? He gave me some help when I was in a bad situation and hooked me up with this job when I got out of jail for drug shit—which was a bunch of bullshit anyway—and nobody wanted to hire my ass, so I *owe* him one, right? And Kelly, I say to Kelly, the time to return the favor is *now*, and my favor to you is this. First of all I'm gonna be the one to cool off your fuckin' *head*, dog, cause you're dead tired and crazy pissed and you have lost your *brain*, so first thing you need is a friend with some rational motherfucking faculties here. Second thing you need is a second, cause there aint no way in fuck you're gonna take that bigass motherfucker by your littleass self. Third thing you need is a *plan*, cause this like take-him-out-and-whack-him Godfather-type shit you're talking about is *simply not enough*. So we're at McDonald's on lunch, right, and we're talking, just brainstorming, understand, and I say look, dog, I know Caleb Quinn. I used to be tight with Caleb way back, known him since we were *this* tall. So I go meet up with Caleb, I say to Kelly, I go meet up with him and I bring him to you. Don't ask me how, I'm gonna figure that out. I have my ways, dog, don't worry about it. I take him up to the park, right? Centennial Park, with the cannon on top of the hill where they killed all those Indians or some shit? We take his car so he feels chill with it. We drive up to the park, and that's where you're gonna be at, and you've got a baseball bat or something. Go get yourself one a them Louisville Sluggers. There's this trail there, right, and the trail goes down a hill, around the bend? You know what I'm talkin about? You be waiting right there around that bend, so you can get the drop on his ass. I aint even gonna touch his ass unless you miss or something and you need my help, but I don't want to cause this is your thing, right? So don't miss, but if you do, just in case I *got* your ass, trust me. So that's the plan, right? And I say to Kelly, you better be out on that trail with a bat or some shit by nine o'clock tonight, and you just sit your ass down and wait. I'll take care of the rest. I say nine cause that's when the sun goes down, cause it's summer. It might take me all night to get him out there cause I don't know how long it's gonna take me to find him, so be ready just in case, is what I tell him. If I got him with me I'm gonna try to call your cell before we get over there so you can get ready, but I'm warning you I might not get a chance to call, so don't expect it, just be ready anyway. And *don't,* I repeat, *don't* go busting nobody's skull by accident cause you're a jumpy motherfucker right now and you think they're Caleb. I'm gonna keep him talkin, and you know his voice, right, and you know my voice, so that's how you're gonna know we're coming. And I'm gonna make *damn* sure he's walking in front a me so I aint the one that gets whacked by mistake. Main thing is, keep your fucking cool, Kelly. And then Kelly asks me if I can try and get Caleb out to the park by eleven so he can still get to work throwing newspapers, and I think that shit's so fuckin funny I just laugh, but then he's all like, I'm *serious*, dog, I can't miss work. So I just say yeah, whatever, I'm gonna try and get him up there by eleven so you can beat his ass and still get to work. But here's what I want you to do now, I say to Kelly. Huh? Yeah, we're still at McDonald's here. I say, go tell the boss you're sick, you *got* to go home right now. You gotta go home cause the most important thing you gotta do now is get you some fucking sleep, dog. Rest up, cause you're gonna need your energy, and you're all nodding and shit right now, I can tell you're tired. So Kelly says yeah, OK I'm gonna go home and get some sleep. We go back to work and he tells the boss he's sick as a dog, and the boss is like, yeah, whatev, Kelly, you look like shit, go home. So he clocks out and I drive his ass home and drop him off. And we're outside his house and all these dogs in the yard next door are going crazy barking and Kelly's getting out of the car and I say, Kelly, promise me you get you some sleep. I don't care fuckall what that bitch has got to say to you when you get in there, just tell her shut the fuck up, I got to get some sleep so I can think straight, you understand? And he says yeah, he promises me, but I can't hardly hear his quietass voice cause of all them crazy dogs barking. So I get back to work and everybody is looking at me all like suspicious, cause they understand some kind of shit is up but they don't know what, but I just say fuck all y'all, and I clam the fuck up and I don't say a goddamn thing to nobody the whole rest of the day, except for shit like, hey, gimme that hammer. The end of the day comes and there's this little bit of shit with the boss wanting me to work overtime cause with a man down that afternoon we didn't get where we was supposed to, but I just say no, man, I got a date, can't stay, sorry. I go back to my gramma's house, say whatup and kiss her cheek and shit and I go downstairs and wash up and change clothes. I get in my good clothes which was a mistake cause they got all fucked up with blood later but that's the least of my problems now. When I leave the house, all I got on me is a shirt and jeans and boots, forty bucks in my pocket, my phone and a pack of smokes. I take the bus downtown, eat a sandwich at Papa Jose's and then I go to the Scumdowner and walk up to the bar and order a beer. There aint nobody in there at first cause it's early, but more people start coming in and I just hang back and shoot some pool. And sooner or later I see this guy I know, Braden Boomsma. I know he knows Caleb. So I see this motherfucker from my past life and I just go up and say hey dog, whatup, and he says I hear you got out a jail a couple months back, and I say yeah, it's good to be back. And then I say, hey, dog, you ever seen Caleb

Quinn round here no more? Whatever happened to that dog? And he's all like, naw, dog, I guess that just means you aint been to the Scumdowner much lately cause he still comes in here all the time. He's working some job fixing swimming pools now. He gets off work about seven and he comes in here about a half hour later. He stick around all night? I say. He says, yeah, he stays a couple hours sometimes, sometimes he's here till last call. It's like six thirty now, and I know Kelly aint gonna be out there at the park with a bat till like two, three hours, so I gotta keep busy. I bet Braden a beer on a round of pool, and I'm winning till I knock in the eight ball, so I go up to the bar to buy his ass a beer and buy my ass one too, and when I get back from the bar who the fuck is standing there at the pool table as Braden's racking the balls? I aint seen this motherfucker in two years, and I never did much like that motherfucker much anyway so it aint like I been seeking his ass out since I been out of jail. Sure enough he's wearing these ugly yellowass boots that he cleans pools in or whatever. And here I am, I'm standin here with two beers full up to the rims in both my hands and I'm all trying not to spill and shit and still for some reason I can't take my eyes off these big yellow boots he got on. And Caleb Quinn says, hey, whatup dog, like we're buds. I put down the beers and we shake, and when me and his hands are doing the whole slap-squeeze thing I feel he's still got a real good arm, and I note this duly. So then I'm all like, I aint seen your ass in like two years, what you been up to, just some bullshit like at. And we're talking, and the conversation's just about shit we used to do, all the girls we used to know. Just a bunch of inconsequential bullshit. And we're shooting pool and shit and talking. But I'm keeping my eyes on the clock the whole time, waiting for it to get close to nine. Caleb's loosenin up and drinking, and I'm drinking too, but I'm trying not to drink too much cause I gotta hold on to my wits. But I get an idea on my own, which is I keep on betting him beers on pool games, and at this point it's just me and Caleb and the pool table cause Boomsma is over at the bar trying to chat up the one girl in the room, and she aint even that hot. And here I am, I keep on losing and losing, cause I'm throwin the games. I keep on sinking the eight ball and shit, playing like shit on purpose. So I let him win and win, and I keep going like, *shit*, dog, it aint my night, and Caleb, this greedy motherfucker can't turn down free booze, especially if he feels like he *won* it off me. So I been going over to the bar and buying his ass beer after beer and then shot after shot when he switches to whiskey, and don't get me wrong, Caleb's a big dude and he's a drunk anyway, so it takes a lot to get him good and shithoused but he gets there alright. And it's like, not even nine yet, but here's Caleb, and he thinks we've been having a grand old fuckin time and I guess he's right, and here I am about to take a shot, and I'm lookin at the cue ball and the cue's slidin in and outta my fingers like a dick in a pussy and that's when I look up all sly and I see Caleb standing there like he's ten sheets to the wind, and I see him put down his beer on the edge of a table, but he like half misses the table and the glass falls, and I don't even remember if it broke or not all I remember is he tried to put his beer down and missed the fuckin table. And that is when I unload the plan on him. And it works like a motherfuckin *charm*, at least the first part does. I make my voice all quiet so he's gotta lean in to hear me, and I look around the room like I'm being all like conspiratorial and I say, you still into yay? He leans back and he's all like, yeah, every now and then, like he's trying to play it cool, but he don't have a very good poker face. See now this is the thing, Quinn (I say to Caleb). My old connection calls me up the other day and says check out all this shit we got. At first I say, naw, dog, I can't get into that shit no more, I'm still on probation. And then he tells me how much and what price, and I freak out, right? Soon as he tells me what he's selling this shit for I'm all like, the *fuck*? cause at first I don't believe him, I think he's shittin me, but I say, I gotta see this shit, so I meet up with him and take a look at it and sure enough he aint shittin me. Shit is fucking *gold*, man. And I'm broke as a joke right now cause ever since I got out of jail I been trying to go straight. If I sold this shit off for even like half what it's worth I'm gonna be in good shape, I think. I can*not* turn this shit down, so I throw down and buy it all off him right then and there for half a grand. And then I go home, and the next day I get a surprise visit from my probation officer. She didn't search the place or nothing, she's just like checkin up on me to make sure I got a job and shit, which I do, but she scares the fuckin shit out of me, right? I'm all standin there and she's talkin to me and the whole time I'm all like shakin in my boots cause alls I can think about is all that yay all rolled up in a sock in my closet, and I'm trying to stay cool, and I do, and she goes away, but soon as she's gone I'm having some extremeass second thoughts about my little purchasing decision yesterday. You know what caveat emptor means? Caleb goes, what? I go, it means don't go round buying a shitload of coke when you're on probation and you got some bitch from the fuckin government coming round at randomass intervals checking up on your ass. So, I say to Caleb, that all happened yesterday. So now I realize how much I fucked up. I bought all this yay, and I realize now, I been in jail for damn near two years, and in that time all my contacts dried up. I don't hardly know nobody in town no more. I don't know who the fuck to sell it to. And for obvious reasons I aint about to try to sell it to some dog I don't know all that well. And that, Caleb, is what brings me to my *unhappy conclusion*. I have *got* to get rid of this shit ASAP, and I figure if I can't turn a profit on it I might as well sell it for what I paid for it just to get rid of it, which is a fuckin steal considering the quality of this shit. So. You interested? And then he lets a couple seconds go by, like he's all busy thinking it over, like he don't want to make it look like his pussy's already all wet over it, but I can see in them little pig eyes of his he's already made his decision. Yeah, he says, yeah, I'm interested. Good, I say. And then we talk details and he says he'll give me the five hunnerd I say I paid for it, which is the best offer I got for a bunch of coke that don't even exist. He says today's my lucky day cause today was payday and he's got the cash on him right now if I got the shit on me. I say good for you, but I don't have the shit on me. My whole unfortunate legal situation's made me *real* paranoid about this kind of shit, and I went and hid it in the woods. He goes, what the fuck? I go, I know, it sounds crazy, dog, but I wanted that shit the fuck out of my house. I put it in a fuckin coffee can and hid it a little ways off a trail in Centennial Park. You know up on that hill off Lookout Road? It's like five-ten minutes from here? He agrees, says yeah, yeah, says he knows it. So I say, you got wheels? I drove the company van down here after work, he says, cause I got the van till close and they aint got no way of knowing what I do with it after. Okay, good, I say. What? Yeah, yeah, we're still at the Downer. I dunno, nine? Nine fifteen? Yeah no. Yeah. Now Caleb Quinn's shithoused, yeah, but I figure he's a pretty good drunk driver from years of practice so I guess he's still basically good to drive. We're only going one way, anyway, I think. So he goes off to piss and I call Kelly on his cell, but it aint on, which kinda scares me a little cause he's supposed to pick up. What? Yeah, I guess it was like about nine thirty, almost ten at that point. Last time I looked at a clock it was nine, don't know where the fuck a whole hour went. I start leaving a message for Kelly but then I stop and put down the phone cause I see Caleb come out of the bathroom. Now I'm thinking if Kelly pussies out on me or some shit and it turns out he aint there when we get there what the fuck am I gonna do if we get out there in the bushes and I aint got nothing to show him? That thought makes me start to sweat a little, so now I gotta work out a Plan B if Kelly flakes. Caleb comes back, says, aright, let's go. First he wants to peace out with Boomsma though, but I don't want nobody being able to say for sure he saw me leave the bar with Caleb that night, and I tell him so, and he agrees, but he don't know the real reason why, he just thinks I'm being all paranoid about the coke and shit. So I swear him to secrecy and then I go up to Boomsma and smack him on the back and say, so long, and he aint really paying much attention anyway cause he's still tryin to chat up the one girl in the bar even though she's not that hot, and I just get the fuck out of there and go wait outside for Caleb. Five minutes later he comes out, too, but before he does I try calling Kelly's cell again and again it just rings and rings. I'm thinking if Kelly pussies out on me I guess I'm just gonna have to say, aw, shit, man, it aint here, some little bird must of took it, but I don't know if I'm gonna be able to act that good to bullshit that bad. We go get in his company van, which is like this pool cleaning van with all these nets and pool equipment and shit on top of it and this picture of a mermaid on the side of it holding a pool net. The mermaid's got nice tits. We go. I'm sitting there tryin to think, and in my head I'm all like, stay rational, dog, and there's all this alcohol swimmin around in my brain cause I fucked up a little and wound up drinking a little too much. I try and see what pocket he kept his keys in, cause now I'm thinking if this here company van's in the parking lot next morning it's not so good, right? And I'm also thinking if he sees I aint got shit on me and I took his ass all the way outta town for nothing, he's gonna get *real* suspicious, and I aint got a getaway car or nothing, and don't get me wrong, I'm plenty confident with just my fists, but this here motherfucker is stacked like a fuckin wall and if he lands a punch on me in the right place it's gonna mean lights the fuck out for me. So all of a sudden I got a lot a shit on my plate and I'm sittin shotgun in this pool cleaning van and we're driving around and Caleb's all swerving around on the road and shit, and that's when my cell goes off. Who the fuck is at? says Caleb. The fuck is it to you? I say. I say, it's my gramma. That was a lie. Of course it's Kelly, calling me back way the fuck too late. I turn down the volume on the phone way way low so Caleb can't hear and then I answer the cell and I make my voice go up like three registers like I'm talking to my gramma. I go like, *Hi, Gramma!* What the fuck? says Kelly on the other line. Oh *shit*, I'm thinking. How fuckin dumb can you get? And I'm like, oh, I'm just out and about, Gramma. I'm coming home soon, yeah, yeah, yeah. Don't worry about me. The fuck are you talking about? says Kelly. I aint your gramma. We been sittin here in the goddamn dark waiting for your ass. Good, good, I think. And I say, okay, love you too, Gramma! Be home soon! Remember to take your medicine when you go to bed, OK? OK. Love you too. And I hang up. Then I says to Caleb (and we're almost at the park now), I turn to Caleb and say, hell, I gotta say it. I love the shit out of my gramma. She practically raised me, cause I was born when my ma was fifteen, and when I was a kid she split and never came back, last thing we heard she was shacked up with some asshole in Tucson. Yeah, yeah, says Caleb, like he's all chill now. Gramma, he says, aint at the shit. Hells yeah, I say. But in my head now I'm feeling totally chill about one old thing but I'm freaking the fuck out about one new thing. I feel chill now I know Kelly's gonna be there alright, cause we're about to be there in about five minutes. But then I'm thinking: The fuck's he mean, *we*?

She took off her shirt and rolled off her jeans and her underwear, and now she was standing naked on a black plastic bag in the middle of the kitchen floor. Seventy-five years before, a man sat in a small white room and sang songs about sex and death and love and murder and the end of the world, and his voice was imprisoned, copied, and pressed onto a vinyl disc that now revolved on a spindle as the stylus tickled over the grooves and resurrected his voice here in Fred's house.

John the Revelator, tell me who's that writing?
John the Revelator wrote the book of the seven seals.

Fred was fiddling with a paint sprayer at the kitchen sink. The paint sprayer was a handheld device with a plastic container for the paint that screwed onto a gun-shaped nozzle with an electric cord coming out of it and a tube with a filter that siphoned the paint out of the container and blew it out the nozzle.

Lana had pale skin and sharp hip bones and a tuft of copper-colored hair in her crotch with a trail of tiny hairs leading up to her navel. Her waist was so thin it looked to Fred like he could fit his hands around it and touch his thumbs and middle fingers together, and her rib cage showed. Her skin had that irretrievable glow and smoothness of youth. She was drinking a beer and smoking a cigarette and snicking the ashes on the floor with her thumbnail.

Fred had bought some special paint for this project, which was kind of expensive and came not in a can but in a big plastic jug. Fred opened the jug of paint, mixed it, and poured it into the smaller container that screwed onto the paint sprayer. He screwed the container onto the nozzle and washed the silver paint off his hands. The wet paint didn't look like much, just like thin gray mud.

"You got any allergies to certain chemicals or anything I ought to know about before we put this stuff on you?" said Fred. He was inspecting the side of the plastic jug of paint for a list of ingredients.

"I'm allergic to penicillin."

"Well, they don't make paint out of penicillin, Little Miss Louis Pasteur. This shit's latex-based, no oil or anything, so I think it should be fine."

"Louis Pasteur wasn't penicillin, Fred. Louis Pasteur was milk. Like pasteurized milk. Some other guy was penicillin. Fleming. Ian Fleming?"

"No, that's James Bond."

"Didn't that girl die when they painted her gold in the James Bond movie?"

"I take it you're referring to the iconic cinematic moment in *Goldfinger* when the Bond girl's been murdered in bed by being painted gold and asphyxiated because her pores are clogged or something. That, hon, is a myth. You don't breathe through your fucking pores. The only way you can asphyxiate somebody with paint is to pour it down their throat."

Fred opened some windows to ventilate the room and pulled the chain to turn on the ceiling fan. He unwound a yellow outdoor-use extension cord and plugged it in across the room. He gave her a bathing cap that he had also bought specially for this project. She put her hair up and scrunched it inside the cap, and edged it up on her forehead as close to her hairline as possible.

"I'm gonna start at the bottom and work my way up."

Lana swigged her beer and finished her cigarette and handed them to Fred.

"Here, take these," she said.

Fred set down the paint sprayer and put the cigarette in the ashtray and the beer on the kitchen table, which had been scooted aside to give them more floor space. Fred wheezed and puffed as he moved around the room, knots of long gray hair falling in his face. Lana stood waiting to be painted, in the middle of the floor on a black garbage bag that crinkled and stuck to her feet.

The song in the next room ended, and in the empty moment between songs there was a brief but oppressive silence in which they could hear the *click-click-click* of the ceiling fan, the pulsing chirrup of crickets outside, and the crinkling sound of the garbage bag under Lana's feet.

"What do you think?" she said.

"Honey," said Fred, "I think I'm fat and old and ugly and you're my sister's kid."

The next song started with that stepping down, down, down and then up that all blues songs seem to start with, and Fred pulled the trigger on the paint sprayer. The paint sprayer made a loud whirring noise, as well as the hiss of the paint coming out of the nozzle, and that brief but oppressive silence was thankfully over. Fred had his painting clothes on: shorts, a moth-eaten Denver Broncos T-shirt, pink plastic Kmart flip-flops. His legs were thin and pale. The flesh on his legs looked like the flesh on the underside of a snail and his toenails were long and flaky and the color of tortoiseshell.

Using a paint sprayer is all about maintaining the right rhythm, trigger pressure, and distance from the painted surface to spread the coat evenly. Fred painted her feet and realized he was holding the nozzle too close to her, so he backed away a few inches.

"It tickles," she said.

He worked his way up her legs and painted her inner thighs and the area between her legs as quickly as possible, and she spread her legs out to facilitate the process. After that Fred began to relax and got absorbed in the work. He went into a trance of narrow concentration, and the more paint he applied to her body, the more of her skin was covered, the more she became an object he was painting, just like a sculpture or a piece of furniture, and he lost himself in the task. She was art, and he was an artist. Fred breathed more evenly, and he forgot himself. He never even touched her.

"Shut your mouth and eyes," he said.

He painted her face carefully, aiming the spray at such an angle that it wouldn't get in her nostrils. Her lips quivered. Her eyeballs vibrated under her eyelids.

"Don't open your eyes or your mouth until the paint is sorta dry," Fred said.

She consented by nodding.

Fred sprayed on a quick second coat holding the nozzle at a farther distance, covering up the thin spots in the paint. Then he unplugged the extension cord, disassembled the paint sprayer in the kitchen sink, gave everything a quick rinse, and left the parts to soak in a bucket of soapy water. He wound up the extension cord and lit a cigarette. The blades of the ceiling fan chopped up the mist of tobacco smoke and paint particulate hanging in the room. The room was suffused with the heady chemical smell of the wet paint. Lana stood silent and motionless in a Hail Mary pose under the jittery fluorescent kitchen light and the strobing shadows of the fan blades, her head down, tilted, her arms not touching her sides, her legs apart, her fingers not touching, her lips and eyes closed, waiting for the paint to dry. With her eyes closed, Fred could allow himself to look directly at her. In the next room, Robert Johnson was singing about the end of the world.

"Dunno the fuck that was," said Kelly.

He clacked his cell phone shut. He'd been pacing around trying to find a place where he could get reception. He'd wondered if maybe he hadn't paid the bill and the phone company had shut it off, or if he had paid the bill and they shut it off anyway. Financial causes and effects were unpredictable to Kelly. The company shut off the phone, or they didn't shut it off. The bank charged him fees or they didn't charge him fees. But then he found a place with reception, and there was a message from Jackson wondering why he wasn't picking up his phone. He called him back and then Jackson said something about his grandma, but Kelly couldn't quite understand what he was saying, both because the reception was choppy and because what he was saying didn't make any sense.

"What?" said Maggie.

"He was sayin' somethin' about his grandma."

"He's probly with Caleb right now and he didn't want to let him know he was talkin' to you."

Kelly felt sick and hot and achy all over his body. He hadn't slept. Instead he'd fought with Maggie. They both broke some stuff. She cried.

The kid cried throughout the duration of the afternoon. The dogs outside were barking.

His stomach was an empty bag twitching with nausea. It was half past ten. The last time he'd slept was about twenty-four hours ago.

"I ain't slep in twenty-four, twenty-five hours," said Kelly. "And I ain't gonna sleep for sum'n like twenty more. I ain't gonna get to sleep for almost a whole nother day."

Maggie didn't say anything.

" 'Cause I gotta go to work after this, and then I gotta go to work again, so the next time I get to sleep is like, what? a whole goddamn day from now."

"Please shut up," said Maggie. "You got a cigarette?"

"We're outta cigs."

Kelly had switched from coffee to NoDoz. He'd been popping them like jellybeans all night and now his heart was rattling against his ribs and his hands were shaking like machines that were about to break. He stretched out the fingers on his hand, made a fist, stretched it out, made a fist, just to make sure it's his, yes, and it's obeying the commands from his brain, yes, it's working, yes. They had dropped Gabie off at Kelly's parents' house. He handed Gabie to his mom while Maggie waited in the idling truck, and Gabie was squirming in a dirty diaper. He handed her the squiggly little shit-smelling, howling kid and said they were going to see a movie. That's right, a movie. Date night. Right. Then he went around to the front of the house and borrowed a crowbar and a flashlight from the garage.

Maggie was sitting next to him just a little ways off the trail, on a mound of dirt, on sticks and leaves and rocks. Kelly was holding the crowbar and Maggie was holding the flashlight. They'd been sitting like this for an hour and a half. The night was clear and crisp and warm and they could see a lot of stars. Maggie was playing with the flashlight, clicking it on and off.

"Don't do that," said Kelly. She made an ugly face at him and he apologized. "I'm sorry. I mean, they're gonna see you. Don't advertise us."

She stopped playing with the flashlight. They were trying to stay silent, so they could hear them when they approached. Cars and trucks clattered by within earshot along Lookout Road, and occasionally they'd hear the crescendo/diminuendo of a vehicle coming/going up and down the road matched with the movement of the long shadows of trees shifting in the headlights.

Thousands of crickets chirping together made a throbbing rhythm all around them. There must have been a cricket hiding under every leaf. The racket they made was deafening, their incessant *krreepa-krreepa-krreepa*.

A heavy truck rumbled by on the road, quietly at first, slowly gathering volume, then the sound changed pitch as it passed and sped off down the other side of the hill, and the noise quickly faded.

"You know why they do that?" Kelly whispered. The crowbar was slick with sweat and warm in his palms from his handling it.

"Do what?"

"Change sounds when they go by."

"No."

"It's called the Doppler effect. When a car's comin' at you, you hear the noise get louder and louder, and when it goes by, the noise changes from goin' up to goin' down. It's got to do with waves. Same reason why you look at a star in a telescope it looks red 'cause it means it's moving away, which means the universe is constantly expanding."

They looked up at the stars.

"The universe is constantly expanding and it's infinite at the same time," said Kelly.

"Why do you think I'm stupid?" said Maggie.

"I don't think you're stupid."

"Then why you talkin' to me like 'at, tellin' me all this mister science shit like you think I'm a fuckin' kid?"

"Oh fuck off."

"Don't tell me to fuck off."

"Sorry. I didn't mean to say that."

"Quit sayin' sorry."

"What the fuck you want me to do?"

"I want you to grow a dick."

They were silent after that.

Kelly squeezed the crowbar till his knuckles whitened and for a moment he wanted not only to bash Caleb Quinn's brains out but all the brains of everybody everywhere and then he'd never have to worry about money or other people and he could go to the mountains by himself and just simply live, and maybe catch some fish.

They had been out there long enough that they had become used to the rhythm of the crickets chirping, so they noticed it when the crickets stopped.

There was a piercing flash of light somewhere in the distance, up ahead, in the trees. It was followed by another.

"What's that?" said Maggie.

"I don't like it," said Kelly.

A snake egg started growing in Kelly's stomach.

There were two more flashes of white light, but they weren't accompanied by any discernible noise. They were quick, slicing pops of cold, silent light. They were happening pretty far away, maybe two hundred feet into the woods, but it was hard to tell.

Then they heard voices of people coming down the trail. They couldn't hear what they were saying, but Kelly thought he recognized Jackson Reno's voice. Kelly gripped the crowbar, loosened his grip, tightened it.

"Get the light ready," Kelly hissed at Maggie.

Maggie snatched up the flashlight and took a few steps back.

Kelly was hot, weak, hungry, nauseated. The egg in his stomach hatched and a snake came out and started swimming around in his guts.

Two people came around the bend in the trail. One of them was wearing heavy yellow rubber boots. He was in front. Jackson was behind him. The one in the yellow boots saw that someone was there. Maggie clicked on the flashlight.

Caleb Quinn winced in the light.

Kelly stepped onto the trail and hit him with the crowbar as hard as he could in the gut. The sound of it was strangely muted, silent: a dull, flat noise of metal smacking flesh. Caleb doubled over, and Kelly jumped back and hit him in the side of the head, on his temple. Caleb pressed a hand to his head and blood came down his face. Kelly tried to get him in the balls, but missed and hit him in the thigh, and Caleb was covering his head and face with his arms as Kelly hit him in the gut again, and when he moved his arms, he hit him again in the head. Caleb fell down, and then Kelly hit him repeatedly all over his body. Kelly flipped the crowbar around and hit him one more time on the side of the head with the uglier end of it, the end with the hook on it, and there was the noise of something audibly breaking and an enormous amount of blood came out of Caleb's head.

Kelly didn't realize that Maggie was screaming until she stopped screaming because Jackson had pinned her arms behind her back and slapped a palm over her mouth.

"Kelly, chill," said Jackson.

Kelly chilled. He looked at Jackson and Maggie. It was dark. Maggie had dropped the flashlight and the beam was pointing uselessly into the grass. She was struggling.

"Let go of her," said Kelly.

"Why the fuck did you bring the girl, Kelly?"

"Let go of her."

"This bitch was screaming her goddamn head off. What the fuck were you thinking bringing the bitch along?"

"Let go of her." Kelly was the one screaming this time.

Jackson let her go. She ran over to Kelly and punched him in the face.

"Fuck," Kelly said, and dropped the crowbar and covered his face with his hands. His nose and cheek where she'd hit him were tingly and hot. "What the fuck you doing?" he shouted.

"You mother*fucker*," she spat. Jackson had her arms pinned again. "You didn't have to beat him up *that bad*, you mother*fucker*."

They all looked down at Caleb Quinn on the ground and the blood spilling out of his head. Nobody said anything for a while. Caleb was still breathing, but his eyes were vacant.

The crickets started chirping again.

Fred screwed the flashbulb onto his 1967 Leica M3, loaded a roll of film, and took a couple of test shots. He sank a fat finger into the button and listened to the precise and delicately mechanical scissor-snip noise of the shutter opening and closing: *Slackit. Slackit. Slackit. Slackit.* He turned off the lights to see what she looked like in the dark. Her body glowed with a glittery silver-blue metallic luster. The thatch of pubic hair in her crotch was a brittle nest of shimmering wires, like tinsel. The way the silver paint looked on her skin reminded Fred of Jack Haley's Tin Man makeup in *The Wizard of Oz.* Lana opened her eyes, and it was like this wild, haunting effect, these two bright human eyes opening up inside something that didn't quite look human.

"It feels weird," said Lana. "I don't feel naked."

Fred clacked the shutter, *slackit*, and triggered a sharp splash of white light from the flashbulb.

"How do you feel?" said Fred.

"Good," she said, stretching, rolling out the muscles and bones that had gone creaky from standing still too long, just like the Tin Man after he's been oiled up, regaining familiarity with autonomous locomotion. She examined her paint-caked legs, her arms, ran her hands over her body, this exoskeleton of dried paint.

"Do you want anything before we go? Like a towel, a blanket or something?"

Fred gradually struggled into a ratty leather bomber jacket that had fit him before he got fat. His keys tinkled as he fished them out of a pocket of the jacket.

"No," she said. Her eyes were alarming, surreal-looking in her head. "I don't need it. I feel like I have two layers of skin."

They went out the front door, which Fred didn't bother to lock behind him: Lana first, then Fred, the squeal and bang of the screen door, no neighbors watching, good, they're all inside, nestled up in their stupid cocoons watching TV, as one can tell from the undersea glow of the walls behind their living room windows. Lana fastidiously picked her steps across the gravel driveway in her bare feet. The sky above was alive with stars. Somebody's dog half barked in a false alarm, more of a guffaw than a bark, and then it tinkled its chain and settled back down behind its fence. In a nearby yard there was the rearing-rattlesnake noise of a sprinkler dusting off a sunburned patch of grass: *tchitcha-tchitcha-tchitcha-tchitcha-tschhhhhhhhhhhhhh——tcht-tcht-tcht-tcht*. It was a comfortably warm summer night with a hint of a coming autumnal chill in it.

Fred unlocked his battered blue '93 Honda Civic, passenger-side door first and then the driver's, and carefully squeezed himself under the steering wheel. Fred had taken out the back seats to maximize storage space, and the back of the car was crammed full of paint buckets, cans, brushes, tins of paint thinner, rags, socks, crumpled fast-food bags, petrified fries, Styrofoam cups, various other detritus, cigarette butts, cassette tapes. It didn't smell good.

"Why is this car so gross?" said Lana.

"Because I'm a slob," said Fred.

She rolled down the passenger-side window. Fred rolled his window down too, twisted the key in the ignition, and kicked the gas, and the engine grumbled on, then settled into a phlegmatic pant. A second later the stereo flickered on, a little too loud, and Fred turned down the dial. There was a cassette of Ornette Coleman's *The Shape of Jazz to Come* in the tape deck. Fred turned on the lights and the car sputtered down the gravel driveway before they turned onto a paved road and Fred shifted into higher gear; the engine sighed in relief and the headlights spat dim yellow light onto the road in front of them as they drove along in the night and Ornette's sax squeaked and whimpered over the rapid *skisha-skisha-skisha* of the cymbals.

"This is like, *nervous* music," said Lana.

"I've always thought the tension in this tune comes from that jittery energy in the rhythm section mixed with the threnodic sound of the horns," said Fred, glad to be talking about music again, where he felt conversationally at home. Fred waited for her to ask what "threnodic" meant; she didn't.

"This is a very important album," Fred continued, "but really you gotta get into Bird and Miles and Monk and Trane before you can truly begin to appreciate what Ornette's doing here. All those guys, Miles and Monk especially, they *hated* this guy when he came out with this album. They were like, what the fuck is this lunatic doing?"

Fred slipped back into American-musicology-professor mode and discoursed on the emergence of free jazz all the way to the park. He talked about Albert Ayler, Don Cherry, Cecil Taylor, Pharoah Sanders.

"You know what threnodic means?" said Fred finally.

"Yeah. It means like, mournful, right? It's like a death wail."

Fred was disappointed.

"Yeah," he said.

They eased off 227 and onto Lookout Road, went about five minutes up the road and came to the top of a hill, where Fred slowed down to look for the turnoff to get into the park. He found it: There was just one narrow dirt road off the main road that led in and out of the park. The car shuddered over the washboards. They passed a sign nailed to an open gate that read PARK IS OPEN FROM SUNRISE TO SUNSET in red block letters above an illegible scramble of fine print.

"Where are we?"

"This is called Centennial Park," he said. "Colorado is the Centennial State because they were made into a state in 1876, a hundred years after the Declaration of Independence. This is supposedly the site of some battle where the National Guard slaughtered a bunch of Indians or something."

Fred pulled into the parking lot, dragged the car to a stop, and crunched up the brake lever. There was a massive cannon, dull green with oxidization, next to the parking lot, with a plaque on it. A half-moon showered light on the faces of the mountains heaving up in front of them to the west and tapering off into the distance to the north and south. Below them in the valley, the lights of civilization curled up the sides of the mountains and dispersed into darkness. A thin worm of railroad tracks coiled around the bottom of the hill, which sloped into fields and woods and a grid of dirt roads. Just below the hill there was an artificial lake and a coal-burning power plant: a tangle of power lines and a squat, ugly building with two char-blackened smokestacks towering from the top of it. The power plant glittered with yellow and green lights that were reflected as cleanly as in a mirror in the lake below.

"It'd be a beautiful view if it weren't for that fucking power plant," said Lana, squinting as if she was trying to imagine what the landscape would look like without the smokestacks.

"Yeah," said Fred. "It'd be dark."

"I like the dark."

They stood in the parking lot of the scenic overlook and absorbed the landscape. Fred turned to Lana, who was standing on the gravel with her hands on her hips, her thin, naked, painted body iridescent in the moonlight.

"You cold at all?" he asked.

"No. The paint's warm. And there's all the beer and whiskey."

There was an old white pickup truck with a crack in the windshield parked in the parking lot. Fred pointed at the truck.

"I don't know if I like that."

"Maybe somebody just left it here," said Lana. "It looks like a piece of shit."

"Well, I don't see anybody."

Fred's camera dangled from a leather strap that cut into the thick flesh of his neck. He got the bag containing the film and his camera equipment out of the car and slung it over his shoulder, stuck the tripod under his arm, its telescoping legs contracted and folded together, and clicked on the flashlight. Fred started plodding down the narrow trail that wound out of the parking lot, down the hill and into the woods. Lana followed. Fred's pink plastic flip-flops slapped against his heels. Together they scrabbled a little ways down the trail, then turned off of it into the grass and brush. Tall sprays of grass thrashed all around them.

"All right," said Fred, turning around to Lana. "Let's take some shots here."

Fred aimed the camera at her and took a picture with the flash. *Slackit*. The flashbulb spat a piercing blank field of light at her, and for a fraction of a second her monstrous shadow stretched high up into the trees. The light of the flashbulb bounced off the paint on her skin; it made her shine with false light, the stolen light of a reflective surface—a mirror, a moon, a satellite.

At first it looked like Lana didn't know what to do with herself. Her skinny adolescent body was positioned in an awkward, unattractive way, her arms cradled against her torso like she wanted something to hold on to.

"What should I do?"

Fred ratcheted back the lever to advance the film, sank a finger into the shutter-release button—flash, *slackit.*

"Just, uh, I dunno. Do whatever," he said. "Relax. Pretend you're a . . . Pretend you're a wild animal or something."

As Fred took more pictures Lana appeared to gradually loosen up and get into it. She started to become comfortable with being his model, with being naked, being vulnerable, on display, outside, in a place she'd never been before in her life, with him. She was hopping around, thrashing around in the grass, being a bunny, being a fox, being a deer. *Slackit, slackit.* Again, Fred was sinking into that trance of concentration that he went into when he was working intently on something, and he began thinking exclusively in images, or how to capture the images. He was thinking about lines, framing, exposures, depths of field, and the distribution of light, and in his mind this stuff pushed away all the thoughts about all the things he hated in the world, and all his problems, and all his troubles: troubles with money, troubles with drugs, not having health insurance, forgetting to pay his bills or brush his teeth or clip his toenails or reregister his car, the government, people who don't love music or art or any of the other things that make life worth living, being an adult in general.

At some point Lana said: "Look."

She was pointing up. Fred followed her finger, looked where she was pointing. An object, like a tiny, dim moving star, was scrolling slowly across the sky. The light moved in a shallow arc, gathering in brightness until it became a bright white flash, and then the light, though still moving in the same direction and at the same speed, began to fade, until it disappeared from the sky.

They were still and silent for long enough that the crickets forgot them and started chirping again.

"*Whoa!*" Fred whispered, awed. "Was that a fucking UFO?"

Lana rolled her eyes.

"No, Fred," she said. "I think it was like a satellite or something."

Then they heard someone, someone not too far away, screaming in the dark.

"Jesus, dog, why you gotta go all psycho on the motherfucker," said Jackson. "I mean you just fucked him up *bad*, dog. I seen some shit before but I ain't never seen 'at much blood come out of a motherfucker's head like 'at."

Maggie squirmed out of Jackson's hold, kneeled down on the ground and hugged Caleb Quinn. She was crying. Jackson picked up the flashlight.

"Let's get the fuck out of here. I can't fuckin' believe you brung the bitch with you, dog. You wanna look like a cowboy and shit in front of her? Is that it? Fucking stupid, dog."

Jackson pointed the flashlight at Kelly, who looked down at himself and saw that his clothes were covered in blood. Maggie was still hugging Caleb, and now she was also covered in blood.

"What time you reckon it is?" said Kelly, trying to sound casual.

Jackson pointed the flashlight at his watch.

"Eleven thirty."

"Shit. I gotta get to work. I should've brung a change of clothes."

"We gotta get this motherfucker off the trail," said Jackson.

"Get off him, Maggie," said Kelly.

"Fuck you," she said.

"Get off him or I'm gonna smack the teeth out of your head, bitch," said Jackson.

Maggie looked at Kelly. Kelly mumbled something too quiet or unintelligible to hear. Maggie stood up. Her face was wet. She was soaked in Caleb's blood.

"Pick up that end of him, I'll get this end," said Jackson.

Jackson picked him up by the legs and Kelly grabbed his limp arms. They were able to pick him up and move him, but he was heavy. It was kind of like moving a couch. They were forced to look at each other. Jackson's eyes glowed pale blue in the dark. They struggled to carry him off the path and into the woods. They carried him about twenty feet through the grass and into a dirt clearing where the trees around were thick, and dumped him there. In the process Jackson got a lot of blood on him as well. Maggie remained on the trail with the flashlight and refused to follow them, so they had to do it all in the dark. They walked back to the trail with the tall grass thrashing all around them. Up above, the sky swarmed with stars. When they got back to the trail they saw that the place where they'd been was covered in blood.

"That was some bad shit, Kelly," said Jackson. "You fucked that dog up real bad. We're gonna have to lay real low, you understand? I mean I *just* got done doing time for my drug shit and I'm still on probation, so I can't be goin' around being accomplice to no goddamn murder and get sent away till I'm an old man. And you too, dog, you understand?"

"What do you mean murder? He's not dead."

Jackson snatched the flashlight out of Maggie's hands like you'd snatch something dangerous out of the hands of a child.

Maggie was crying again.

"Kelly, you have got to shut up your bitch, dog. I can*not* fucking think straight with all this bawling."

"Please be quiet, Maggie."

"Please be quiet? 'Please be'? What the fuck kind of shit is that? *'Please be quiet.'* If you don't shut your bitch up *I'm* gonna have to shut her up."

"Don't you fucking touch her."

"Oh, what, so killer here goes all batshit on some motherfucker with a crowbar and now all of a sudden he thinks he can take me? *Fuck* you. Don't insult me, dog."

Kelly didn't say anything to that. He reached out to touch Maggie—just to touch her—and she flinched and shivered and flicked her hands like she'd been touched by something so loathsome she'd have to wash herself later, and she walked faster up the trail away from him.

They made it up the hill and back to the gravel parking lot and scenic overlook at the top of the hill without anyone saying anything to anyone else. Kelly's truck was parked in the far corner of the parking lot under a tree. A pool cleaning van with a mermaid on it holding a pool net was parked in the opposite corner.

"Fuckin' A," said Jackson. "I gotta go back down there and get his goddamn keys off him and move his van. Should've took the money he said he got on him, too."

"No. Please no, no, no," said Kelly. "We ain't got time for that. We gotta get the fuck outta here. I gotta go home and clean up and get to work. I ain't slep in twenty-five hours. And I ain't gonna sleep in like twenty more."

Then they noticed that there was another car in the parking lot. A little blue Honda Civic. Jackson pointed at it.

"The fuck is that all about?" he said. "That little blue piece a shit wasn't here when we pulled up in Caleb's van."

There were needles of fear under Kelly's skin.

"I don't like that," he said.

"I hate you," said Maggie.

"Ain't nobody talkin' to you," said Jackson.

Kelly threw the crowbar, which was slick with blood, into the bed of the truck and it landed with the hollow clunk of metal against metal.

Maggie was wearing a dark green hoodie with a kangaroo pocket in it, and was hugging herself with her arms in the pocket. She was refusing to look at him. Jackson stood in the parking lot with his arms akimbo, looking at the little blue car and then at the pool cleaning van.

"Let's just shut up and get the fuck out of here," said Kelly. "I *do not* like that there's another car here."

"No shit," said Jackson. "We should bolt."

They got in the cab of the truck. Maggie said she didn't want to sit next to Kelly, so she sat on the passenger side, Kelly drove, and Jackson sat in the middle. If they hurried, there would still be enough time to drop Jackson off at his grandma's house, go home, wash up, swing by Kelly's mom's house to pick up Gabie, drop him and Maggie off at home, and then tear back up the highway to report to work. Kelly's palms were wet. They were getting blood all over the seats. Maggie sat still with her hands in her lap and stared straight ahead out the windshield.

Kelly jingled the keys out of his jacket pocket, inserted them into the ignition, turned them, and prayed. The motor didn't come on the first time, or the second time or the third or the fourth time. Then, it did. Sometimes it did, sometimes it didn't. The headlights came on and the engine groaned as Kelly pulsed the accelerator. The radio came on. It was playing "Friends in Low Places."

I'm not big on social graces
Think I'll slip on down to the O—asis
Oh, I got friends in low—places.

The song lightened the mood a little. (A little.) Kelly mouthed along to the chorus out of habit.

The truck's fat, soft tires rocked over the dirt road, bits of gravel popping under the wheels. They crept down the hill toward the stop sign. The red octagon flashed in the headlights and went dark again as they passed it. No cars coming in either direction. Kelly goosed the engine and the truck rolled out onto the main road and died.

The truck died across both lanes of the road, without enough space on either side to drive around it. The first car nearly plowed into them at about fifty miles an hour. Tires screamed, the sulfurous odor of burnt rubber. The driver jammed a fist into the horn. Then another car coming from the other direction did the same thing.

Kelly kept trying the engine, and the engine kept making a chortling noise and then choking off, until it failed to start completely, and then there was just the sound of the starter clicking, and then that stopped too, and now he turned the key in the ignition and absolutely nothing happened.

A line of cars began to stack up around them in both directions. There were four or five cars on either side of them, then six, seven, eight, and then there were two long trails of headlights and winking red brake lights on either side of the truck. Idling motors panted up and down the hill like tired dogs. Horns honked futilely. A few cars peeled out of the line and turned around.

Kelly didn't want to get out of the truck with all the blood on his clothes. He just kept trying to start the engine. He put the transmission in neutral and tried to coast out of the way, but the truck didn't move much. It took up a lot of space, and the road here had no shoulder. Jackson and Maggie were talking to him the whole time, but Kelly wasn't listening to what they were saying. Kelly's vision seemed almost to be flashing with white light, and all he could hear was a thin, high-pitched, nearly silent whine.

Somebody rolled down a window and shouted, "What the hell's going on here?"

It was a stupid question, and Kelly didn't answer it.

Kelly sank his forehead into the wheel and prayed. He silently prayed to God to start his truck. Then he tried the ignition again: silence. The radio came back on, though.

Just wait 'til I finish this glass
Then sweet little lady
I'll head back to the bar
And you can kiss my ass—

Kelly looked at the lit green displays on the dashboard—radio, heater/AC, speedometer, odometer, check oil light, fuel gauge—and realized what the problem was.

"We're out of gas," he said.

Maggie was laughing. Kelly started laughing too.

Jackson slammed a fist into Kelly's ribs. He wasn't laughing.

"Ha ha ha *ha*," he said. "You fucked us over, Kelly, but you fucked me over most of all. So figure out how you gonna move this goddamn truck or I'monna fucking *kill* you. You under*stand* me, *dog*?"

Kelly only kept trying to start the car, hoping that enough gasoline fumes were wafting around in the tank to kick-start the engine, which had happened before. If he could fire up the engine, he could pull out and coast all the way down the hill in neutral to where he knew there was a gas station, or thought there was, maybe. He thought there was a gas station down there.

The red and blue lights of a police cruiser flashed beside them. The police car emitted a truncated hoot from the siren, just a single, short rising-pitch *wooop*, and they heard a cop get out of his car and shut the door.

The cop's face materialized in the driver's-side window. He clicked his knuckles against the driver's-side door because the window was down.

"Damn thing won't start," said Kelly, half laughing, smiling as much as he could. "Hell of a place to break down, in'n it?"

Unsmiling, the cop aimed a flashlight into the car. He was a young cop, his throat thick with dense cords of muscle, eyes taciturn, cheeks scraped smooth. Kelly turned the key in the ignition, listened to the engine not starting, staggered the accelerator with his foot.

Somebody up the hill buried a fist into a horn. Farther down the line there was the snarl of somebody juicing a motorcycle. The cop trained the flashlight on Maggie and Jackson, then at their laps, and saw that all three of them were covered in blood. The cop's eyes darted to the bed of the truck, where there was the crowbar, and more blood.

Kelly was looking up at the cop, and he could see the exact moment, the slight change of expression on his otherwise emotionless face, when he must have thought something like this: Looks like this is going to be more interesting than I thought.

The cop kept his flashlight on Kelly as he unsnapped his holster and rested his right hand on the handle of his gun.

"Would you please step out of the vehicle, sir."

Kelly turned to the cop.

"I ain't slep in twenty-five hours." Kelly knew it was obvious, it was obvious to everyone from the hideous croak in his voice that he was about to cry. "And I ain't gonna sleep in twenty more."

The cop repeated: "Sir, would you please step out of the vehicle."

Somebody was screaming. Fred and Lana looked at each other. The screaming stopped. There was a long silence. Everything around them was still and dark. Lana and Fred stood ten paces away from each other, still, listening. There was another scream. It was a woman's voice, screaming in either fear or fury.

"What the fuck is that?" Fred whispered.

Fred and Lana stood there in the grass without moving or speaking. The screaming had stopped, but there were some faraway but audible voices somewhere.

Amid a mumble of things they couldn't understand, a male voice shouted: "Let go of her."

Neither of them spoke. Fred and Lana listened to each other's breathing.

The voices came closer. There were at least two male voices, talking. It sounded like the two men were angry at each other. Or Fred thought so, anyway.

Then they saw, a little ways off, maybe two hundred feet or so, the yellow light of a flashlight traveling along the ground, and they saw the shadows of legs, a few people walking up the path to the parking lot. Fred wasn't sure how much time had passed.

"Fred?" Lana whispered. "I'm kind of freaked out now."

Fred shushed her. "Let's just be quiet and wait for them to go."

They couldn't hear what was being said, but the dominant voice was of a man who sounded angry. There was a woman, and it sounded like she was crying. They watched the beam of the flashlight move along the ground, up the path and into the parking lot. The light shut off, and after what felt like a very long time, they finally heard car doors slamming. The white pickup truck in the parking lot. Then somebody trying to start an engine. It took four or five attempts, four or five times the truck made an ugly chattering noise and died before they heard the *froom* of the engine coming on. Then there was the sound of heavy tires rolling on gravel.

"Huh," said Fred. "Weird."

Silence.

"I think we should go," said Lana. "Actually, yeah. I want to go."

Silence.

"Actually I want to go right now, Fred."

"Yeah. Fine, okay," said Fred. "Okay. Right. Yeah. Let's go."

They had trouble finding the path again, though. They had wandered farther into the woods than Fred had thought, and while Lana had been running around in the grass and he was busy taking pictures, it turned out neither of them had been paying much attention to where they were. After walking for a while in the general direction of where they thought the path was, they realized they were in a place neither of them recognized. The trees were closer together here. It didn't look familiar. Fred was shining the flashlight on the ground as they walked and Lana kept close beside him, behind him. They walked for a while more before they came into a small clearing in the woods where there was a man lying in the dirt in a puddle of blood. There was blood trickling freely from the man's head. He had spat out some teeth, which were lying next to his head. Fred trained the flashlight on his head, framing it in the annulus of pale yellow light, and they saw that his eyes were open, though one of them was caked in blood and swollen almost shut. He was alive, and awake, and breathing, though there was a sort of gargling noise in the back of his throat as air whistled in and out of it. He was a big guy, tall and thick, probably weighed more than two fifty, could have been three hundred easily. His lower jaw hung open. The man pushed the blood out of the corner of his mouth with his tongue. He tried to speak, but whatever he was trying to say came out unintelligible. He coughed on the effort to force up words and spat some blood. He was wearing yellow rubber boots.

"Can you. Um. Jesus, dude." Fred cleared his throat. "Can you move?"

The man shook his head, slightly: No.

Fred was kneeling beside the man with the flashlight. He clicked it off and heaved to his feet. He stood the tripod on the ground to rid his arms of it. Fred looked up into the sky. It swarmed with stars.

Fred looked at Lana. She was standing far away from the beaten-up man, eyeing him with terror, and covering her breasts and her crotch with her hands, looking like Eve walking out of Eden. Fred had forgotten about that.

"We have to call nine-one-one," she said.

"Exactly. That's a wonderful idea, my dear," said Fred. "So, just curious, here: *What* were you doing trespassing in the park in the middle of the night, Fred? Well, you know, Officer, I was just getting my sixteen-year-old niece stoned and drunk and then we came out here to take naked pictures of her. Nothing wrong with that, is there?"

"This is art."

"This *is* art, *goddamnit*. You expect the cops to get that? I can just see it. Oh, I'm sorry, Fred! Here we were gonna book you for supplying drugs and alcohol to a minor, driving drunk, probably, trespassing on government property, and, and, uh, *and* child pornography! Looks like we can scrap that last charge, boys. We didn't realize this was just some tasteful erotic art photography you're doing here."

"So we should leave him here and not tell anybody?" said Lana.

"Well—" Fred started, and stopped.

"This guy's head is like, bashed in. He can't even move. If we leave him here he'll die. We have to help him."

At this point the man on the ground tried to say something, but he choked, coughed, spat up a sluice of blood, and was silent. Fred waddled into the middle of the clearing, the flip-flops slapping under his heels. He crossed his arms. He was still holding the flashlight. Fred was thinking. His breathing was pained and heavy. The temperature had dropped a few degrees.

Fred set the flashlight down in the grass, went over to the man on the ground, and grabbed his hands. Fred yanked hard on his arms, trying to move him. The man growled in pain.

"What the fuck are you doing?" Lana said, or more half screamed.

Fred didn't answer. He yanked on the man's arms again and succeeded in moving the body an inch or so. The man grunted. A violent convulsion rumbled through him. Fred huffed and blew out some air, looked up at Lana. She looked back at him. Fred sopped his face with the corner of his shirt and blinked a few times.

"Well, princess, you gonna stand there and watch, or help me move him?"

"Move him *where*?"

"To. The. Fucking. *Car*," said Fred.

"*What?*"

Fred dropped the man's arms to explain. He spoke slowly and melodically because what he was saying was so obvious. "We're going to drop him off in front of the door at the hospital and then get the fuck out of there."

Lana laughed, theatrically.

"That," she said, "is *such* a bad idea."

Fred snorted and picked up the man's arms again.

"We won't even be able to drag him up there," she said. "Look at this guy. He's fucking huge. There's no way we'll get him all the way up that hill."

"Not by myself we're not. Come on, princess. I get the hands, you get the feet."

"No," she said.

Fred dropped the man's arms again. He'd only been able to drag the man a few inches, and now he seemed to be in much more pain than when they'd found him. The exertion had left Fred out of breath. He braced himself against a tree.

"Fine," said Fred, turning to her again. "We go home. We clean up. Wash that shit off you, get some clothes on, then we call the cops and give like an, uh. I dunno. Give an, an anonymous tip or something, I guess. I guess that's the best thing to do."

Lana nodded.

"Fine," she said. "But now we've still got to get back to the path."

"Easy, hon. We just follow this trail of blood."

Fred had meant it as a joke, except it wasn't a joke. The man on the ground was gurgling and moving around, trying desperately to say something to them as they left the clearing, Fred carrying the camera and flashlight and the bag full of film and camera equipment, Lana carrying the tripod. Fred held the beam of the flashlight shivering on the ground in front of them. There was so much blood on the stalks of grass, it really was easy to see where those people had come from, and whoever that guy's assailants were, they apparently had a better sense of direction than Fred, because by following the blood they quickly got back on the trail and started back up the hill. Fred walked sluggishly on the way back, snorting and puffing up the trail in his flip-flops, and Lana stayed close by him. They made it back to the parking lot. The white pickup truck was gone, but now there was another car in the lot. It looked like a service van for a pool cleaning company, with a bunch of equipment strapped to the roof rack and a picture of a mermaid holding a pool net on the side. They didn't comment on it. They got in the car, and shortly after that Fred was piloting the vehicle back down the hill along the narrow dirt road, and again they were shuddering over the washboards.

Neither of them said anything. The stereo played Ornette Coleman's *The Shape of Jazz to Come*. The tension in the music came from the jittery energy of the rhythm section mixed with that threnodic sound of the horns. Lana curled herself into a fetal ball, her knees squeezed to her chest and her arms wrapped around her ankles. Her face was turned away from Fred, looking out the window.

Fred ended the silence.

"You know," he said. "I am not happy."

She didn't say anything.

As they rounded a curve and approached the turnoff to the main road, Fred saw the flashing red and blue lights of a police car on the trunks of the trees by the roadside. The white pickup truck they had seen in the parking lot was parked across two lanes of traffic, and two long lines of cars, headlights glaring and engines idling, were stacked up bumper to bumper on either side. A man and woman were sitting on a grassy berm to the side of the road with their heads between their knees and their hands cuffed behind their backs. Another man was standing with his legs planted apart and his palms flat against the side of the truck, and a cop was frisking him with one hand and holding a radio to his mouth with the other.

Fred stopped the car.

"What," Lana said in a sleepy voice. Her eyes blinked open. Had she been asleep?

She looked at him over her shoulder, still curled away from him toward the window.

"You gotta get out of here," Fred informed her, in a thin voice that was shrill and sick with panic. "You gotta get out of here right now before anybody sees you, those cops are gonna want to talk to me. I can't have you in here. They'll throw me in jail if they see you in here like that. Way way way way way too much to explain to the cops. Get out. Please please please get the fuck out of here right now please."

"What? Where am I gonna go?"

"I don't know. I don't fucking— I don't know, uh—"

The cop seemed to be looking in their direction. Fred cut the headlights, and then the cop was really looking at them.

"Wait," said Fred. "Wait wait wait wait, okay. I know. I got an idea. Go up there and hide in that cannon. Nobody'll ever look in there."

"What?"

"You know the cannon in the parking lot on top of the hill? Commemorating the slaughter of Indians or whatever, hide in there, hide like in the barrel of the cannon, you're skinny, you'll fit in there and then I'll know exactly where to find you when I come back and if they throw me in jail I'll use my one call to call up my buddy Craig, and he'll come get you. I'll tell him where to find you but I don't think that'll happen because I'm basically pretty much sober now anyway and I can talk my way out of this, just please please please please get the fuck out right now."

Lana got out of the car, slammed the door, and ran back up the hill along the dirt road. When she slammed the door the cop down on the road looked up and aimed his flashlight in Fred's direction. Fred turned the headlights back on and eased the car forward.

She did like the dark. She didn't make the Platonic mistake of associating the good and the beautiful and the light with the truth. That was saccharine and deceptive, like using a euphemism for something more accurately expressed in grubbier, more direct language, like saying "passed away" instead of "died," or "make love" or "sleep with" instead of "fuck." Her parents' house in California vibrated softly all over with fake sweetness and light. She hated their money, hated their tasteful well-matched furniture, hated their sterile Thanksgivings. After Lana learned the word *bourgeois* she took enormous pleasure in applying the adjective to her parents. Lana was more interested in darkness and ugliness—the juice of life, the life/death force, the yin/yang, the eros/thanatos, the duende. She wanted to do and to have, in part to do and to have and in part to have done and to have had. She wanted to be a bohemian. Like Baudelaire. She wanted to be bisexual, and maybe commit suicide after doing or creating something brilliant. But at this particular moment she wished she were in her parents' house in California, taking a tropically steamy shower, sneaking a glass of wine, and blazing through the satellite channels on her parents' TV. Then she would sneak another glass of wine, smoke a joint, surreptitiously blow the smoke out the bathroom window, light incense, and read the diaries of Anaïs Nin in bed.

Lana had, in fact, found the cannon with the plaque on it again, but the opening of the barrel was so narrow that no one but an infant could have possibly fit in it. And then she had thought she heard somebody coming, so she ran into the woods and immediately proceeded to get lost. She walked through grass and woods, in a part of the country she had never been before; she could not have even located her position within a hundred miles on a map. She was alone. An hour ago, all her blood had been singing with the wildness and wickedness and novelty of everything she was doing. The silver paint on her skin reflected the moonlight. Her body glowed with otherworldly light and darkness yawned all around her.

She walked slowly. Twigs and rocks drove horribly into her bare feet. She walked on the edges of her insteps to minimize their surface area. Maybe because the alcohol was burning out of her system, the air began to feel much colder. Goose bumps prickled her body beneath the paint.

She had no way of telling time, but she guessed that hours were passing. She lay down in the grass. She stared at the ground, curled into herself like a snail, hugged her legs to her chest, flesh against flesh, warmth to warmth. She was exhausted: There was sand in her veins, all her inner machinery slogging along at half its regular rhythm. And she was hungry. She was very hungry, a sucking hollowness clawing at her gut. She didn't exactly feel drunk, not anymore, but the universe pitched around like a ship in a storm when she shut her eyes. Yes. No. Yes. She was still drunk. She lay on the ground and looked up, imagined that gravity had inexplicably reversed itself, that her back was pressed against the ceiling of the sky and the clouds she saw were sailing over mountaintops six miles below her. She couldn't lie down anymore; being still nauseated her. She had to stand up and move around. She got up, and all the blood gushed into her brain. She felt acutely conscious of her internal organs sloshing around in her body, everything out of balance and out of time. She might have fallen asleep. She couldn't tell. The stars had shifted positions, the moon had moved. But it was still dark, and she had nothing to hold on to, mentally or physically, figuratively or literally. She tried to remember what had happened, but only decontextualized blots of memory remained of the night, certain noises, sense perceptions, images with contours inconstant and definitions blurry as if seen under water, a cloud and a tree and a car and a cannon and a hand and an eye and a blast of smoke and a sudden eruption of light and the warbling sound of a man singing songs about sex and death and love and the end of the world seventy-five years ago in a noise field of pops and crunching static, and in her consciousness the memories smeared continuously into dreams about fathers slitting the throats of their children on mountaintops thousands of years ago, and somewhere between waking and sleeping she had a vague thought that there is nothing as elemental as an unexplained light in the sky, or the sound of a voice screaming in the dark.

Then she looked to the north, along the distant ridge of mountains and across the rippling, light-dusted plains, and saw a cloud of fire in the sky. She looked, and saw four spirals of fire, blazing bright and revolving clockwise, like whirlpools of flame. The four spirals of fire hovered high in the sky, and they were moving. They darted from one place to another, and there were flashing white tendrils of electricity in the sky. And she looked below them, and saw four enormous gold machines below the four spirals of fire in the sky. The machines went where the fires went, darting rapidly from one place to another. Each of the machines had the appearance of a wheel inside a wheel. The inner wheel of each machine was perpendicular to the outer wheel, and the outer wheel spun clockwise while the inner wheel spun counterclockwise. The wheels were alive with light, and innumerable human eyes studded the rims of the wheels, and all the eyes looked in different directions, and blinked at different times. Inside each of the four machines was what looked like a living creature. Each of the living creatures had four wings and four faces. The living creatures moved inside the machines, but did not touch the wheels that revolved around them. Wherever the spirals of fire went, the machines went beneath them, and the creatures within went with them. Then everywhere the fields were consumed in fire, and she saw blood running in rivers from the gullies between the mountains. She saw a desert of white ash.

Lana looked around her, and saw that she was standing in a field of tall grass. She looked behind her, and saw the hill: Beyond that was the road. She heard the sound of a truck rumbling down the road and letting off pressure from its gaskets in short, sneezy hisses. To her left she saw the power plant—the squat, ugly building with its two char-black smokestacks. She realized that at some point she must have crossed the railroad tracks, because now she saw that they were behind her. Now the half moon shone big and low above the outline of the mountains. She thought she could see the beginnings of dawn skirting the eastern horizon. Ahead of her, across the field, she saw a row of utility poles, standing along a thin dirt road like a fence of crucifixes, connected by positive parabolas of wire drooping from one to the next. She saw a tall, narrow house at the end of the field where two dirt roads intersected, and there were lights on in a few of its windows. She walked through the field toward the house. The grass thrashed around her. It was still dark when she reached the house. The wooden boards of the front porch felt comfortably flat and hard under her blistered, bare feet. She pushed a button beside the front door and heard the doorbell sound from inside the house. She heard movement inside. After a while, she heard the clunk of a bolt being unlatched, and the door shrieked open on dry hinges.

An old woman peered through the mesh of the screen door at her: She was small and frail, and the texture of the skin of her face looked like crumpled silken paper. She pushed open the screen door and stepped out of the house on tiny white bare feet. The old woman wore a dark blue bathrobe. Her face was the face of someone who has just seen something terrifying, or sublimely beautiful. It was the expression of religious experience. She was breathing heavily and unevenly. Her chest shivered, it seemed her lungs were struggling to draw oxygen. Her hands were shaking.

Lana stood before her in the dark, on the porch. Her body was glowing with an otherworldly light. The woman's lips quivered. Her eyes were wet. The woman took a step forward and reached out to her with delicate white arms.

THE FAT ARTIST

All art is quite useless.

—Oscar Wilde, *The Picture of Dorian Gray*

I, Tristan Hurt, am a Fat Artist. This is a modus of being quite distinct from "fat person." Obviously, I am that as well; at my peak weight I believe, though unfortunately I cannot prove, that I was the *heaviest* (such is the admittedly crude rubric/analogue I have necessitated to adopt to read: "fattest") person alive, moreover, possibly ever to have lived. While fat person indeed I may be, in my anomalous case, that of the Fat Artist, the adjective *fat*, applied to the noun *artist*, modifies not so much the man as the art. *Fat* is not (not *just*) a descriptor of the matter contained within my corporeal boundaries (i.e., my *body*—what in the quaintly benighted days of mind-body dualism would have been called on the gravestone I do not at this late stage hope to have, "'all that [was] mortal' of Tristan Hurt"). I am an artist, and *fat* is the medium in which I work. I have made my body into an art object.

I certainly do not presume to suggest my project is an unprecedented one.* (I bore myself with the usual mentions: Abramovic, Acconci, Finley, Burden, Orlan, et al.) However, I shall maintain unto my death, which—as I sit here on this rooftop, unable to move, without food or water, alone and naked (as opposed to nude†), abandoned, forgotten and forsaken by the world—I presume is imminent, that I have suffered *uniquely* and (if I may so flatter myself) more terminally than other artists who have adopted their own bodies as their primary medium.

I am thirty-three years old (please, should there be any gloss of the messianic over the age of my death, know that it is entirely accidental) and I am about to die.

When I was young—and at thirty-three I am young yet, although (*Nos morituri te salutamus*) I am about to die—I was a handsome man. In my late twenties my hairline began its slow vertical creep up the corners of my forehead and thinned on top, but that is all; my hair has always been this dusty-brown color and my eyes have always been these pellucid swirls of whale gray and celadon (every lover who looked into them described

* What, at this late stage (or any other), is truly unprecedented? The anonymous eyes, minds, and hands that overlaid extra-semiotic images on the raw found walls of Lascaux merely forged after the forms of nature, and only because of this very forgery of form is such anodyne work (still!) exalted: typical of self-serving bourgeois approval, then, I'm sure, as now, and my sympathies are with those early cave artists. ("Ooh," I imagine their naïve fellows saying, "it's a horse! It's a buffalo!")

† "The English language, with its elaborate generosity, distinguishes between the naked and the nude. To be naked is to be deprived of our clothes, and the word implies some of the embarrassment most of us feel in that condition. The word 'nude,' on the other hand, carries, in educated usage, no uncomfortable overtone. The vague image it projects into the mind is not of a huddled and defenseless body, but of a balanced, prosperous, and confident body: the body re-formed"(Kenneth Clark, *The Nude: A Study in Ideal Form*). I myself was once *nude* (I was a work of art), but now have become again merely *naked*: as embarrassed and defenseless as Adam out of Paradise.

them as "sad"). My face—now swollen with loose pouches of fat that merge smoothly into my fat neck, which merges smoothly into my fat shoulders, and they in turn into the squishy mammarian saddlebags of my chest—used to sport robust and angular features, a boxy jaw, sharp cheekbones. In those bygone days when I was physically able to stand, I stood six feet and one inch and weighed about 200 lbs (91 kg). I was a relatively big man, and for most of my life had enjoyed the slight deference of authority that is paid to the substantial occupier of space—but I was not fat.

I would always lie to interviewers about my upbringing, and I never repeated the same lie twice. When they pointed out inconsistencies, I glibly manufactured more lies. Of course they knew I was lying, but that was part of the game, n'est-ce pas?, the Moriartian cat-and-mouse of it.

I was born (this is, so far as such a word means anything, the truth) in Hartford, Connecticut, and raised in a leafy, moneyed Nassau County suburb on Long Island, a child of considerable wealth and privilege. My father was an investment banker, and my mother's pedigree stretches back to a Mayflower Compact signatory. I tolerated my mother and hated my father. I'm half-Jewish on my father's side; the wrong side, as far as Rabbinic law is concerned. We did not practice any religion, though. Nothing was worshiped in the many rooms of my father's house; each December we erected both a menorah and a Christmas tree, and both were rather secular suburban objects, signifying only a certain season of the year. As a child I saw no conflict in displaying them together in the same room: Both were good, both were the harbingers of an increase in material abundance for me. I was lucky to have two older sisters to demystify the feminine for me early. I was a spoiled and intelligent child and a rebellious teenager, impotently upset that all the usual paths of rebellion had been trodden flat by the pioneers of twentieth-century male adolescence before me: Marlon Brando's leather jacket of 1953 presaged Sid Vicious's leather jacket of 1977, and by the time I donned the article, the thing had become a dead signifier,* the sign having long ago devoured itself (like Beethoven's Ninth; once a paean to religious ecstasy, later blasted from loudspeakers as the Third Reich marched down the *grands boulevards* of Paris). My adolescence was, though I was too naïve to realize it at the time, an off-brand cliché: cigarettes, drugs, safety pins, early attempts at sexual experimentation, interests/indulgences in the French avant-garde, German Expressionism, New York punk, high fashion, self-mutilation, Dada, Fluxus, etc., etc., sigh, etc. My mother wrung her worried hands over her troubled baby boy, while my father—stoic, implacable, cadaverous with sangfroid—did not seem to care; he seemed to regard his three children as household pets that his wife had purchased whimsically but promised to care for. Once, over dinner, I informed my father that he was a stooge of late-capitalist oppression of the third world. My father shrugged and took a sip of wine, as unfazed as if he had not heard me.

Expensive college, hypocrisy, expansion, experimentation, hypocrisy, growth. Baudelaire, Apollinaire, Bataille, Duchamp, Tzara, Céline, Artaud, Klein, Marinetti, Cage, Adorno, Debord, Foucault, Derrida, Lacan. Italian Futurism, Situationism, Lettrism, Bauhaus. The usual.

I was frustrated with Dada (and its children) in the same way I had been frustrated with the leather jackets of Brando and Vicious, spoiling the thing for future generations with too many layers of irony or recycled sets of meaning. A middle finger to the art establishment means very little in a time when the middle finger has long become de rigueur; after rebellion becomes fashionable, then fashion becomes expected—art collapses from rebellion fatigue, and collectors come like buzzards to pick at

* Somewhere (and where on earth does one hear such things?) I heard that, if one is dying of dehydration (in the desert, or wherever you are), one may drink one's own urine once: There is more water than poison in it the first time round, and it will hydrate the body for another revolution. But don't drink the next batch: It's more toxins than hydration. I'm afraid my own leather jacket was just that: twice-recycled piss.

the remains. I found the dithyrambic had so entirely replaced the Apollonian that the prospect of taking a shit in someone's living room and charging everyone to look at it wasn't even fun anymore. My rage was impure; beset by second- and thirdhand rage anxiety. "Make it new," as Pound said—easy for a high modernist in the first half of the twentieth century to say, isn't it? How to make it new when making it new is the new old? The anxieties of the contemporary artist. Fuck it all—just get an MFA, or (a sunnier option) kill yourself.*

One weekend close to my graduation from college, I took my parents on a tour through the modern wing of the Metropolitan Museum of Art. I was getting along well enough with my parents at the time. I was twenty-two, and I had the adventurous feeling that my future lay splayed out before my feet like a resplendent red rug.

We came, I remember, to an Yves Klein monochrome (the only one at the Met): a vertical rectangular slab of material hanging on the wall, coarsely textured and painted thickly and uniformly in International Klein Blue.

Had I, Tristan Hurt, at that moment been elected to the honor of choosing an object to include in a durable capsule to be shot into outer space under sway of the vain hope that perhaps one day billions of years from now some alien race might find it, crack it open, examine the things therein, and ponder the *geist* of whatever creatures produced these beautiful objects, I might very well have selected that Klein monochrome (my choice would be different today, but, again, I plead the romance and enthusiasm of youth); and maybe, if their organs of visual perception

* Suicide is the last remaining method by which an artist might claim original authorship; the risk is, of course, that one will never know whether the gamble worked.

happened to be sensitive to the same band of the light spectrum as ours, they would understand that human beings had been animals who were indeed capable of artificing beauty so sublime as to compete with (rather than merely imitate) the forms of nature.

My father stood before the painting. I watched him look at it. The filmy annuli of his nacre-colored eyes (I was born last, late, probably accidentally, and he was old even then) examined it as blankly as they would have the floral-print wallpaper in the dining room of a New England bed and breakfast. He tipped his head back and sleepily blinked at it; pale, swollen eyelids opened and closed on the image like the mouths of garden snails eating blueberries, and the flat zero line of his bloodless lips soured into a sardonic affect of boredom. He leaned forward to read the wall text with his hands clasped behind his back, as if he was thinking of buying it for me for my birthday if (though he couldn't fathom why) I liked it so much, and was just checking the price tag. The placard beside it read:

> **Yves Klein. (French, 1928–1962) *Blue Monochrome*. 1961.**
>
> Monochrome abstraction—the use of one color over an entire canvas—is a strategy adopted by painters wishing to challenge expectations of what an image can and should represent. Klein likened monochrome painting to an "open window to freedom." He worked with a chemist to develop his own particular brand of blue. Made from pure color pigment and a binding medium, it is called International Klein Blue. Klein adopted this hue as a means of evoking the immateriality and boundlessness of his own utopian vision of the world.

My father read the title aloud: *"Blue Monochrome."*

He emitted a brusque, equine snort, and delivered his judgment: "No shit."

That was all he had to say: quote—"No shit"—end quote. I tried to explain to him why the painting was beautiful. I probably proceeded to bloviate at great length about Yves Klein, about the unexpected violence in his work, the conceptual playfulness, even the dark sexiness of it, the deliberate provocation. *Le Saut dans le vide*. I fired every bullet of critical art theory at him that my education (which he had paid for) had loaded the chambers of my brain with. My father's face slackened with contempt, a slowly deflating gray bag. The more I spoke, the further his understanding and interest in what I was saying got away from me, chugging indifferently into the distance.

When I finally fell silent, he waited a beat, and said:

"I guess it's supposed to be art if you have to explain it."

Perhaps, I thought, art needs the bourgeois in order to react against it. As long as there is a bourgeoisie to afford art without bothering to understand it, that underpinning rage of the artist may flourish, the rage of the captive animal biting the feeding hand, no matter if originality has been done to death. In that moment I more clearly understood the depth of the poverty in my father's soul, and in that moment I more fully realized my father was a man with a worldview so far removed from anything worth loving that hating him was hardly worth the energy.

New York City. The *enfant terrible* loose in the art world, playing his role, making work, plucking strings, sucking on glasses of wine at gallery openings and committing long and unusual words to heart for use in the immediate future. Fashion, alcohol, cocaine, heroin, but never (I'm mildly embarrassed to admit) any real addiction: subsidized struggle, an MFA somewhere in there. My luck snowballed, then avalanched, was off and running on its own. Basel, Miami, Hong Kong. London. LA. Venice Biennales. Seven years later, I was famous (at least in some—the right—circles). Critics praised my work as ugly, angry, abrasive, disgusting, violent, scatological, pornographic, antisocial, and antihuman. It's not terribly easy, mind you, to get called these things anymore. I lived as if my parents were dead.

Four thousand pink latex casts of artist's testicles and (erect) penis covering entire interior of large, hollow, womblike enclosure illuminated from exterior by cunt-pink neon tubes, which viewer enters via spiral staircase through door in bottom of said enclosure. Artist mixes vat of artist's own blood, urine, feces, semen, and vomit, stirs in block of melted wax; crystal chandelier is delicately submerged in heated mixture, then suspended from gallery ceiling such that cooling fluid coagulates in mid-drip; unsightly puddle collects on floor directly beneath, cools, hardens. Two thousand Manhattan telephone directories are shredded and scattered over gallery floor, artist spends five days living in gallery space intoxicated on various drugs, masturbating, urinating, defecating in shredded paper, scrawling obscenities and crude pornographic cartoons on white walls with Magic Markers. Artist films self defecating directly onto lens of video camera, projects footage onto four walls of darkened room, in reverse and slow motion; dark walls slowly recede into four giant, luminous images of artist's anus.

My work was exhibited by Deitch Projects; my pieces found homes in the collections of Charles Saatchi and Larry Gagosian, among others. I became very wealthy. I squandered money lavishly, publicly.

Behold: Tristan Hurt, standing at gallery opening, glass of wine in hand, slovenly dressed in thirty thousand dollars' worth of dirty clothes, face carefully peppered with four days' stubble. I am pictured en medias schmooze with several other people as-or-more-famous than myself. This photograph appeared again and again in many similar variations, and the fame of the people with whom I stand in the photograph gradually increased; as it did, boat lifted by rising tide, so did my fame, so did the prices of my work, and so did my wealth. At a certain point I ceased to be Tristan Hurt, the blasé, angry young man infused with his perfectly suburban father-hatred, and became Tristan Hurt: Tristan Hurt, whose name stands alone.

One night my parents did come unannounced to an opening. They wanted to "surprise" me. Pleasantly, I suppose they assumed. I was, of course, busy, standing naked (rather, nude) in the middle of the gallery floor, masturbating into a raw steak folded in my fist when I saw them walk in. (This was a performance of my piece *Pursuance*: Artist stands nude in gallery and masturbates into holes cut in slabs of raw meat, which latex-gloved assistants then dunk in tubs of shellac and hang with clothespins, dripping, from suspended wires.) My father's expression did not change as my mother fled the room. My father calmly walked out of the gallery after her. I was twenty-eight years old at the time.

Later, sometimes I would meet my mother for lunch when she was in the city, but I would not see or speak with my father again.

There is such a thing as a fame drive. Or call it a glory drive. Like the ability to sing, like a taste for cilantro, it's something you either have or you don't. With the exceptions of people who happen to be caught standing in exactly the right place at exactly the right time, or people who happen to be caught standing in exactly the wrong place at exactly the wrong time, almost everyone who ever becomes famous has it, while very few of the people who have it ever become famous, which is why to have it is a curse: It means you will probably feel like a failure for most, if not all, of your life. I have it. I envy and admire those who don't. Those people can go to bed knowing that they are alive, healthy, and comfortable, and can be perfectly content with that. Those of us who have the glory drive cannot be content with just that. We are not happy unless the number of people we have never met who know our names is increasing. As with money and sex, only too much fame is enough, and there is never too much of it, hence never enough, hence we are never happy. A therapist once told me that people who have this doomed and repellant personality trait have it because of certain kinds of childhoods. What kinds, I asked him. He theorized that it happens to children whose parents tell them they're wonderful on the one hand and on the other treat them as if they're never good enough. They pump up your tires, take away your training wheels, and push you down a hill so you can go forth and live a life of restlessly straining to fulfill an inflated self-image, constantly making up for an inward feeling of inferiority. I thought: Mother, encouragement; father, denial—that's right. That's me. Feral children are lucky in that they don't have to worry about this. God, to be raised by dingoes in the wilderness. That's the best way to do it—this, life: Grow up thinking you're a wild dog. If these children are out there, I hope for their sakes we never find them.

The fame, or glory, drive is, at least in men, a relative of, and collaborator and coconspirator with the libido. (Perhaps in some women as well—but I can't speak to that; I only know that female sexuality is usually more complicated and interesting than that.) I won't bore you with a locker-room litany of the models and actresses whose interiors I have explored. And I can attest that like the goose that laid the golden eggs, it's just ordinary goose inside. The pleasure of fucking a model isn't fucking the model, it's showing up at the party with the model. That's a pleasure in its own right, of course, but the real pleasure of sex while famous is fucking people who are less famous than you.

Olivia Frankel taught creative writing at Octavia College, and wrote quirky, bittersweet short stories about the doomed love affairs of artists. Or so I surmised; I never actually read them. She twitched and babbled in her sleep, talked too much in conversation, and ground her jaw when she wasn't speaking. She had a thin, squeaky voice that sounded to me like an articulate piccolo. She was pale, and skinny as a bug, and always sat with her shoulders slightly hunched. We were not in love—not exactly—and the relationship did not last very long. We casually dated for maybe about five months. She was initially attracted by my accomplishment, my fame, my easy charisma, my intelligent conversation and sparkling wit, but eventually grew into the realization that I am, in certain respects, a fraud. They always do wind up scratching the gold leaf off the ossified dog turd, don't they?—the smart ones, anyway, and the dumb ones will eventually bore me.

As a person, I was nearly as lazy as I was self-absorbed.* I had never actually read very much. Almost nothing, really. All that critical theory in college and graduate school? All that heady French gobbledygook? Not counting the front and back covers, I probably read maybe a cumulative fifteen pages of it. That may in fact be an overgenerous estimate. I was, however, blessèd with the gift of bullshit—a blessing that took me far indeed. I knew the names of the writers I was supposed to have read, and could pronounce them with a haughty accuracy and ironclad confidence

* *Was, was*: As I sit here, alone, naked, and unable to move, with the summer sun roasting the flesh of my enormous belly and my backside rotting against my mold-blackened bedsheets, I have begun to think of my life in the past tense.

that withered on the spot those who had actually read them. Believe me, I could slather it on so thick and byzantine that most people—even those who did "know" what they were talking about—were dazzled to silence by the fireworks of obfuscation that burst from my mouth when I spoke.*

Olivia, however, learned to see through it, and was probably a bit irritated with herself for having been at first seduced by it. A few friendly interrogations over dinner on matters approaching the erudite were enough to reveal that I probably had not finished a book since high school. So, in the first few months of our nearly meaningless affair, back when Olivia was still at least ostensibly entertaining the possibility of allowing herself to love me, she bought me a present: a volume of the collected stories of Franz Kafka. Written on the inside front cover, in her filigreed female handwriting (but in rather assertive black marker), was the businesslike inscription: "Tristan— Here you go. Most of them are pretty short. Olivia."

That sign-off was characteristic of her, by the way. No "love," no "with love," not even a tepid "best wishes." Just her first name followed by a period, as if that alone constituted its own sentence.†

* I can at last admit, now that I am probably about to die, and now that the New York art world has as far as I can tell ceased to exist (for the city appears to have been depopulated), that the New York art world was a house so haunted with bullshit that wandering its darkened hallways we sometimes felt like pseudoscientists with silly pieces of beeping, blinking equipment, searching empty rooms for something we wanted to be there, but wasn't. Admittedly, under any closer than the most pedestrian scrutiny, whole paragraphs of criticism could vanish, like grasping at smoke, as they either meant nothing or expressed ideas so simple they hardly needed to be articulated. Where else but in art criticism was there so little to say and so much space to fill? All of it is gone, now. Do I mourn it? Yes, for even now I remain confident there were babies to be found alive in that sea of bathwater.

† We have time for an amusing anecdote: Sometime later, in her apartment, I was perusing Olivia's bookshelf while she was in the shower, and found two identical copies of *Kafka: The Collected Stories*. One was battered and dog-eared, with multiple creases in the binding—clearly her own—and the other was brand new. On the inside front cover of

For her I was probably at most a brief, interesting infatuation or experiment. I don't think she was ever really in love with me. She did once tell me I was the most, quote, "fake and pathetic person [she] ever made the mistake of fucking." Much later, she also told me she would, quote, "call the cops on [me] if [I were to] show up [at her apartment] coked out of [my] mind [in the middle of the night] again."

But all that is beside the point. I mention Olivia only by way of explaining how it was I came to admire Kafka's haunting allegory, "A Hunger Artist." A man sits in a cage and refuses to eat. He is gradually forgotten by the public. He starves himself for so long that everyone ceases to care. But his art goes on—unto his death. His last words are: "I couldn't find the food I liked. If I had found it, believe me, I would have stuffed myself like you or anyone else." When he dies, they sweep out his cage and replace him with a young panther. "The food he liked," writes Kafka, "was brought him without hesitation by the attendants; he seemed not even to miss his freedom." The people crowd around the cage that now contains this creature so ardently alive, and "they did not want ever to move away."

Starvation—my goodness, is that a dark metaphor, Mr. Kafka. Take a look at the cover of the book: Kafka peers out at you in grainy black and white, his dark hair slicked back from his temples, his eyes wide, wet, hunted-looking. His cheekbones are high and brutally sharp, his cheeks sunken. He looks malnourished already. We know his sisters died in Auschwitz, which is doubtless where this man's skull would have wound up, scrabbled in a ditch along with thousands of other Jewish skulls, had

the brand-new one the exact same inscription appeared, only this one was signed, "Love, Olivia." Clearly she had bought the book, inscribed it in this way, then had second thoughts, bought another copy, and signed it *without* "Love."

tuberculosis not mercifully knocked him off at the age of forty in 1924. He died of consumption, as the Victorian euphemism goes—because the disease *consumes* one from the inside out—whereas I, Tristan Hurt, would set out to die of a different kind of consumption. What if—I wonder—Kafka had not coughed himself to death, but had lived long enough to be herded onto a cattle car bound for Poland, where the writer/insurance underwriter (who, like me, bitterly resented his father) would have been stripped, shaved, tattooed with a number, starved, and forced to dig his own grave? It would not have taken this wan, skinny little man very much time at all to begin to look like the men lying on the bunks and wincing at the daylight as the doors of Auschwitz, Buchenwald, and Dachau rolled open in the spring of 1945: horrifically thin, eyes sunken, ribs like claws. He was halfway there already. This man himself resembled the hunger artist. But in those penetrating but deeply sad eyes, evident even through the poor exposure and the fuzzy focus, there is a hunger beyond the merely physical—this man was starving not only because he felt caged in by his oppressive family and besieged by the zeitgeist of his interwar Prague, but was suffering a starvation of the soul, an insatiate hunger of the spirit.

The story was also very short, and while I quite honestly did not read very much of that book, I did at least read that story, and the beginnings of several others.

After Olivia terminated relations with me—citing as she did some pointed critiques of my personality and lifestyle—I gained a tremendous amount of weight.

Should you ever want to nearly treble your magnitude in a relatively short period of time, I recommend the following regimen: morbid depression, sleeping thirteen or more hours a day, addictions to alcohol and barbiturates, and lots of eating.

I spent much of the next year in bed. My finances were comfortable. I could afford it. I disappeared from public life. I ordered food in daily. Initially I relied heavily on pizza and Chinese food. Sometimes I ate large quantities of fried chicken. Sometimes I ate four to five canisters of Pringles snack chips in a single sitting. Sometimes I ate two or three gallons of ice cream for dessert. A typical day during this period might go something like this:

4:30 P.M.:	Rise, shine
5:00 P.M.:	Pick up phone, order three pizzas
5:10 P.M.–9:30 P.M.:	Sit on couch, watch TV while eating three said pizzas
9:35 P.M.–1:15 A.M.:	Naptime
1:15 A.M.–5:00 A.M.:	Wake up sobbing and chilled in sweat with wildly beating heart. Gobble fistful of benzodiazepines and crouch over laptop, drinking whiskey, eating ice cream, smoking cigarettes, and enjoying pornography until sleep comes again to take the artist away from this awful place

Groceries, drugs, liquor, laundry, etc.—it was almost astonishing how nearly everything that might require my leaving my home I was able to have someone from the outside bring to me (only in New York!). I spent most of my time in the nude; I donned a bathrobe to meet deliverymen at the door (sometimes). I kept the curtains drawn. No light came into my space. I did not wash my sheets either. They grew sticky, filmy. I expanded rapidly.

Ten months later, I weighed nearly five hundred pounds. Not that I was keeping track. This initial period of massive weight gain, while I was dimly aware of it, was more or less unintentional. I was not yet a Fat Artist—I was merely an artist who had allowed himself, by way of a largely sedentary and unwholesome lifestyle, to become extraordinarily fat. I was merely a fat artist.

Throughout this year I communicated with practically no one. It was surprisingly easy to drop off the face of the earth in a luxury loft apartment in a converted warehouse in Greenpoint. I did not come out, I called no one, never returned a call, nor did I answer anyone by e-mail or any other medium of communication, and I quickly became—by choice—friendless.

What drew me out of my malaise was not love, nor was it fear (not, at least, for my life), nor was it the intervention of friends or family, as I had no real friends and was estranged from my family. Rather, what drove me back into the world was the most powerful but prosaic mover in human civilization: money.

I was broke. I had been consuming a great deal, and I'd had no source of income for nearly a year. I had not sold a single piece, I had not done any hobnobbing, I had not appeared in a single photograph holding a single cocktail in *Artforum*'s "Scene & Herd." I was missing in action in the art world.

I did not realize at the time that my refusal to communicate with anyone or even leave my home for a year had lent a mysterious luster to my absent celebrity. I had not been—as I had thought (as I probably should have been)—forgotten. Rather, my long and unexplained absence had acquired a strange quality of presence. I had created a vacuum of myself. At every gallery opening that year to which I had been invited and did not attend, there was a Tristan Hurt–shaped hole in the room, a phantom, a shadow, a void that was more glamorously conspicuous than my presence would have been. As if my prolonged disappearance were in fact an ingeniously crafted publicity stunt. Clearly an artist who chooses to abruptly vanish from society before the zenith of his career must be a creative genius locked in a fit of feverish productivity that ordinary people cannot ever hope to truly understand.

I do not know if they thought I was working. I do not know if they thought I was in a torturous state of nerves, for which I needed the dark romance of my solitude. I do not know if perhaps they thought I was sleeping until four in the afternoon each hateful day and then spending my waking hours shoveling gooey clumps of General Tso's chicken between my industrious jaws and watching videos of big-dicked men ejaculating onto the waiting faces of girls while I soporated my brain with Ambien and bourbon with my listless penis sleeping in my hand like a beanbag. I do not even know if this knowledge would have detracted from, or in fact somehow added to, their newfound romantic notion of me as an eccentric recluse.

But as I said, it was nothing more—or less—romantic than a matter of grubby economics that drove me from my long hibernation. I had not checked up on my personal finances in many months. I simply had not been thinking about it. I'd had so much money at the outset of my long period of torpidity that I had somewhat blithely assumed my bank balance would remain always as inexhaustible as the horn of plenty of legends old. I did not open my mail for nearly a year. I kept a year's worth of unopened mail in a black plastic trash bag in a closet. Whenever a piece of mail arrived, I immediately stuffed it in the bag. For a year I was, on some level, distantly terrified of how much money I was spending, and so I was disinclined to look.

Tax day came and went without my so much as bothering to call my accountant. Eventually I received an unpleasant call from the Internal Revenue Service. This prompted me to finally steel enough courage to investigate the state of my accounts.

With great trepidation fluttering in my weak heart, I exhumed the contents of the garbage bag in which I had been keeping all my unopened mail. I ensconced myself on the floor and ripped open each cursed envelope. Every piece of mail I opened revealed my financial situation to be graver than the last. Over the past year, the fortune I had acquired had diminished to nil. It was gone. Gone! Gone up my nose and down my gullet, gone through my idleness, gone into images of naked women subjecting themselves to hideous acts of willful degradation, gone into my brain and my veins and the fat of my body and splurted out of my anal sphincter and my penis, often into my dirty socks. The cost of the pornography alone that I put on my credit cards came out to something in the order of nine thousand dollars per month, to say nothing of the drugs, the alcohol, and the food, the food, the glorious food.

I was destitute!

I looked around my home. What did it look like? First, imagine a loft space in a converted warehouse in Greenpoint with twelve-foot ceilings, large, arch-shaped west-facing windows, a beautiful view of Midtown Manhattan, white walls and warm-toned glossy oak floors, track lighting, designer furniture, granite countertops, everything tastefully accented with objets d'art. Now make it dark. Draw curtains shut over windows so that no light gets in. Take considerable quantity of soiled clothing, drape pell-mell over furniture, scatter across floor. Fill room with empty beer bottles, empty whiskey bottles, stacks of oily pizza boxes. Moldy, soiled dishes should litter floor, coffee table, dining table, countertops; heap high in sink. Leave to rot for many consecutive months. When artist runs out of clean dishes, add top layer of paper plates, soaked transparent with grease. Add thick stench of sweat, semen, smoke, garbage, etc. Add generous quantity of cockroaches. Add mice. Add rats. Allow mice and rats to skitter freely across floor. Cease to care about cockroaches, mice, rats. Cease to notice cockroaches, mice, rats.

Add cloud of flies. Do not even attempt to swat/shoo flies if/when said flies land on artist's skin.

And it wasn't only the massive weight gain: I had been ignoring all avenues of personal hygiene. Give artist long, tangled beard and long, knotted hair. Give him long, sharp fingernails and long toenails that curl under toes like demonic yellow hooves. Do not wash the artist. Make the artist's skin sickly pale from long period of entirely interior and nocturnal existence.

Behold the artist.

First I made a feeble attempt at tidying up my living space, but quickly became discouraged by the overwhelming complexity of the mess. Next I turned my attention to my person. I trimmed and groomed my beard, cut my hair, clipped my nails (both finger- and toe-), showered, brushed my teeth, spat a brown spume of filth and blood into the sink and brushed them again, laundered some clothes and donned them. I was now a much more presentable man, albeit nevertheless a grotesquely obese one. I even liked the rich chocolate-brown beard I had grown. A good, thick beard has a way of dignifying a very fat man.

I reentered society. I reconnected with old friends. It was not hard to get back in the scene. The art world was appropriately appalled, revolted, saddened, intrigued, amused, and delighted with my new body.

My monstrousness made me highly visible. I went back to the parties, back to the VIP openings, returned to the photos in which I stood in the company of the hypermoneyed and/or famous, holding a glass of wine—and damned if I wasn't bigger than ever.

Through whisper campaign and providence of gossip it became known that I, Tristan Hurt, had spent almost a year in monastic seclusion, working steadfastly on my most ambitious and important project to date: myself. I had spent the last ten months sculpting my body, working as hard on my physique as might an athlete, a bodybuilder, a dancer—but not for the sake of vanity, nor for agility, not to make my body stronger, more robust, or more beautiful. Like my sculptural work before it, my body art was to be deliberately grotesque, and, as Wilde opined all art is, quite useless.

Thus it was that I conceived the installation piece that would revitalize and conclude the career of Tristan Hurt, the Fat Artist.

I obtained generous financial patronage for the project from the Guggenheim Foundation. I worked closely with Italian "starchitect" Emilio Buzzati to design the structure in which I would be kept. A large glass cube, each side twenty-five feet long, was constructed according to our plans atop the roof of Frank Lloyd Wright's famous Solomon R. Guggenheim Museum at Eighty-Ninth and Fifth Avenue. My exhibit was constructed on top of the long, flat roof of the rectangular addition to the museum that was constructed in 1992. Each side of my glass cube except the floor was constructed of thin steel girders structurally reinforced with crisscrossing steel cables, forming a grid of twenty-five five-by-five-foot squares, which were inset with plates of glass. The floor was concrete, poured in place, sanded smooth. The room was perfectly transparent all around. Visitors would enter through two wide glass-and-steel double doors in the east wall of the cube. An extravagant bed was constructed in the center of the room, with the back of the headboard flush against the north wall, such that the person sitting on the bed—that is, the Fat Artist himself—could gaze either in a southerly direction across Central Park at Midtown Manhattan, or up through the glass ceiling at the firmament above.

The bed unto itself was a work of art. I designed it. My bed was my last piece of inorganic sculpture. In style, it is deliberately imitative of Louis

Quatorze-period furniture, except that those luxurious mid-seventeenth-century beds tend to feature tall posters and canopies with thick curtains, whereas my bed allowed none of these, as I demanded maximum visible exposure of my repulsive body from every angle in the room. In a visually musical series of symmetrical filigrees, the headboard slopes upward into a central peak eight feet from the floor. It is fashioned of mahogany, ostentatiously carved with decorative designs, and gilt with a thin film of gold. The bed is longer and slightly wider than a California king, and its frame was reinforced with sturdy steel rods, in order to support the extraordinary weight that would be pressed upon it. The mattress also had to be custom-made to fit the unusual dimensions of the frame, and also required a three-inch-diameter hole through its upper center. The mattress was designed to be firm and strong, but as comfortable as possible, three feet thick and vacuum-stuffed with a hardy and pliant foam insulation. The bed was covered with a sumptuous sheet of glossy purple velvet, and then piled high with a mountain of matching purple velvet pillows with tasseled fringes of gold thread. The bed was built inside the room on top of an industrial platform scale of the sort used to weigh automobiles and shipping containers. We affixed the scale's large digital readout to the west wall of my exhibition chamber: accurate down to the fourth digit to the right of the zero, with data presented in both imperial and metric, numbers aglow, red on black. The bed was then weighed by itself and the scale's zero reset so as to measure only any additional weight.* Behind the bed—obscured from the public's view of the installation—a hole was cut in the bottom-center panel of glass in the north wall, and we ran a thick rubber tube through the hole, wound it under the bed and up through the hole in the mattress. On the outside of the exhibition chamber, the tube connected to a low-pressure vacuum that would suck waste out of my

* I.e., "taring" the scale.

body and into a septic tank that flushed into the museum's plumbing system; inside the exhibition chamber, the tube emerged from the hole in the mattress and bifurcated into two smaller tubes, one narrow and one thick: my urinary and rectal catheters. Additionally, an eighty-gallon-capacity water tank was affixed to the north wall, beside my bed. A filtered hose siphoned clean drinking water from the building's water supply into the tank, and another rubber hose ran from the bottom of the tank and was kept coiled around a hook within my reach on the headboard. A metal ball plugged the lip of the hose when I was not drinking. When I needed to drink water, all I had to do was put the hose to my mouth and push the metal ball in with my tongue to let the water dribble into my mouth. It was essentially a large-scale adaptation of similar drinking apparatuses commonly seen in the cages of hamsters, guinea pigs, and other pet rodents. In this way I would always be kept well hydrated.

On the roof of the Guggenheim Museum, on a sunny, pale blue day in mid-May of a year sometime in the spirit of the twenty-first century, I, Tristan Hurt, removed my clothes and handed them to an assistant, and with great effort hefted my 493 lb (224 kg) frame onto my bed. I gingerly maneuvered my body as museum staff workers inserted my penis into the narrower of the two rubber tubes, made a seal of adhesive silicone putty, and wrapped the bond in gauze for double reinforcement. Then I slowly turned over and allowed the workers to insert the other rubber tube into my anus, a good two inches deep, and likewise seal the bond with sticky silicone putty. The hole in the mattress was situated directly below where I was to sit, such that I could partially sit up on the bed with no discomfort, my back resting against the plush mound of pillows piled against the headboard.

Although I was naked, I was not indecent, as my genitals were obscured between my enormous thighs and beneath the rolling folds of my lower torso. I spread my legs on the glossy velvet bed and playfully wiggled my distant toes. I reflected on my luxurious comfort. I mentally remarked upon the pleasantly crypto-erotic sensation of the vacuum tubes sucking ticklishly at my penis and anus. I gazed at the faces of the museum workers surrounding my bed. That night the world would get its first glimpse of me at an invitation-only VIP opening exhibition. I was prepared to eat.

The concept was elegant in its simplicity: to turn Kafka on his head. "A Hunger Artist" in part derives the power of its allegory from the sheer horror of self-abnegation. Why on earth would anyone deliberately starve himself to death? But in a culture of abundance and affordable luxury, bodily self-abnegation no longer retains this primeval horror. Rather, the twenty-first-century middle-class American must actively labor *not* to become fat. Thus eating becomes moralized behavior. How often have you heard a woman describe a rich dessert as "sinful"? To *eat* is to *sin*—in secular society, the body replaces the soul. Good and evil are no longer purely spiritual concepts—these words have been transubstantiated into the realm of the flesh. At other times it seems as if the very process of eating has even become a chore—something associated with work. How often has a waiter at a restaurant asked you if you are "still *working*" on your meal? Perhaps eating for us has therefore also been stripped of the especial joy it might retain in a culture in which people are immediately conscious of the threat of want. In a culture such as ours Kafka's story becomes deflated of much of its sting—we fail to feel the poison of it, because food exists for us in a different psychological space than it did for Kafka: We are a culture that moralizes the diet. Thus "A Hunger Artist" cannot strike its contemporary readers with the same fascination and revulsion. Indeed, far more apropos to an age of overabundance is a Fat Artist.

And I, Tristan Hurt, the Fat Artist, vowed to become the fattest human being in known history.

As I have said, I was forced by the necessity of objective measurement to equate "heaviest" with "fattest." Before me, Carol Yager of Flint, Michigan, was widely thought to be the heaviest human on record. Prior to her death at age thirty-four in 1994 from massive kidney failure, Yager was estimated to have peaked at about 1,600 lbs (726 kg). Just below Yager was Jon Brower Minnoch of Bainbridge Island, Washington, who died shortly before he turned forty-two in 1983, having attained a peak weight of approximately 1,400 lbs (635 kg). I, Tristan Hurt, began my journey at a comparatively scrappy 493 lbs (224 kg), which meant I had to gain 907 lbs (411 kg) to even tie for second place, and I had to gain 1,107 lbs (502 kg)—*half a ton*—to tie the record, though preferably much more if I was to comfortably surpass it. The work I had before me was nothing short of daunting.

The parameters were thus: Anyone could bring me food of any sort—rather, the public was greatly *encouraged* to bring food—and I would have to eat it. There was but one rule for the visitors, that their offerings had beyond all reasonable contestability to be *food*—i.e., nothing inedible, impotable, or indigestible. No chewing gum, mouthwash, motor oil, cigarette butts, packing peanuts, cotton balls, chewing tobacco, shaving cream, rubber bullets, small toys, leather, paint, etc. Aside from this one broad guideline, any cuisine was permissible. And there were but two rules I designated to myself, the Fat Artist: (1) any food that is brought to me I must consume; and (2) during museum hours, I must be in the process of consuming (eating or drinking) at all times.

My exhibition chamber also contained a glass table on rollers, long enough so as to stretch wider than the industrial scale beneath my bed, high enough to come up to my midriff when wheeled over the bed, and transparent, so as not to obscure my fat beneath it. My dining table. Waiters were employed. The waiters wore black bow ties and tuxedo vests, and worked in shifts to attend to my dining experience at all times, clearing away my dirty dishes and continually presenting me with more food. The visiting public was to bring me offerings, which the museum workers kept on a table nearby to await their imminent consumption. The table was equipped with heat lamps to keep warm food warm, and a refrigerator underneath it for chilled items. The waiters would bring me the food when I was ready for it and clear away the refuse of whatever I had just consumed.

The VIP opening of the exhibition was held on a Thursday night in May. It was a beautiful evening. The temperature was consummate, hovering at about 70° F. The museum employees propped open the doors of my exhibition chamber, and the people milled about on the roof, ambling in and out of the open doors of my glass cube. My opening meal was specially prepared under the supervision of Philip Laroux, the chef de cuisine at the West Village's preeminent three-Michelin-star restaurant, Pleonexia. Laroux also supervised the preparation of the hors d'oeuvres that were arrayed on a long table on the roof outside my glass exhibition chamber. The theme of the evening was food, and thus naturally I demanded that the hors d'oeuvres represent the height of culinary excellence. The hors d'oeuvres table was laden with colorful displays of foie gras, crystallized seaweed, oyster vinaigrette, carpaccio of cauliflower with artichoke and chocolate jelly, scallop tartare and caviar, white chocolate velouté, braised rabbit dumplings in broccoli ginger sauce and chili oil. The centerpiece of the display was an ice champagne fountain, 3D printed after my deliberately garish design: Five female nudes lay basking in sumptuous repose around the base of the fountain, which sloped curvilinearly upward into a deep bowl; the sides of the fountain's bowl were studded with five erect penises carved from ice and complete with testicles; the fountain was filled with a great quantity of champagne, which tunneled through the hollow flutes of the ice penises and squirted in smooth golden arcs into the open mouths of the five nudes at the base of the fountain; the champagne gargled and frothed in their icy mouths and dribbled down their chins into the lower basin, where it was thrust back into the fountain bowl by a recirculating pump. The guests would catch the champagne by holding their glasses under the streams jetting from the constantly ejaculating penises of ice.

Meanwhile, for added effect, a string quartet played *Eine kleine Nachtmusik* in continual repetition. Achingly beautiful clothes abounded. Some people wore designer gowns and others, ripped neon mesh T-shirts. Jewelry flashed at slender throats. A photographer slithered through the interstices between bodies with his camera slicing at the night with blank razors of light. High heels clapped on the asphalt surface of the roof. Wineglasses tinkled. Hands shook hands, bodies embraced bodies, lips kissed cheeks. New inamorata were introduced to friends and colleagues. As the string quartet played, mellifluous songs of lovely female laughter rose and fell amid the burble of general conversation, in incidental accompaniment to the violins lacing their high sweet notes through the luscious velvet of the viola and the cello.

The roof of the 1992 addition to the Guggenheim was never designed as an exhibition space. We could not have constructed the exhibit on top of either of the two smaller towers included in Frank Lloyd Wright's original building because they were not big enough, and we demanded the exhibit be constructed outside, for important aesthetic reasons I do not presently recall. Pipes, antennae, ductwork, and unsightly things like that crawl out of the hot, tar-spattered surface of the flat rectangular roof, and there really isn't much room to move around. Before the opening, certain cautionary procedures were taken to assure the safety of the patrons, including a temporary guard railing to keep people from straying too close to the edge of the building. All night people awkwardly squeezed past airshaft ducts while trying not to dirty their clothes or spill their drinks.

The attendees of the VIP opening crowded at my bedside like family round a dying patriarch, munching the hors d'oeuvres they cradled in folded napkins in their hands, sipping champagne and murmuring with reverently muted conversation, while I sat nude on my enormous purple bed and ate.

My opening meal began with a bottle of '97 Château d'Yquem and a modest tomato soup with minted crème fraîche, peekytoe crab, and julienned bacon. This was followed by a plate of langoustines and snails glazed in a light Hollandaise with cracked Basque pepper and parsley. I ate every one of them, scraping the puffy white meat from the sharp ridges of the lobster carapace, delicately sucking the slick mollusks from their shells. Following this, a course of veal cappelletti and truffles stuffed with ice-filtered lamb jelly, sweetbread, and mussels. At this point I swallowed the last of the Château d'Yquem and switched to a velvety yet robust 2000 Châteauneuf-du-Pape recommended to complement my main course, which one of my tuxedoed waiters forthwith displayed to me with a flourish while the other swept away the remains of my previous course, and I wiped my oily fingers clean with a moist towelette: an entire goose, braised in a champagne-butter reduction and stuffed with chestnuts, shiitake mushrooms, and venison sausage. For maximum effect two silver candelabras softly illuminated my meal, and I ate with fork, knife, and spoon, although I neither wore a bib nor draped my lap with a napkin, which would have obscured part of my fat body, for which I wanted maximum visibility; it did not take long before I took to wiping my hands on my plush purple bedsheets. Crumbs tumbled between my legs; drippings of sauce streaked my belly. It took me about an hour and a half to devour the entire goose. I had to work very slowly so as not to overstuff or exhaust myself. I did once have to move my bowels in the middle of the meal. This is something I would learn over time to feel less squeamish about. It is an oddly exhilarating sensation to defecate in full view of spectators while actually eating at the same time: to eliminate the arbitrary and bourgeois separation between not only the physical, but also the *psychological* spaces designated for the body's admission versus evacuation of material.* My excrement, liquid and solid, simply slipped out of me when it was ready to go, with minimal effort on my part, and was immediately whisked away unseen, vacuumed straight out of my body via the tubes concealed beneath me. I don't think anyone present even noticed. When I had slurped the last remaining edible sinews from the last remaining bones and ligaments of the goose, the dish was borne away and immediately replaced with a glass of forty-year-old tawny port and my dessert: a whole cheesecake, which I hacked apart and shoveled into my mouth one dainty forkload after another, dampening my bites with glass after glass of port. By the end of the night, this cheesecake took me longer to finish than the main course. Several times I nearly vomited, but each time I felt the bile racing up my throat, I clenched my mouth shut tight, steeled myself, closed my eyes, swallowed, and recovered—ready to eat on.

By the time I had almost finished the cheesecake, most of the VIP opening's invitees had left. I was feverish, ill, sweating profusely, slightly delirious. As I sat nude on my giant purple bed, the edges of things had

* Again, I make no claim to the originality of this observation; Luis Buñuel of course beat me to it with *Le Fantôme de la liberté*. Vanity of vanities; all is vanity.

begun to acquire a silvery haze, like a faraway desert horizon, and my vision of the world before me kept sliding off its axis, stopping, getting back on, sliding off again. The exhibition was closing for the night, and my scale reported that on that first night, I had gained 23 lbs (10 kg) in one meal alone, finishing out the evening at a formidable 516 lbs (234 kg). Although I knew that in order to reach my goal of becoming the heaviest human being in known history I had approximately another 1,200 lbs (544 kg) to gain, and although I very well knew much of this initial weight gain was only temporary, as it would soon be evacuated from my perilously engorged digestive tract through the rubber vacuum tubes connected to my body's lower egresses, I felt then an enormous inner swelling of pride at my achievement.

The last stragglers left the museum employees to clean up after the party as I sluggishly chased the remnants of my cheesecake across the platter with my fork and nipped at the dregs of the port. From my bed, in delirium, I watched the museum employees pick up the discarded fingerprint-fogged, lipstick-smudged wineglasses, sweep away debris with push brooms, dismantle the hors d'oeuvres table, and throw out the basinful of tepid water that my champagne fountain/pornographic ice sculpture had long since become. As if from twenty feet under water I looked languidly at my waiters, who stood leaning against the outer glass walls of my exhibition chamber with their shirts now untucked and unbuttoned at the throats, and the flaps of their undone bow ties dangling down, as they joked and chatted. They were smoking cigarettes and blowing the smoke into the warm May air, and looking out across the dark expanse of Central Park and the Upper West Side's glittering wall of light. They did not look back at me. Nor did they think to speak to me as they wheeled away my long glass dining table, misted it with Windex, and wiped it down with squeaky rags. I watched them sweep and mop the smooth concrete floor of my exhibition chamber while passing a bottle of wine left over from the opening back and forth between them, and I faintly heard them make plans to join some of the other museum employees for a drink after they were done with their work. When they had mopped the floor, one went to return the mop and bucket to a janitorial closet while the other surveyed the room for anything they might have missed, and, finding nothing, pulled the doors shut, snaked a heavy chain through the door handles, secured them with a padlock, and left—all without looking at or speaking to me or acknowledging my presence in any way. He was simply at work, and I may as well have been an inanimate object in the room. I settled my weight against the pile of pillows at my back and watched him go. From my vantage point, propped up on the plush purple bed of my own design, inside my glass exhibition chamber atop the roof of the Guggenheim, I could see clear across the park, and gaze at the towering luminous rectangles of Midtown Manhattan to the south. Jets flew low overhead, red and green lights blinking, engines droning low streams of colorless noise as they gently descended toward JFK and LaGuardia. The city at night sparkled and hummed with heat, with light, with life, ardent life.

In the morning I awakened to the clinking sounds of a museum employee fiddling with the padlocked chain on the doors to my exhibition chamber. That day my exhibit was to open to the general public.

The roof was thick with humanity all day, from the museum's opening at 10:00 A.M. until it closed at 5:45 P.M. The exhibition was hotly anticipated, as it had been hailed as a groundbreaking cultural event, preceded by a long campaign of advertising that had culminated with a massive billboard draped across the west-facing side of the Condé Nast Building. The opening-day visitors had purchased their tickets months in advance. The line to get into my exhibit coiled twice around the block, I'm told, with an average wait time of two hours. Once visitors made it into the museum, they were directed into two streams of traffic: one line to enter the regular museum, and the other line for those who had come only to view the Fat Artist. Still others had purchased tickets that allowed them to also see the exhibits in the rest of the museum before or after viewing the Fat Artist, and these people were allowed to choose their line, though most of them, for fear of not being able to make it to my exhibit later, chose to see me first. Velvet ropes corralled the line into the museum's addition and stopped at the elevators, to which visitors were admitted in small groups of ten to twelve by museum employees who communicated with the staff on the roof through walkie-talkies that crunched and squawked in their hands. The elevators then ascended to the top floor, where staff herded the visitors outside onto the roof. And the people came, crowding into my exhibition chamber to watch the artist eat. Museum staff tried to keep the number of people on the roof to forty at most, but there were too few of them to properly police the behavior of the visitors, and the people thronged around my bed in such numbers that many were forced to stand outside of my exhibition chamber and peer in with faces puttied to the glass, breath blowing spots of fog. The late spring was slouching into early summer and the temperature was warm, and with the pulsing flux of sticky, sweating skin moving in and out of the room it quickly took on the thickly biotic aromas of a bath house, a public locker room, a zoo. Soon the interior of the box had become so opacified with condensation that it was difficult for those outside to see in. Tremulous beads of moisture gathered on the ceiling and dripped desultorily onto my bed, my body, my food. There was a constant, rushing din of people—so much humanity in all its vivacious grotesquerie—taking pictures, talking, giggling, pointing, watching me eat.

Food and drink of any sort is ordinarily prohibited in the museum, but special exemption was made for those who had come to view my exhibit.

I was astounded—heartwarmed, even—by the magnificent variety of offerings the visitors brought me. They brought me shrimp cocktail. They brought me T-bone steaks. They brought me spare ribs, glistening with barbecue sauce. They brought me spaghetti and meatballs. They brought me pepper-blackened ahi tuna. They brought me to-go cups of split pea soup. They brought me chocolate cake. They brought me greasy paper boxes full of tandoori chicken. They brought me snickerdoodle cookies. They brought me waffles, soggy with whipped cream and blueberry compote. They brought me kebob. They brought me deli sandwiches. They brought me hot pastrami on rye. They brought me club sandwiches. They brought me egg salad sandwiches. They brought me Reubens. They brought me bagels with lox. Others came bearing fast food. They brought me Big Macs. They brought me Whoppers. They brought me Chicken McNuggets. They brought me Frosties. They brought me Baconators. They brought me Crunchwrap Supremes. They brought me Blizzards. I am told the street vendors quickly learned to capitalize on my exhibit, and clustered their carts on Eighty-Ninth and Fifth near the entrance of the museum for all the visitors who felt acutely embarrassed, seeing other people's offerings, by not having brought any offerings themselves, and thus I saw a great abundance of New York street food: They brought me hot dogs, falafels, puffy cheese-stuffed pretzels, roasted corn nuts. Still others touched me with the personal warmth, the unexpected hominess of their offerings. These ones brought me dishes made from cherished family recipes for casseroles, for fudge brownies, for lasagna, for manicotti, for scalloped potatoes, for jambalaya, for lemon meringue pies, for key lime pies, for pecan pies, for rhubarb pies, for butterscotch cookies. They brought me plates of deviled eggs. They brought me dozens of raw oysters. They brought me chips: They brought me crinkling cellophane bags of Doritos, of Fritos, of Ruffles, of Lay's. They brought me tubes and tubes of my beloved, orderly-stacked Pringles: They brought me

Cheddar & Sour Cream, Honey Mustard, BBQ, Memphis BBQ, Jalapeño, Pizza.* They brought me chorizo burritos. They brought me shrimp tacos. Naturally, star chefs from gourmet restaurants all over the city also sent up meals, desirous that the delicate works of their own ephemeral art, the culinary, be incorporated into this gastronomic spectacle, this stationary one-man saturnalia, this unmovable feast—that the fruits of their labor should be enjoyed by the Fat Artist, physically and spiritually sublimated into the flesh of his body. They sent me their choicest dishes. They sent me saddle of venison seasoned with celeriac, marron glacé, and sauce poivrade with pearl barley and red wine. They sent me duck breast with spaghetti squash, almond polenta, and pomelo molasses. They sent me cippollini purée with pickled onion vinaigrette. They sent me smoked lobster garnished with snap peas, mussels, and lemon-mustard sauce. They sent me crispy pan-seared red king salmon steak with parsley. They sent me anchovy-stuffed bulb onions with sage jus. They sent me za'atar-spiced swordfish à la plancha with chickpea panisse. Such heights of the culinary arts were amusingly offset by the more lowbrow offerings, which I also enjoyed and consumed. They brought me family-sized buckets of fried chicken from KFC and Popeye's. They brought me pyramids of diminutive hamburgers from White Castle. Hostess snack products were popular offerings, selected surely for their artificiality, nutritional worthlessness, nostalgia value, and sheer cultural vulgarity: They brought me Twinkies, they brought me Hostess Cupcakes, they brought me Ding Dongs, they brought me Ho Hos. They brought me Mallomars. They brought me candy. They brought me Butterfingers, Three Musketeers, Snickers, Milky Ways, Whatchamacallits. They brought me Reese's Peanut Butter Cups. They brought me cartons of chocolate chip chocolate

* Pizza-flavored potato chips? Yes. One food may be flavored like another. Third-stage simulacra, what Baudrillard called "the order of sorcery."

ice cream with caramel fudge swirl, sweating in the sun. They brought me bags of sticky Campfire Marshmallows. They brought me dozens upon dozens of donuts, with pink frosting and sprinkles. They brought me jars of mayonnaise, jars of jelly, jars of peanut butter, jars of Grey Poupon mustard and bottles of Heinz 57. I have not even mentioned the beverage offerings. They brought me boxes of wine. They brought me chocolate malts. They brought me six-packs of Heineken. They brought me Perrier. They brought me two-liter bottles of Coca-Cola, of Pepsi, of Dr Pepper, of Mr Pibb, of Mountain Dew. They brought me bottles of fine French champagne. All this they brought me and more.

And I ate and drank all of these without even the deftest nod of consideration for harmony of the palate or of the stomach. I simply ate my offerings in the order in which they came to me, and if that meant following a box of powdered chocolate donut holes with a platter of eel and salmon sashimi followed by a grilled BLT dripping with sizzling bacon fat and American cheese, all while alternately sipping a lukewarm bottle of Budweiser and slurping noisily from the straw that punctured the plastic lid of a strawberry milkshake from Shake Shack—then so be it. And so it was.

Soon the table in the corner of my exhibition chamber on which the people lay their offerings was piled so high with foodstuffs that they began to tumble over the edges and onto the floor, where they were kicked around and trodden flat by many feet. A few hours after opening, there was no room left in the refrigerator reserved for chilled items, and so cartons of ice cream quickly became containers of warm, sweet milky glop in the early-summer heat. When my waiters were not busily clearing away refuse or transferring the food and drink items from the on-deck table to my dining table, they were employed in swatting away the flies that had discovered us. The visitors would linger on far beyond their allotted viewing time, hoping to wait long enough to watch me insert into myself some of the food they themselves had brought—but more often than not they waited in vain. I simply had too much to eat. I had such a backlog that it often took me hours after the offerings had been left for me to get around to eating them. The museum staffers, equipped with their institutional walkie-talkies, would frequently have to remind the dawdling visitors that there was still a very long line to enter the exhibit, and that they should be considerate of others and give them a chance to see the Fat Artist. Later they erected a sign warning visitors they were allowed only a maximum twenty-minute viewing period. When the people finally had to go, they would slowly back away from the exhibit, slightly disappointed—but only slightly, for although they would not get a chance to witness me actually ingesting their food, they left knowing they had caught a glimpse of something great.

No one—not one person—ever attempted to speak to me, and I certainly did not ever initiate conversation with them, nor did I ever deign (or dare?) to make eye contact with the visitors. To them I was a like a wild, exotic animal, like a panther pacing ferociously behind his bars—a being not to be interacted with, but marveled at. Once, I recall, only once, a curious child reached out a finger and curiously poked the flesh of my thigh while I was eating. I did not react. The child's mother tore his hand away and, her fist shaking the offending arm, scolded him in a severe voice, saying, "Never, *ever* touch the art in a museum. You know better than that. Do you understand me?" The child nodded silently and held back tears.

I ate on.

I became keenly attuned to the secret rhythms of the cosmos in the course of my consumption, digestion, and excretion. I had to. I would of necessity eat very slowly, in order to prevent vomiting. *Do not pause*—I told myself—*you may eat slowly, but you may never* stop *eating*. This mantra I inwardly repeated to myself over and over as I ate. *Just keep the food flowing*. I learned how to keep the muscles of my bladder and sphincter permanently relaxed, so that it required no conscious effort of my own to expurgate my bodily wastes. My urine and feces slid easily out of my body and disappeared down the rubber tubes, vacuumed away into oblivion. The input–output relationship between eating and defecation, between drinking and urination, became as unconscious and as physically effortless as the inhalation and exhalation of air. My body was an ever-flowing continuum, connected at both ends to the material effluvia of the external world. I achieved a Zenlike state of serene hypnosis, a harmonious fusion of being and becoming, oblivious to all but the hands that brought the food before me to my mouth. In, out, in, out: like an element of nature, like a river, like the waters of the river flowing forever and anon unto the sea, where it rises to the heavens and falls again to the earth, a never-ending samsara cycle of death and rebirth, entering and exiting, my body nothing more than a passive and temporary holding chamber for the things of this world.

I ate on.

In this way the days continued. Days following days compiled into weeks following weeks, and with every passing minute I grew fatter and fatter. In the first few weeks of my exhibition the constant surge of curious visitors abated only slightly. My weight skyrocketed. After the first week I was already up to 712 lbs (323 kg), having comfortably surpassed my personal goal of gaining 200 lbs (91 kg) from my starting weight of 493 lbs (224 kg) in the first six days. Maybe because of my initial hubris, I faltered a bit during the second week—whatever the reason, I succeeded in gaining only another 51 lbs (23 kg), ending week two at just

763 lbs (346 kg). However, during week three I rebounded from that disappointing second-week slowdown, going full steam all the way up to 870 lbs (395 kg). My body mass index was estimated at 114.8.*

I was pleased with my work, but obviously, if I was to reach my ultimate goal of breaking the record for the fattest human being in known history by well surpassing the 1,600 lb mark (≈726 kg), I still had a very long way to go: I would have to nearly double my weight.

I steeled my innards for the journey ahead, and ate on, ate on.

As my weight increased, I lost my sense of linear time. Because of the monotonous nature of my days, my entirely stationary existence, and the oneiric effect that a life purely devoted to eating works on the mind, sunrises and sunsets became events that only barely registered in my consciousness. At first I counted the days, but after a few weeks I completely lost track of how much time was passing, like someone forced to live deep in a cave or a windowless prison. There existed only the food before me and the readout of the scale affixed to the wall. The boundary blurred between my sleep and my wakeful life. Soon I dreamt nothing but dreams of sitting in my bed and eating.

By the time I had surpassed 1,000 lbs (454 kg), I had essentially lost all significant autonomous mobility. I could not have gotten out of bed unaided even if I had wanted to. I could still move my legs a little, certainly, and I could shift slightly in bed. I could wiggle my toes, and I could move my head. But aside from that, I had now successfully eaten myself utterly immobile. I was now less like an animal and more like a plant, rooted to the spot, helplessly subject to changes in my external environment while passively accepting whatever nourishment the world brought my way.

* (For reference, a BMI above forty is considered morbidly obese.)

I could still move my arms as well, although the procedure of using my arms to move food from the table to my mouth was an increasingly wearying one, encumbered as my bones and muscles were by the pendulous bags of limp flesh that dangled heavily from them. Although I never rested from eating during museum hours, I sometimes had to rest my feeble arms. During these times it was necessary for my waiters to climb onto my bed and feed me by hand, gently guiding forks and spoons laden with food into my open mouth. My knees had disappeared from view beneath my stomach, and my nipples had long ago retreated from view somewhere in the many folds of fat in my chest. Breathing—mere breathing—had become so difficult that it physically tired me.

For the first month or so that the exhibition was open I had been capable of rolling over in bed by myself, but this now being quite impossible, museum employees had to do it for me. I assume and hope they received some extra compensation for this unpleasant chore. When the museum closed at the end of each day, five or six male museum workers pushed me over onto my left side, in which position I spent the night. First thing in the morning, another five or six museum workers would push me onto my right side, in which position I stayed for another three hours or so, until the museum opened at 10:00 A.M., when they returned to push me onto my back again for public viewing. This was done to prevent bedsores.

The museum closed on Thursdays. I considered Thursday my sanctioned day of rest. I did not have to eat anything on Thursdays—or, rather, no one came to feed me, until the midafternoon, when the interns would come to clean the exhibition chamber, feed me a modest meal, and bathe me. I came to—well, not exactly *look forward* to these calm, reflective days, for as I said, I had lost my sense of time, and when these days came they were always a pleasant surprise—but certainly relish them when they came. These five strong young people were ebullient college students with nonpaying internships at the museum. I enjoyed their company. They felt free to converse with me, and I came to know them each by name: Christine, Dave, Nora, Lindsay, and Geoff. They worked only on Thursdays, which most of the museum employees had off. They would arrive bearing a meal on a tray, which I consumed with gusto while they swept and mopped my exhibition chamber and squeegeed the glass walls. After I had eaten, they would wash me. I cherished their weekly bathing of my body—afterward I always felt so cool, fresh, and reinvigorated. First they cut my hair, clipped my fingernails and toenails, trimmed my beard, and swept away the leavings from my body and from my bed with little brushes. Then they would heave me onto my side, and all working together they would sponge wash and dry my back and my side. Three of them would stand on the bed and hoist up one of my enormous legs for the other two to bathe. Then they would roll me over onto my other side to wash the parts they had missed, then roll me onto my back and wash my front, lifting up my giant arms to scrub my armpits, cleansing my body of all the bits of dried food that had fused to my chest and stomach, always remembering to lift up my many heavy flaps and rub the damp sponges in those hard-to-reach crevices where mold would develop if the weather had been humid. Then they left me, all high fives and waves and sunny smiles.

Then Friday came, and on I ate.

By the end of the second month, I was up to 1,345 lbs (610 kg).

I ate on.

As I have said, I no longer retained a reliable sense of the passage of linear time, but I believe it was around the end of the second month when I noticed the stream of visitors to my exhibit had steadily decreased. I suppose the initial hype over my exhibit had died down, and public interest had begun to fade.

There were even some brief stretches of time when I had nothing to eat, because too few visitors had come bearing offerings to me. During these times I had to ask the museum staff to order food for me. There was a dark period during which I actually *lost* about fifteen pounds, and was unable to gain them back: For nearly a week my weight appeared to have plateaued at around 1,360 lbs (617 kg)—which worried me deeply, as I still had quite a long way to go, and yet had already come so far. I had only to gain another 240 lbs (109 kg) before reaching 1,600 lbs (726 kg). Due to the relative dearth of visitors, the only way I could get my weight gain back on track was to each day send my waiters out to pick me up nine or ten buckets of KFC, which I requested they dump out before me on my dining table in a big pile. These emergency food supplies were generously paid for by the Guggenheim Foundation. My waiters, being otherwise unneeded, would take long breaks, leaving me in my solitude to forlornly snack upon my mountain of fried chicken parts. Several days of repeating this procedure did the trick nicely, and my weight began to climb again. But still. I found this sudden drop-off in my public appreciation troubling.

I ate on, anyway.

Then one day it happened: an entire day when no one came. My waiters unlocked the doors to my exhibit in the morning, and the hot sun slowly climbed all the way to the zenith of the summer's pale blue proscenium of sky and began to fall back down the other side, and not a single person visited me.

I cried. I was stricken with a sharp panic—which expanded into a dull terror as the evening at last came on—that the world had forgotten me. And then, I was angry. To hell with "angry"—I was enraged. A hot flower of fury bloomed in the fertile soil of my wounded heart. I screamed and railed at my waiters. I waved my fat fists in the air, and in a voice hoarsened with bitter tears I demanded to know why Tristan Hurt, the inventor and sole practitioner of Fat Art, had become subject to neglect.

They shut my exhibit doors and turned their faces away.

I ate on.

Days passed. No one came to feed me. So I ordered my waiters to bring me great steaming piles of chicken, to bring me hundreds of pepperoni pizzas, hot and sodden with grease. Indeed, I had almost reverted to the diet of my year of solitude, the very foods that had made me fat to begin with. I looked down at my body. One would scarcely believe, seeing me, that buried beneath all this flesh was the stalwart and handsome man of six feet and an inch in stature and a mere 200 lbs (91 kg) that I had once been. Except for my head, I scarcely any longer resembled anything identifiably human. It would have been unjust to compare my body even to that of, say, a hippo. My body looked more like some large aquatic mammal that had washed up on a beach and died—it had the same floppy lifelessness to it, the same squishiness and dimpled, pulpy, rotten-looking texture. My flesh had developed a pallor and stickiness that seemed almost amphibian. My body was so soft and so giving that I was able to stick my arm into the folds of my stomach and sink it in all the way to the elbow before meeting any resistance.

Still, I had more weight to gain. I ordered my waiters to bring me food. They brought me eighteen pizzas for lunch. They brought me thirty-five Big Macs. They brought me forty packages of kosher beef franks and three gallons of half-and-half with which to wash them down. I do not know if the foundation was still paying for my emergency rations. I think my waiters had been given some sort of company expense card. They were probably out buying themselves three-martini lunches with it when they were not delivering me my own endless lunch. Parasites. They brought me twenty racks of pork ribs. One day they merely brought me thirty loaves of Wonder Bread, forty pounds of shaved Black Forest ham, and a gallon tub of mayonnaise. They told me to make sandwiches for myself, and then they disappeared for three days. No one came. They didn't even leave me a knife. I had to spread the mayonnaise with fat, clumsy fingers. The ham spoiled fast; I ate it anyway. When they came back, they started putting their cigarettes out on me for fun. My nerve endings were buried many layers deep; I felt no pain.

I ate on.

A week or two later—though really, I had no idea how much later, but if I were to hazard a guess—Olivia visited me. I had not seen her in nearly a year and a half.

When she came, my preliminary food table had nothing on it. Like the forgotten idol of a vanquished tribe, no one had brought me any offerings for many days. The only visitors I had received in the past week or more were people who had come to visit the main wing of the museum and had somehow wandered into my exhibit by accident. My exhibition chamber was out of the way and difficult to find for ordinary patrons of the museum. To see the Fat Artist required museum visitors to follow signs taped to the walls directing them to an emergency stairwell and into the service elevators, which were the only elevators that went all the way up to the roof of the building, and if the people were not following a large crowd—as had been the case in the early days of the Fat Artist, when the exhibition first opened—then it was easy for people to assume they were in the wrong place, or were somewhere they were not allowed to be, and they would turn around. I had begun to suspect that the signs directing visitors to the Fat Artist had been mistakenly removed, perhaps by some well-meaning janitor who was not aware the performance piece on the roof was still ongoing.

On certain days, my waiters would simply open up my exhibit in the morning and then disappear, returning only twice in the day: once, at lunchtime, to drop off the food I had requested of them earlier that morning, and then again only when it was time to close the doors in the evening. I usually smelled beer on their breaths when my waiters came back in the late afternoon to shut the exhibit for the night. Sometimes they would not even show up to unlock my chamber until it must have been close to noon.

I worried that I would never achieve my minimum goal of 1,600 lbs (726 kg). I had managed to fatten myself all the way up to the impressive—but insufficient for my purposes—weight of 1,491 lbs (676 kg). I knew this weight comfortably put me in the positions of (1) the fattest human then known to be alive, and (2) second fattest human in all recorded history (Carol Yager was still well ahead of me). But with this knowledge came two piercing little fears. The first was the fear that I would not be able to surpass the daunting record set by the great Carol Yager in 1994. I had a mere 109 lbs (49 kg) to go before I tied with her, but my weight gain was slowing with every day of the public's persisting disinterest in my important art. My second fear was that no one would even record it when I attained my desired peak weight—as it seemed that I, Tristan Hurt, had been forgotten, even by my caretakers. The ebullient young interns employed to bathe my body on Thursdays no longer turned up. I was extremely dirty, and much in need of a bath. My body had not been shifted in a long time, and I feared the bedsores that might be developing beneath me.

A few days before Olivia visited me, I had found myself begging a lost-looking group of Japanese tourists for food. They were the first visitors to my exhibit in many consecutive days. At first they seemed not to understand. They took pictures of me pointing to my open mouth and pantomiming the act of eating by picking up an invisible object on my barren dining table (my waiters had been negligent) and bringing it to my mouth, then histrionically rubbing my leviathan belly with both hands as I made yummy-yum-yum noises. One of them eventually figured out what I wanted, and, in a hesitant way that suggested she was not entirely sure if it was "okay" to interact with me, she opened her purse and produced a packet of M&M's, which she tore open and dumped into my waiting palm. I crammed them all at once into my mouth, chewed with quick, greedy chomps, and swallowed. They laughed as they searched themselves for more food and took more pictures.

Olivia came to me wearing a pretty and simply cut white dress. My waiters had come back not long before to deliver my lunch—which was, as per my usual request, nine buckets of fried chicken and four two-liter bottles of Dr Pepper—and then left. I didn't know where they were. They probably wouldn't be back for the rest of the day. I had come not to rely on them to be there for me. They were not even bothering to clean my exhibition chamber anymore. They simply allowed the chicken bones and pizza boxes to lie on the floor exactly where they happened to land when I ineffectually threw them from my bed. The floor hadn't been swept in weeks. A black and thrumming swarmcloud of flies was my only company.

I believe I was up to a respectable 1,510 lbs (685 kg) when she came to visit me. Unfortunately, she did not come bearing any food. My waiters had at least been courteous enough to arrange the nine buckets of fried chicken within my arm's reach all around me on my bed. This is what I was eating when Olivia came to visit me. Rather than any food offering, she was holding a bouquet of blush-colored roses. Her off-blond hair was bound in a ponytail. I watched her emerge from the door to the roof and walk toward my exhibition chamber. It was a muggy, overcast day, the sky smeared with thick gray clouds and threatening rain. A purple umbrella in a compressed state dangled by the strap of its handle from one of her thin, knobby wrists. Olivia is a small woman, and I considered the fact that I was then about fifteen times heavier than her; and then, having nothing to do with the thought considered, put it away. On her feet were black and glistening medium-heeled shoes with an open toe. They were the most beautiful shoes I had ever seen her wear, and I wondered what, if anything, occasioned this outfit: the dress, the shoes, a string of pearls, I believe (though that may be my imagination encroaching on my memory). She looked as if she were on her way to a charity dinner. I listened to her shoes clop on the asphalt-and-tar surface of the roof as she crossed it on her way to my exhibition chamber.

Olivia stood at the foot of my bed, holding the bouquet of fat-petaled roses shieldlike before her chest. Her face was scrunched into a look of timid wonder admixed with patent revulsion.

I ignored her. I could not have possibly stopped doing what I was doing: I was both artist and art. I continued to slurp bits of meat from the chicken parts heaped high before me.

Olivia cleared her throat.

I did not look up.

"What are you doing?" she said. That thin, squeaky voice that had always reminded me of an articulate piccolo bounced off the glass walls of my exhibition chamber, filling the room with a mellifluent tintinnabulation of tinny echoes.

I looked up at her from my bed. The beautiful shoes she wore added little confidence to her posture; she still carried herself like a hunchback. She looked, as she always had, uncomfortable in her skin.

I swigged from my massive plastic bottle of Dr Pepper, emitted a thunderous belch, and continued, unmovable and impervious to language, to snack.

Olivia stood at the foot of my bed, nervously fingering the pink petals of the flowers.

"God, it smells so bad in here," she said. "Do you even realize how you *smell*?"

I made a dismissive snorting noise and squeezed a shrug out of my amorphous shoulders. The exertion exhausted me.

"This room smells like death," she said.

I said nothing. I was busy peeling the skin from a leg of chicken—I've always loved the way fried chicken skin slides so easily away from the pale wet meat beneath, like a silk slipper. I lowered the chicken skin into my always-hungry mouth.

"This whole thing isn't about me, is it?" she said.

I said nothing. I licked the last bits of meat from a chicken leg and tossed the bone from the bed to join the others on the floor. There was a soft drumming of thunder in the sky.

"Anyway. I won't stay long. I came for two reasons," she said. "The first reason I came is to tell you some bad news. I'm really sorry. I don't know if anyone has told you . . . ?"

The rest of her sentence was implied by raised eyebrows and widened eyes. I'm sure the curious look on my face belied that whatever her bad news was, I had not heard it.

"Your father died," she said.

Olivia walked up to the side of my bed.

"Here," she said, and handed me the flowers. I accepted them mindlessly. I rested the flowers on the rolling dunes of my torso.

"He had a brain aneurysm," said Olivia. "Apparently it was very sudden. I happened to see his obituary, and I called your mom. I always read the obituaries. They're my favorite part. So, I just thought you should know."

Olivia stood there and looked at the filth scattered all around the room.

"What day is it?" I said, distractedly fingering the damp petals of the roses.

"Friday," said Olivia.

"No—what is the date?"

She dug her cell phone out of her purse and looked at it.

"August twenty-ninth," she said.

I had entered the exhibit in May. Had I really been here nearly four months?

Time passed. Above the glass ceiling the sky was a snake pit, squirming with thick muscles of green and black vapor. Soon the clouds broke into rain. Pebbles of rain came down on the roof of my exhibition chamber in pulsing waves of crackling water. The echoes of the rain warbled in the big cubical glass room and lines of water chased each other down the walls, warping and distorting the view of Central Park.

"I'm going now," said Olivia.

"Please don't go now," I whined.

"I have an umbrella," she said. "I'll be fine."

"Please."

She looked at me with unmistakable contempt.

"Okay," she said.

Her voice was barely audible over the clatter of the rain echoing in my glass box. The room had become dense with fog, and the glass was nearly opaque with condensation. The inside of my glass box was a small, self-contained universe—nothing had to exist outside of it. I could be bounded in a nutshell and count myself the king of infinite space. This room was my kingdom, over which I both presided as monarch and all by myself constituted my only subject.

"Hold me," I pleaded. I could hear the infantile croak in my own voice.

Olivia scooted aside my rolling glass dining table, removed several buckets of fried chicken from the strategic places where my waiters had nestled them against my flesh, and lay down beside me on my bed. She slid her feet out of her shoes, they tumbled *clop-clop* to the floor, and with careful movements she curled herself beside my mass. She put a hand on my chest and stroked my greasy wet hair with the other. She nuzzled her hair in the crook of my armpit. Rain pummelled the roof. I permitted myself to weep.

When the rainstorm abated, Olivia sat up in the bed, rubbed her eyes, and looked at her watch. She sat on the edge of my bed and put on her shoes.

"Please, Olivia," I said.

"I'm sorry," she said. "I have to go."

She stood up.

"Wait—" I said. "What was the other reason you came? You said there were two."

"The other reason was that I wanted to see if anyone had come to get you. But I see now there's nothing I can do. I just don't see how it's possible. I'm sorry."

"Come to get me? What do you mean? Come get me for what?"

"I'm so sorry," she said again. "Good-bye."

Olivia turned and walked out of my box and into a sunny, newly wet world of petrichor and flashing puddles. The light outside had that steamy, crisp, golden quality it sometimes does when the sun breaks out after a long torrent of rain. I watched her go. I don't know whether or not I would have tried to follow her, even if I had been physically able to move.

Where were my waiters? It was very late. The angles of the shadows were low, stretched long over the wet, golden world.

After Olivia left, I ate the flowers she had brought me. I peeled them apart, petal by petal, put them in my mouth, chewed, and swallowed.

They had a velvety texture. I felt their lush, wet kisses of life on my tongue. Their strong, sweet odor was undercut by a pointedly acrid taste. I munched slowly on the flowers, internalizing them, making them part of my body.

No one came to feed me.

LEFTOVERS

Phil Grassley—still strong, healthy, and handsome in the year of his imminent retirement—stood six feet on the mark in bare feet and khaki shorts on the kitchen floor of his home in a suburb of Houston, cooking enchiladas. Veronica had just called. Phil could tell from the in-and-out reception that she was on her cell phone and driving with the top down. She had called to say she was almost there. She was in the neighborhood, but had managed to get lost in this labyrinthine subdivision of courts and runs and drives and lanes and culs-de-sac lined with behemothic white houses, and needed further directions in order to locate the behemothic white house that belonged in particular to Phil.

Phil was thinking about the fact that he was about to retire. On the one hand, after so many years of working, he'd been greatly looking forward to spending the rest of his life sailing his catamaran, fishing, and drinking beer. On the other hand was Veronica. This meant that, at least for now, the scales were just about balanced. Not that he couldn't continue this affair with her after he retired, but for some reason it seemed like that would be hard to do. If he wasn't working, then excuses not to come home on certain nights would be more difficult to conjure up. He had met Veronica three weeks ago. She was new at the office. They'd had sex last weekend. She was thirty years old. When she was born—*born*—Phil had already been married to Diane for six years. Just to put it in perspective. Veronica wasn't beautiful. She was frankly a bit on the pudgy side. She was attractive, yes, but not in a way that turns heads on the street. Take a look at her picture on the laminated ID card she wore at work, and then take a look at the girl wearing it: The camera wasn't kind to her. What she had instead of beauty was a certain glow, a certain verve, a certain fun, sexy energy, which was more powerful than just run-of-the-mill physical beauty. Phil's wife, in her day, had been a beautiful woman—in that run-of-the-mill way. In thirty-six years of marriage, he had never once had anything with Diane quite like the night and subsequent morning he spent one week ago today with Veronica. She had, for instance, given him a blowjob. Bam! First night, first thing, right out of the gate. He hadn't asked her to. No sooner were their clothes off than his old cock was in her young mouth and she was sucking on it ferociously, until he had no choice but to squirt his come between her cheeks. Diane had never, ever, not once in thirty-six years of marriage, thought to do that without being asked.

Phil's wife was out of town. Phil was drinking a beer and cooking enchiladas, reasoning, through an admittedly complicated act of moral calculus, that at any one time a man was entitled to one *active* secret from his wife. He was allowed one. See, secrets can be active or dormant, like volcanoes. A dormant secret, like a dormant volcano, is essentially harmless. An affair he had ten years ago, for example, was a dormant secret. Veronica was his one current active secret. Phil didn't cheat on Diane very often. In thirty-six years, he'd had plenty of Veronicas on the side, and Diane had never once found out. (Or said anything, at any rate.) These Veronicas did not mean that Phil did not love his wife. It's just that Diane, to Phil, was not *for* sex. She was for wife. Veronica was for sex. Phil thought of his occasional Veronicas as gifts he gave himself every once in a while, well-earned vacations from his otherwise decent record as a faithful and functional husband.

There is nothing that brings two people closer together faster than doing something wrong together, and that's the greatest psychological kick you get out of infidelity. One criminal acting alone has to live with guilt by himself—but two people, a man and a woman, doing something wrong together? These things wouldn't be nearly as interesting if Phil *didn't* love his wife—of course Phil loved his wife, in the repetitive and boring way a husband does, and he did hope that one day, hopefully not too soon (he wanted to get in a good couple decades of unhampered fishing, sailing, and beer drinking), as he lay in some white bed hooked up to all kinds of wires and tubes, it would be her hand, Diane's, that he would squeeze in his as he breathed his last, as his basically successful but less than remarkable existence was blotted out forever from this earth. But for now, there was Veronica.

The doorbell rang. She was peeking through the sandblasted window next to the front door like a neighborhood kid who had come over wanting to know if his sons could "play." Phil opened the door, and Veronica immediately dumped her big body into his. His nostrils sucked in the sappy smell of her. She had on these knee-high black lizard-leather boots with zippers running up the sides, and a candy-apple-red jacket buttoned over those bounteous earth-mama breasts. Her tongue twisted together with his and he found his hand pawing the plump pillow of her ass. In one hand she held a bottle of mezcal. It was about three-quarters full.

"I bought this in Mexico," she said, offering the bottle as if it were proof. "It's the kind with the worm in it and everything."

A pale, bloated bug was indeed drifting around at the bottom of the rectangular bottle, which glowed gold in her hands in the early-summer sunlight.

"Let's make margaritas," she said. This had been the plan, as discussed yesterday over lunch at Dave & Buster's.

Veronica went to work on the margaritas at the kitchen counter. She found limes in the refrigerator, Cointreau in the liquor cabinet, salt in the cupboard. Phil rifled around in the cabinet under the kitchen sink and found the blender, which was dirty and dusty. For some reason the blender was an appliance that didn't see much use in the Grassley household. Veronica eyed the condition of the blender.

"Gross," she opined. She flipped her hair over her shoulder with her fingers. Her round face was framed in long, thick waves of glossy black hair. Her ditzy tic of flipping the stuff over her shoulder was something that might have irritated him if one of his sons had brought her home to dinner in the office of a girlfriend. Veronica was in fact about the same age as his oldest son. But when Veronica did it, he understood what his sons saw in girls like this one.

The blender washed, he gave it to Veronica and returned to the enchiladas. The enchiladas were nested side by side in green chili sauce in a rectangular Pyrex pan, and he was grating cheese over them. Veronica jammed the lip of the blender's glass container against the plastic lever in the hole in the refrigerator door where ice cubes come out. The light came on, and the machine hummed and churned, but no ice came out. Phil covered the Pyrex pan of enchiladas with a sheet of aluminum foil and put it in the preheated oven. Veronica was still pressing the blender container against the lever in the refrigerator. The refrigerator was still humming and churning, and no ice cubes were coming out. Veronica tapped her foot.

"Maybe it's broken?" she said.

"Give it a minute. Sometimes it takes a little while."

"I like your house."

It occurred to Phil that she had never seen the inside of his house before. If she were anyone else, he supposed he might have taken her on a tour or something. But as it was, he invited her in like she'd already been here a hundred times.

Phil didn't worry too much about his house. It was a gated community; he often forgot to even lock his door at night. If she'd just walked right in, he wouldn't have been surprised.

"Thanks."

"It's cute."

"This is all Diane's shit," he said, waving a hand to indicate the décor.

"It's cute."

"You're cute."

He pawed and squeezed her ass again. She still had the lip of the blender pushed against the lever in the refrigerator door; the ice machine still grumbled and hummed, and no ice was coming out.

"What the fuck is wrong with this thing?"

Phil opened the freezer door and immediately identified the problem: no ice. The way the automatic icemaker thing worked was there was this reservoir that emptied through this chute and into your cup when you pressed it against the lever in the hole in the front of the refrigerator door. Above the reservoir was the icemaker, which made ice cubes and spat them out into the reservoir. There was a metal lever on the thing that you could pull up or down to turn the icemaker on or off. The lever was, as a matter of fact, in the "off" position. The on/off lever on the icemaker was in the "off" position because Diane was fucking constantly putting the goddamn icemaker in the "off" position because she had at some point fallen under the benighted impression that this infinitesimal reduction of their carbon footprint would somehow help to allay global warming, and now, as it often happened, there were no fucking ice cubes in the fucking ice cube reservoir.

"Jeez-a-loo!" said Veronica. "We can't make margaritas without ice!"

"Hold your horses. I think there's a bag of ice in the other refrigerator."

There was an old refrigerator in the garage. The bottom compartment contained a mini-keg full of impotable swill left over from Phil's passing hobby with homebrewing. The freezer contained the stiff, gray, freezer-burned slabs of three fish; two black sea bass and an amberjack—and, he remembered, a plastic sack of ice. The ice was left over from a barbecue they'd had a while ago. Phil had bought several bags of ice at the gas station and dumped the bags into a rust-caked red Radio Flyer wagon left over from his three sons' childhoods. This particular bag of ice had been auxiliary. For all its life as one of Phil's possessions it had sat forgotten and unneeded in the freezer of the spare refrigerator in the garage—until today.

"Catastrophe averted," said Phil, and thunked the bag on the kitchen counter. "We got ice."

"Oh, goodie."

Phil ripped the plastic bag open. Months of storage in the freezer had caused the ice in the bag to compact and solidify, all the individual ice cubes settling together into one big rock-hard, bag-shaped hunk of ice. He clawed with his fingers at the shapes of the glued-together ice cubes sticking out of the mass of ice, but failed to wrest them from their foundations. Veronica watched as he searched the kitchen for something to crack the ice apart with. He found a rubber meat-tenderizing mallet, which only bounced pathetically off the ice. Then he tried a wooden cooking spoon, with which he was able to hack off a few chips and shavings, but he realized he needed something much harder and heavier to break the ice into several smaller, more manageable chunks, which could then be more easily broken down into chunks small enough to put into the blender for the margaritas. He opened and closed the kitchen drawers—this was Diane's territory, he'd never really bothered to learn where anything was—until he landed on a wooden rolling pin, which did the job nicely. It fit in his hands well; it had the right shape, gravity, hardness, and heft. He held the rolling pin by the bottom of the shaft with the handle fulcrumed against the base of his palm, shimmied the skin of the plastic bag back over the hunk of ice, held it down on the kitchen counter by the mouth of the bag, and whacked at it with the rolling pin as hard as he could. He felt the ice crack apart cleanly into two chunks. Beautiful. This is the sort of thing he would always try to teach his sons, helping them with their batting, or their tennis strokes or golf swings or whatever. How to manipulate matter, how to gracefully command the movement and force of an object in your hands, how to handle a racket, a club, or a bat such that you minimize your entropy and maximize your results; and what a beautiful feeling it is, when you feel all the atoms lining up just right, when you hit it right in the sweet spot and hear it go *crack*, that priceless moment of impact when the thing you're trying to hit makes contact with the thing in your hands, the physical music of violence. He broke the ice into several smaller chunks, and then hammered it to a crumble with the rolling pin. Veronica was laughing so hard at Phil bashing the bag of ice with the rolling pin that she had to brace herself against the refrigerator. She had a bright, loud, pretty song of a laugh that set her massive breasts to quaking. She was gasping for air. Phil triumphantly poured the ice, now all crumbs and sand, into the blender, sent a burbling golden braid of mezcal in after it, then the Cointreau, then squeezed the halves of the limes that Veronica had earlier bisected on the cutting board into the ice and liquor, then affixed the lid of the blender and pressed the button that instantly filled the spacious white-walled house with its electric shudder, rattle, and roar, then gradually worked his way up the row of buttons, increasing the speed of the motor and the blades to whip the solution into a finer and finer slush. Veronica was on a laughing jag, her brain had come unhinged, she was sick with laughter and couldn't stop, and now it seemed she was laughing at her own laughter, because there wasn't anything funny anymore except for the fact that she was still laughing. Veronica's hand fluttered to her chest, she struggled for air and flung jewels of water from the corners of her eyes with her fingers. She tried to force the laughter to die in her chest by putting on a "serious" face and willing herself to breathe normally. Phil slid a wedge of lime across the lips of the two margarita glasses, ground them upside down in a saucer of uniodized sea salt, set them on the counter, glooped the pale yellow frozen sludge into the shallow glasses, and pierced lime wedges onto their salt-speckled rims: margaritas. He handed one to Veronica. They were tchotchke margarita glasses made of thick Mexican hand-blown bubble glass, with green glass stems designed to look like the trunks of saguaro cacti, with appendages sticking out of their sides, crowned with tiny flowers of red glass.

"What should we toast to?" he said.

"To us," she said. "To me. To your retirement. To enchiladas. To margaritas. To us fucking."

"That'll do."

They chimed the glasses together and drank their margaritas. Phil put on James Taylor's *Greatest Hits*.

"Where *is* Diane?"

Veronica was looking at a framed photo on the kitchen wall, an old picture, showing Phil, Diane, Garrett, Julian, and Kyle standing on the deck of the boat, the old one that Phil sold about a year ago, before he bought the catamaran. They were all wearing bright yellow boating gear. The wind pushed their yellow jackets flat against their left sides and made them flap behind them to the right. The boat was docked at the marina. Phil and Garrett were holding up a dead swordfish. They held it upside down between them with their arms over their heads, clutching the end of the tail together, with its ramrod of a nose grazing the deck of the boat. Kyle, a sunny twelve-year-old in the picture, had his shirt off and was standing next to them with his fists on his skinny hips. Julian was sitting next to Diane, with long dyed black hair and a bored, sullen face.

"Diane's at this, uh, conference or something," said Phil. "I don't really know what it is. Said she'd be back on Monday."

It was Saturday.

"Are these your kids?" she said.

Phil didn't want to talk about his kids.

"Uh-huh. That picture was taken a long time ago. They're grown now."

"Which one's which?"

"That's Garrett," he said, pointing at the lean, muscular young man helping him hold the swordfish in the picture. "He's the oldest. He's a good kid. He's at Harvard Law."

"Following in his daddy's footsteps."

"Not really. He wants to go into constitutional law. He wants to be a good lawyer. Kid's drunk the liberal Kool-Aid but good. He's a good kid, though."

"Are you a *good* lawyer, or a *bad* lawyer?"

"I'm a bad lawyer."

By *bad* Phil meant the word in a moral sense, not a technical one. Phil was a corporate defense lawyer for ExxonMobil, and he was quite good at it.

"That's Kyle," said Phil. "He's the youngest. He's a good kid, too. He's in his junior year at Tulane."

"And this one?"

Veronica's vermillion fingernail clicked against the glass at the only seated figure in the picture: the ugly and melancholic teenager with long, limp black hair, sitting closer to his mother than to his father.

"That's the middle kid, Julian," said Phil. "Nobody knows where he is."

Veronica did not inquire further on the matter. Phil did not explain any further, either. He thought about it, and then refrained, mostly because he just didn't feel like talking about it, but also because for some reason he didn't want her to think he was a bad father—not that he was afraid she'd care. Phil wasn't so sure he was a "bad" father, anyway, just like he wasn't so sure he was a "bad" lawyer. That's how he felt all the time—like the world was a schoolmarm wagging a moralizing finger at him all the goddamn time: bad, bad, *bad!* Phil was sick to goddamn death of people who didn't have the first fucking clue what they were talking about thinking he was "bad" just because he did what he did. If the goodness of a father is judged by the goodness of his sons, then two out of three wasn't bad. The fact that he had two good sons and one bad one he thought might just be an indication that Julian was the fucking problem, not him. He wasn't a bad father; Julian was a bad son. He'd done all he could for the spoiled, miserable little shit, and now he was done. Paying for college was fine. Paying for rehab, less fine. Nobody in the family had seen him for a good while. It had been months. They were used to these silences. He might be on his knees in a bar bathroom in San Francisco sucking cock for heroin. San Francisco's where he was last, in any case. Garrett said he talked to him on the phone a few weeks ago, said it seemed he was in as bad a shape as ever. If Julian didn't want his help, then fine. Phil was pleased to find himself not thinking about Julian much anymore, although Julian was still an unpleasant fixture in his dreams. The main problem with Julian was that Phil couldn't relate to him at all. He had no idea what was ever going through the kid's head. Phil could be a good father to Garrett and Kyle because they were at least halfway normal kids. He could at least vaguely imagine what was going on in their heads. He could understand them. Julian, though, never liked normal kid things. Julian didn't like fishing. Julian didn't like sailing.

Julian didn't like sports. Julian didn't like girls. Apparently Julian didn't like school either, dropped out after his freshman and only year at Sarah Lawrence. What did Julian like? Apparently Julian liked a hypodermic needle in his arm, pumping poison into his veins. That's what Julian liked, and Phil didn't understand it.

He didn't mention any of this to Veronica. At this point, Phil just wanted to have fun, relax, and grow old disgracefully with a margarita in his hand, watching the sunset on the deck of his boat. He had retired from thinking about Julian in the same way he was about to retire from his career. Letting himself retire, letting himself quit thinking about Julian, letting himself buy that beautiful catamaran, and letting himself fuck Veronica—these things were all somehow connected, these were all things he decided to treat himself to after a life of hard work well done and responsibilities met, and he felt he deserved them—he deserved these things, and he didn't give a shit anymore if anybody thought he was "bad."

They ate the enchiladas on the table out on the back deck.

"This is *soooo* good," she said, drawing out the word *so* and making it the emphasis of the sentence. She spoke in that frivolous, childish way that young women speak these days, and Phil loved it. They were already well into margarita numero tres and Phil was drunk enough that he wasn't really all that hungry anymore, but he ate anyway. The green backyard sloped down a long hill toward a fence, behind which was a road, behind which were a couple of other houses, behind which was a brick wall, behind which was a stretch of land, behind which was a beach, behind which was the Gulf of Mexico, which they could see from the back porch, and which stretched clear out to the horizon. The sun was going down in the other direction, and the sky above the sea faded from blue to yellow to orange to red to purple. At the bottom of the hill, toward the back of the fence that divided Phil's property from the rest of the surface of the earth, there was an old swingset and a sandbox. Every time he looked at his backyard he saw the swingset and the sandbox and, now with all three boys out of the house (for better or worse), thought about how he ought to get rid of them. Maybe he would once he retired and had time for things like that. It was almost nine now, the sun setting late in the day in the summer. Veronica looked gorgeous in this light. Phil was in love with life in general right now. She looked gorgeous in this light, with her margarita in her hand and her jaw working on a clump of chicken enchilada. It was June of 2005, and the world had its problems, but Phil felt great.

Phil went to the bathroom to drain some margarita, and when he came back into the bedroom Veronica had already taken off everything except for her jewelry and was on the bed on top of the pastel-colored patchwork quilt Phil's mom had made, half sitting propped up on the pillows, still drinking her margarita. Her clothes were strewn all over the bedroom floor, except the candy-apple-red jacket, which she had hung on the back of a chair. Pictures of his three kids, of himself and Diane on various vacations, of himself and Garrett with various fish, of various relatives he barely recognized by sight, of his parents and Diane's parents, were all over the walls, peeping down at them, as if watching. Let them watch. Veronica put her margarita down on one of the two matching bedside tables, and Phil unbuttoned his short-sleeved Oxford shirt, took off his khaki shorts and his underwear, and, thusly naked, climbed onto the bed and fucked her.

The windows were open, and a hot salty breeze blew in off the gulf over their bodies. Their two naked bodies lay spent and slack on top of the quilt, and they fell asleep together without even bothering to cover themselves.

• • •

Phil was woken up by noises coming from downstairs. First he noticed that his tongue was dry and he had a mild headache. Then he looked at the red numbers on the screen of the digital clock next to the bed, which said it was three thirtysomething. The second two digits were partially obscured by the saguaro cactus-shaped stem of the empty margarita glass on the bedside table. The red numbers of the alarm clock illuminated the margarita glass with the green cactus-shaped stem and made it glow as red as if it had just been pulled from a furnace. He turned his head and looked at Veronica. Her fat pale breasts were flopped over to the sides of her chest, and a sparkling rivulet of drool had slid out of the corner of her open mouth and made a spot of dampness on the pillow under her head. He heard noises of banging, shifting, rattling downstairs. He heard footsteps. He heard something being scooted around. He thought he could hear breathing. He was being robbed.

Then he panicked. He wondered if he had remembered to lock the doors before going to bed, and concluded—being as he had been at the time somewhat intoxicated and preoccupied with Veronica—that no, he had not remembered to secure the premises. And now there was someone downstairs, inside his house.

Phil eased his body off the bed, trying to get up without rocking the mattress too much, without waking Veronica. No need to freak her out. He would go downstairs to investigate. His junk was glued to his thigh with their fluids, and Phil had to wiggle around a little bit to shake everything loose before tugging and yanking his underwear and shorts back on. He crept, fastidiously and silently, out of the bedroom.

There was definitely someone downstairs. He grew surer of it with each step.

From the top of the stairs he could see down into the living room.

There was nobody in it at the moment. There was a wall in front of the couch, where there should have been a flat-screen TV. Instead, there was just a naked white wall. Yes, he was being burgled. The light from the streetlights made orange rectangles across the floor of the living room. Phil made it to the bottom of the stairs and curled around the corner into the living room, hugging close to the wall. He heard a noise coming from the other side of the house, in the kitchen. He crouched behind the marble countertop that separated the kitchen from the living room. The kitchen was glowing with blue-white light, which meant the refrigerator was open. Phil peered above the countertop.

Phil had never been robbed before. Frankly, he had been expecting to find a black person of some sort. Instead, it was a white guy who was standing in his kitchen. He had his back turned to Phil. The guy was tall, skinny, and gangly, in a white T-shirt and jeans. He had an ugly, narrow shaved head, like a baby bird's, with wiry little prickles of hair sticking out all over his pink scalp. Phil rose to his feet and walked noiselessly into the kitchen. The burglar was standing in front of the open refrigerator, with one hand holding the door open and the other dangling down by his side, so Phil could see both his hands, and assumed this meant he was unarmed. He was just standing there, looking into the refrigerator.

What the fuck kind of burglar was this, who would steal his TV and then decide to make himself a snack? With the door open like that, the refrigerator kicked on and began to hum. He heard the icemaker dump a cluster of ice cubes into the ice cube reservoir in the freezer.

The burglar continued to stand there, motionless, gazing into the bright space of the open refrigerator, as if temporarily mesmerized by the combined sensory effects of its chill and hum and light. Phil stood behind him in the kitchen. Slow, careful, no sudden movements, no noise. He thought about sliding open one of the kitchen drawers and grabbing a knife. He decided against it because the noise of the drawer opening would probably alert the burglar. He looked at the kitchen counter and saw the following objects: the empty plastic sack that had contained the ice, a dirty blender, a cutting board on which there lay a few chopped-up, dried-out limes, the knife Veronica had used to cut the limes—which was sharp, but much too small to adequately threaten a burglar with—a bottle of mezcal that was empty except for the bloated worm at the bottom, a bottle of Cointreau, and a rolling pin. Phil picked up the rolling pin.

The part of the rolling pin that had been lying on the counter was wet from the ice dust that had skittered across the counter and melted. He held the end of the shaft with the handle butted against his palm. Phil walked up behind the guy with the rolling pin. He swung as hard as he could and cracked the rolling pin against the back of his skull. He raised his arm to do it again, but the guy crumpled under the first blow. The guy additionally banged the front of his head against a shelf in the refrigerator on his way down and caused a half-full bottle of white wine to tumble out of the refrigerator and explode on the kitchen floor. The guy was knocked out.

"Phil?" Veronica called from the stairs.

Veronica came downstairs and into the kitchen wearing Diane's robe, a slippery and shiny thigh-length thing made of blue silk.

"What's going on?" she said. "I heard a noise, and you weren't in the bed."

She came into the kitchen.

"Phil?" she said, and snapped on the light. They both cringed at the sudden brightness. She saw Phil dragging the inert body of an emaciated young man across the kitchen floor by his feet. She screamed.

"Who the fuck is that?" she said.

"Veronica, meet Julian."

Phil dragged Julian by his skinny ankles into the living room. He was white-knuckled with rage, and still talking.

"The little fucking asshole'd probably think he can blackmail me if he knows daddy's having an affair. Fucking asshole."

Veronica thumped through the house in bare feet, turning on lights. Phil dragged Julian through the living room and lifted him—Julian was so skinny, so dangerously light, much easier to lift than a twenty-four-year-old man should have been (was that right?—was he twenty-four?—twenty-five?)—and laid him out on the couch that faced the wall that used to prominently feature a very expensive fifty-inch Pioneer Elite Plasma HDTV.

The kid looked like complete shit. His arms and neck were spectrally thin. There were gray bags under his eyes. His skin was pale and sickly-looking. His head and face had pimples all over them. There was about a four-inch purple streak running up one of his forearms. He had new tattoos on his arms now, which Phil hadn't seen yet. He smelled like cigarettes. He was out cold.

The front door of the house was open. Outside, Phil saw Veronica's sparkly toothpaste-blue Mazda Miata parked on the street in front of his house. Then there was a nondescript little white car that Phil had never seen before parked in his driveway. Phil looked in the backseat of the white car. It was a shitty little old Toyota Tercel. A dim overhead light came on when he opened the back door of the car. There, sitting on the tan backseat of this mysterious off-white Toyota Tercel, was his TV. Phil carried his TV back inside, set it down on the floor—goddamn thing was heavy—and slammed the door.

Julian had woken up. Julian was sitting up on the couch and vomiting into a small plastic garbage can that he held in his lap. Veronica was down on the floor on her hands and knees next to the couch, wiping up vomit from the hardwood floor with a damp rag. Diane's blue robe was too small for her. Veronica was bigger than Diane in every dimension and direction, and the bottom of the robe rode up above her ass, and in the position she was in Phil could see her pussy peeking out between her plump, naked haunches. Julian's body twisted up in a hideous way as he emptily retched a few times before dumping another torrent of puke into the garbage can in his lap.

"I'm sorry," said Veronica from the floor. She climbed from kneeling to standing with the rag wadded in her hand. "As soon as he woke up he started throwing up. I got him the trash can from the bathroom."

"Thanks," said Phil.

Julian looked at him from over the rim of the garbage can. His eyes were swampy and bloodshot.

"You done?" said Phil.

Julian nodded, weakly wiped his mouth with the back of his hand, and swallowed. His hand was shaking. His whole body was shaking. Phil took the trash can from him.

"How you doin', son!" he said, in a voice chipper with sarcasm. "Good to see you! Been a while, hasn't it? Long time no see. Yessir. Matter of fact, nobody's known if you were alive or dead for a month. Heck, it's been so long, seems everybody just quit giving a shit one way or the other. Good to know you're still feeling well enough to come on back home and steal my shit."

"I'm sorry," Julian said, or maybe croaked. He held his face in his hands and started to cry. His protrusive shoulder blades trembled. He cringed into himself, drew up his knees, and cried.

"Boo-hoo-*hoo*!" said Phil in a sweet little voice. "Boo-hoo-*hoo*! Boo, hoo, fucking, hoo. I see you've already met Veronica. Or should I introduce you formally? Veronica, meet Julian," he said, gesturing from Veronica to the miserable figure crumpled on the couch, a pantomime of manners. "My deadbeat junkie son. We're all *very* proud of him. Julian, Veronica."

Phil was still holding the garbage can full of vomit. Veronica was standing to the side, about ten feet away, with her hands clasped in front of her.

"You're cheating on Mom?" said Julian.

"Fuck you," said Phil, and upended the garbage can into Julian's lap. "Got a lot of high moral ground to stand on, don't you. What with robbing your parents and all. The little boy who was just too special for this wicked world."

Julian stood up. When he got to his feet, his eyes rolled back in his head until his pupils disappeared and his eyes were only bloodshot whites, and he passed out again, falling forward onto the floor.

"God*damn*it!" Phil screamed, and gave the again-unconscious Julian a savage kick in the side.

"Jesus *Christ*, Phil!" said Veronica. "Calm down! It's okay now. We'll deal with this. Come on. Calm down."

Phil threw the empty garbage can at Julian's body. It bounced off him and brattled across the floor. He flung his hands up in the air and left the room. He stomped into the kitchen with a plan to steady himself with a drink and immediately stepped on broken glass. He heard the kiss and crunch of it under his bare feet right before the pain registered in his nerves.

"FUCK!"

"Jesus Christ, what *now*?" Veronica called from the living room.

"I just cut the shit out of my feet on all this goddamn glass all over the floor!"

Phil sank to the floor, sat down cross-legged, and began to try to pick the shards of broken glass out of the bottoms of his feet. Already bleeding like a stuck hog.

"Good *God*, Phil," said Veronica, stamping into the kitchen. "Lemme see it."

To avoid the glass on the floor, she quit stamping and instead tiptoed over to Phil, sat down in front of him, and put one of his bloody feet in her lap.

"Try not to get blood on that thing," said Phil, referring to Diane's blue silk robe.

"You can get her another one."

"Not by Monday. It's monogrammed."

"It's not that bad," she said. "Show me the other one."

Phil switched feet.

"I think you got all the glass out. Look, it's not that bad. Lemme get you cleaned up. Have you got Band-Aids and alcohol?"

"I think there's some stuff like that in the drawer under the sink in that bathroom."

She went down the hall into the bathroom. Phil heard drawers squealing open and rolling shut, heard her digging around in the contents of the drawers. She ran the water in the sink for a moment. She came back balancing in her arms a damp washcloth, a brown bottle of rubbing alcohol, a bag of cotton balls, some cotton pads, and a roll of gauze tape in her arms. Veronica sat down in front of him. She wiped his feet with the wet washcloth, then put a cotton ball to the neck of the brown bottle, dumped it once upside down, and stung his wounds with the alcohol.

Phil winced.

"It's okay. The bleeding's already stopping."

She pressed the cotton pads to the bottoms of his feet and wound the gauze tape around them, securing them in place.

"What did you hit him with?" she said.

"A rolling pin."

"It's not a good sign that he threw up. He might have a concussion."

"What, did you used to be a nurse or something?"

"Yes," she said.

"Oh."

Veronica got up and gave him her hand and helped him climb to his feet.

"*Son*ofabitch." He grimaced at the pain.

"It's not bad. Your feet'll be fine in a couple of days. I'm more worried about your son."

"*Fuck* him, the fucking asshole. Haven't seen him in a year. Haven't heard from him in a month. No phone call, nothing. Could've been dead for all anybody knew. Then he comes back in the middle of the night to steal my goddamn TV."

"Do you love him?"

"What do you mean?"

"Do you have a broom or something?"

"In the pantry. Down the hall to the right."

Veronica swept the broken glass on the kitchen floor into a dustpan and poured the tinkling debris into the big garbage can under the kitchen sink.

"The hell with him," Phil said. Remembering his original intent on coming into the kitchen—a drink—he opened the liquor cabinet, uncorked a bottle of Scotch, and took a slug from the bottle. He coughed and cleared his throat. His breath was staggered and shallow, his hands were trembling with anger, and now his feet hurt like a motherfucker.

"Shhh," said Veronica.

Phil was leaning with his back against the kitchen counter. The floor swept, Veronica walked over to him, wrapped her arms around him, and said, "Shhhh."

She stroked the arches of his wounded bare feet with her own bare feet. She entwined her legs with his, and he felt the skin of her smooth, thick young legs rubbing against the skin of his thin hairy legs, and felt the smooth coolness of the fabric of the silk robe against his bare torso.

She reached her face up to his and kissed him seriously on the mouth, and bit his lower lip as she disengaged. She reached around him, grabbed the open bottle of Scotch, and took a drink from the neck of it.

"Let's calm down, okay?" she whispered carefully, and wiped a trickle of Scotch from the corner of her mouth. "We'll clean him up, put him on the couch, and deal with it in the morning. Okay?"

"Okay," said Phil.

Phil and Veronica went back into the living room. It didn't smell good. Julian was lying on the floor in front of the couch, right where he had passed out the second time, with his cheek pressed flat in the vomit. They took off his shirt—God, he was so skinny—and wiped him down with the rag, then mopped up the puke that was all over the floor with the shirt, threw the rag and the shirt in the plastic garbage can, and dumped the whole mess in the garbage. Then they picked him up—he got the arms and she got the feet—and laid him out on the couch again. They covered him with a yellow wool afghan that Phil's mom had knitted, which had been draped over the back of the couch. Julian, sleeping under that yellow afghan on that couch—despite his shaved head and skinny, bruised, tattooed junkie arms—looked like he had when he was a kid, home sick from school, watching TV all day: It was the same yellow afghan, same couch, same kid. Phil and Veronica turned off all the lights and went back to bed.

When they got up in the morning he was dead. Phil, for his part, hadn't slept well. Veronica, amazingly, even after all the hubbub in the middle of the night, had just conked right out again and slept like a baby—but Phil had sweated and thrashed around in bed with an angry heart hammering at his ribs, guts in a snarl, and blood galloping in his temples until the windows began to grow light and the birds began to tweet, and Phil finally decompressed into a nauseated vertigo of half sleep that eventually became full sleep, and he woke up just a few hours later at about nine in the morning, with his headache from last night still not completely gone and the bottoms of his blood-blotted-bandaged feet swollen and smarting.

Phil and Veronica showered and dressed in turn. Veronica rebandaged Phil's injured feet for him after his shower. Veronica put on the clothes she had worn yesterday, and Phil put on another pair of khaki shorts and a pink short-sleeved Oxford, clothes that were very similar to, but different from, what he'd had on yesterday. Phil shaved, spritzed his armpits with deodorant, and combed the hair that over the course of his life had thinned to near baldness but stopped with enough left over to still comb. They went downstairs and inspected Julian, who still lay supine beneath the yellow afghan on the couch in the living room. His eyes were closed, and his face was pale and bluish, with a mouthful of white vomit that was leaking out of the corner of his lips and had dribbled down onto the couch beneath his head. It seemed that in the night he had thrown up again without waking up, choked on it, and died.

Veronica checked his pulse, though it was so obvious just from looking at him that he was dead that there was hardly any need to, and confirmed that there was nothing moving in him. The blood was cold; the organs were motionless. The electricity that had animated this matter was gone. He had stopped.

"Huh," said Phil.

They continued to stand over the couch and look down at Julian's pale, skinny body. Veronica looked back and forth from Julian on the couch to Phil standing a few feet away at the foot of the couch. Phil's hands were submerged in the pockets of his khaki shorts. Veronica's eyes were huge and scared and she was biting the knuckle of her forefinger.

"What should we do?" she whispered.

Phil didn't say anything. He was rolling his tongue around in his mouth. He could see in his peripheral vision that Veronica was trying to make eye contact with him. He kept looking at Julian's pale blue face. Phil had never seen a dead body before, for one thing. He'd made it through all these years without ever actually having seen a real dead body. Well, actually, he'd been to a couple of open-casket funerals, but that didn't seem to count. He'd never seen his father's body; it had been cremated by the time he'd made it home. Phil's mother was ninety-one years old and somehow not dead yet. Thus, Phil had never actually seen a dead body—a raw, unembalmed, un-cleaned-up one—until now. Phil pulled the yellow afghan over Julian's face.

"I need some coffee," said Phil.

He went into the kitchen, noticed that the floor was sticky from where the wine bottle had broken and spilled last night, replaced yesterday's soggy filter and grinds with fresh stuff, filled the glass pitcher of the coffeemaker with cold water—not from the tap, but from the spigot in the refrigerator door next to the automatic icemaker, which was filtered and extra cold and made for better-tasting coffee—poured it into the percolator, replaced the pitcher, and flipped the switch, and in a moment a thin brown thread of liquid began to dribble through the hole in the lid of the coffeepot and steam up the sides of it.

"You want some coffee?" he said.

"Yeah," said Veronica from the other room.

When it was ready he poured the coffee into two mugs. One was a conference-swag mug that said BAIN CAPITAL on it, and the other had a picture on it of Snoopy wearing a scarf and aviator helmet pretending his doghouse was an airplane.

"Milk or sugar?"

"Little of both."

Phil glooped some two-percent milk into the mugs and shot a few dashes of sugar into each from the sugar dispenser, opened the silverware drawer, selected a spoon, rattled the spoon around in the cups, and watched the ribbons of milk in the black coffee eddy and blur into homogeneous shades of tan.

The items of the night before—the blender, the limes, the mezcal bottle, the ice bag, the cutting board, the bottle of Scotch, the rolling pin—were still sitting on the kitchen counter. Phil put the two cups of coffee on the kitchen table. Phil and Veronica sat at the table and sipped their coffee. It looked like it was going to be a beautiful day: a sunny, wet, thick-aired, late-summer Texas Gulf Coast kind of day.

They drank the coffee, and Phil told Veronica everything she needed to know about Julian. When he was done, she said, again:

"What should we do?"

"What's this *we* stuff," he said, Tonto to Lone Ranger. "This is my problem. If I were you I wouldn't worry about it."

"I want to help."

"That's sweet."

"It was an accident."

"Sort of."

"It was an accident. There was somebody robbing your house, and you hit the guy and knocked him out. Case closed. It's not your fault. It's totally understandable. You have nothing to hide. You have nothing to fear."

"Jesus. All this is gonna be a barrel of laughs to try to explain to Diane. For one thing, you weren't here. Let's get that straight."

Apparently for lack of anywhere else to look besides at Phil, Veronica looked down into her cup of coffee and said nothing.

"Is that gonna be a problem? Is it? I need you to promise me that, at least. Anybody asks, you weren't here last night."

"Phil. It was an accident. I'm a witness. I saw what happened. I'm the only one who knows it was just an accident."

"No. Period. No. How many surprises at once do you want me to spring on Diane when she comes home tomorrow?"

"I don't want you to get in trouble. Just call the cops and we'll tell them what happened."

"Look," said Phil. He pinched the bridge of his nose with his fingers, drew a breath, and let it out slowly. Veronica rubbed his arm, which was resting on the kitchen table holding the cup of coffee. After a long time, he said: "None of this had to happen. Why do this to our lives? Why do this to my life? Why drag you into all this? Why put Diane through all this? This didn't have to happen. Right now, it might as well not have happened. Nobody knew where the hell Julian was for a month, or more. He was totally incommunicado. We still don't know, actually, and probably never will at this point. Point is, this didn't have to happen. You see what I mean?"

Eventually, she saw what he meant.

A cardinal landed on the birdfeeder outside.

They prepared and ate breakfast. Phil cut two bananas into slimy pale yellow chips and fanned them out on top of two bowls of Wheat Chex. They had orange juice and toast with butter and raspberry jelly, and finished off the pot of coffee.

Veronica washed the dishes from breakfast and from last night while Phil rooted around in a linen closet—comforters, blankets, fitted sheets, pillows, pillowcases—until he found a ratty old blue bedsheet. They never used it anymore. It was thin and threadbare and washed-out and had a bunch of little moth holes in it. It wouldn't be missed.

Phil came back downstairs. From the kitchen, noises of running water and clinking plates. Phil pushed some furniture aside and billowed the sheet out flat on the living room floor. He threw off the yellow afghan, picked up

Julian, who had already begun to stiffen, laid him down on the sheet, and rolled him up in it. Then he went out to the garage and found a roll of duct tape. He unpeeled long strips of the tape and wound them around the bundle. He propped open the door to the garage, picked up the taped bundle, heaved it over his shoulder, took it into the garage, and dumped it in the truck bed of his silver Chevy Silverado. He scooted the plastic truck bed cover on top and drummed on it until he felt it snap down into place.

Veronica was done with the dishes.

Phil squeezed his wounded and bandaged feet into his boating shoes and put on his yellow all-weather boating jacket and the blue Beneteau cap he received as a prize the time he won the Wednesday-night Galveston Yacht Club Open Regatta, which he always wore when he went sailing, for good luck.

"I can do this by myself, but it'll be easier if I have another pair of hands," said Phil.

"I know," she said. "I want to come."

Veronica sat on the bottom step of the stairs and began to pull on and zip up the black lizard boots she had left by the front door the night before.

"I've got an extra jacket you can wear," Phil said from the foyer closet, flipping through a rack of coats and jackets. He pulled out another yellow boating jacket.

"Oh," he said, looking at Veronica. "You can't wear those boots. The soles'll scuff up the deck. What size do you wear?"

"Women's nine."

"Uh-oh."

Phil sorted through the white-soled boating shoes in the bottom of the closet.

"Diane's would be too small for you." He found the pair that Garrett wore when he was home. "Try these on."

She took the shoes.

"These are way too big. They'll be like clown shoes on me. Can I just go barefoot?"

"Mnn," Phil growled. "Well, you need traction."

She put her feet in the big shoes and laced them on.

"These are ridiculous on me. Look—" and she pressed down the toes of the shoes with her thumbs. "There's like two inches of space in the toes."

"They'll have to do."

Veronica rolled her eyes and acquiesced, then put on the yellow jacket, which was also Garrett's, and also too big for her. The sleeves drooped past her hands.

Phil unhooked the keys to the Silverado from their peg on the cute stupid rack by the door that had a row of pegs to hang car keys on. Diane had bought it at Crate & Barrel, and Phil doubted its necessity.

They went out through the door to the garage and got in the truck. Phil pressed the button on the garage door opener clipped to the driver's-side sun visor, and the garage door roared to life and rolled open to let the light in. Phil started the engine, put it in reverse, and nudged the gas, and immediately almost backed into the little white car that was parked in the driveway.

"Oop. I forgot about that. Sit tight," he said to Veronica. "I gotta do something."

He got out of the cab, snapped off the plastic truck bed cover, hopped into the truck and ripped the tape off the middle of the bundle, whipped open the sheet, dug through the pockets of Julian's jeans, and fished out his car keys. He got out, walked over to the car, opened the driver's-side door, and got in. The car was disgusting. There were cups and coke cans and papers and clothes and all kinds of shit all over the floor of the passenger's side, and a Styrofoam cup in the cup holder between the seats was half-full of old coffee, with a bunch of waterlogged cigarette butts floating in it. The car started, with a little trouble.

"God*damn*it," said Phil. "Kid treats his things like shit." Phil could tell from the raspy sound of the engine that the fucking fan belt in this piece of shit was about to snap, and there was a goddamn idiot light on on the dash, telling him to change the oil. Just to *change the goddamn oil*—pretty basic stuff.

Phil backed the car out of the driveway and onto the street, then turned back and reparked it on the other side of the driveway. He shut it off, pocketed the keys, got out, hopped back into the truck, haphazardly taped the sheet shut again, hopped out, pounded the plastic cover back onto the truck bed, and got back in the cab.

Veronica was listening to the radio.

It was a beautiful day. Sunny, with a good warm breeze, but not too gusty. Perfect day for sailing. People were out in the neighborhood, walking their dogs and jogging, on this bright, quiet Sunday morning. It was about eleven by the time they made it to the yacht club and marina. They stopped at a gate with a booth. Phil rolled down the window, and the attendant waved.

"Morning, Phil," said the attendant.

"Morning. This is my niece, Veronica," he said. Veronica waved at him across Phil from the passenger seat.

"Howdy," said the attendant. "Good day for a sail, huh?"

"Yep," said Phil. "Great day. Hey listen. I got some stuff in the truck I want to put in the boat. You mind if I pull the truck up by the boat? It's right over there."

The attendant ducked into the darkness of his booth to look at some paperwork. His cabbage-like head came back into view in the window.

"Sorry, last name?" he said.

"Grassley."

"That's right. Sorry."

The man's head disappeared again, and then returned to the window.

"Nope," he said. "That's all right with me."

"Thanks," said Phil.

The attendant waved them through, and Phil guided the Silverado around the palm trees planted on the median of the roundabout by the front entrance to the yacht club, through the parking lot, and onto a little road that stretched along one of the concrete jetties of the marina between a row of warehouses and the docks. He parked the truck between two warehouses and they got out. The riggings of the boats clinked against the mast poles and the languid water slapped against their hulls.

Phil popped open the truck bed cover, dragged the taped-up bundle out of the bed, heaved it into his arms, and slung it over his shoulder. He led Veronica past the warehouses and down a long, bright white floating pier. They passed a couple of people walking in the other direction down the pier, and everyone smiled quickly and waved at each other.

They stopped at Phil's boat.

"There she is," said Phil. "My pride and joy."

And Lord, was it ever a beautiful boat.

"This is a thirty-eight-foot 2005 Lagoon catamaran 380 S2. Twin inboard engine."

"Wow," said Veronica.

"Wow is right," said Phil.

He laid the body down on the pier and gingerly stretched out one foot and then the other onto the surface of the boat. There was a big blue plastic tarp tied to the rings at the edges of the boat, to cover the wooden deck. Phil untied it and thundered it aside, uncloaking the brilliant white body of the catamaran. Phil held out his hand and helped Veronica step aboard. Phil made preparations to sail, then stepped back onto the pier and threw the bundled body into the mesh net strung between the twin hulls of the boat.

Sailing was one thing Phil loved and loved absolutely, without any complications or equivocations at all. He loved the equipment, for one. He loved the learned skill required to master its complexities, knowing what to touch and how to touch it and by how much to make the craft obey the commands from your hands. He loved the language that went with it; he loved how one can immediately tell a sailor apart from the rest of humanity by his correct usage of all these technical shibboleths, the singsongy jargon for all things nautical, these words whose blunt, silly choppiness denotes their Anglo-Saxon and Germanic roots, and hence their ancientness, which ancientness reminds one that the craft and science of seafaring is intrinsic to every human culture that ever found itself living beside open waters, and thus none ever had the need to filch words from other languages to explain its particulars—no Latin, no Greek, no French terms were ever imported by necessity to delineate its phenomena or to name its things: abaft, abeam, astern, bight, bilge, binnacle, bobstay, boomkin, bowsprit, capstan, coxswain, daggerboard, gollywobbler, gunwale, jib, lazyjack, leeway, mainsail, mizzenmast, portside, rudder, scupper, spinnaker, starboard, topsail, transom, traveler. Phil loved driving out to his boat in the Galveston Marina on a beautiful Sunday morning like this one, finding it bobbing proudly right in its special place between two less expensive and less beautiful boats, waiting to be maneuvered out into the choppy green gulf, waiting for his hands, for his touch. He loved untying and unfurling the dew-dappled blue plastic tarp—the noise it made, *ba-boom*, like a drum—then carefully rolling it up and placing it in its proper storage compartment. He loved when he got out into the deep water, after he had gently piloted the boat, helped along by the river water draining into Galveston Bay, through the channel between Galveston and Pelican Island and then past Port Bolivar and out past the jetties and the seawalls and the breakwaters and into the gulf, over the line that you could see, you could physically *see* dividing the light blue from the dark blue water, where the sloping floor of sand below dropped steeply down and the water got deep and the waves got high. He loved the shrieking of the seabirds circling above them. He loved the sound and the feeling of the seawater lapping against the hulls of the boat. He especially loved when it was time to cut the engine and hoist the sails—the pulleys and winches wheeling until the ropes and rigging snapped taut and the sails ballooned into shape—and he tacked the vessel into the wind and felt the force of the rushing air thrust them into serious motion, the newfound silence, the sun, the wind whipping his hair around, the boyish sense of adventure. Out here he felt extraordinarily alive and at peace, out here his mind raced with great thoughts and his heart surged in his chest and he felt like a man feeling like a man was supposed to feel.

Veronica wasn't a sailor. He could tell that at once. She didn't have the lust for the wind and the sea in her blood. You can tell that immediately about people. Even if they've never sailed before in their lives—and Phil considered the souls of such people to be unknowingly and infelicitously impoverished—you can take them sailing and know instantly whether they've got the potential but unused love for it buried inside them. Some people immediately understand the greatness of what they're doing. Other people—and Veronica appeared to be one of them—seem to fear the feeling of the boat's constant pitching and rolling, its rising up and slapping heavily down again into the water, they are afraid of the sea, they miss the land—they miss the way gravity and the solid properties of the earth cooperate to firmly and comfortably station their bodies in space. Phil could move around aboard the boat quite naturally. Veronica, though, for the most part timidly kept her ass rooted as if nailed down to the semicircular wooden bench set in the bridge deck between the helm and the cabin. Meanwhile Phil stood at the helm, gleefully tilting the wheel of the boat in such and such a direction, now in another direction, cooperating with the wind to take them farther and farther out into the hot, breezy gulf, and the black and green and blue water chopped and frothed all around them for miles.

And Lord, was it a pretty day. To be honest, Phil didn't really mind the fact that Veronica didn't appear to love sailing. He liked that there were still some things, certain experiential preferences, which divided the psychology of men from that of women. The more girlish she acted, the more of a man he felt. More than anything, he liked for her to *see him* enjoying this.

Soon they had sailed far enough away from the land that the coast of Texas—Galveston Island, and beyond it, the southern suburbs of Houston where he lived—was now just a flat brown line on the horizon to the north. To the south, the moisture in the air blurred away the line between the sea and sky. Somewhere in that blue-gray blur, the water bent out of sight over the surface of the planet. Although the radius of visibility at sea, on a perfectly clear day, is only twelve miles in any direction, for some reason you grasp the bigness of the world when you're out on the open water more than you ever can on land. It has something to do with the absence of any references by which the eye might measure the depth of the space, the perfectly unbroken flatness of your field of vision.

There were now no other boats around anywhere within easy eyeshot.

"She's in a good place, now," said Phil. "Come on up here."

Veronica timidly rose from the wooden bench, groped and picked her way across the deck to the front of the helm.

"All I need you to do is just keep your hands right here," he said. She put her hands on the spokes of the wheel where Phil's hands were. Phil stood behind her and wrapped his hands around hers, demonstrating to her the right amount of pressure to apply and the right amount of resistance she should be feeling. Her thick black hair flew into his face and tickled his nose and lips. He breathed in the smell of her skin and hair.

"Just keep her right there."

"Like this?"

"That's right. Just like that. You want to feel about this much resistance. That's it. You want to be pushing on it, but not too hard. Easy does it. Now keep her right there. If all of a sudden she gets too hard or too easy on you, then you know something's wrong."

With Veronica positioned at the helm, Phil stepped out onto the back of one of the twin hulls of the boat. He reached out into the net strung between them, where he had put the body. He dragged it toward him, got a good grip on it, and rolled it out of the net into the sea. It dropped into the water. The body floated briefly, and the bedsheet dampened, then it turned over several times, and began to fall under. A gust of wind came and puffed the sails up like fat wings, and took the boat away from the place where the body was falling, sinking from an active secret into a dormant one, a secret that would sleep forever on the floor of the Gulf of Mexico.

Phil came back to the helm and took over from Veronica.

"Good job," he said.

She hurriedly sat down again.

There were a couple of other loose ends to take care of before Diane would come home tomorrow. Such as, for instance, that shitty little Toyota still parked in front of the house. It would be easy enough for Veronica to follow behind him while he drove it to some far-flung place and parked it there, and then drive him back home. He would ask her to do that when they got back ashore.

He looked at Veronica. She wasn't looking at him. She was watching the sea. Her head was half turned away from him. Lord, she was beautiful. She was so full of energy and brightness and life. Look at how the light just bounces off that smooth young skin. Her hair blew around behind her like streaks of ink. Phil was, in fact, in love with her. Of course he was in love with her, and of course he assumed this meant she was in love with him, too, and of course she would never tell anybody about all this. This secret was dormant; it would sleep forever. Once again, Phil had just one *active* secret, and Veronica was it.

And then Phil noticed an amazing thing: Up ahead of them, obviously moving very fast, and yet seemingly not moving at all because of the lack of visual references all around them, there were several dolphins—they looked like bottlenoses but he wasn't sure. Just hopping in and out of the water. There were three or four of them. Their sleek silver bodies were looping in and out of the water in perfect sequence, moving together all at once, as graceful as—what, as ballerinas?—no, ballerinas hobble like gimps next to the dazzling physical grace of these creatures. They were traveling through the water in a perfect wave, each one coming up and going down at the exact same time, their athletic bodies working with the material around them, harmoniously collaborating with the media of the world as they moved through it, constantly accounting for the gravitational difference between air and water, their heads, necks, noses, fins, and tails all working together with physics to make them move, and move beautifully. How the hell do they know how to do that? Where'd they learn that? Who taught them? Why do they all jump out of the water and dive back in again at the same time? Surely there's a reason for it. Surely there's a real and important reason. An animal's body does everything it can to maximize its results by minimizing its entropy, always conserving its energy. Everything like that has some kind of reason. Animals don't do things without a good reason for it.

VENUS AT HER MIRROR

Men look at women. Women watch themselves being looked at.
—John Berger, *Ways of Seeing*

The Representative was dead. He would have been one of Rebecca's oldest clients, except Rebecca had long ago ceased to think of him as a client. Yes, he was generous—he always paid for everything, that was a given—but he had not directly paid Rebecca for her services in years. They weren't services, anymore, they were just things they did together.

The Representative was dead. Rebecca Spiegel had known him for eleven years, and she was no longer sure what one would call their relationship. What began, long ago, as a rather businesslike arrangement between two people—one of them paying money for services rendered, the other receiving the money and rendering services—had over the years turned into other things: a deep friendship, a partnership, a secret bond that somehow because it had begun as a balanced relationship between equals was truly closer than most romances ever are. Sometimes, they had sex. Now, sometimes (though rarely), they had ordinary vanilla intercourse, without role play, without restraints, without toys, without make-believe. It wasn't that she had quit charging him. One day, about two years ago, he seemed to have forgotten to pay her (the usual stack of hundreds in an unmarked white envelope on the kitchen counter was not there), and she had not reminded him. Since then, he no longer paid her, and she no longer accepted payment—which, she supposed, made their relationship perfectly legal now, though it was still fraught with secrecy. Was she, in a sense, his mistress?

The Representative was dead. If she had heard of his death from a friend (which would not have happened—the only friend they had in common, the one who had introduced them, she had not spoken to in years), or (more likely) from the news, she would have cried. As it was, she was not crying—not yet—because she was alone with a mind locked in a rattrap of fear and anxiety surrounding the facts of the Representative's death, and her presence for it.

The Representative was dead. The Representative had been a good man. He'd had that yacht-club swagger, that easy arm around the shoulder. He had never been someone who could be described as a simple man. No, he was a complicated man. But under that there was essential goodness. Under the armor of public life was someone who cared deeply about the poor, minorities, women, the exploited, the underserved, the uninsured, the unemployed, the disempowered. He'd hated Bush passionately, had been against the war. At the bedrock of his many-layered life, he fought on the side of the good. Social injustice drove him to rage, and it was that rage that drove him into politics more than his vanity or his ambition: the desire to do good. And he had done good. He would do no more good, now. The Representative was dead.

Rebecca was sitting in a leather armchair, looking at his body. The Representative had paid, as he always had, for her airfare to D.C., and put her up in her usual suite in The Fairfax at Embassy Row. She had flown in that morning and was scheduled to leave the next day. The hotel was a thirty-minute walk away, at most, or two quick stops on the Metro. She had barely moved in the last hour. The Representative, for his part, had not moved at all in the last hour.

Rebecca Spiegel—Mistress Delilah, once, sometimes—continued to find herself in this unusual and undesirable situation: slumped in an armchair in spike heels, fishnet stockings and garter belt, a leather corset, and the red wig she had always worn when she was Mistress Delilah with the Representative—staring, without really looking, at the body of the Representative, which lay motionless, faceup and (except for the alligator nipple clamps and the rope around his wrists) naked on the concrete floor of the apartment. It was in a luxury high-rise on Virginia Avenue, a newly built mixed-use steel and glass structure with a balcony view of the National Mall and Arlington National Cemetery across the Potomac, which proceeded unhurriedly toward the Chesapeake Bay thirty stories below, flowing under the arches of a squat stone highway bridge, its rippled surface glowing yellow in the slant-light of the golden hour.

The apartment was furnished almost in the way a Realtor would furnish a model home: a hollowly perfect simulacrum of a human dwelling that clearly no person actually lives in. It was decorated as if the Realtor were trying to sell it to fussy upper-middle-class yuppies who happen to be into BDSM. The expensive, unused furniture all matched tastefully: Everything was metal, blue-tinted glass, and black leather. The bed had been fucked on, but no one had ever spent a night sleeping in it. The decorative touches were the Representative's, and he'd had a good eye: rows of photographs framed in ornate tarnished silver frames that surprisingly harmonized with the sleek designer furniture; all the pictures were sepia-toned early-twentieth-century porn—women with round, sweet faces and full, fleshy hips, sleeping masks, riding crops, student-teacher scenarios, naughty maids in the mistress's boudoir. The floors were smooth, cool concrete. There were iron rings and chains installed in the ceilings and walls. Mistress Delilah rarely made use of them. Likewise the closets were stocked superabundantly with various equipment: whips, ropes, chains, leather hoods, ball gags, harnesses, collars, handcuffs, butt plugs, cock rings, and many other devices more unique and harder to describe.

The Representative had loved his toys. He had liked talking shop with her about different kinds of whips and so on. He had always had a fawning regard for her opinion as a professional. She didn't especially share his collectorism, his fetish for connoisseurship, except as it related to psychology. (Rebecca found dominance and submission play that leaned heavily on toys a bit graceless, gimmicky. A whip and some good sturdy rope can go a long way. The art of sexual domination is not in the material; it's in the mind.) The idea of grades and progression excited him, of different sorts of whips for different purposes. Men seem to like seeing tools lined up in a rack ranging from smallest to biggest, they get some sort of primeval kick out of confronting a problem requiring the widest-gauge socket in the socket wrench set. The Representative had recently acquired a whip that Mistress Delilah had to admit was an impressive item (Rebecca herself was more aloof to it). He'd been so excited for her to use it on him, the object had probably occasioned the visit: It was a genuine South African *sjambok*, a hard, semiflexible three-foot-long whip, traditionally made from twisted rhinoceros hide, originally meant for driving cattle, later infamous as the police and military weapon of choice during apartheid. These days they make them out of plastic or rubber—the real ones are illegal because they're made from the hide of an endangered animal. The Representative got off on that, and also on the weapon's troubling symbolic place in a brutal history of colonial subjugation. He'd bought it from a South African antiquities dealer, and it was the real deal—long, stiff, heavy, the handle embroidered with some African pattern—the object was electric to the touch, alive with sleeping evil. Thing was not a toy—when she started using it on him, she immediately realized that the difficulty would be to hit him hard enough to get him off without seriously hurting him.

Mistress Delilah had also brought along, as always, her own special black bag. A professional brings along a bag of tools: the country doctor making a house call, the plumber come to fix the sink. She only brought it because she knew it excited him just to see it in her hand. It was laughably gratuitous—at this point only a reminder of the way things used to be between them. (Once, she'd had to endure a TSA employee spreading the contents of her bag on a counter: She'd stood there while the woman scrutinized her ball gags and nipple pumps with turquoise latex gloves and had to ask someone to check if a cat-o'-nine-tails violated FAA regulations; it did not. Now she just checked the bag.) The black bag sat, rumpled and deflated-looking, in the corner of the living room, the zipper open, the only things she'd removed from it lying in disuse on the glass coffee table: handcuffs, muzzle, nipple pumps. The sjambok, she realized, looking down, was still in her hands, lying sideways across her lap.

Rebecca guessed it was a heart attack. She asked new clients for medical histories, and wouldn't risk taking them on if she thought something like this might happen. But the Representative had been her client when she was new and green in the business, and not thinking about things like that yet. And he had been forty years old and in better health back then. The years had puffed him out, and he was not really her client anymore, but her friend, confidant, sometime benefactor, and the most complicated lover she'd ever had. Now he was fifty-one, on the hefty side, and not in the best health. Did he have a genetic history of heart disease? Maybe it was a brain aneurysm? She had tried to revive him with the basic CPR she knew. She'd tried to administer mouth-to-mouth resuscitation, but it had been of no use. He had, quite literally, died in her arms.

• • •

Rebecca had the first inkling that something was wrong when she noticed the Representative convulsing under the scarlet sole of the Louboutin pump squished against his face in a way that did not seem sexual in nature. She glanced behind her and saw that his cock had gone slack. He'd taken his hands off it—his hands were tied together, which restricted the movement of his arms, but he was limply whacking his wrists against his chest, like someone pretending to be retarded. She took her foot off his face, but didn't break character.

"Oh? Something wrong, cuntface?" she said in her belittling-the-baby voice. "Aw, whatsa matter, sweetie-poo?"

The Representative was making a worrisome gakking noise in the back of his throat. He sounded like a dog choking on a bone.

She nudged his shoulder with the toe of her shoe.

"Seriously. You okay?"

He hadn't used the safe word—he didn't appear capable of using it or any other word at the moment.

She knelt down beside him. His swollen choking face was red, flaming. A bright sweat had broken out on his forehead.

She said his name—his real name. She said it twice with question marks, and a third time with an exclamation point. Then she was shaking his shoulders, screaming his name. He was unconscious.

The thought would haunt Rebecca afterward—probably for years, maybe for the rest of her life—that if she had called the paramedics right away, maybe they could have rushed him to the hospital, and maybe he could have been revived—by those electric paddle things they use to restart hearts in TV medical dramas, and presumably also in real life (and what is that, really?)—and maybe his life could have been saved, by heart surgery, by a stent, a pacemaker . . . Instead, she had hesitated. She had hesitated because the Representative had a wife and a family who knew nothing about Mistress Delilah—who knew nothing of his other life, or however many other other lives he had. That was to say nothing of his public life, the things he stood for, his political career, the careers of others he was connected to—a chain of influences that went all the way up to the Oval Office, and, this being an election year, it would not be good to have a Democrat humiliated this way, possibly shamed out of office . . . God knows how many outward threads of the web would tremble when this hit the news cycle.

There had been a narrow window of time in which there may have been a chance that if she'd made the hasty decision to pick up the phone and dial the three digits every American child learns in kindergarten, she might have saved his life. But instead, because of the world outside—rather than inside—this luxury apartment overlooking the Potomac, she had hesitated, and now, as she had confirmed and reconfirmed and reconfirmed again in the hour since she'd first taken her foot off his mouth, with her thumb on the inside of his bound and motionless wrist and her head on his silent, motionless, cooling chest, the Representative was doubtlessly dead.

It was a sensation of paralysis, sitting in that chair. This must be a little of what it feels like to be paralyzed, a conscious vegetable—the sort of person the Representative may have become had she acted instead of hesitated: seeing, feeling, hearing, thinking, unable to unroot oneself from the spot—passive, helpless, stuck. If she looked down at her legs and arms and willed them to move, they would not.

The plush black leather armchair accepted her body like a gently swallowing mouth. The leather felt smooth and cool on her bare thighs. The back of her leather corset rubbed against the leather of the chair, grunted and squealed if she adjusted her back. Her goddamn back was killing her for some reason. What the fuck she'd done to it she did not know, but this pain in her lower back seemed to return for a few days once a month like a muscular-spinal period. Every time it came back she made a mental note to see a chiropractor, but it always went away before she remembered to make the appointment—and then the motherfucker came roaring back again the next month. Maybe putting on the tight corset today retriggered the back pain. Was this aging?

She had a lot of decisions to make. Some urgent, some middle, some distant. She felt so overwhelmed, so suffocated by the unmade decisions crowding around her that she was for the time being incapable of doing anything but staring at the body of the Representative that lay on the concrete floor in front of her and letting the late-afternoon light fail as she sat in this leather armchair beginning to grow hungry.

In her mind, she began to sketch out a To-Do list. It was an easy exercise suggested by a therapist from years back that she still found a useful way to compartmentalize her problems when she was feeling overwhelmed, and it helped to calm her. When she made these interior To-Do lists, she put items into three categories, according to the urgency of their concern. High Priority, Medium Priority, Low Priority. Her eyes unfixed, she gazed out the window at the river many stories below her. She could see the streetlights beginning to come on, and the colorful lights that spookily underlit the monuments at night: She could just barely discern, not far away on the Mall, a solemn and tired-looking Abraham Lincoln glowing in his cage of columns, sitting perfectly still in his own armchair, as if immobilized for centuries by the weight of his own difficult decisions.

TO DO

HIGH PRIORITY

1. Deal with current situation

What were her options? She would admit, later, that the thought did occur to her of simply changing into her street clothes, packing her bag, and leaving. Who would know she was ever here? What if the Representative had happened to be alone in the apartment when he had his heart attack, or whatever it was? Well—there was the doorman, who knew her, and had seen them come in together, and who would see her leave alone. But who was to say this didn't happen after she had left? Did anyone else know about this apartment? The Representative had tight, important connections everywhere—he would be missed, conspicuously and immediately. How many hours or days could he lie there decomposing on the floor before anyone found him? She couldn't do that. Even if she could, what good would it do? The apartment would be discovered, the closets full of BDSM gear, the South African sjambok made out of fucking rhino hide . . . Questions would arise, and before long, they would be answered. He would be humiliated in his death. He would be a laughingstock, an easy punchline in Leno's opening monologue. The scandal and embarrassment would come sooner or later; it was inevitable now. In a sudden, brief flutter of hope, she entertained a fantasy of somehow getting in touch with his congressional aides, moving the body to his office, covering it up—which fast spiraled into an oblivion of logistics so delicate and dauntingly complicated that it immediately overwhelmed her. No, that would not work. The safest recourse was the blunt truth. One way or another, she was going to have to pick up the phone and tell someone what happened, hand off the situation to the outside world. She herself had done nothing wrong—except perhaps hesitate past the critical moment when an emergency call might still have been useful. And whom should she call now? Nine-one-one? A bit late for that. Should she tell the doorman? He probably already knew enough about the Representative to infer the general gist of what was going on. The cops? She was loath to talk to "the authorities." The phrase alone nearly made her shudder. She would want to explain everything deliberately and calmly, not leaving anything out, beginning at the beginning—and she knew that if she were talking to such people, she wouldn't be allowed to do that—she would struggle against the current, being brusquely cut off over and over by arrogant, unlistening men interrupting her with questions about things that happened on square twenty-seven when she's still on square one—if they would only shut up and listen to her, she could explain everything—but who would listen? What if—what if, what if, what if—she called his wife? Tracy—Tracy, of whom she had heard a great deal over the last decade—complaints, compliments, grievances, and guileless confessions of enduring love—but had never met. How much did she know? Probably nothing. How much did she suspect? Who could say? If Rebecca were to call his wife and start explaining a lot of very-difficult-to-explain things to his family, it might be possible to keep the whole thing within the inner circle, not let it out into the public sphere . . . Save his reputation, spare his family the humiliation, and not hurt the Democrats' image . . . She chased this line of thought all the way to the bedside table, where the Representative's iPhone was plugged in, charging. She heaved herself out of the chair—wincing at a sudden spike of back pain—and slogged across the swamp of floor space between living room and bedroom, picked up the phone, slid the lock on the screen, and was immediately confronted with a four-digit passcode. Obviously a man who lived with so many secrets would not have an unpassword-protected phone. She went to the desk chair on which she'd earlier that afternoon ordered him to fold and carefully place his clothes. In the pocket of his pants she found his wallet: driver's license, ID cards, debit card, credit cards, a few business cards, photos of his wife and children (no help there), health insurance card, Metro card noticeably absent (never slums it on the Metro, always takes the car service home from the Capitol), slightly under $280 cash—a recent trip to the ATM minus maybe a cup of coffee. No phone numbers. Of course. No one writes down phone numbers in the year 2012. All information is consolidated on our mobile devices, these guardian angels in our pockets that guide us, protect us, control us. She put it back and returned to the chair. Was 911 really her only option? If she really called the cops she must remember to flush the coke down the toilet before they arrived. It wasn't hers, but before they started (before Rebecca became Mistress Delilah), he had offered, she had declined, and the Representative had shrugged amiably, chopped out a long fat line on the marble countertop, and sucked it up through a crisp twenty, which now that she remembered it rounded out the amount in his wallet to $300, and was still lying in a gossamer curl on the kitchen counter. Come to think of it, that gulp of cocaine may very well have been what pushed his heart over the edge. Rebecca looked with dread at the cordless landline weakly blinking a green light in its cradle on the kitchen counter. The little green light blinked, and the gulf of dread inside her grew deeper and wider with every second that distanced her from the Representative's time of death.

2. Eat something

Hunger was coming on fast. What had she eaten that day? That morning, sitting in LaGuardia's Delta Shuttle terminal waiting for her one-hour flight to Reagan National, she'd had a latte and a disgusting premade hummus-sprouts-and-tomato sandwich on an everything bagel that came wrapped in a cellophane package; the pale hard slice of tomato had tasted as though it had been grown in a petri dish. The Representative had treated her to a lobster roll and a glass of Sancerre for lunch. (He'd wanted to buy a bottle, but she said she only wanted a glass, and even that she only sipped at. This abstemiousness was uncharacteristic of her; the Representative had thought nothing of it.) Evening was falling and her belly was beginning to gurgle. Acid, gas, something—chemicals weren't getting along in her stomach. She eased one cheek off the sticky leather seat cushion to let a fart slide out. Why not?—she was alone, now. She needed to eat.

MEDIUM PRIORITY

3. Call Richard back

It could be important. She had no fucking idea what the fuck Richard had called her about, but whatever it was, it was most likely something she did not remotely, pardon the understatement, want to deal with at the moment. It was probably either about the divorce or the apartment. He had called earlier in the afternoon and left a message. She had been pre-occupied. Mistress Delilah had one shoe on the back of the Representative's neck, hissing insults at him and thwacking his ass with the sjambok while he was bent over in worshipful genuflection, licking up the puddle she'd just pissed for him on the bathroom floor (purely as a professional, she was impressed by the sjambok—it had a pleasing heft and grip, and she appreciated the clear, crisp note of its whistle before the crack: What it sang through the air on its way to strike flesh was a love song); meanwhile, a distant, separate, and ever-alert corner of her consciousness (Rebecca's) registered the faint buzzing sound of her phone vibrating in the next room, and made a quick mental note to check it later; and later, when she had a moment—she put a blindfold on the Representative and ordered him to jack off awhile, but denied him permission to come—she fished the phone out of her purse and glanced at the screen, just to make sure it wasn't urgent. (It might have been about Severin, was what she feared most—her sister was watching him while Rebecca was away on this quick trip to D.C., and Severin's regimen of pills was complicated.) It was Richard. And he'd left a message. She could not bring herself, even now, to listen to the goddamn message. The message almost certainly had to do either with the apartment or with their endless divorce. The two issues were closely interrelated. In broad abstract, the conflict about the apartment (third-story two-bedroom, one-bath in East Village with balcony and nice view of Empire State Building, short walk to First Avenue L, pets OK, laundry on-site) was this: (1) they bought and own it together; (2) Richard, who now finally has tenure and lives in Connecticut with the woman he left her for, wants to sell it; (3) Rebecca, who lives in it, does not. It was a never-ending sideshow to the circus of animosity that was their divorce. Richard and Rebecca had separated four years ago, and it seemed now the divorce was finally coming through. She was so used to its terrible weight, at this point it was getting difficult to imagine what life would feel like with this grindstone cut from around her neck. Were one to unwind all the knots and lay it out along the ground, the string of unanswered e-mails and unreturned messages—from Richard, from Richard's lawyer, from her own lawyer—would stretch for miles. The divorce was a backyard running out of room to bury bodies in. When she asked herself if, at the age of twenty-one, when she met Richard, she had known that it would end like this, would she have still done it?—the answer was no. All those years of love and cooperation and contentment with him were not worth this. It was a bum deal. She had been a twenty-one-year-old college senior in love with a brilliant (so she'd thought) grad student seven years older than her (an age difference that had seemed significant then, and it was laughable to her now that she'd ever thought so), and she wished she could let that person know she would be in love with that man for fifteen years—fifteen years, with a marriage in the middle—if not of bliss, then of relatively functional happiness—that she would give her youth to this man—and he will violate the one rule you will ask him to obey, which he will have agreed to—and he will leave you, and here you'll be, thirty-nine and single, your married friends cluttering their Facebook walls with baby pictures while you are thinking daily about sperm donors, about freezing your eggs, the window of fertility shrinking, dimming, closing, every day dogging you with worries about having a child in your forties, the rising risk of birth defects, bringing into the world some rubber-faced mutant with flippers and a tail and raising it alone, and you'll post pictures of you and your malformed freak-child on Facebook and your friends will "Like" them. From the ages of twenty-one to thirty-six, when she and Richard separated, she'd had someone, and had lived her life pretty much as she always assumed she would. And he had been her best friend—that was what made his betrayal doubly horrible: She'd lost both her husband and her best friend. Where would she find someone like that again? How, now, nearing forty, was it possible that she would meet another person who could ever know her that intimately? Someone with whom she had shared so much history, so much of her growing up? It simply wasn't possible anymore. Not now. It was such a strange feeling, to have these sickening waves of anger toward the one person in the world with whom she'd shared more of herself than anyone else. What she'd wanted, vaguely, but on second thought, specifically (and in retrospect, thank God it never happened), was a child with Richard, to mix their DNA and make a person whose face shared their features, not a cup of frozen come from a stranger, a stranger who at some point had been paid to come into a cup. Remember, Richard, how we'd talked about having kids—a kid, or kids plural, whatever—and you didn't want to until your career was more settled, until you had tenure? Of course, I said, that's fine—I didn't want to yet, either. We would wait. We would have our fun. And boy did we have fun. There was the threesome with Harriet, for instance. When we shut ourselves up in that cabin in the Catskills for a long weekend and smoked opium—whose idea was that, smoking opium like Frankfurt School philosophers in Paris? Where did we get *opium* of all drugs, anyway? And we all got high as emperors and had a languorous three-day threesome with my former college roommate. Don't think for a moment that that wasn't mostly for you. I'm not actually really bisexual like I said I thought I was back then. When I fucked other women, even the ones I fucked without you around—you know what?—the only way I could really get off on it was to imagine a man watching. Male fantasy is a curved mirror that warps female fantasy. We are all at once bodies and mirrors, and our minds are the curves in the mirrors. And then there was that creepy couple we met on the Internet that one time—we went to their hotel room, they were visiting from Toronto—something funny about us fucking a couple of Canadian swingers—and that woman freaked out at you for not switching condoms. And she was right, Richard. What the fuck is the point of safe group sex if you take it out of me and put it right in her without switching condoms? *Think*, Richard. Richard and Rebecca had had an open relationship. Well, they were supposed to have had an open relationship. The whole *open* part necessitates that we tell each other when we fuck other people, doesn't it, Richard? It was supposed to mean no secrets, no lies, no jealousy, honest communication. That was the idea. Rebecca had thought it was working. The one thing I asked of you, Richard, is don't fuck your students. And you agreed to that. Yes, I took advantage of the open relationship a lot more often than you did. Could I help the fact that I was young and hot and you were such a fucking pussy? You never told me you didn't want to hear about it. You were with me when I had the job working for the phone sex line. It was the nineties, first Clinton administration, news about Bosnia on the TV, and Rebecca put on her husky honeydrip voice and got off strangers on the phone while Richard cooked paella or whatever for dinner. That was in the toddlerhood of the Internet, when it was still possible to make okay money working for a phone sex line. You were with me when I started working as a dominatrix. You even said you liked it. You helped me put up the website. You helped me pick out the name, you scholar of comparative religions, you. Rebecca had chosen the name Delilah for a range of reasons: The name sounded sexy, and the biblical reference was a private nod to her Jewish upbringing; she liked the nightmare labyrinth of misogynist connotations—Delilah the emasculator, the woman who renders the strongman weak with the snipping of scissors—the symbolic castrator. You said you *liked* the idea of me tying up and whipping other men. You said you liked to imagine me dominating other men when you slapped me around and shoved my head down to suck your cock . . . You even asked to watch that one time—with the Director, who fucking adored me, by the way—and I asked if he minded, and mind, hell, he *loved* the idea of my husband watching. That was fun, wasn't it? You sat there rubbing yourself through your jeans while I rammed my fake dick up his ass and that avant-garde theater director who's famous enough to have his own Wikipedia page now and who liked to be called sissyboy clutched the pillows and came like a woman. I told you *everything*. That was supposed to be the way it worked. You were the one who was hiding things. Or you were in the end, anyway—who knows what you successfully kept hidden. We know you kept it hidden that you were violating the only rules we had: (1) no outside relationships; (2) you don't fuck your students; and (3) no lying—all three of which you were doing. It's kind of funny how we thought we were going to have this freethinking bohemian marriage between a couple of people determined not to become another boring bourgeois couple with an interesting but dead past pushing one of those ergonomic mother-facing anti-autism strollers down Wyckoff Street—and yet, and yet, in the end, it all fell apart because of the most boring bourgeois reason imaginable. You had an affair and left me for a younger woman. Unoriginal, Richard. Tawdry. Gross. Predictable. Fucking *classic*. And now you've called me about something, and left a message. It's probably about the apartment, which is of no use to you as it sits around unsold on Avenue C not making you any money while I live in it. You want to sell it off for less than its current market value—and keep in mind we bought that place pre-gentrification and now it's worth almost twice as much and prices in the neighborhood are only going up—and you want to pocket the windfall and take it back to Connecticut with the grad student you cheated on me with and never have to see me again. Shove it up your ass, Richard, we will sell when I'm ready, and I'm not ready yet. And yes, I know I haven't yet returned your last message about it. You cannot fucking begin to fathom how unimportant that seems to me right now. I am in a very strange situation—a life-and-death situation (well, now it's just a death situation)—and I probably won't be getting back to you today.

Rebecca didn't know how much longer she could keep on doing this. She had been doing more pro-Domme work recently because she was short on money. She wasn't young anymore. She had relaunched her website last month. It had been dormant for years, as she hadn't needed it. She'd had the same roster of ten to fifteen clients for nearly a decade now, and they kept her in business. All the pictures on her site were taken six years ago. She was opening the door to new clients for the first time in a while. She was staring forty in the face. It stared back at her: her face. It was beautiful, but Venus in the mirror had deep laugh lines now, and two vertical creases in her forehead above the bridge of her nose. She hated looking at photos of herself from just five, six years ago—such as, for instance, the ones on her website. Mistress Delilah, specializing in whipping, caning, flogging, bondage (light or heavy), leather and/or latex fetish, foot fetish, anal femdom, face sitting, cock torture, pissing, edgeplay. She'd gotten Ike, the photographer who always gave her the friend discount, to take those newer pictures in his studio: corsets, wigs, masks, leather boots that laced up to the thighs . . . She looked gorgeous in them, and that was just six years ago. Was it false advertising to still be using those pictures? It wasn't an illusion: She had aged perceptibly in the last six years. Stress accelerates the effects of aging, doesn't it? And with the divorce, the apartment, the being broke, the Severin getting cancer, the hurtling childless and single toward menopause, the possibility of never getting to share the common experience that has united women since the days of goddamn pagan moon rituals and the Venus of Willendorf, for the last few years she had been pretty stressed out. There was a time, in her early twenties, when she looked at small children with confusion and maybe mild disgust—only mild disgust, the way you would look at something that is visually interesting but which you're not planning to touch, like a slug; they were cute things in the strollers that took up a lot of space on the subway, brief obstructions in the path of a young woman who was on her way to spend a night careening barefoot around Manhattan with her heels in her hands and eventually spill out of a cab at dawn, drunk and shaky with blow, to curl up in the arms of the fiancé who'd been dealing with his own demons all night. Later, when she was in her early thirties, and had been married a few years, her heart, to her own self-reflective annoyance, would gelatinize at the sight of an infant—the cooing, gurgling, finger-grabbing monkey-faced goblins with bright, smooth, smooth, smooth, soft skin that were beginning to emerge from her friends, she looked at them with warmth and tenderness . . . And now? The other weekend, she woke up at noon on Sunday, parked herself at the kitchen table to eat breakfast in front of her MacBook Pro, and when she looked up, the sun was setting and she had lost the entire day to YouTube videos of babies: a video of a baby being weirded out by a talking Elmo toy, a montage of babies tasting lemons for the first time, a montage of babies laughing hysterically, a baby laughing hysterically at a person jingling car keys, a baby laughing hysterically at herself tearing up a piece of paper, a baby laughing hysterically at an ice cube, a baby laughing hysterically at absolutely nothing, a video of a baby petting a cat, a video of a baby being petted by a cat, a video of twin babies in diapers flapping their hands and squawking at each other in their own strange made-up language, a video of two babies on a couch, holding each other and laughing, hysterically. Feeling like the false mother at the judgment of Solomon. Elohim! Yahweh! Let me conceive like Sarah at the age of ninety-nine! She was irritated at herself for feeling all this maternal yearning, in the same way she was irritated at herself for fantasizing about male fantasy, for getting off under the male gaze. One of the regular crazies who peregrinated Rebecca's chunk of the East Village between Tompkins Square Park and Stuy-Town was a woman with frazzled crazy-person hair bundled in ratty shawls who walked around in clogs all day, murmuring to herself and pushing a baby stroller full of broken baby dolls with clicking eyelids. The woman terrified her.

She'd voiced these complaints to Colin, her brother—her younger, her only brother—last time she was visiting their mother, in whose basement he dwelled with his lovingly hand-painted *Doctor Who* memorabilia. Colin!—five years younger than her at his still-virginal thirty-four. A lost cause, a lost soul, a lost child. Colin lives in the dark—sticky and pale like a grub, eating garbage, fearing sunlight, sleeping till noon, one, two, three in the afternoon on a soggy futon in the wood-paneled half-finished basement of that shabby split-level ranch house in Caldwell, New Jersey—the very same room in which she had eaten mushrooms and lost her virginity to her boyfriend at fifteen (and hell, he slept on the very same futon). There Colin lived with his eyes glued to the Internet, a man (strange as it sounded to call him that) who would likely leave little behind in the world but an exhaustively complete collection of *Doctor Who* and *Red Dwarf* figurines and a really impressive *World of Warcraft* Gear score. She had come to visit because her mother, long since divorced from her father, a long time alone, a long time lonesome, was in poor health, recovering from hip surgery. (Mom—why do you let Colin live like that? Why do you allow him to treat you like a live-in servant when you are old and frail, when *you* should be the one in bed, not doing his goddamn laundry and making him sandwiches for lunch, which you leave on the top step of the basement stairs for him to find when he gets up, as if feeding a troll?) Anyway. She'd sat with Colin in his moist underground lair, drinking most of a box of Mom's Chablis while he drank a liter of Mountain Dew, unloading her heart to what had become of the little boy whose hand she'd held on the way to his first day of school. And it was Colin, Dorito-munching amateur psychoanalyst who dwells in Mom's basement, to whom she confessed her anxieties about growing older alone, about the terrible dread she felt facing her imminent fortieth birthday. And you were so understanding, and so helpful, Colin, when you shrugged, and offered what I guess was the most reassuring thing you could think to say: "It's merely the accident of a base-ten number system." I think it was that "merely" that made me throw your fucking Dalek at you. I didn't mean to break it. I'm sorry. I love you. I wish I could help you, but you seem to be beyond help. In a way, your problems are worse than mine, even though sometimes it's hard to find sympathy for a thirty-four-year-old man whose sick and elderly mother washes his underwear.

4. Severin

Severin was dying. Severin was dying of cancer. Poor thing was only eleven—not that old for a dog. He was a shih tzu, a boutique breed notorious for chronic health problems. She was pretty sure he was mostly blind. He had respiratory issues, too—he grunted and grumbled, fighting for breath as he scuttled around the apartment, or lay in bed with her snoring like a jackhammer all night long: She'd grown to tune it out, while every boyfriend she'd had since Richard left had whined about never being able to get to sleep with this stinking, wheezing, farting, dying little dog curled into a ball at the foot of the bed making weird, gross, and for such a small animal, astonishingly *loud* noises. (No, not boyfriends—she hadn't had any boyfriends, only New York single men, who were all the same in the end: selfish, childish, spiritual weaklings, commitment-phobic assholes who wanted to fuck her occasionally but kept their distance wide enough to never be called anyone's boyfriend—say the word *boyfriend* and watch them skitter down the drainpipe like a roach when the light's flicked on.) Her sister, Liz—her much younger half sister from her dad's second marriage to the younger woman he left her mother for (boys will be boys, won't they?)—was watching Severin while Rebecca was out of town for the weekend, and even that much time away made her nervous. It wasn't an ordinary pet-sitting job: Severin had a daily regimen of medications he had to be tricked into taking that was as complicated as that of a dying human's, and came in the same tray of little plastic boxes labeled by the time of day they had to be given. They were supplementary to the chemo somehow, and Rebecca followed the vet's orders with religious obedience. No, Severin's hair didn't fall out—that doesn't happen with dogs in chemo for some reason—and yes, she had a shih tzu in chemotherapy, and if you just rolled your eyes at the idea of "wasting" money on chemotherapy for a shih tzu then fuck you, I don't care what you think. Have you never loved a dog? Have you never loved anyone? All her life Rebecca had given out love, and Severin was the one creature alive to which she gave her love who honestly and reliably and unconditionally gave it back.

Then she remembered she had gotten Severin at the same time she had met the Representative. Eleven years ago. She had not thought that Severin would outlive him. What had gone on between them in the last couple of years no longer felt like a performance she was being paid to give, but a mutual give-and-take between friends (they had always been equals), between almost lovers. In a certain way, they had loved each other. They were lovers who could do certain things with each other because they had started out without the usual invisible walls, the walls that are there when people meet each other in the "real world," out there in the wild, with all the complex uncertainties of sex and power and emotion unspoken and unsolved between them—the way it is between two people who are not sure, or who are afraid to say, exactly what it is they want from each other.

However, that simplicity, that clarity, had thrillingly, unsettlingly, gone away. This was not ordinary. This was not responsible. Rebecca had no other relationship like this with any other person who had begun as a client. The first time they'd had sex (ordinary, unadorned sexual intercourse) was two years ago—afterward it had felt to her deeply, inexplicably wrong, almost like incest. She could not forgive herself for a long time, and had refused to see him for months afterward. He had acted in an appallingly unprofessional manner, and she had not stopped him, which was appallingly unprofessional of her. She had allowed the boundary between them that had kept things simple to drop. He had flooded her voice mail with messages, sent her strings of increasingly desperate e-mails, sent her flowers. Eventually, she allowed him back. She had genuinely missed him. She missed his company. She missed his very genuine wit and charm, his warm, confiding conversation in the apartment, sitting around drinking wine after a session, or in one of the restaurants where he wasn't likely to be recognized. When she returned, something between them had changed forever. There was a new sense of intimacy between them; now they could never go back to the satisfying but emotionally safe relationship they'd had before. They had ruined one thing, and made something new, something else. They showed each other their souls as well as their bodies, and this was when he quit paying her. He still paid for her airfare, her meals, her drinks, her hotel room—everything extraneous that needed paying for—but this was when he quit paying her any money directly, and she never asked for it or expected it again. It was different, now. This became the new norm. Sometimes she would be in character as Mistress Delilah, and sometimes she was herself, Rebecca Spiegel. The Representative was in love with both women, but in very different ways. When they had ordinary sex—when she was Rebecca—she didn't wear her costumes: no corsets, no wigs, no whips or bondage or toys. They were two people naked in bed together in the most predictable arrangements:

an affair that was perfectly legal, but came with all the usual lies and complications of infidelity (on his part). Rebecca had quite recently realized that she had something with Sam (for that was the Representative's name) that she had never quite had with Richard.

A month earlier they had been in Rebecca's hotel room in The Fairfax. It was risky for Sam to be seen there, even by the desk clerks. It was after a session at the apartment. The risk was stupid, but they had wanted to have sex as Rebecca and Sam—without Mistress Delilah or the Representative around—and he didn't want to do it in the apartment, because he wanted to keep his fantasy sex life separate from his other sex life, which was in turn separate and kept secret from the rest of his life. (It was frightening how many lives Sam juggled.) When he came, she felt at once that the condom had broken. He pulled out, and they both looked down at the sleeve of latex with a broken flap loosening its grip around his softening penis. He had a sheepish, embarrassed look. In that moment, Sam, still breathing heavily after coming, naked in her bed in her hotel room, fat and white and growing old, on his knees with his cock retracting between his legs, looked helpless—less than ever like a powerful and influential and principled man, and more like a fragile adolescent boy who did not yet know himself. He began to stammer his way through saying he was clean as far as he knew, and, um, well.

"Don't worry," Rebecca had said. "I'll take care of it."

LOW PRIORITY

5. The secret

How did she come to be here?—sitting in this chair at the age of thirty-nine, not dead broke, but zero nest-egg in savings, single, growing older, wanting a child but having no one to have it with, and no career outside of sex work, which had always felt like a side career anyway. She'd never really planned on making a living off it. Mistress Delilah got her start back in the nineties, working in a fairly aboveground dungeon in TriBeCa—there were private rooms where things could get a little more intimate, but it was all low-grade stuff—mostly fantasy, role-playing. Nobody came; no fluids other than sweat and maybe a little blood were expurgated from anyone's body. It was all light whipping and caning, usually with sleazy Eurobeat crap blasting through the speakers. The place had a façade that made it clear what it was. It was a legitimate business, the building passed code. It was decorated to evoke a medieval castle (or something), black iron chains, fake stone walls, spooky candelabras dripping red wax: something about the aggressive fakery of the place she'd found distasteful. She felt the décor called attention to the fantasy rather than melding it with the real. The joint was even still there, though in a reduced state, one of the few true BDSM clubs that survived Giuliani's Disneyfication of Manhattan. Sometimes gawkers would come just to hang out at the bar and watch. After a year or so there she'd moved on to working at a much sketchier sex club, behind an unmarked metal door on a nondescript side street in Chinatown. You had to get buzzed in, and then push your way through two layers of black velvet curtains and down a set of stairs, then another door, where the guy who scrutinized you and then maybe let you in sat on a stool in the hall. That place had class, a sense of reality, of a little real danger. People really got hurt there. Not badly, of course, but there were definitely patrons who left with marks they would want to conceal with strategic clothing for at least a few days. She'd liked the aesthetic of the place: mirrors everywhere, red floors, all the furniture ornate and old-fashioned, fake Louis Quatorze chairs and tables—it had a very *Story of O* look. You had to know someone to get in. It was the kind of place where people who were hard-core into the BDSM scene went; you would never see a lifestyle tourist there. That was where Mistress Delilah started picking up her first private clients, and from there she set off on her own. She got Ike to take the first set of photos, got Richard to help her set up the website. That was how she'd met the Representative, through a referral from someone at the club who knew him. Back then he was getting ready to run for city council. He only met dominatrices in private sessions—he was too afraid to show his face at even the most secretive, discreet sex clubs. When Mistress Delilah did private sessions, she let her clients come. Usually not until the very end, due to the nature of the male orgasm, with its punctuative finality. But that was not usual. Those were the ones who made the most money—the ones who let their clients come. It was slightly dangerous: The involvement of an orgasm pushes the session into the gray area of what may or may not be prostitution. Legally, it's a hard thing to define. Sometimes she let a client see her breasts, or she would push her underwear aside to piss on the floor or a client's face, but she almost never took off any more of her costume than she began the session in. There was a foot fetishist she had who got off simply on giving her a foot massage and a pedicure. At the end of the session, she would relax in the recliner, wiggling her toes, tufts of cotton stuck between them, toenails freshly filed and lovingly painted valentine red, kissable as lips—why not let him come? Admiring his handiwork, that Goldman Sachs executive on his knees at her feet inhales the toxic sweetness of the drying nail polish and plants timid, delicate kisses on her feet while he masturbates with the feverish, trembling hands of a starving man fumbling with the cellophane packaging of a premade airport bagel sandwich. It had been a jarring contrast, to be pampered, adored, worshiped in this theatrical way by powerful men who paid her to let them do so, while at home, when Mistress Delilah was folded in the black bag in the closet and she was only Rebecca Spiegel, she was being taken for granted and lied to by her husband, treated like shit—treated merely (*merely*, Colin) like someone's wife. At times she wished she could step through the mirror's membrane where fantasy touches the fingertips of reality.

How did she come to be here? How was it that she was dressed in fishnet stockings, a garter belt, a leather corset, and a red wig, holding a creepy South African rhino-skin whip and sitting alone in a luxury apartment in Washington, D.C., with the dead body, which was naked except for the rope on his wrists and the nipple clamps still on his nipples, of a US congressman?

There was more. Rebecca had begun to experience an inexplicable feeling that she had never quite felt before. It was a vaguely pleasant feeling, and hard to describe: a warmth—a sense of calm she had not felt in a long time, if, in just this way, ever. For various reasons, she had not thought it likely, but suspicion had driven her to the drugstore down the block from her apartment, and earlier that day, she had met Sam for the first time with a secret of her own, one she very literally carried inside her. She had not yet made a decision. Until today, she had been leaning one way, and now, she was leaning another.

Rebecca thought again of her mother. Well, Mom, she said to her, so it goes. We don't plan to be disappointed. We don't plan to be betrayed. We both know that. Nobody plans to suddenly leave a lover with a body on her hands and the eyes of a watchful nation to face, to be seen by, to stand before naked, nude, on display, Venus looking back at them in the mirror, gazing at her gazers. They will not understand. You will not understand. We are all at once bodies and mirrors, and our minds are the curves in the mirrors.

Rebecca Spiegel went into the kitchen and picked up the phone.

BEAUTIFUL, BEAUTIFUL, BEAUTIFUL, BEAUTIFUL BOY

The Dakota, 1 West 72nd Street. Edward Cabot Clark, head of the Singer Sewing Machine Company, commissioned the building's design from architect Henry Janeway Hardenbergh; construction broke ground in Manhattan's then-undeveloped Upper West Side on October 25, 1880, and was completed four years later. Its layout and floor plan reflect French trends in interior design popular in New York City in the late eighteenth century, and its decorative exterior shows strong influence of North German Renaissance architecture: high gables, deep roofs, turrets, dormers, terracotta spandrels, panels, niches, and balconies with balustrades. Square-shaped and eight stories high, it fills the city block between Seventy-Second and Seventy-Third Streets on Central Park West, with a porte cochere leading to a courtyard that served as a turnaround for carriages. No two of the building's sixty-five luxury apartments are alike, as many of them were designed to the specifications of their first occupants, which would have included Edward Cabot Clark himself had he not died two years before construction was completed.

Soon after its construction it became a point of pride among New York high society to live in the Dakota, and it is still among the most exclusive and expensive addresses in Manhattan. Famous residents have included Leonard Bernstein, Lauren Bacall, Rosemary Clooney, Judy Garland, Lillian Gish, Boris Karloff, Jack Palance, and John Lennon and Yoko Ono.

One hundred years, one month, and thirteen days after construction on the Dakota began, Mark David Chapman spent most of December 8, 1980, waiting outside the building's gated south entrance on Seventy-Second Street between Columbus Avenue and Central Park West with a copy of *The Catcher in the Rye*, a Charter Arms .38 Special loaded with hollow-point bullets, and a copy of John Lennon and Yoko Ono's album, *Double Fantasy*, which had been released three weeks before. Around mid-morning, Chapman met Lennon's housekeeper, who was returning to the building from a walk with Lennon and Ono's only child together, Sean, who was then five years old. Chapman touched the child's hand and said, "Beautiful boy," quoting the song Lennon had written about his son, the final track on the first side of *Double Fantasy*. Around 5:00 P.M., Chapman met Lennon as he and Ono were exiting the building on their way to a recording session. Chapman silently handed him his copy of the album for an autograph; Lennon obliged and handed it back, saying, "Is this all you want?" Chapman accepted the autographed album, smiled, and nodded yes. At about 10:50 P.M., Lennon and Ono returned to the Dakota. Ono passed through the gate of the reception area leading into the courtyard, Lennon following a few steps behind her. From directly behind him, Chapman opened fire, discharging the revolver five times in quick succession. The first bullet missed and the other four landed in Lennon's back.

• • •

Derek Fitzsimmons spent most of December 8, 1980, sixty-six blocks south of the Dakota at the Sheridan Square Playhouse, in dress rehearsal for a production of Charles Ludlam's Ridiculous Theatrical Company's *Love's Tangled Web*, which Ludlam had written and was directing and starring in. Derek was twenty-four years old. He had graduated from the Fashion Institute of Technology a few years before, and was living with his boyfriend, Tom, in a studio apartment in Forest Hills. He was dressing the actors backstage at the Ridiculous, and performing small onstage roles in Ludlam's productions. Ethyl Eichelberger was in that production. He had met Ethyl earlier that year when he was doing wardrobe at the Lucille Lortel Theatre for a production of Caryl Churchill's *Cloud 9*. Ethyl had just moved back to New York from Rhode Island, where he'd been the lead character actor for seven years at Trinity Rep. When she came back to New York she changed her name from whatever it was before to Ethyl Eichelberger, and got a tattoo of himself as an angel on his back. That tattoo was somehow an important part of Ethyl's becoming Ethyl. Ethyl was only hired to make the wigs for that show at the Lucille, though she had already been in a few of Ludlam's Ridiculous productions, and was beginning to do her solo shows. They became friends backstage at the Lucille, and wound up working together often. They both performed in drag, and Ethyl invited Derek to perform in some of her shows. Ethyl was, though only for a brief time, a mentor to Derek.

Six months after John Lennon was assassinated, Derek was at Club S.n.A.F.U. on Sixth Avenue and Twenty-First Street, standing onstage while Ethyl did her Lucrezia Borgia show. Ethyl always beat him to the finish line in the dressing room. Derek's approach to his makeup was delicate and precise. He wanted every false eyelash in place. His lip liner looked machine-etched on. Derek would lose himself in the mirror, falling into his reflection like Narcissus: spacing out, spending fifteen minutes alone perfecting his foundation. Ethyl, eleven years his senior, found this fastidiousness of his silly and endearing—a mark of his youth and relative inexperience. Ethyl's drag aesthetic was decidedly old-fashioned, as far as it could be said that there are conservative schools of the art form. She found it distasteful that some of the younger drag queens seemed to really want to be able to pass for women, with their rubber breasts, worshiping at the style altar of Diana Ross. For Ethyl, the whole thing was supposed to be redolent of the circus, of Weimar Republic cabaret; he wanted a face painted halfway between clown and whore. Ethyl slapped her makeup on in twenty violent minutes: ghost-white foundation, that night, glittering triangles of gold eye shadow with metallic magenta streaks, false lashes like tarantula legs dragged through the black mud of her mascara, red lipstick she stabbed on in three bellicose jerks of the wrist.

Derek was emceeing that night. It was his job to introduce Ethyl, then simply stand back and become a living set piece as Ethyl turned the tiny stage into a lavish spectacle—pure *Satyricon*. Sometimes, before the show, Derek would open with his Rosemary—his first, and admittedly not his most tasteful, drag persona: Rosemary, the retarded Kennedy sister lobotomized by Dr. Walter Freeman and shamefacedly sequestered out of sight, drooling in a rocking chair and gazing vacant-eyed out of some attic window. Rosemary was a combination of a drag performance, a satire on moneyed Cape Cod, and a playground-quality retard act on the maturity level of why-are-you-hitting-yourself, and of course it brought the house down every time.

But on that night, he just did a short stand-up routine before introducing Ethyl. Derek was wearing drag he'd mostly made himself: a tight leather miniskirt and a sequin-spangled silver top with long shimmering tassels swishing down his thighs, sequined pumps that matched the top, chandelier-drop earrings, and his fussily done face of makeup. His hair was his own, long and blond, teased out and gelled up with egg white, scrambled atop his head in an early-sixties Brigitte Bardot sort of thing. He was *en costume*, as the obnoxious professional actors he and Ethyl had dressed at the Lucille Theatre would say. After nattering a while at the audience over a jungle of hoots and whistles, he retreated to the side of the stage and very nearly forgot that he himself was part of the show—albeit an ancillary part—and not a spectator, so riveting was Ethyl's Lucrezia.

Derek thought it appropriate that she changed her name to Ethyl, with that spelling, which reminded him of the technical suffix of a chemical: her performances were high-octane spectacles. Ethyl had begun doing these shows because he said he wanted to portray all the great ladies of the stage and history: Jocasta, Clytemnestra, Nefertiti, Medea. His Lucrezia Borgia had something to do with the infamous femme fatale of the Italian Renaissance, but even to call it a character study would be misleading: No two performances were alike, and they always involved half-improvised songs in which she accompanied herself on a big silly accordion that reminded Derek of *The Lawrence Welk Show*. Her repertoire was vast: song, dance, fire eating, cartwheels. Sometimes he would hire a set painter to paint the backdrop live while he performed, as he did that night.

When the show ended, the DJ put on a Chaka Khan song, "I'm Every Woman," and like a snake shedding a skin the ambiance of the night slid from performance space to dance party. S.n.A.F.U. was a galaxy of glitter and confetti in a black room that shimmered like outer space, and was as fantastic with alien life: feather boas, leather skirts, wigs, star-shaped sunglasses, boys in ball gowns and girls in pinstripe suits, those slender Audrey Hepburn cigarette holders, the night floating ever higher on champagne and amphetamines and a tremendous lot of cocaine and whatever else was around, strobe lights blitzing, the disco ball throwing spinning multicolored points of light all around. It was nights like these that Derek would later remember as the halcyon days, that flash-in-the-pan golden age of no more than a few years in the late seventies and early eighties between punk and the plague that came, pure Fellini in Technicolor, the sex and fun and wildness without restraint, without shame.

And out of this melee there came a woman. From amid that dazzling spectrum of genderfuck and drag there came a woman, dressed in women's clothing, floating like a ghost in Derek's direction—gliding—for she had the primly postured gait of a woman who had once been a little girl made to cross a room with a book balanced on her head. This woman looked as out of place as a Q-tip in a Crayola box at S.n.A.F.U. She was probably about thirty-five and very Waspy. She seemed to have stepped freshly powdered out of a garden party in the Hamptons. She was short; her impeccably groomed, naturally wavy brown hair was pulled up in a tortoiseshell clip that came up to Derek's midriff (though granted, Derek was five foot ten and in five-inch heels). She wore a starchy white blouse with puffed sleeves, pleated khaki trousers, tasseled Italian loafers, carried an Yves Saint Laurent handbag. All terribly soigné. Thin white-gold bangles trembled on her slender wrist and caught glints from the disco ball as her bony fingers rose and indicated Derek's outfit, waving without quite pointing up and down his body, and she said, in a feathery voice scarcely audible over Chaka Khan: "I like . . . *this*."

She came closer, and Derek suddenly felt like he was meeting someone else's mother at a wedding. She held her hand out to him, not vertically, like a salesman about to make his elevator pitch, but horizontally, as if inviting one to kiss it. Derek took the little hand in his—this tiny, perfect hand with tiny, perfectly manicured, lightly blush-colored nails—and did not shake it so much as simply hold it for a moment, soft, cool palms brushing smoothly together. She introduced herself to him as Marianne.

They talked. Her voice was deft and quiet and her speech grammatical, softly chiming with years of education and centuries of wealth.

"I would very much like for you to come to my home to have your picture taken," she said. Marianne spoke with a hint of that upper-class East

Coast accent that was dying out it seemed even then, what used to be called the Transatlantic accent. That voice reminded Derek of Agnes Moorehead from *Bewitched*. (Thank God he hadn't done Rosemary that night.) "I do portraiture, you see, and I am very interested in photographing entertainers."

Entertainers—that was the word she used. Not drag queens, not cross-dressers, but "entertainers." Did she use this gossamer euphemism out of timorousness or politeness? Or some other reason?—some upper-crust noblesse oblige sort of decorousness, which Derek certainly knew about but was not overly familiar with. Derek was the second-to-last of seven children from a blue-collar Irish Catholic family in Poughkeepsie. His had been a childhood of hand-me-downs, burnt steak and baked potatoes, fiercely measured portions at mealtimes. His father died of a heart attack when he was nine, and after that his sisters raised him and his mother wore a green dress and drank herself to sleep on the couch in the afternoons. One of his older sisters was a nun now, and to her, Derek was not an "entertainer," nor even a "drag queen," but a sinner, and to his older brothers, he was a freak, a pervert, a queer, a faggot.

A card materialized between his fingers, the apparition vanished, and the night roared into oblivion. The many points of light spun around the room and became a vortex of streaks, smooth horizontal lines of color and whiteness, flashes of fake diamonds and the orange tips of cigarettes. Even here there was a hint of money in the air, or of carelessness, at any rate. Money: the ailment and panacea of the eighties, the real drug we should have said no to. Reagan had told us we had it, and we liked to hear that. Everyone did, including drag queens in squalid basement bars on Sixth Avenue and Twenty-First Street. Derek's memory of that night would fade around three or four in the morning and come back to him when Sunday's dishwater light of about noon slanting in through venetian blinds on a window in his friend Scott's East Village apartment woke him. He was naked and looking directly at Scott's pillow, which he had smeared with the makeup he hadn't removed before bed. Scott was still snoring as Derek picked his things off the floor, and when he made it back to the dingy studio in Forest Hills he shared with Tom, he discovered he had miraculously retained that card. It was a stark beige rectangle of starchy, quality stock, with a name and phone number in crisp gold lettering, and an address, at the Beresford on the Upper West Side. With the card in hand, he sank a finger into a plastic hole in the rotary dial of his bedside telephone and fought back an apprehension tightening his throat that surprised him.

The Beresford, 211 Central Park West. With one hundred and seventy-five apartments, this preeminent prewar landmark is the largest of four luxury residential buildings on Central Park West designed by the notable Hungarian-American architect Emery Roth, who decorated the massive structure with then-fashionable beaux-arts and art deco flourishes of style. The Beresford stands twenty-three stories tall between Eighty-First and Eighty-Second Streets, with three separate entrances, and four copper-capped towers. The building provides sweeping layouts with ballroom-sized rooms, ten-foot ceilings, wood-burning fireplaces, and private elevator landings. Its mass is relieved by horizontal belt courses in the masonry and features detailing reminiscent of late Georgian facade work. In the late eighteenth and early nineteenth centuries, the advent of steel frames gave rise to skyscrapers, and the citizens of New York, finding themselves living increasingly in shadows, passed the 1916 Zoning Resolution, which outlawed tall buildings from blocking air and light to the streets below; this resulted in Beresford's expansive setbacks, with fifty-foot-wide flagstone terraces overlooking Central Park. Thus, the higher-up apartments on the building's east-facing side are among the most expensive and prestigious residences in New York City.

Derek was curious to see the inside of it.

• • •

Derek stood before a doorman in a stately lobby of gold-veined white marble, Derek in jeans and a T-shirt with his long hair knotted loosely in a ponytail and a sparkly purple foil dance bag slung over his shoulder and sagging at his waist, watching the elderly man in his bottle-green uniform with brass buttons murmuring into a desk phone. The doorman's uniform, with its symmetrical and military ceremoniousness, reminded him of a Christmas nutcracker, an impression helped by the deep-creased jowls that made his chin look separately attached to his face by hidden hinges. Derek had agonized over what to bring. He had figured Marianne would be interested in seeing a few costume changes, so he had brought along as much of the best of his best as would fit in the bag. Lots of makeup, brand-new silver stiletto sandals, the leather miniskirt he'd had on at S.n.A.F.U. the night Marianne had introduced herself to him, jewelry, hairspray, a navy-blue top he'd also made himself, which he called his Balenciaga top because of the way he'd cut it—it had ruffles at the bust, and a wonderful way of swinging out in back.

The doorman hung up the phone, smiled, gestured him toward the elevator bank. He rode the elevator with an elevator man dressed in a bottle-green uniform similar to the doorman's. The three walls of the elevator that were not doors were floor-to-ceiling mirrors, creating an illusion of the infinite, Derek's and the elevator man's reflections diminishing into the distance on either side of them. The doors opened onto a small private hallway with a coatrack. There was only one door in it, which was open, and Marianne was standing on its threshold.

Marianne ushered him inside with a courtly "Good afternoon," and in a moment he was standing in the most luxurious interior space he had ever stood in. Marianne was at his elbow in an outfit similar to what she had been wearing at S.n.A.F.U.—her hair up, the sleeves of her beige silk blouse rolled up, houndstooth wool trousers, and a thin braided leather belt. She would probably have offered to take his coat had he been wearing one. He wasn't, as it was late May: It was humid and overcast outside, a dull, dark day, but warm and sticky, the heavy sort of atmosphere that begs for rain all day and doesn't get it until dinnertime, and then steam rises from the hot streets when the downpour finally splashes them. She didn't have many lights on, which contributed to the melancholy mood in the vast apartment. They stood in a circular foyer; under their feet was a classic compass design of black-and-white marble. She led him in and around, in and around, deeper into the apartment, apologizing all the while for the mess, Derek half-beside and half-behind her, half listening to her and half ogling their surroundings. She was explaining, in her trim patrician accent, that her husband, Ken, was an architect, and that he had designed the apartment's renovation himself, and they were just now moving in and putting on the finishing touches. Derek would remember that thick, sleepy smell of wet paint: Everything was freshly done, immaculate, not yet lived in. There were no workmen in the apartment that afternoon, but there were signs here and there of unfinished jobs that someone soon intended to come back to: a paint-speckled ladder, plastic drop cloths, power tools. Unopened cardboard boxes were stacked up in some of the rooms. Most of the rooms had furniture in them, but all the Louis Quatorze tables and chairs seemed to be floating aimlessly in the middle of the parquet and marble floors, awaiting someone's decisions on where they would go. He saw a Chagall painting in a recessed frame leaning against a living room wall, waiting to be hung.

He followed Marianne as she glided across spotless floors that reflected almost as crisply as a mirror. Derek quickly got lost in the space. He'd been in the apartment less than five minutes, and already, if he'd been asked to find his way back to the door he couldn't have done so. He would remember lots of rounded shapes, lots of moldings, lots of warm, pale colors: ecru, apricot, champagne. She led him in and around, in and around: living room, dining room, hallway, another living room, another hallway . . . and finally, into a bathroom. This bathroom was, it may be said without hyperbole, more spacious by the square foot than Derek and Tom's apartment. Everything blinding white marble: his and hers sinks, toilet, bidet, tub, one of those giant showers you can sit down in, which blasts water at you from the sides as well as from above. The bathroom had an adjoining dressing room—a boudoir, he supposed, with a large vanity table. It was a gorgeous piece—Derek guessed it was something late nineteenth century and French. Three wide mirrors winged out in triptych, their silvered surfaces faintly veined with age. The surface of the table was, what was it called?—*ormolu*—finely gilt with a coating of high-carat gold.

Marianne gestured toward this museum-quality piece of neoclassical furniture and said, "Please. Do what you do." And then, "Would you like a drink?"

Derek would not remember what he said then, if anything, but Marianne floated out of the room and a while later floated back in again with a Campari on the rocks in a crystal lowball, in which time Derek had unzipped his sparkly purple foil bag and spread his makeup across the vanity, undressed, and slipped on his pantyhose. He would wear one pair of nude pantyhose to cover the hair on his legs, and then his fancy hose—that day it was a pair of stretchy powder-blue fishnet stockings that he rolled on very carefully, as they ripped easily. He began to put on his makeup. The whole apartment was as hushed as a library, the deft clickings of Derek opening and shutting his compacts or popping the cap off a mascara brush the only audible sounds in it. Derek's own face looked strange to him in the three antique silver mirrors, as if he'd just taken some hallucinogen whose effect he was feeling but hadn't started tripping yet. His downmarket makeup—all his little drugstore compacts and cheap Brucci lipsticks—looked so absurdly out of place rolling around on Marianne's ormolu vanity table.

So he sat barechested in pantyhose and fishnet stockings at the vanity, sipped his glass of Campari, a tinkling red liquid with a spiral of lemon rind in it, and painted his face.

"If you don't mind, I should like to begin," said Marianne.

"Oh? No, I don't mind at all," he must have said.

As he leaned into the mirrors and worked on his face, he began to hear the mechanical snips of an aperture opening and shutting, opening and shutting. He glanced up in the mirror and saw the neat little woman hovering behind him, her face hidden by a big, black, expensive-looking camera—the most masculine object in the room.

Derek had already been photographed this way many times. All these photographers seemed to love shooting you as you were getting ready, capturing the transition from male to—not female, exactly, but whatever it was on the other side. Drag, for Derek, was not an imitation of the feminine, but its own third category. Derek had done so many of these in-transition shoots. Every photographer seemed proud of the idea, confident no one had done it before. Derek had begun to find them tiresome. Every goddamn fashion photographer he had met liked to think of himself as David Hemmings in *Blow-Up*, barking *yes!* and *no!* at you as you did your best Vanessa Redgrave, writhing around on the studio floor. He had begun to feel queasy about it. Something lurid or voyeuristic about how those photographers loved shooting you in half drag. There is a photograph of Ethyl this way, curled in a bathtub somewhere in the East Village. He's wearing a kind of crenulated tutu, his fishnet stockings—the old-fashioned kind, you can tell by the line in the back of the leg—and an impractical pair of six-inch pumps Derek knew he cherished (and would years later remember him shuffling onto the stage in with tight little baby steps, a six-foot-three beanpole under his towering Marie Antoinette wig and polka-band accordion). He doesn't have any trademark wig on, just his own nearly shaved bare head and wild wings of makeup around his eyes, the angel tattoo visible on his bare back, failing to look comfortable in that cramped bathtub, not smiling, but almost sneering. Derek's favorite touches in that photo are the half-visible studio portrait of Ethyl hanging above him in the background, and the drink balanced on the rim of the tub, probably likewise given him presession by the photographer. Every drag queen in the early eighties got photographed in a bathtub at some point.

But with Marianne, he didn't mind. There was very little bluster about this quiet, tiny, middle-aged woman in slacks and slippers who floated around him as he applied his makeup, so quiet he nearly forgot she was there, concentrating, completely losing himself, as he always did, in the mirror. Coral lipstick, electric-blue eye shadow that more or less matched the color of his stockings, rouged cheeks, Cleopatra eyeliner that swept out in elegant strokes of black. When he finished with his face, he strapped on his open-toed silver stiletto sandals and his chandelier-drop earrings. They were real crystal teardrop beads from an old chandelier, mismatched (that was part of their charm), and so heavy they had to be kept on by a wire that curled around the back of the ear. (Ethyl had taught him that trick.) Derek stood to go fishing in his bag for his leather miniskirt, but Marianne lowered her camera and beckoned to him from the doorway.

"If you don't mind, I'd like to photograph you just as you are right now."

Derek shrugged, took his drink, and followed.

The gray afternoon outside the windows suffused the palatial black-and-white rooms in soft pale light. Derek followed Marianne as she looked around the apartment for a good place to shoot him. The spikes of his stilettos made a racket on the parquet floors, echoing solemnly around the half-moved-into apartment.

"I would like it if you would just—just lie down. Right here."

She gestured toward a smooth circular curve in the ivory-colored paneled hallway. It was just a little niche, an architectural hiccup of space between rooms. Derek guessed when the apartment was fully moved into they might put a marble table there with a vase on it or something. The curved wood was what Derek would remember. He'd heard somewhere about the process of making a curved piece of wood like that, how you warp it with steam. There was a round silk carpet on the floor, and he would remember the soft smooth coolness of it against his back and chest and arms as he lay down on it in a fetal position as Marianne instructed him to do, a position much like Ethyl in that bathtub. The royal-blue rug was as soft and silky as a kimono, with a pattern of vines or birds on it. Marianne stood over him, her face behind the camera.

"I love the way your body looks," she said in a near whisper.

Derek writhed around on the floor in slow motion, conforming the contours of his body to the curved white wood.

"Please just move your head," said Marianne.

Obeying her command, Derek quit his full-body squirming and just held still in the pose she wanted, moving his head around. Up, down, side to side, toward her, away from her. In the silence punctuated only by the camera clicks, Derek became acutely conscious of the sound of his own breathing. He looked around at the Escheresque intersection of rooms they were in, at the high ceilings and lighting fixtures, out the windows, which he could see were thinly streaked with the light rain that had broken and was softly pattering the Beresford. He moved his head and looked around at things, and the camera snipped and clacked, followed by the ratcheting sound of Marianne pulling back the lever that advanced the film, followed by a long pause—and then another snip and clack. She went out for a moment and wiggled a stepladder in from another room, climbed it a few steps, and shot downward at Derek as he looked up at her from the floor. The camera snipped and clacked.

"Thank you," she whispered.

Derek felt a head rush as he finally stood, a tingling of blood, a little sore from lying on the floor. He started off toward what he guessed was the direction of the dressing room, to go get *en costume* in his leather skirt and homemade Balenciaga knockoff. But a feeling made him turn back, to see Marianne putting away her camera equipment, and he realized that "Thank you" meant good-bye. That was all she wanted.

As a child, Derek had mistaken the black spiral in the opening sequence of James Bond movies for a camera aperture rather than a gun barrel. It was not such a far-flung mistake: What is more symbolic of espionage—a gun or a camera? There is a kinship between the two machines. For one, both are "shot." There is a dialogue between them as symbols. The camera is a hidden eye, whereas a gun is an element of positive space, a protrusion, male. A camera is negative, a hole, a trap. The silhouette of a man saunters into the viewfinder, stops, swivels, and fires directly into the camera, blinding us, the counterspies, the voyeurs, with our own blood.

A couple of weeks later Marianne invited him back to a party at her apartment.

"The apartment is finally done," that quiet voice said through the honeycomb of holes in the plastic receiver. Derek was lying in bed in the early evening, very high on hashish, carefully dipping Chips Ahoy! in blueberry yogurt and trying to eat them without getting crumbs on his sheets. Derek was in a state of limbo: Tom would be out all night at his bartending job, and Derek was in want of company, but unfortunately he'd already made himself way too high to leave the apartment.

"Ken and I are having a few friends over," the phone said. "It's a housewarming of sorts, I suppose."

"Mn?" he said. "Oh, sure. Why not?"

It could have been a paranoid note from the hash bubbling in his nerves, but he sensed a question lurking behind the invitation, possibly a sexual one. These were days of widespread experimentation; Derek had been on the balcony at Studio 54, and was well versed in threeways with straight couples. Which he didn't mind, necessarily, but in any case, as a sort of buffer, he invited Scott along to the party. Tom knew Derek occasionally had sex with Scott. They weren't "supposed to," as they were both in relationships with other people, but again, these were days of widespread experimentation. He knew Tom had his own dalliances. Sometimes Derek would feel a wave of guilt, and would say to Tom, "You know, um, I think we really ought to be monogamous." To which Tom would say, "Yes, I think you're right about that, yes, absolutely." And two nights later Derek would be putting on his jacket with his hand on the doorknob, saying, "Oh, I'm just going over to Scott's to watch *Dallas*."

(Well, Scott actually did like *Dallas*. Derek didn't. He never watched *Dallas* and never spent a second of his life wondering who shot J.R.)

Scott and Derek climbed out of the Eighty-First Street subway station and into the early summer night. It was the time of year when everyone is still joyfully surprised that the sun is setting so late in the evening, later every day, meaning only more summer to come. The sky was in what photographers call the golden hour; the faces of the buildings glowing like, well, ormolu, and the shadows of the skyscrapers were long across Central Park. Derek was wearing sandals, a faded black T-shirt with a neckline he'd roughly cut out to bare one shoulder, and red Zouave pants tied at the waist with a knotted sash. He loved wearing those pants, especially in warm weather, all that breezy fabric billowing around his legs. Minimal makeup that night—eyeliner, red nail polish, and a touch of glitter on his temple and on his exposed shoulder. He was wearing iridescent dragonfly-wing earrings, and his hair was pinned up but loosely falling about his face in a couple of well-placed tendrils that he'd coiled a few times with the curling iron. Altogether his outfit was a little genderfucky, but certainly not drag. He wasn't trying to look like a girl. He never tried to look like a girl. He didn't want to look like a girl, and he didn't want to look like a boy—but simply something other. Not even something in between. Just something else.

Marianne was standing in the marble compass-rose foyer with her husband, Ken, greeting the guests, proper host and hostess. Ken was an attractive man—older than her, about forty, forty-five, maybe, and imposingly tall. So this was the architect. He wore a genuine smile and didn't seem to talk much, was balding but well built, with eyebrows as white-blond as hoarfrost and kind but arresting blue eyes. He wore khakis and a blue blazer. He had that aura of worldliness architects often have—Derek wouldn't have been surprised to learn Ken had a passion for sailing, or had climbed Mount Kilimanjaro. Marianne was in her usual elegant but restrained attire. Pearls, that night. Derek introduced Scott, shook Ken's large hand, lowered himself to Marianne's face for kisses on cheeks.

Scott was jittery for the bar, and hunting for a drink he quickly disappeared into the fabric of the party, thereafter abandoning Derek for most of the night. Derek would remember emerging into the living room without anyone to lean against socially, Scott already gone and Marianne occupied in the foyer with her husband: that initial lost feeling of walking into a party at which the other guests know one another well, but no one knows you. It wasn't a big party—though granted, one would have to invite quite a lot of people to make that apartment feel crowded. There were maybe thirty people or so, most of them older than Derek, closer to Marianne's and Ken's ages. The apartment had been transformed. If it was impressive when Derek had seen it not quite finished a couple of weeks ago, now it was nothing short of majestic. Everything was in its place: pictures on the walls, furniture all in position. It was complete. The sky had begun to turn purple, and the windows were open to the warm summer night, as were tall French doors that led onto a terrace overlooking the park, and a magnificent breeze blew transparent voile curtains back into the rooms. Somehow a flute of champagne came to be in Derek's hand. Truly, it was a lovely evening. That breeze blew the sheer curtains around, there was laughter here and there, cocktail glasses clinking and chiming, kisses on cheeks, soft conversation. Derek stood by an open window holding his glass of champagne, a line of golden bubbles as thin as a necklace chain ascending to its surface from the stem where he held it, and he looked out at night falling across Central Park from the twenty-third floor of the Beresford. *Double Fantasy* was playing, and he would remember that, too. *Double Fantasy* was playing at many cocktail parties in the summer of 1981, but this one was playing at a cocktail party on the Upper West Side, ten blocks away from where John Lennon had been shot six months before, at a stately, named apartment building similar to the one he was standing in. Lennon sang: "Beautiful, beautiful, beautiful . . . beautiful boy." It was a disquieting feeling to be living now in a world in which a Beatle was dead. Derek had guessed Marianne was in her midthirties, which put the year of her birth sometime in the late forties, right in the generational crosshairs to be someone for whom the Beatles had truly changed the world: She could have been one of those shrieking teenage girls waiting on the runway at what used to be Idlewild Airport, but had then recently been renamed JFK in the shadow of his assassination (death beatifies). To Derek, the Beatles had never been anything new, but something that simply played in the background of his growing up, as it now played in the background at this party. He had not imagined it would be so soon that he would be listening to this particular dead man's voice. He liked the album. But to listen to that album on the Upper West Side in the summer of 1981 was not just listening to music, but a table rapping, a séance. It was an album of love songs, unexpectedly sweet and guileless ones, without Lennon's usual cast of irony, that drop of venom that made his songwriting so much darker and meaner than McCartney's. And now these love songs had become haunted. The voice of a man who had recently been murdered sang: "Beautiful, beautiful, beautiful . . . beautiful boy." Death beatifies.

It took Derek a little while to realize that many of the people at the party were very ordinary (some of them very large) men who were dressed in women's clothing.

It wasn't drag at all: They were simply wearing women's clothing. They were *en costume* as women who had just come from their jobs at a law firm, or an advertising agency, or perhaps they had picked up their children from school that afternoon. They were wearing conservative, pedestrian outfits: navy-blue polyester skirts with little matching jackets, shoulder pads, salmon-pink pantsuits, ruffled silk blouses with bows on them, sensible, low-heeled pumps, pearl chokers, thick black tights. They wore wigs styled in pageboys and bob cuts and whatnot.

Marianne was at his elbow, introducing him to someone. Hands were stuck out to be shaken. He was introduced to a man named Bill in a mousey-brown curly wig. Bill wore an indigo dress with white polka dots, and a little gold woman's watch on his thick, hairy wrist.

"This is my wife, Margaret," said Bill, lightly putting a proprietary hand on the back of the woman who stood beside him, similarly attired.

As they stood there in that opulent apartment with their drinks, Derek looked around at Bill and Margaret and Marianne, and at the other men around them, at their wigs and skirts and dresses, their makeup. Bill's makeup was of a perfunctory sort, appropriate for the office: lipstick, a little powder and mascara, a hint of rouge on the cheeks. It was poorly applied—he could tell Bill really didn't know anything about the craft of applying makeup. The lipstick spilled over the lines, and his foundation didn't quite match his skin tone. He had probably borrowed his wife's makeup. These men were not trying to be beautiful—they were only trying to be female. But not even that, exactly. There are drag queens who change completely when in drag—an inside-out mental, physical transformation. The voice changes, as do the mannerisms. You instinctively do things such as examine your nails by looking at the back of the hand, with fingers outstretched, instead of looking at the palm with the fingers curled in, the way a man does. Bill was *en costume*, but not *in persona* as a woman. The blue polka-dotted dress he wore had pockets, and the hand that didn't hold his drink he kept casually sunk in one of them as they chatted. Men and women mingled together, couples, friends, some of the men in men's clothing, but most of the men dressed in their pedestrian women's clothing. No one did or said anything that indicated they even noticed anything unusual at all was happening.

He was introduced to another guy, whom he wound up talking to for much of that evening. The man stuck out a hand in an elbow-length black satin glove and said in a deep voice, "Hi, I'm Cathy."

He had a good, strong handshake. He was a tall, squarish man in a houndstooth skirt and a puffy silk blouse the faintly yellowish color of a white key on a very old piano. He wore black hose and white peep-toe slingbacks he must have thought matched the blouse, a quiet string of pearls, and a wig of waxy black hair in a China-chop style, chin length on the sides with straight, tight bangs, like Louise Brooks.

"Beautiful place, isn't it," said Cathy. Derek noticed that Cathy had missed a spot shaving that day; there was a line of tiny mustache hairs just under his nostrils.

"Oh, yes," said Derek. "It's gorgeous."

"Ken did all this himself," said Cathy. "Really dynamite work. Ken is a detail-oriented kind of guy. There's a guy who sweats the details. I can imagine the hell he must have put the contractors through."

It turned out that Cathy was also an architect, a friend of Ken's from "way back," as she put it, "way *way* back."

"This is her virgin voyage," said Cathy. "This little soirée is Ken's way of showing off his work, you know. And it's damned impressive work, I'll say that."

They stood in the apartment and talked about the apartment. Somehow, Cathy fell into taking him on a tour of this apartment neither of them lived in, which Cathy in fact was seeing for the first time and Derek was not. Cathy pointed things out to him, talking about how such and such a detailing element was constructed. Derek glazed over a bit, drinking but trying not to let himself get drunk, finding himself on the receiving end of a lot of prattling straight-guy *explanations* of things. The difference between Greek and Italian marble, things like that. The apartment looked so different from the last time he'd seen it that he couldn't be sure whether or not it was the same place where Marianne had shot him, but it was that same smoothly curved wall that Cathy ran his satin-gloved hand across while explaining how this was done, how they steam the wood to get that curve.

"Damned impressive work," said Cathy, again, for emphasis.

It was fully night, now. People were laughing and smoking on the terrace with the city glittering all around and below them, everyone milling about, waves of people moving through one another. He watched Marianne moving around the rooms, gracious hostess making sure all her guests were enjoying themselves, lightly touching backs and elbows and shoulders, gliding across the radiant parquet and marble floors. She moved so quietly, so elegantly. If there were a pencil attached to her head she could have drawn a straight line across a wall. She reminded Derek of those bar games where you push the stick and the little hockey player moves across the ice: She moved as if she didn't have feet, as if her body rolled along a fixed track in the floor. She was such a serene human being.

Scott had vanished to who knows where, leaving Derek on his own to make it from the Upper West Side all the way back to his shitty apartment in Forest Hills, which would mean spending at least an hour drunk on several subway cars and platforms in his sandals and Zouave pants and eyeliner, and it was getting late. It would involve a lot of kissy faces and fag-bashing from gangs of teenagers to be resolutely walked past, through, away from. Not the safest prospect, but he'd done it before, and what else could he do?

So when Cathy offered him a ride, of course he took her up on it. Cathy had mentioned that she lived in, what was it?—Connecticut? Some tony exurb of New York—Greenwich, perhaps—to which he would be driving home over the series of tolled bridges that would bear him back to a gabled Tudor colonial, to wife and children and dog and cat.

It was hardly out of her way, said Cathy; she didn't mind dropping him off at all.

People were collecting their spouses and jackets and purses, slowly filtering toward the door. Cathy, with her blouse and satin gloves and China-chop bangs, excused herself to the restroom, where she was gone for a very long time. Perhaps she was in that same enormous white marble bathroom with the adjoining dressing room, with that nineteenth-century French ormolu vanity table on which Derek's cheap cosmetics had looked so hilarious a couple of weeks earlier. Derek was talking with the host and hostess on a couch in one of the living rooms as the party wound down around them, waiting for his ride. Ken was sitting in the corner of the couch with a leg crossed, holding a half-drunk Old Fashioned on his knee, looking on with comfort and a gentle aura of ownership (Derek by now suspected Ken was wearing lingerie under his clothes) as Marianne perched beside him, depressing the white couch cushions just as much as if she were made of air, Derek nodding along as she talked, trying not to reveal that he had drunk too much. She had the floppy black-and-white contact sheets from their session in her bony little hands, was telling Derek he could come back and have any prints from the shoot he wanted. He would never take her up on the offer. It wasn't because he didn't care, but because he never sufficiently got his shit together for long enough to make that long subway journey back to Eighty-First and Central Park West, and the more time and silence he let pass, the more his embarrassment grew, and the greater became the courage it would have required to pick up the phone and get back in touch with her. Many years later—years after most of his friends had died, and years after he had gotten sober—a friend would call and tell him she thought she saw his picture hanging on a wall in the Bowery Bar. It wasn't a far walk from his apartment in the East Village anyway, and out of curiosity he went in and scanned the walls until he found it. And there he was, nearly thirty years ago, twenty-four, in fishnet stockings and sparkly silver stilettos, makeup, chandelier-drop earrings, and nothing else, lying in a fetal position against the curved white wall on that blue silk rug (which you can't tell because the picture is in black and white). It only has her name credited on it, and the date: 1981. Derek was one of the ones who would survive the years that followed the shutter that opened and closed on that image. AIDS wasn't even called that yet. It didn't have a name. It was only a dark rumor that most people mistrusted. Ethyl would fire him soon after that picture was taken. Despite his calculated ridiculousness, Ethyl was a very serious performer. He didn't want anyone involved with his act who had problems with drinking or drugs, which naturally soon came to preclude Derek from performing with him. They lost touch afterward, though he bumped into her occasionally, and sometimes went to her shows. He saw her at Charles Ludlam's funeral in 1987, which he attended in drag. They chatted awhile outside the funeral home, Derek having swept aside his netted black veil to smoke a cigarette. Ethyl would die three years later. A suicide, but he had AIDS too. He was on AZT, the only drug available then, and it ravaged his body. He was starving and going blind. Ever the control freak, Ethyl was unwilling to wait for the disease to kill him. Derek heard he had died from Black-Eyed Susan, who had acted with the Ridiculous and still kept in touch with Ethyl. She'd found him in the apartment he was sharing with a roommate in Staten Island. "He slit his wrists like an old Roman in the bath," Susan had said. That phrasing he would remember: "like an old Roman in the bath." She saw Ethyl, emaciated and naked, lying in a bathtub in Staten Island, blood marbling the water, swirling about his body. *Exit Ethyl.* Death beatifies.

Cathy returned from the bathroom, and it took Derek a moment to recognize her. Or him. It was the man beneath the Cathy. He had removed his perfunctory secretary makeup, and his wig, and changed out of his skirt, hose, heels, gloves, pearls, and blouse. He was a tall and blandly handsome man with short blond hair, dressed in a tucked-in yellow Lacoste polo shirt with the little alligator over the heart, khaki shorts, and boating shoes with no socks. He carried an oversized gym bag, which must have contained Cathy. It looked as if he were coming out of the locker room after a tennis match.

They bid good-bye to Marianne and Ken, then rode the mirrored elevator to the lobby. He was parked on the street, not far from the Beresford. He stuffed the gym bag into the trunk of his gold Buick, and they got in. Ken drove them through the park and over the Fifty-Ninth Street Bridge out to Queens. The night was still warm and the windows were rolled down. Wind roared in the car, and behind them the blue and yellow lights of Manhattan on a crisp clear night were mirrored upside down in the East River. There wasn't much conversation in that car, in part because it was loud with the windows open, and in part because of something else. At first Derek's aim had been to make it home without getting propositioned, but he sensed an alteration in the mood between them that told him Cathy was completely uninterested in him sexually. They had been chatting quite a bit at the party, and Derek had very lightly flirted with him, as Cathy—but now, they were only a gay man and a straight man who didn't know each other very well in a car together. The man's left arm hung out the window, resting on the side of the door, and his right hand was on the wheel; Derek's hands were in his lap. The space between them had become awkward and stilted. He had learned the man's name by then, but wouldn't remember it: It was something like Chuck, or Charles, or Chase. Chase seemed to fit him, anyway. In striving after things to talk about, they wound up in desultory intervals of conversation discussing the various neighborhoods of Queens, the tennis stadium, the Unisphere in Flushing Meadows. He seemed comfortable talking about buildings and landscaping and things like that—those concrete, emotionally neutral subjects that straight men gravitate toward in conversation, the histories and properties of things. Well, a certain kind of things. There are of course feminine things, such as makeup and chandelier-drop earrings, and there are masculine things, such as buildings and machines. One thing Derek would remember about the 1980s was that there seemed to always be a great deal of the discussion of things going on. Stick and carrot, yearning and having, desire and possession.

Derek tried to draw personal information out of him—gently, not wishing to pry, but spurred ahead by frustrated curiosity. What had been bizarre to him was seeing drag that was somehow still inside the box of heterosexual gender relations. This man was not gay. Chase did not want to fuck him. His offer of a ride home was just him being friendly. Derek asked if he was married.

"Uh-huh," said Chase. "The Big Ten's coming up this fall."

"Do you have children?"

"Uh-huh. Two. A girl and boy."

By this time they'd come off the highway, and the Buick was idling in front of Derek's squat, cheap apartment building on Jewel Avenue. The odds of ever seeing this man again felt low, and perhaps that was what prompted him at last to just ask him directly.

"What does—" Derek faltered. His hand was on the door handle, and it was late. "What about Cathy? What does your wife think about her?"

"Oh, no. She doesn't know anything about that."

"Oh? She thinks you're—?"

"At a club."

"A club?"

"You know. Athletic club."

"So—you don't identify as gay, or . . . what?"

Chase smiled and shook his head. He shrugged. The explainer was out of explanations. He didn't seem to like talking about it. He made a sort of gesture toward the back of the car with his head.

"Cathy stays in the trunk. I think it's best that way."

THE MINUS WORLD

"I saw this documentary? About DARPA?"

Greg obligingly nodded for him to go on. Megan was watching the ceiling. Peter had spent the evening nervously shoving conversation across anxious waves of silence.

"You know DARPA? Defense Advanced Research Projects Agency. They're involved with all kinds of black helicopter shit, like training spies to do ESP, invisibility shields, the Montauk Project, all that shit, but okay, so they've developed this thing called the Exoatmospheric Kill Machine—it's this satellite with a really, *really* fucking powerful laser on it that can just zoom in on anybody anywhere in the world and kill them from outer space. One second you're walking around, hum-de-dum, doing your thing, then all of a sudden, *bzzzzt*, you're dead. That's our fucking tax dollars at work."

Megan was lying on the couch with her bare feet in Greg's lap and Peter sat hunched on the edge of a chair, rapidly bouncing his leg on the ball of his foot. Since they'd gotten home from dinner he'd been sucking down glass after glass of orange soda so quickly the original ice cubes hadn't had time to melt. It was getting late. Megan gave Greg a seemingly meaningful look that Peter couldn't interpret.

"I really don't think they have the capability to do that," said Greg.

"Do *not* be a fool," said Peter. He could feel how agitated his voice was. It had a quivering edge of emotion that he couldn't swallow. "It's the fucking government. They have the money. They have the power. Do *not* be naïve."

"I'm going to bed," Megan said to Greg.

It was the first night Peter would be staying with Greg and Megan. They had picked him up from South Station that afternoon and taken him out to dinner in Boston, then come home and talked for a while. Greg had had a beer with dinner, and that's it. Megan was pregnant, and Peter of course was not drinking. The air was awkward with sobriety.

Peter kept on trying to think of interesting things to say. Every time he tried to make conversation Megan looked at him like he was crazy.

During his exit interview, Robin had told Peter he needed a fresh start. Robin was the counselor-therapist woman. She was nice to him but he never believed anything she said. She always did the therapist thing of being nice to you but not getting remotely emotionally involved. Her face was round and so deliberately earnest looking that there was obviously nothing earnest in it at all. She was wearing this sort of low-cut shirt, and Peter's eyes kept getting stuck in her cleavage. During the interview she shrugged up the shawl thing she was wearing and wrapped it across herself, and Peter wondered if she'd noticed him looking at her breasts. She probably had. Peter had finally learned that women are better at knowing when you're looking at their breasts than you think they are. He was a little embarrassed but it wasn't like he was ever going to see her again. This was his exit interview. She told him he needed a fresh start.

Yeah, well. Peter was edging up on the realization, the main part of him had already admitted it, but out of fear he'd not yet let his conscious mind admit it, that there is no such thing as a fresh start. Not in life. In a Nintendo game, if you fuck up beyond the hope of ever pulling your shit together again you can always press the reset button, and you're back at the beginning, and Mario is little again and running down the brick pathway ready to encounter the mushrooms and the turtles, but you, playing him, now know exactly when and where the dangers will come. When the mushrooms and the turtles slide onscreen from the right-hand edge of the TV, you will be ready for them. At least until you get to the last place where you died. Life is not like that. No matter how badly you fuck up, you cannot ever press the reset button and start over. All you can do is pull the plug.

Peter needed help. His parents wouldn't help him anymore, his sister wouldn't help him, his ex-girlfriend, Gina, wouldn't help him, his friends wouldn't help him, and he wasn't sure he had any more friends. Other relatives were out, too. All of the possible people who might help Peter had been overfished, like a sea that has no more fish in it. But Greg, Greg had fish left for him.

As soon as we can, Peter promised himself, we will pay Greg back for the many times he's helped us when we didn't deserve it.

(Ever since he was a kid, Peter had always talked to himself using the first-person plural. The we was always the external, rational voice talking to him, Peter. Superego talking to id. He only did this in his head, though, or out loud when he was alone. If people had heard him talking to himself in the first-person plural they might think he was crazy.)

"As soon as I can," he said to Greg, "I will pay you back for this."

"Don't worry about it," said Greg, and went upstairs to join his wife (the word *wife* still sounded weird) in bed.

Greg clearly didn't expect to ever be repaid. Part of Peter also knew he'd probably never repay him.

"We have to pay him back," said Peter to himself when he was alone. "We have to pay him back."

Greg's wife disliked Peter. She had her reasons.

Most people disliked Peter. Peter disliked Peter. Even Greg seemed to dislike him sometimes, although he always helped him. Greg "loved" him. Some people still loved Peter. He wasn't sure about his mom, but his dad loved him. His sister loved him. Even his ex-girlfriend loved him. But, coming to the point, they wouldn't give him any money.

Greg wasn't giving him any money, either. Just a place to stay, rent free and indefinitely, and a job, which with time and patience and work and saving and not fucking up would turn into money. Greg was doing the whole teaching him to fish instead of giving him fish thing. Peter had never been any good at fishing. He was good at staying up all night doing drugs and playing Nintendo. That he could do.

Greg had gone upstairs, said goodnight, and turned off the light. It was dark all over the house except for the weak white kitchen light above the sink. Greg and Megan's house was in Somerville, Massachusetts. This was the first time Peter had ever been to Massachusetts. He'd been on a Greyhound all day and the previous night, and hadn't really slept at all except for little naps in the bus seat for the last like, thirty hours. Megan had made up the futon for him in the basement. That's what he was going to sleep on until he had enough money to move out. Which was probably going to take awhile. The basement was full of boxes and Christmas ornaments and vacuum cleaners and things like that, and a futon. Peter and Greg had stayed up talking awhile after Megan went to bed. Megan was really, really pregnant. They had gotten married like, a year ago. Peter hadn't been there. Unless a miracle happened, like finding a magic bag of money that always has money in it, Peter was definitely going to still be living in the basement when their kid was born. This was the newest of the various reasons Megan disliked Peter.

It was a little after midnight. Peter wasn't tired at all. Peter had a meeting with his prospective employer the next morning at eight.

"Why so early?" he'd asked his brother.

"They've already been working for two hours by then," said Greg. "They get to the lab around six. They have to start working that early because the fishermen bring in the catch even earlier than that."

The job was driving this truck with a tank full of salt water on it from the marine biology lab at MIT to the docks in New Bedford to pick up all the squid the fishermen hauled in along with the fish. The fishermen just threw the squid back and kept the fish, but MIT needed squid to run experiments on. So he was supposed to get there early in the morning, before the boats came in, ask them to give him their squid, then drive back to MIT, deliver the squid. He would be paid by the squid.

Greg said he had put the word in for Peter. He said they weren't interviewing anybody else. The job was as good as his; this interview was basically a formality. He said they'd been trying to get students to do it, but none of them wanted the job because it didn't pay that much and you had to get up at three in the morning to do it. Greg said he'd seen the thing for the job on the job-posting thing, the bulletin board, in the student quad cafeteria whatever area for weeks and weeks and nobody had torn any tabs off it. So he went to the marine biology lab and asked the guys who worked there what the job was and what it entailed and how much it paid. And then he asked them if they'd mind giving his younger brother, Peter, a job.

"What did you tell them?" said Peter.

"Not everything. I said you were in kind of a tough spot and needed to make some money, get back on your feet."

"What do you mean back?"

"I told them you'd be a reliable worker. So please don't embarrass me."

So they didn't know everything. Everything was that Peter was a twenty-seven-year-old addict with ten thousand dollars in credit card debt, a criminal record, and no college degree, who'd been living in a half-way house in Illinois until last week. But now he was here. So?

Actually, that wasn't everything, not even close. But those were the big things.

Okay, so we have to be there at eight. It takes like, twenty minutes to get there. Okay, so let's get up at seven. That means we should go to bed now.

Peter opened his brother's liquor cabinet. Inside it was a sight that amazed and ashamed Peter, a sight that probably always would: a bunch of bottles of liquor that were half full, three-quarters full . . . you know, bottles that have been opened, but aren't empty. Greg was the kind of person who could pour himself a glass of Scotch or whatever, drink it, and then stop drinking and go to bed or whatever, instead of drinking until either there was nothing left to drink or he physically couldn't drink anymore.

Peter got a glass out of the cupboard and poured himself about three fingers of what looked like expensive Scotch. He looked at it, set it down, and poured another finger. He took a sip, put the glass back on the kitchen counter, and started looking around the kitchen for something he could turn into a funnel to pour the Scotch back into the bottle with. He ripped a page out of a *National Geographic* with a picture of whales on it and rolled it into a funnel. He stuck the skinny end into the neck of the bottle and dumped the glass into the fat end. The page instantly got all damp and floppy. Some of the blue ink from the whales slid off the page and got in the Scotch, tiny ribbonlike clouds of whale-colored ink in the Scotch. Oh no. We're fucking this up. The whisky was running down the sides of the bottle and getting all over his hands and the counter. While Peter was doing this it occurred to him that his mom had a funnel that she used for cooking somehow. A funnel had some sort of cooking-related function. Remember we used to play with it when we were a kid? When we would make potions? Peter had once covered it in aluminum foil and worn it as a hat when he was the Tin Man for Halloween, and Greg had been the Scarecrow and Lindsay had been Dorothy. There was no Cowardly Lion. This led to the thought that Greg and his wife had a pretty nice house and everything, full of grown-up stuff, and they cooked, and they might have an actual funnel somewhere in the kitchen, one that was made to be used as a funnel, made out of metal or plastic or something. But it was too late now.

He put the stopper back in the bottle, wiped the bottle and the counter off with a paper towel, put the bottle back in the liquor cabinet, thought about how weird it was that they even had a liquor cabinet and if they had a fucking liquor cabinet they probably had a fucking funnel, then he looked in the liquor cabinet and realized there was in fact a funnel *in* the liquor cabinet, washed the glass and dried it and put it back in the cupboard, went downstairs, set the alarm clock Megan had given him for seven, took off his clothes, got in bed, and stared at pink tufts of fiberglass insulation stapled to wooden beams in the basement wall until the alarm clock went off.

As soon as he hit the button that shut off the buzzer he was suddenly incredibly sleepy. He heard Greg and Megan moving around upstairs. He fought his way into the same clothes he'd worn the day before, went upstairs, pissed, splashed water on his face, and combed his hair with his hands. His skin looked pink and puffy, and his eyes were narrow and swampy looking. The whites of his eyes were dull gray. He joined them in the kitchen.

"How'd you sleep?" said Megan.

"Bad," said Peter.

"I'm sorry."

She was making coffee. Their coffeemaker looked like a futuristic robot or a spaceship or something.

Greg and Megan were both healthy, good-looking people. Greg had always dated girls who were way above Peter's looks-bracket. Megan had small hands and buggy eyes and skin and hair right out of commercials for skin and hair products. She looked like a pregnant woman on TV. Some pregnant women get fat feet and things like that. But Megan just had a perfectly compact, round belly, like she had a beach ball under her shirt. It looked like when she gave birth it would just kind of make a harmless popping sound like the sound of a cartoon bubble popping, and then she'd go back to exactly what she looked like before.

"You want a ride to the campus?" said Greg. "I'm going to my office early anyway."

Fuck. We can't say no. There's no point. We're going to the same place anyway, it doesn't make any sense for us to walk now.

He'd planned on smoking cigarettes while he walked to the campus, and if Greg drove him that meant he wouldn't get to do that and he probably wouldn't have time for a cigarette until after the interview.

"Thanks," said Peter.

They were eating bagels and cream cheese. Peter couldn't eat anything. He was hungry, but he couldn't eat anything. He drank four cups of coffee and afterward was light-headed and slightly nauseated.

Greg was reading the newspaper.

"Can I have the funny papers?" said Peter.

Greg slid the cartoon pages out of the newspaper and gave them to him. Peter gulped coffee and read *The Far Side* first, then *Calvin and Hobbes*, then started working his way through the other ones, which are never, ever actually funny, like *Hägar the Horrible.*

"So," said Megan. "Are you going to start looking for a place soon?"

"Megan," said Greg.

"Well, yeah," said Peter. "I'll be out of here pretty soon."

Greg read the newspaper, ate his bagel, and began to fiercely ignore their conversation.

"I figure maybe a couple weeks," said Peter. "Depends on when I get my first paycheck and stuff like that. Really soon though."

"Where are you thinking of living?"

"Well, okay, this one time I was driving by this storage place. You know, where they have all those storage lockers? I once helped a buddy of mine move his shit out of one of those things. Some of them are pretty big inside. His was temperature controlled too, so it was even warm in there. You know what the rent for those things is? It's like fifty bucks a month. And I thought, fuck, man, I could just rent one of those and live in it. Just put a mattress in it or something, a thermal sleeping bag, maybe get one of those electric camping lanterns. Boom. There you go. Super-cheap place to stay."

"What about taking showers?" said Megan.

"Thought of that. I'd take showers in the locker room at the rec center. Just like once or twice a week. I read this thing about how modern Americans take way too many showers anyway. It kills the good bacteria. You don't really need to shower more than once a week."

Greg folded his newspaper.

"You're not going to live in a storage locker," he said.

"Why the fuck not?" said Peter.

After breakfast Greg drove him to the campus. Greg was thirty years old. He worked in a chemistry lab at MIT where he did something that involved testing chemicals on rats. Their sister, Lindsay, was twenty-five. She was in her first year of law school. Peter was twenty-seven, and he was nothing.

"Go in there and ask, they'll tell you where it is."

"Okay," said Peter. The car door was open and Peter was halfway out of it. The car was making a soft, irritating *bong-bong-bong* sound because the door was open.

"I'm going home after I finish in the lab," said Greg. "If you wait around till then I can give you a ride back, but it'll be a while. I don't know how long you'll be. You can walk around and explore the campus if you want. Or you can go into Cambridge. There are bookstores and coffee shops; you can kill a day there. Or you could come by my office before noon and we can get lunch. Or you could just walk home, it's not that far."

Peter started to freak out a little. Greg was giving him too many options. Too many choices to make. When Peter started to get freaked out, when he started to feel like a loosely put-together thing unraveling uncontrollably in every direction, he tried to use a trick they'd taught him in therapy: Try to boil everything down to just one decision at a time. Just choose one item from a pair of options, then go on to the next. Either this or that. Pick one. Next decision.

"I don't know," said Peter.

"Well, if I don't see you later I'll assume you went home. Okay?"

That made things a little easier. Peter walked up to the building.

It was early and not many people were on the campus yet. It was November. The weather was wet and bleak and made the grass look greener. It was a cold morning. It was an ugly day. Or beautiful. Whatever. It wasn't either. He never thought of a day as beautiful or ugly. He knew what beautiful and ugly days were supposed to look like, but he wasn't the sort of person who really cared about the weather.

He could see a clock on another building. We should buy a watch, he thought. He had about five minutes. He lit a cigarette and realized that it might take awhile to find the place he was supposed to find—that he might not be able to just walk in and instantly be there. So if we smoke this cigarette, we might be late for the interview.

Decision: He put out the cigarette even though he'd only just lit it, and went inside. Decision made. He had analyzed the situation, weighed the options, and made a decision, like an adult.

"Can you please tell me where the marine biology lab is please?"

Peter was embarrassed by how small and weak his voice sounded. He was trying to be polite. The girl behind the desk didn't hear him.

"I'm sorry?"

She craned her neck and slightly tilted the flap of her ear toward him with her finger. She was a sweet-looking, pudgy girl. She was drinking coffee, or some kind of hot drink in a paper cup that steamed up her glasses. Maybe it was tea.

"Can you please tell me where the marine biology lab is?"

"Which one?"

"Um. I don't know. The one where they do stuff with, um, squid?"

"*Do stuff* with squid?"

"You know, do like, experiments? Study them?"

She looked down at something on her desk, somehow figured out what he was talking about, then gave him directions. His shoes were wet and they squeaked on the hard vinyl floor. The halls were dark and he didn't see anyone else in the building. He found the right room eventually. He didn't know what time it was when he knocked on the door. He was probably late. Nobody answered. He opened it and stuck his head inside.

"Hello?"

He was afraid of raising his voice too much.

The marine biology lab was all tile, plastic, stainless steel surfaces, garishly bright, and smelled like brine and fish. The best thing Peter had in his bag of experience to compare it to was a seafood grocery store. It smelled more nautical than the sea itself. The seaness of the smell of the sea was compacted here, concentrated. The smell was sickeningly thick.

Peter hadn't bothered to dress up for the interview or anything. He figured they wouldn't expect somebody applying for a job that was basically just driving a truck to wear a suit and tie to an interview. He'd look silly if he did. Plus he didn't have any nice clothes anyway. Peter was wearing jeans, a button-down borrowed from his brother, and a smoky-smelling Goodwill denim jacket. It turned out he wasn't under- or overdressed. The scientists in the lab wore jeans and T-shirts. Peter was met by a woman in her late twenties, not much older than himself. She shook his hand. She was wearing a fleece pullover. She had blunt features and blond hair she wore in a thick braid behind her head. She looked like a Viking. She looked like Hägar the Horrible's wife.

"Peter Cast?" she said.

"Yeah, hi."

"Emma. Nice to meet you."

She had a friendly, slightly husky, lower-register voice. Something about her made Peter wonder if she was a lesbian. The phrase "lesbian Viking" popped up in his mind and stayed there.

"You're Greg Cast's brother, right?"

Not many people were in the room, just four or five that looked like grad students sitting around looking at paperwork. Two of them were huddled over an old computer with a green-on-amber display screen.

"So you're ready to start getting up wicked early in the morning?"

"If that's what I gotta do," said Peter, trying to sound game, trying to sound like the kind of guy who liked getting up at three in the morning to drive a truck. He wasn't really ready to start doing anything.

She led him to a big cylindrical tank with an open lid. The lip of the tank came up to their chests. Its sides were thick, pale green metal. The insides were smooth wet ceramic. An air-filtration pump thing beside it made a low white humming noise. It was full of squid. They varied in size—some were the size of a handspan, the biggest ones looked about ten inches, maybe a foot long. The squid aimlessly darted around inside the tank. Their head flaps undulated, and they languidly propelled themselves through the water with their pumping tentacles like slow-motion darts. It was at once fascinating, beautiful, and ridiculous to see how gracefully they moved, until they bumped their stupid heads into the sides of the tank. Some of them swam around a lot, some of them just floated. They looked bored.

Emma unhooked a long mesh net from a holder on the wall and dipped it in the tank. She swirled it around slowly, causing the squid to come alive with agitation, shooting every which way, bouncing off the walls, making the water wobble.

Emma snagged a couple of squid in the net and brought them out of the water. The heavily sagging net drooled water back into the tank. The squid hung limp and slimy in the net, weakly writhing their tentacles, trying to move their poor boneless bodies, totally out of their element. Emma dragged her hand in the tank to wet it, reached into the net, and grabbed one of them. Just like that. She held it by its tubular, torpedo-shaped head. She dropped the net back in the tank. The squid's slick, shiny body was red and gold, like an apple, flecked with metallic sparkles. The thing wiggled its tentacles, dangling feebly in her hand. Its flat, weird yellow eyes glistened dimly, like silver foil, like dirty sequins. It was disgusting and a little terrifying. The smell was overpoweringly putrid, almost to the point of making him gag.

"These are the guys we're after," said Emma. "Want to hold it?"

Peter hoped this wasn't some kind of test. Because no fucking way was he going to touch the squid. If that were the case he'd just find some other job, one that didn't involve squid-touching.

Emma dropped the squid back in the tank. They walked around the lab while she explained the experiments they were running on the squid.

Some of the squid were separated in smaller tanks. Peter listened to her talk and nodded comprehendingly and didn't understand any of what she was saying.

She showed him the truck. It was behind the building, through a back door, parked at the bottom of a delivery ramp. It was an F-450 with a huge rectangular metal tank in the bed. There was an aluminum ladder bolted to the side of the truck bed, leading up to the rim of the tank. Peter climbed the ladder and looked inside. It was about half full with salt water.

"We have to change the water once in a while. It's not ideal, but it's what we've got right now. Basically, we need as many squid as we can get."

She explained the job to him. Drive to New Bedford, get there around six, when the fishermen bring in the first catch. Get the squid. Bring them back. There were maps, directions, instructions. She gave him the keys to the truck and watched him drive it around the parking lot a few turns to make sure he could maneuver the vehicle.

"A lot of the squid are going to die," said Emma. "They go into shock, and they're dead by the time you make it back from New Bedford. So you gotta get the squid back as soon as you can. The dead ones are no good. We can only experiment on live squid. We pay you for every live squid you bring back."

"So—you want me to speed?"

"No," said Emma. "Definitely not. We're not asking you to do anything illegal. I'm just saying, the longer you spend on the road, the more squid are going to die on your way back. We pay by the living squid. Interpret that however you want."

The phrase "by the living squid" finally replaced "lesbian Viking" in Peter's head. Of course she was saying, in a winking way, in a *I'm not actually saying this but yes I am saying this* kind of way: Yeah, speed.

"You're hired," she said, and gave him a tight handshake that made Peter self-conscious about his own feeble handshake. He thought of the limp, slimy squid in her hand. She sent him to accounts and payroll to sign tax forms and other formal documents. For technical reasons he had to be signed on as a contractor. To make the paperwork simpler or something. No benefits. So he pocketed the keys, followed her directions across the campus to payroll, got lost a couple of times, asked directions, found it, signed a bunch of stuff, went outside, chose a marble staircase to sit at the top of that overlooked one of the main lawn quad whatever areas of the campus, and smoked three cigarettes in a row, lighting the second off the first and the third off the second while watching the campus come to life, the students shuffling across the damp grass in their coats and hats with cups of coffee and satchels and backpacks, on their way to their first classes presumably, or labs, or wherever they were going. These kids were in their late teens and early twenties. Later they would probably go on to work on projects like satellites with giant lasers that kill people from outer space, and make a lot of money. While Peter, who was seven, eight years older than they were, would continue being broke and desperate. What he felt toward these kids walking across the grass while he sat on the steps smoking wasn't quite hate or resentment. There was too much self-loathing mixed into his feelings for that. It requires more self-respect to hate and resent, it takes some self-confidence to believe that they've been blessed and you've been gypped by a capricious universe. No, Peter mostly blamed himself. He'd started the game on Go with two hundred dollars, same as anyone else, but had bungled it through bad moves and reckless investments. How do other people do it? How do other people navigate the world so easily, as if they already know the way, and never feel unmoored, lost, frantic, like their compasses have been fucked up from too much holding a magnet under them to watch the needle spin and spin, searching for a north that seems to be everywhere at once?

• • •

"Sometimes I think about just not talking for a while," Peter said to Greg at lunch. Greg had taken him to lunch to celebrate his getting a job. Peter had thanked him effusively, even though it wasn't really an unusual thing for Greg to buy him lunch, because Peter had no money. They were eating at a nice-ish place in Cambridge. Their table had a tablecloth and a flower arrangement on it. Greg ordered a calamari appetizer as a joke. The breaded calamari rings were tough to chew. They didn't really taste like anything. The sauce they came with was good, but the calamari itself tasted like nothing.

"I mean, like, not talk for a long time. Like six months or a year or something. I heard that Buckminster Fuller did that. He just decided not to talk for like a year."

"Why would you do that?" said Greg. "What good would that do?"

"Just to be silent," said Peter.

Peter was slightly self-conscious about sitting in this restaurant, being ragged and dirty-looking and reeking of smoke. The undersides of his cuticles were perpetually dirty. At some point in his life he'd acquired yellowish-gray rims of filth around his fingernails that never went away no matter how much he washed his hands.

"You know, to figure shit out in my head until I'm ready to talk again."

"If you can't figure shit out talking, why do you think you'd be able to figure it out not talking? What have you got to figure out anyway?"

"What I'm going to do with my life."

"Plus it would be difficult logistically."

"What do you mean?"

"I mean, okay, say you walk into a store, you need to buy something. How do you communicate with the guy at the counter?"

"I'd carry a notebook and a pen around with me everywhere."

"If you're not talking for some Zen, self-searching reason, if you're writing everything down and showing people the notebook, wouldn't that mean you'd actually be spending way more effort just to communicate with people? What's so Zen about that? It's ridiculous. You're just inconveniencing everybody else for no reason."

Peter felt cornered. He had ordered a cup of coffee with his club sandwich. He'd only eaten half the sandwich, and that alone had been a labor, but had asked the waitress for three coffee refills. The cup was pretty small. With each refill he ripped open a sugar packet and dumped a fresh silken thread of sugar into the coffee, then separated the flaps of the sugar packet along the glued seams, flattened it, and tore it into strips, which he wadded into tiny balls with his fingers. When he ran out of sugar packets he went to work on the flower arrangement, fastidiously denuding the daisies of their petals and wadding those into tiny balls too.

"Um," said Peter. "I guess so. I mean, you know. I don't, um. Shit. I don't know."

"It sounds like you haven't really thought this through."

Half the daisies in the glass flute of water were now naked, sad-looking yellow circles on sickly thin stems. A pile of weird debris had accumulated on the tablecloth next to Peter's plate, wadded-up bits of pink sugar-packet paper and daisy petals.

"Dude. Quit fucking with their flowers."

"Sorry."

Peter's hands shot back from the half-stripped flower arrangement.

He put his hands in his lap like a reprimanded child. Then he started unwadding the tiny balls he'd made.

"I don't think I'm gonna do it anyway. The not-talking thing, I mean. Not right now, anyway."

Greg smiled deftly and nodded, like a therapist being nicely encouraging, only Greg did it with condescending irony.

"I think that's a good plan."

• • •

Peter did manage to sleep a little that night. Emma had said it was a bit over an hour's drive from Cambridge to New Bedford, plan for an hour and a half, and he was supposed to get there before six in the morning. Plus the walk to campus took about twenty minutes. Peter didn't see why he couldn't just park the truck at Greg's house, but he hadn't thought to ask about it that morning. Maybe it had something to do with rules about campus vehicles off school property or something. We should ask about that. So that means we should get up at about three thirty to be on the safe side. Especially since it's our first day and we should leave some slack time in case we fuck something up. Eight hours counting backward from that means we should go to bed at seven thirty.

It didn't feel like it had been dark out for long when Peter went to bed. He lay there for four, five hours, not sleeping. Megan was watching TV upstairs, and the living room, where the TV was, was directly above the futon in the basement. The volume wasn't loud but he could almost hear what was happening on the TV. But he must have fallen asleep eventually, because the skull-grinding electric throb of the alarm-clock buzzer dragged him out of a nightmare he was having about a guy with his arms and legs cut off who was stuck inside a refrigerator shitting blood into a hole in the bottom of it. He opened his eyes and didn't know who he was or where he was. He saw the red digital numbers 3:30 glowing somewhere in the darkness outside his body and didn't know what they meant. As he slowly recalled who he was, what was going on, and what he now had to do, he realized he would probably never get used to this.

He doused himself with cold water and struggled with Megan's fancy, complicated coffeemaker, muttering the word *fuck* over and over as he fiddled with levers and buttons. At last he was able to make it make coffee, but it tasted weird. He'd probably done something wrong. He poured it into one of their plastic travel mugs and left for campus in the utter dark. The streets were empty and as silent as the streets of a semi-urban place like Somerville get. The sidewalks and buildings were dull orange from the streetlights. It was cold. Peter turned up the collar of his denim jacket and hugged it to himself, shivering. He walked with hunched shoulders and a quick, short, screw-tight gait, slurping the weird-tasting coffee and smoking cigarettes in continuous succession while he walked, concentrating on his feet. He had a headache that came at him in fuzzy broken radio waves of pain and his thoughts were like a screeching horde of freaked-out bats flapping around frantically, going nowhere. A part of him still worried constantly about whether he would ever feel life was still worth living if he could never get drunk or high again. He hoped there would come a time when he had no desire to get fucked up, and wouldn't even think about it, and would be totally fine with being sober, but he doubted it would ever happen. It was like being offered the choice between a death sentence and life in prison. It's like, I'll choose life, I guess.

He found the truck parked by the delivery ramp by the back door to the marine biology lab. He climbed up into the truck. It was battered and clunky, everything in it rusty, oily smelling, with puffy shreds of foam poking out of cuts in the bench seat and sticky hand-grime coating the steering wheel. He started the engine, switched the heater on full blast, and turned on the radio. He unfolded the sheet of yellow notepaper on which he'd written the directions to the commercial fishing docks, smoothed it out on the dashboard. As he drove the truck, he could both hear and feel the great quantity of salt water sloshing around in the tank in the back of it. If he stopped too abruptly at a light he felt the water heave against the front of the tank, and heard it splash over the sides. He wondered why there wasn't a lid on it or something. It was a particular feeling of strange calm, driving a giant truck around in the middle of the night, completely alone—not sadness or loneliness, but a warmer feeling, a tingling-belly melancholy. For the most part he found his way, cautiously easing the enormous vehicle into the turns. He was pathfinding, trying to memorize the route. There was one hard-to-find turn that he fucked up and had to double back to take. He lost five or ten minutes, but learned that part of the route much better. Once he'd climbed onto the highway he was fine. He sat back in the seat and breathed easier, turned up the radio and twisted the dial, the green needle scrolling back and forth along the FM band, looking for anything halfway decent. It was the late nineties, and the airwaves were clogged with Alanis Morissette, Bush, Līve, Collective Soul, fucking *Moby*. Comfortably south of Boston the highway began to cut through areas less and less urban, and more fields and trees appeared on each side as the landscape opened up. He passed other cars from time to time, but mostly it was just trucks out on the highway, twinkling juggernauts, roaring engines and sighing gaskets. The last long stretch of the drive was on a smaller highway, through rural country that surprised Peter. He was surprised by the bucolic pleasantness of this part of Massachusetts—being a Midwesterner, Peter thought of the whole Northeast as a place paved over from one massive metropolitan area to the next, cities and suburbs connected by stark gray spiderwebs of industry. The sky was no longer black, still dark but gradually lightening. He could make out cows standing in clusters in green and brown fields off to the sides of the road. Like a lot of things in New England, Peter was realizing, the cows were more ideal, more picturesque than they were in other parts of the country. Back home in Illinois the cows were all nondescript dull brown ones—but these cows were the classic black-and-white kind, cartoon cows, the kind of cow a child would draw if you asked a child to draw a cow. They looked like what cows are supposed to look like. Peter appreciated that. He liked clouds that were fluffy, fire engines that were red, and cows that were spotted black and white.

Soon the sky had brightened into morning light, though because it was overcast the dawn was a more gradual process than usual. He could smell the sea. As he got closer to the shore, the forests and farmland fell away into more developed areas, houses, concrete. This looked more like what he expected of the East—a gray-and-brown place, metal and brick, drifts of mushy litter packed against the corners of the concrete barriers along the roadsides. The clouds looked yellowish green, tortoise colored. He made it through New Bedford: an old town, all that stately New England stodginess, all the little architectural filigrees corroded by time and weather, more recently overlaid with colorless industry, which had also already gone largely to rust. And there was the sea.

He drove through the open gates of a chain-link fence and onto a wide asphalt blacktop by the docks. Rigging clinked against mast poles, the docks creaked, waves softly slapped against the seawall. The sky was cluttered with seagulls. The water was choppy and the ugly green of oxidized copper, the line of the horizon an indistinct gray smear. It was barely daybreak, and there were fishing boats anchored at the docks, already come in from their first catch, and more in the harbor that looked to be on their way in. Peter parked the truck as close to the docks as he could, killed the engine, and stepped from the truck cab's soporific cocoon of artificial warmth into the sharply pointed cold of the morning, made colder by the sea. Here again was that overpoweringly putrid smell of fish and brine.

He walked timidly out onto the dock with his hands crammed in his jacket pockets. The boat lurched in the water. The boat was a huge, complicated piece of machinery, rigging, nets, enormous gears for releasing and dragging up the net. Everything on it was wet and filthy. Fish everywhere, slapping their bodies, dying on the embossed sheet-metal deck. Machinery creaked, squealed, hummed. Peter could hear the fishermen working on the boat, their boots clanging on the deck, their voices shouting over the din of machines. He was nervous about approaching them. He didn't quite know what to say, and was afraid they would make fun of him.

The dock swayed very slightly. In the boat, fishermen in caps and bright yellow foul-weather gear were sorting through fish on conveyor belts. On the conveyor belts and here and there all over the deck, fish flopped around, their mouths and gills gaping, their blank, disclike eyes seemingly looking at nothing. Peter found it a little amazing how long fish survive out of water. They take so long to die.

"Hey," Peter called down to the fishermen on the boat from where he stood on the dock.

They hadn't heard him.

"Uh—hey? Um—?"

One of the men looked up at him. The others kept picking through the fish with their work gloves. There were rows of big blue plastic barrels, the size of garbage cans, full of fish, lined up on the deck alongside the conveyor belts. The men tossed some of the fish into the barrels, some back into the sea, and let some move past them on the conveyor belt and fall into a hole that emptied somewhere inside the hull of the ship. There seemed to be a system.

"Good morning," said the fisherman who had looked up at him.

"Um," said Peter. "I'm from the biology lab at MIT? Can we have your squid?"

This last sentence felt strange in Peter's mouth, but the fisherman was unfazed. Peter imagined fishermen as having big, bushy beards. A couple of the men on the boat did in fact have beards, but not this one. He did have a sharp New England accent, though. At least he had that.

They gave him their squid. Peter followed the fishermen's lead during the process of getting the squid. They had done this before and were used to people from MIT coming for their bycatch.

"Where's Emma?" said the man who'd spoken to him.

"I'm her new squid man," said Peter, and imagined a superhero named Squidman.

They invited Peter on board. On the deck of the swaying anchored boat he stepped gingerly among the dying fish, trying not to squish them. They were gross, alive, frightening. The fishermen largely ignored him, but Peter still felt inadequate and embarrassed among them. These were men who had real jobs, *really* real jobs, who got up before dawn and worked with their hands and knew how to do things. These were men who knew how to operate complicated machines, who knew how to do practical, useful things, who knew how to catch fish. There were fish out there in the ocean, and these guys got in their boat and went out there and got them and brought them back. Just like that. These were men who were not easily frightened, not easily overwhelmed. Some of the fishermen looked younger than Peter, and Peter was ashamed that he was as old as he was and didn't really know how to do anything useful.

Soon the wire handle of a heavy plastic bucket full of squid was sinking painfully into the flesh of his hooked fingers. The squid wriggled and squirmed in the bucket. Their tentacles stretched, thrashed, suckers sticking to the sides of the bucket. It was like holding a bucket full of aliens. The smell was pointedly sickening. Peter tried to breathe through his mouth. Sometimes when you see animals that are hurt or trapped, you wonder what they're feeling. You wonder if they're in pain, if they're afraid. Peter found that it wasn't easy to do that with squid. It was hard to anthropomorphize them, to project human emotions onto them. They were just too scary, too weird looking.

Peter dumped the squid into the tank on the truck and went back for another bucket, and so on, feeling less uncomfortable with the task with each bucketful. He did the same with a few other fishing boats that were docked there that morning, and began to feel like an old hand. It was fascinating to watch these animals that were so helpless and awkward when slopped together in a bucket instantly come alive when he dumped them in the water, suddenly moving with otherworldly graceful ease. He got back in the truck and began the task of following the directions in reverse, which was harder, especially in New Bedford, a town he had even less familiarity with than Cambridge—as in, none—plus he'd driven in in the dark. But he felt good now. He was at work. The fishermen had understood, and helped him, and given him their squid. He turned the radio up and found a station that played a stretch of non-suck songs, and was back on the highway, looking at the trees and black-and-white cows standing along the fences.

On the fairly long and boring drive Peter's mind fell into patterns of thinking about Gina, the way iron filings filter themselves into magnetically predictable patterns on a vibrating surface. Last fall and winter, before things completely fell apart, Peter and Gina had been living together in a squalid apartment in a fairly sketchy area of Humboldt Park. He was working twenty, thirty hours a week at a music store in Logan Square, and Gina was going to school part-time at UIC and waitressing at a steakhouse. There was this one time, though, when it was almost the end of the fall semester for her, and Gina had invited over a friend of hers from school and his girlfriend. Peter couldn't remember either of their names now. They'd only met that one time. They were nice people. Peter couldn't really remember anything about them. It was a Saturday afternoon in a Chicago December, which means it was brutally cold with an arctic windchill. The weather had been flirting with the idea of snowing all day. They had all holed up in Peter and Gina's apartment, smoking weed and drinking and playing Monopoly. Their apartment was on the second floor of a half-dilapidated wooden house that had been divided into dubiously up-to-code apartments. It was cluttered with desiccated houseplants with dust-coated leaves that the previous tenant had left, and poorly insulated and poorly heated, such that they spent that winter always draped in blankets and wearing hats inside, and had two space heaters going at once, cheap ones from the hardware store, metal boxes with grates of glowing orange filaments that hummed and made clicking and clinking noises, as if broken parts were rattling around loose inside them. And still it was fucking freezing in the apartment. Peter had landed on a trick that seemed like a good idea at first, which was to boil water. He'd been boiling a pot of water on the stove for mac and cheese, and noticed that the steam raised the room's temperature. So he would keep a soup pot full of water boiling on the electric stove all afternoon and night until they went to sleep, filling the apartment with hot moisture, fogging it up like a bathhouse. It was strangely pleasant to breathe the warm, humid air; it felt good in the lungs and on the skin. It was probably good for all those half-dead houseplants too. One night both Peter and Gina passed out dead drunk—not an uncommon occurrence that winter—and forgot to turn the stove top off. When they woke up the next day the pot was ruined, the red coil of the stove eye having burned away all the water and then gone to work on the pot, causing the Teflon coating to crackle and peel in curdled flakes, turning the outside of the black pot a brassy reddish-brown color. The insides of the kitchen windows were glazed with sheets of ice as thick as fingers.

They had been so much in love, remembering it made Peter almost physically sick with regret. Peter would always remember this one particular time, when he and Gina had first gotten together, when they were having sex, and they had looked into each other's eyes and said "I love you," which they had just started saying to each other—there was something about that one time, it was hard to explain. It was hard to explain because it was such a commonplace-sounding thing when you're describing it, something predictable, that anyone could experience, that anyone could say. That's one of the irritating tragedies about being a person these days, is that love is a clichéd emotion, sadly, something used to sell stuff, and it's hard to talk about it earnestly without sounding like somebody on daytime TV. But this feeling had happened to Peter exactly once in his life, then. It was a moment that, Peter felt, no matter if he and Gina stayed in love or not later on, would tie them together forever. He knew he might not have a moment like that ever again with anyone. In retrospect he was glad it had happened to him at least once. But by the time the thing with her friends from UIC happened, Peter had lost all agency in their relationship. At first it had felt like they had been moving forward, together, at the same time, but by then, Gina was leading and Peter was tottering along behind her every step of the way. She decided when they would have sex and how, she decided what they ate, what they were going to do, what they were going to watch on TV. Sometimes she even walked a pace ahead of him on the street when they were out together. Peter had relinquished any control, and was now helpless, dependent. She removed the need for him to make decisions, she protected him, made him feel loved, safe, taken care of. And she had slid into nagginess, was always castigating him for something, sniping at his every fault, from his pitiful inability to ask his boss at the music store for more hours to what shirt he would wear, and whether or not he would button the collar. Once, when they were driving to a party, trying to follow some complicated, barely sensical directions a stoned friend had given them, Peter, who was at the wheel, had accidentally called Gina "Mom." But Peter still loved her, even now. Since they broke up she had quit drinking and using on her own. She had never been as bad as he was. He saw her the last time he was in Chicago, a few months ago, during the couple of days he had free between rehab and the halfway house. They had lunch together. Lunch. The least intimate meal of the day. She had been impenetrably distant and polite. As if they were acquaintances. Gina hadn't seemed happy or unhappy. She was just flat. Flat as the green line of a dead person's heart monitor on a hospital show on TV. She wasn't the same person anymore. It was totally *Invasion of the Body Snatchers*, when the aliens replace someone you love with an eerily disaffected doppelgänger, a person who looks exactly like the person you love but who you know just, just isn't.

• • •

The people at the marine biology lab were a little disappointed with him when Peter made it back to Cambridge. Just a little, which was okay. Peter was used to people being disappointed with him. It turned out a lot of his squid had died on the way back. He hadn't realized how quickly they could die when they were in shock. Peter watched as the lesbian Viking marine biologist fished around in the tank for the squid with a long net. Standing on the ladder on the side of the truck, swishing the long, skinny net in the tank full of squid, she reminded him of one of those guys in Italy with the striped shirts and the hats who do the thing in the boats with the long poles. One netful at a time, Emma raised the squid dripping and squirming from the water and carefully dumped them out into five-gallon plastic buckets that one of the grad students who worked in the lab held out for her. They counted the squid as they collected them. They were paying him five bucks a squid. He'd picked up almost forty squid at the docks that morning, but by the time he got back, apparently only eighteen of them were still alive enough to pay for. The ninety-dollar take that day was the first money he'd made since he got fired from the record store, almost a year ago, when he was living with Gina in Chicago. Emma told him to get the dead squid out of the tank and put them in these special buckets they used to throw away dead animals. As Peter stood at the top of the ladder in the cold, fishing with the net for dead squid, these sad-looking, bloated lumps of jellied fat, he wondered if he couldn't make some money on the side by taking the dead ones to a Chinese restaurant or something. He didn't see why not. Maybe they wanted live ones too, like how you're supposed to cook lobsters alive. Squid are dead when you eat them, right? A dead squid's a dead squid. Maybe he could sell them to the restaurant where he ate calamari with Greg. He counted twenty dead squid. That meant his haul was overall more dead than alive. If he'd made it back with all the squid alive, he would have made almost two hundred dollars.

Peter finished putting the dead ones in the special buckets. Then it was like, well, guess it's time to go now. He walked through the building toward the front entrance, the way he'd come in the day before, and was in the sort of lobby area when he remembered that he'd wanted to ask Emma if it was okay to park the squid truck at Greg's house, so he didn't have to get up even earlier than crazy early to walk to campus and get the truck. He stopped in the middle of the floor of the lobby area and looked at the front door. He'd heard once that there was a phrase in French, because they have a lot of phrases for those kinds of weird feelings that are hard to describe but are incredibly specific, for that weird feeling you get when you realize you just forgot to say something you'd meant to say to somebody before you left, and at the moment you realize this, you're not so far away from the place you just left that there's no point in going back now, but you *are* far enough away that if you did go back and say it, it would be kind of awkward. Peter stood there for a moment, then turned around and started walking back to the lab, then thought, whatever, fuck it, we'll just try to remember to ask her about that tomorrow, and turned around again and started walking back toward the front door of the building. But then he had the thought that, knowing him, he would probably also forget to ask tomorrow, and he should probably just ask now because he was already fucking here and it was fresh on his mind, so he turned around again and again stalled out when his increasing anxiety about facing the awkwardness of going back to the lab dragged him to a halt. Maybe we can write a note to ourselves on our hand, he thought, to remind us to ask Emma about the truck. Let's write it in permanent fucking marker, like a Sharpie, and if we write it today, then it'll probably still be there tomorrow, and even if it washes off a little then the mark will still be there, which will be enough to remind us. So he turned back around.

"Are you okay?" said the girl at the front desk who'd given him directions yesterday. "Can I help you?"

Peter realized that to an outside observer, such as the girl at the desk, he'd just been slowly staggering back and forth in the lobby of the building looking confused.

"Um," he said.

He walked up to the desk. The girl was drinking a hot liquid again, which might have been coffee or tea. It steamed up her glasses. She was a little on the heavy side, but she was very sweet looking and had bright, smooth skin, and Peter began to think she was kind of cute. Her glasses were ugly, though, and took away from her face. He tried to imagine what she would look like without the glasses. Peter hated it when he caught himself thinking things like this, because they made him feel like an asshole. He couldn't help it; they just popped up. When Gina broke up with him, a period of time began that started with a time of utter darkness, during which he got fired from the music store, evicted from the apartment, crashed his car, got beaten up outside outside of a bar and fell asleep in the snow. Then he went to rehab, and then the halfway house, and now this. During that whole period of his life, that kind of thing—girls, love, maybe even sex, that stuff—had been so far out of the question that there was no point in even thinking about it at all, except for small things he almost couldn't help, like looking at Robin's breasts during his exit interview.

"You look like you're looking for something," said the girl at the desk. She smiled broadly at him, in a way that suggested she might want to talk to him in a friendly, non-I'm-at-work way.

"Are you drinking coffee or tea?"

She gave him a look that wasn't an are-you-crazy look, just a low-grade jitter of the needle on her what-the-fuck-o-meter.

"That's why I was trying to decide back there. I mean what, not why. When I was walking back and forth."

"What?"

Peter wondered if he was trying to flirt with her. If so, that coffee/tea thing was a train wreck of an opening line.

He remembered that he'd wanted to write a note on his hand with a permanent marker.

"I mean, hey, uh. Can I borrow a pen?"

She offered him the gnawed-on Bic that was in her hand.

"Actually, do you have like a, a permanent marker, like a Sharpie or something?"

She glanced at a mug on the desk that was Garfield's head and full of pens. She found a black Sharpie in it and gave it to him. Peter uncapped the marker and thought about sniffing glue when he was really young. He held the wet, sweetly stinky point of the marker poised above his palm, but had totally forgotten what he was supposed to write on it. He stood there awhile trying to remember, couldn't, and just pretended to write something on his hand while worrying about how obviously fake the gesture was, gave her back the marker, and slowly wandered out the door like a zombie looking for brains. He figured that from now on he should probably just leave out the back door to the parking lot to avoid her.

So Peter went home and spent most of the day drinking coffee and watching TV and making the air in the house crackle with uncomfortable tension between him and Megan, who sat at the kitchen table sorting through baby shower presents, such as baby clothes and one of those things with the big brightly colored beads on it that you can push around on the metal things.

In the afternoon Megan went upstairs to take a nap, and when she'd been up there long enough for him to assume she was asleep, Peter silently poured himself a generous swallow of vodka from Greg's liquor cabinet, and as soon as it was in him Peter instantly felt calmer and happier and more at peace with himself than he had in a year.

The next morning he was surer on his feet with the fishermen. Peter had slept well that night. He still didn't like getting up at three thirty in the morning, but he felt less like death warmed over, and made the drive to New Bedford in significantly less time than the day before. Then it was down to the docks, say hello to the yellow-jacketed soaking men in the boats, the same situation and same faces, dump the squid in the truck and he was off, hauling fucking ass down those adorable little New England highways to get the squid to the lab alive. His foot kept the pedal planted to the floor, the engine roared, and all those trees and fences and black-and-white cows wailed past him like he was playing *Tempest* and flying through space, hell yeah, warp speed, motherfucker, we are on a *mission*.

And when he got back to the lab, the scientists were pleased. Emma the blunt-faced Scandinavian counted thirty-two, we repeat, *thirty-two*, living squid out of the fifty or so he'd brought back. That meant a hundred and sixty bucks in his pocket. That could pay for at least two months' rent in a storage locker. At this rate maybe it wouldn't be so long after all till he could move out of Greg and Megan's basement. He was getting good at this. He cheerfully fished the dead squid out of the tank, stuffed them himself into the special dead animal buckets, no longer icked out by it all, and before leaving he even remembered to ask Emma if he could park the squid truck at Greg's house so he didn't have to get up so early. She said no, because of some rule about school-owned vehicles being parked off campus property. Okay, whatever. At least he asked.

In the hallway he took a pull from the water bottle full of vodka and 7UP he'd brought with him, to give him the courage he needed to talk to the girl at the front desk in the lobby.

He smiled at her when he was in the lobby. She smiled back.

"Hi, weirdo," she said. Peter figured there was a high probability she was flirting with him.

"What do you mean, weirdo?"

"You act weird. You do weird things. You're a weirdo. So what did you write on your hand yesterday?"

"Nothing. I just pretended to write on my hand."

"I know. I could tell."

He explained to her about the squid truck, told her about the job.

He made her laugh. There is no better feeling in the world than making someone laugh. Her name was Amy. She thought the whole situation was kind of funny. She wasn't wearing those ugly glasses today, and she really was pretty cute. She was a senior at MIT. Working the desk in this building was her work-study job. It was ridiculously easy, she said. All she had to do was just sit there for four hours on weekday mornings. She mostly just did homework. She also said she was in "biochem." Peter asked her if she knew his brother. She blanked on him till he said, "Mr. Cast?" (Greg wasn't the kind of PhDickhead who wants everybody to call him "Doctor.") Of course she knew him. First she seemed a little impressed that Greg was his brother, and then Peter thought he saw something behind her eyes wonder what Gregory Cast's brother was doing driving the squid truck, as if she expected the brother of a young professor at MIT to be making something of his life. But she seemed to find the fact that Peter was a loser kind of charming. Maybe it was refreshing to meet him, considering all the other guys she met around here were probably hyperambitious type-A types who didn't expect to be crashing in their brothers' basements and getting up at three thirty in the morning to drive a truck full of squid when they were twenty-seven. That's what Peter told himself, though admittedly he was counting unhatched chickens. Then he surprised himself by throwing himself off a cliff and asking if she wanted to get a cup of coffee sometime.

"Or tea," he added. She laughed. That was clever. Peter had actually successfully said something that sounded cool and was flirty and kind of clever. She said yes. If she had said no, then Peter really would have had to start leaving the building through the back door. But she said yes. She said yes. She said she was free tomorrow afternoon. With Amy's logistical guidance, they arranged to meet at a coffee shop in Cambridge at three in the afternoon tomorrow. Peter left the building in a state of elation.

His days at this job would apparently be oddly structured: getting up insanely early in the morning, then a few hours of frenzied activity, then a long stretch of time in which he had nothing to do between getting off work and letting exhaustion take him under. Walking around and drinking the vodka and 7UP from his water bottle, he wandered the campus, he wandered the town, he wandered. He went back to Greg and Megan's house and stole more vodka when Megan wasn't looking. He took the whole bottle into the basement and, his mind racing with energy, he spent the afternoon drinking by himself in the dark basement while pacing around in circles until he passed out on the futon.

When the alarm woke him up at three thirty Peter was beyond hungover. A hangover doesn't even adequately suggest what he was feeling. It was an evil black cloud. There should have been flies buzzing around his head. He tried to get out of bed and fell on the floor. In the bathroom his eyes were so heavy-lidded and bloodshot it looked as if he'd been punched in the face, twice. He got in the shower, even though he didn't have time for a shower, and took a shower anyway, his logic going something like, Maybe if we take a shower, time will stand still and at the end of this shower it will still be now. He downed a glass of water and puked it out half a minute later. Hair of the dog, he thought, and twisted open another bottle of vodka, gulped down a few shots, and instantly felt a hell of a lot better. He dumped half the vodka in the bottle into his water bottle, filled up the rest with 7UP, and he was off, feverishly smoking cigarettes and speedwalking through the dark, empty streets of Somerville and Cambridge, occasionally unscrewing the cap of his water bottle and taking a sip of his tepid vodka-7UP mixture, trying not to think about how late he was, there's the truck, keys, ignition, let's go.

The fishermen at the docks smelled something funny with him, maybe literally, though Peter figured the general ambient stench of the fish was enough to mask any alcohol on his breath. It was like the fishermen knew there was something too buoyant about him today, too gung ho let's-do-this. He wasn't his usual anxious, timid, exhausted self. His usual self? How would they even know? This was only his third day on the job.

There was the usual haul of forty, fifty squid in the bycatch buckets. Back in the truck now, *vroom, vroom*, tearing ass down the highways back to Cambridge as fast as humanly possible, making up for lost time, working every twitch of horsepower the clunky old truck had in it, doing eighty, ninety, edging up on a hundred miles an hour, which he could do because there were almost no other cars on the road yet, the sun coming up perceptibly later today as it was still quite dark, barely daybreak, though it was hard to tell because the sky was overcast again, a sheet of hammered iron with the newly risen sun a fuzzy white blot in it. And again on the drive back his mind careened back to Gina. Peter thought, in a swirly-headed half-hungover, half-drunk way, about the girl he was supposed to get coffee with later that day, in the afternoon, and figured that today he definitely should leave the building through the back, one, because of the state he was in, and two, because of some sort of like, groom not seeing the bride before the wedding type reason. He would have time to go home, go back to bed, catch a desperately needed chunk of beauty rest before his "coffee date" with Amy. This "coffee date" officially made Amy the first girl who had shown any interest in him at all since Gina dumped him. He would have traded anything to be with Gina again, though of course he had nothing of any value to trade. He again remembered that time in the winter, in December, when those people, the couple, these friends of Gina's from school, were hanging out with them on a Saturday afternoon, celebrating the end of finals, or something. They played Monopoly on the floor, everybody in socks and hats and draped in blankets with the two space heaters roaring and clinking and water boiling on the stove, and still it was cold. Peter was the ship. Peter was always the ship, because when they were kids, Greg had always gotten to choose first because he was the oldest, and he always chose the top hat, because, duh, it was the coolest piece, and Lindsay had always gotten to choose next because she was a girl, and she always chose the dog for some reason, which left Peter as usual with the leftovers, and he always chose the ship because he thought it was the next-coolest piece after the top hat, and being the ship became a private tradition with him when he played Monopoly. They smoked a couple of bowls and drank hot cider and rum, though they didn't have all that much rum left, and when that ran out they broke into the beer, and when they ran out of beer they sat for a while around the game board, having crapped out on the game and long ago forgotten whose turn it was, discussing who would brave the elements and death-march it the three long blocks down the street to the store to get more beer. The wind was rattling the sides of the house and the temperature hovered somewhere in the ballpark of zero. Peter volunteered. The guy, the friend of Gina's from school, offered to go with him, help him carry the beer back, but Peter waved him off, said, Don't worry, man, I got it. They pooled their cash and Peter crammed the ball of ones, fives, and tens into the pocket of his coat, which he squeezed on over a hoodie, a sweater, and a scarf. Outside, the streets had that desolate, moondust look that very, very cold days sometimes have, puddles fossilized opaque and white into the sidewalk cracks, the wind sifting powdery old snow in wispy waves across the road. He hadn't worn gloves, and he alternated the hand he was smoking with—when his right became numb he'd stuff it in a pocket and switch to the left, then go back to the right when the left was numb. Instead of going to the store to get more beer, he found himself ringing the bell at Dominick's place. Dominick lived on the next street over, halfway between their apartment and the store. Looking back on it, Peter supposed that one could call this building a "crack house," but Peter simply thought of it as Dominick's place. Then he was inside Dominick's place, stamping his boots, shaking off the cold, though it was cold inside the house too, colder than Peter and Gina's apartment. And then Peter was forking over to Dominick all the cash he had just been given.

And now a cow was standing in the road. Peter saw it, of course, and knew what it was. It was a cow, one of those picturesque black-and-white New England cows, and it was standing in the road, in the middle of the lane that Peter was currently driving in. It might have been that Peter was going so fast that he wouldn't have had time to stop anyway, but Peter didn't even brake. The sight of the cow just confused him. The few long fractions of seconds that passed between seeing the cow and hitting the cow with the squid truck were just like, Hey, that's not supposed to be there. That cow is supposed to be over *there*, behind the fence with the other cows.

The cow made a hideous noise that was a combination of mooing and being hit by a truck, rolled into the air, and smashed the glass of the windshield. Peter was stomping on the brake and the accelerator at the same time, the truck was on its side now, and now, after maybe blacking out for a moment, Peter was heaving open the driver's-side door, pushing it against gravity, realizing how drunk he was and wondering how badly he was hurt. His hands were shaking. He crawled out of the wreck as fastidiously as he could. He put a hand to the side of his head, which hurt, and his fingers came back red. It was almost unbearably painful to inhale breath, which maybe meant he had broken a rib or two against the seat belt, and one of his knees seemed to be so fucked up he could hardly walk—one leg of his jeans was dark red and he didn't even want to look at it. Okay, so. What now?

He saw where the cow was lying in the road, and limped over in that direction. Several hundred gallons of salt water had splashed onto the road, along with a streak of diffusely strewn chunks of metal and the dust and crumbs of blue-green glass blasted scattershot across the asphalt. The cow was alive. It was lying on its side in a pool of blood made thinner by the water. It was wet—its hide was sleek and glossy with blood and water. Blood trickled from its open mouth, and its chest rose and fell like bellows, the air rushing in and out of the mouth and nostrils. Its shiny black eyes were desperate and scared. All around them, draped bizarrely over the cow's body and lying inert in useless, slimy piles of tentacles, were the squid. The squid, in perhaps a collective dying gesture, had all released their ink sacs, and had covered the whole scene with their ink. The water and the cow's blood and Peter's blood mixed with the oily, briny-smelling squid ink. The runny puddles of ink had rainbows swirling in them. It was about seven in the morning.

Peter sat down on the shoulder of the road, and watched the cow dying and the squid dying.

A farmer, presumably, a man who at least looked like a farmer, who looked to be in his fifties maybe, in heavy rubber boots and a Mackinaw, had hopped over the wooden fence by the roadside, the fence that separated what was supposed to be the car space from what was supposed to be the cow space. The glittering stardust of shattered glass crunched under his boots as he approached the scene. With his hands on his hips, he looked at the dying cow, and looked at the squid flopped pell-mell across the road, squirming their tentacles and squirting their ink into the blood and water. He went to Peter, and offered him a hand.

• • •

It had been dark in that crack house in Chicago, even darker for Peter because his eyes were still adjusting to the indoors. The only light on was in the kitchen, where he could see a couple of plump girls sitting at a table, smoking and talking rapidly in Spanglish, and a bunch of black dudes were sitting in the living room in puffy, metallic-gloss coats. They were all drinking forties they kept in their laps and some of them were smoking. They paid no attention to Peter. Peter recognized some of the guys, some he didn't. The couple of guys on the couch were playing *Super Mario Bros.* on a dusty, beat-up-looking NES, the original console, which you didn't see much anymore even then, passing the controller back and forth between them, switching turns when Mario died, which happened often because they sucked. Peter watched them play Nintendo while Dominick was counting the money, going into the kitchen, coming back with Peter's crack. The guys playing *Super Mario* were drunk and high and not putting much effort into it. The only sounds in the room were beer swishing around in bottles when somebody took a swig, the music on the game, and the silly *boing!-boing!-boing!* noises Mario made when he jumped. Soon Peter was also high and sitting on the couch, and thinking about how weird it would be if there was a loud *boing!* whenever a person jumped in real life. They were on one of the underground levels, with the "scary" Mario music that goes *do-do-do-do-do-doot* . . . *do-do-do-do-do-doot* . . . Peter held his lighter to the pipe and felt that hot, corrosive froth in his lungs and the beautiful feeling that went with it. In a way, smoking crack makes you feel like when you get the star of invincibility in *Super Mario.* Suddenly the music speeds up really fast and you're flashing with inner energy and anything that touches you dies. And then it wears off, and you're back to being normal Mario—the same as before, but now you feel less than you should be, or could be. Peter watched them playing the game: Mario kept sliding off the bricks and falling into chasms, getting killed by the plants that go up and down in the tubes, just running right the fuck into the turtles and mushrooms. Peter was getting irritated watching them play. It's like, dude, come *on*, it takes a pretty fucking remedial player to let Mario get killed by a fucking mushroom. When they finally exhausted all of Mario's lives and got a Game Over, Peter asked if he could play. They gave him the controller, and watched him sail through World 1-1, as he had done so many thousands of times since his childhood that the landscape of the first level was etched in his brain, in his soul, he probably could have done it with his eyes closed, going by sound and muscle memory alone, collecting every coin and bumping every secret box, getting every 1-Up Mushroom, Fire Flower, and Invincibility Star to be got. When he came to the end of World 1-2, just to show off, he entered the Minus World. The guys on the couch were astounded. They had seriously never seen that shit before. "The fuck you doin', motherfucker?" said the guy next to him. "Walking through rocks and shit?" Peter glowed with pleasure, with pride. The Minus World is a glitch in the game at the end of World 1-2. At the end of the level—the very, very end, where the green tube is that you go into to leave the level—you can stand on top of the tube, crouch jump, move slightly to the right, and moonwalk into this secret space, and it looks like you're gliding right through a solid brick wall and into the space where the three Warp Zone tubes are, and there's this hidden tube you can go down that takes you to . . . the Minus World. It takes you to World –1, World –2, and so on. The Minus Worlds are a bunch of fucked-up, unfinished, or rejected levels that the programmers left floating around in the game, and some of them are almost, what, like, *psychedelic.* Mario swims through a level of black water where all the tubes are neon pink, shooting fireballs at neon-blue plants and white squid, and there are these big blank blue rectangles where there's simply nothing there, like a hole in the universe of *Super Mario*. It's as if Mario has traveled to the distant, frayed edges of space and time. He must now look into the void. It's a little frightening. At some point in *this* world, the

Plus World, the world outside, it had begun to snow, and snow in earnest, coming down in thick, heavy clumps of snowflakes so big they were almost snowballs. The snow was piling up in the corners of the windows, and the house acquired that still, densely muffled acoustic quality a house gets when it's covered in snow. The guys on the couch had become enrapt in watching Peter play the game, and Peter himself was in a shamanlike trance, his mind had been sucked into the game's vortex, he had fully broken through the living membrane and entered the pixelated otherworld. Being high on crack probably helped this. He took hits off the pipe between worlds, when Mario pulled down the flag and entered the castle and the game tallied up his coins as fireworks went off. He was being cheered on now, all the guys were rooting for him. He was racing, racing through the game, heart pattering, the controller hot in his hands, the buttons getting slippery with sweat under his thumbs. He was winning. He was going to beat the game. He was a star. He was a hero.

Then someone stood in front of the TV.

Peter loosed a warbling, inarticulate shriek and ducked his head to see the screen.

He looked up, refocused his eyes on the Plus World, and was genuinely astonished to realize that the person who stood between him and the Nintendo was Gina. *Astonished* wasn't even quite the right word. It was more like, like cognitive dissonance, a feeling of seeing a certain thing in a context so unfathomably out of place that it simply *does not register*, and your subconscious spends a few seconds doubting whether you're really seeing what you're seeing before your conscious mind can catch up.

"What the *fuck* are you *doing* here?" said Gina.

Uh-oh: language. Brain problem. Brain-related problem. Language receptors not good right now.

"Uh . . ." said Peter. "What?"

Peter blinked, trying to think. The game screen still left a rectangular wake of light in his vision. Gina was covered in snow. She was wearing snow boots, a coat, a hat, a scarf. He flicked a glance outside. Snow. It was dark out. What time was it? The past was trickling back to him.

"I'm getting more beer," he said.

Peter had been sort of planning on smoking a little bit here and then going to the store and buying the beer with his credit card. He wasn't exactly sure if he had any credit left, but that was a bridge he'd cross when he came to it.

He tossed aside the controller and stood up. Head rush. His knees were trembly and weak. He realized he was very hungry.

"Okay," he said. "Let's get the beer."

"Forget the fucking beer." She was furious, but quiet, almost whispering. He knew she was afraid of the guys who hung out at Dominick's place. "Dan and Jessie left a long time ago. You were gone for *five hours.* I was *so* worried."

"Uh—" Peter looked around the room. Everyone was staring at him. He didn't know where to put his hands.

"What the fuck were you thinking?" said Gina. "Do you still have the money we gave you?"

Peter must have known, somewhere in there, that hours, not minutes, were passing. Later, he thought the whole thing was kind of like the *Star Trek: The Next Generation* episode where Captain Picard dies in this world, and then he wakes up in another world, and lives out a full, happy life as a flute maker on a rustic, primitive planet, and then dies in that world and wakes up again just a couple seconds later on board the starship *Enterprise* again. Only this was sort of the opposite of that. Only it wasn't really like that at all, actually, because when Peter had entered into a separate time-space, into the Minus World, real time was still going on without him just like normal, and Gina had been embarrassed, at first, when he was taking so long, and then embarrassed and nervous and scared when he'd kept on not showing up and it had begun to snow, and then mortified as her friends gave up on him and were putting on their coats and leaving, and then Gina had been stomping around for hours, panicked and desperate, in subzero weather and rapidly accumulating snow, calling his name in the streets, calling out his name as if he were a lost child.

Acknowledgments

This book was written very slowly over the course of the last ten years or so. Some of these stories I began a long time ago, and others are newer. They appear more or less in chronological order. Because this book came together so gradually, I've been in a lot of places over the course of writing it, and a lot of people have helped me.

Thanks first to Brian DeFiore and Cary Goldstein for being my team in publishing—whose support and confidence I've come to rely upon.

I am gratefully beholden to Bard College, both for the Bard Fiction Prize in 2012 and later for welcoming me back to teach, and to my colleagues there, especially Robert Kelly and Mary Caponegro.

A special thanks is due to Bradford Morrow, a tremendous editor and friend, and *Conjunctions*, where several of these stories, in slightly different forms, debuted in print. Great thanks is also due to Lorin Stein for publishing one of these stories in *The Paris Review*.

I want to vociferously thank Lan Samantha Chang, Connie Brothers, and everyone at the Iowa Writers' Workshop. Thanks also to Tobias Wolff, who helped me fix a broken part of one of these stories. Thanks to Brian Morton and Sarah Lawrence College. Thanks to T. Geronimo Johnson, and everyone at UC Berkeley's SCWP (it was great while it lasted).

I am grateful to Kathryn Hamilton and her theater company, Sister Sylvester, with whom I spent a very weird couple of weeks in Detroit in 2013, out of which one of these stories emerged, and I am particularly indebted to Terence Mintern.

Thank you, Micaela Morrissette, for staples, tape, pens, countless other favors, and general help with just about everything.

Thanks also to the following people, each for their own different and important reasons: Jonathan Ames, Matt Beckemeyer, Christopher Beha, Caroline Bermudez, Ethan Canin, Edward Carey, Eleanor Catton, Sam Cooper, Moira Donegan, Jennifer DuBois, Cara Ellis, Julia Fierro, Gwenda-lin Grewal, Kevin Holden, William Melvin Kelley, Alexandra Kleeman, Chris Leslie-Hynan, James Han Mattson, JW McCormick, Eric Morgan, Sara Ortiz, Andres Restrepo, Karen Russell, Kate Sachs, Maggie Shipstead, Bennett Sims, Alexander Singh, Ted Thompson, Sergei Tsimberov, Graham Webster, Chris Wiley, and Jenny Zhang.

Endless love and thanks to my parents and my brothers.

And thank you, Caitlin Millard. You know what for.

About the Author

BENJAMIN HALE is also the author of the novel *The Evolution of Bruno Littlemore*. His fiction and nonfiction have appeared, among other places, in *Conjunctions*, *Harper's*, the *New York Times*, the *Washington Post*, and *Dissent*, and has been anthologized in *Best American Science and Nature Writing*. Originally from Colorado, he is a senior editor of *Conjunctions*, currently teaches at Bard College, and lives in a small town in New York's Hudson Valley.